PRAISE FOR TAWNA FENSKE

ABOUT THAT FLING

"Fenske's take on what happens when a one-night stand goes horribly, painfully awry is hilariously heartwarming and overflowing with genuine emotion . . . There's something wonderfully relaxing about being immersed in a story filled with over-the-top characters in undeniably relatable situations. Heartache and humor go hand in hand in this laugh-out-loud story with an ending that requires a few tissues."

—Starred review, *Publishers Weekly*

MAKING WAVES

Nominated for Contemporary Romance of the Year, 2011 Reviewers' Choice Awards, RT Book Reviews

"Fenske's wildly inventive plot and wonderfully quirky characters provide the perfect literary antidote to any romance reader's summer reading doldrums."

—*Chicago Tribune*

"A zany caper . . . Fenske's off-the-wall plotting is reminiscent of a tame Carl Hiaasen on Cupid juice."

—*Booklist*

"This delightfully witty debut will have readers laughing out loud."

—4½ stars, *RT Book Reviews*

"[An] uproarious romantic caper. Great fun from an inventive new writer; highly recommended."

—Starred review, *Library Journal*

"This book was the equivalent of eating whipped cream—sure it was light and airy, but it is also surprisingly rich."

—*Smart Bitches Trashy Books*

BELIEVE IT OR NOT

"Fenske hits all the right humor notes without teetering into the pit of slapstick in her lighthearted book of strippers, psychics, free spirits, and an accountant."

—*RT Book Reviews*

"Snappy, endearing dialogue and often hilarious situations unite the couple, and Fenske proves to be a romance author worthy of a loyal following."

—Starred review, *Booklist*

"Fenske's sophomore effort is another riotous trip down funny bone lane, with a detour to slightly askew goings on and a quick u-ey to out-of-this-world romance. Readers will be enchanted by this bewitching fable from a wickedly wise author."

—*Library Journal*

"Sexually charged dialogue and steamy make-out scenes will keep readers turning the pages."

—*Publishers Weekly*

FRISKY BUSINESS

"Up-and-coming romance author Fenske sets up impeccable internal and external conflict and sizzling sexual tension for a poignant love story between two engaging characters, then infuses it with witty dialogue and lively humor. An appealing blend of lighthearted fun and emotional tenderness."

—*Kirkus Reviews*

"Fenske's fluffy, frothy novel is a confection made of colorful characters, compromising situations and cute dogs. This one's for readers who prefer a tickled funny bone rather than a tale of woe."

—*RT Book Reviews*

"Loaded with outrageous euphemisms for the sex act between any type of couple and repeated near intimate misses, Fenske's latest is a clever tour de force on finding love despite being your own worst emotional enemy. Sweet and slightly oddball, this title belongs in most romance collections."

—*Library Journal*

"Frisky Business has all the ingredients of a sparkling romantic comedy—wickedly clever humor, a quirky cast of characters and, most of all, the crazy sexy chemistry between the leads."

—*New York Times* and *USA Today* bestselling author Lauren Blakely

let it breathe

ALSO BY
TAWNA FENSKE

let it breathe

TAWNA FENSKE

Montlake
Romance

ROM
Fenske

Published by Montlake Romance, Seattle

www.apub.com

Amazon, the Amazon logo, and Montlake Romance are trademarks of Amazon.com, Inc., or its affiliates.

ISBN-13: 9781503949553
ISBN-10: 1503949559

Cover design by Shasti O'Leary-Soudant

Printed in the United States of America

To Dixie and David Fenske:
for showing me what an amazing marriage looks like
and then being my tireless source of love and support
while I figured it out for myself.

CHAPTER ONE

Reese Clark ducked out of her house and made a beeline for the picnic table beside the winery barn. In one hand she held a bowl of Cocoa Puffs. In the other, a bowl of mealworms.

The magazine she'd tucked under one arm slipped a little, but Reese pinned it in place with her armpit. The movement made the small black bird on her shoulder ruffle his feathers and squawk as Reese squished across the damp grass. It had rained all night, but sunlight seeped through the clouds as Reese savored the hug of her comfiest jeans and the thrill of being blissfully alone with her breakfast.

"Here, try this."

Reese jumped, losing her grip on the magazine but saving the mealworms and Cocoa Puffs. The starling on her shoulder chirped again and fluttered to perch on her head. Reese frowned at the man emerging from the winery barn with a glass in one hand and his ponytailed blond hair held back by a blue bandana.

"Dammit, Eric—why are you here so early on a Tuesday?"

"It's not early, it's six thirty."

"That's early. And it's your day off."

She plunked down on the picnic bench and set her cereal and mealworms on the table. Eric bent to snatch the magazine by its cover, keeping the wineglass clenched in one hand.

"Hey, the new *Wine Spectator*," he said. "Mind if I—"

"Yes, I mind." Reese grabbed the magazine back and flipped the end of her long, gold-brown ponytail out of her cereal bowl. The bird held his ground, its tiny claws anchored in Reese's hair. "I haven't read it yet. You'll get it later, but only if you let me eat my breakfast in peace."

He dropped onto the picnic bench beside her and scratched his chest through his SpongeBob T-shirt. He studied the two bowls.

"Which one's your breakfast?" he asked.

"The mealworms. Bluebirds love Cocoa Puffs."

He pushed the wineglass in front of her, knocking the spoon out of her cereal.

"Mealworms go great with Viognier—come on, just a sip," he urged. "I think it's a bit too brassy, but I want your opinion."

"Eric, I—"

"Don't be a grump, Riesling. Drink the fucking wine."

She slugged him in the shoulder. "Don't call me Riesling." She was more annoyed by the use of her full name than by the cursing or the suggestion she was the sort of girl who drank wine at seven thirty in the morning.

She *was* that sort of girl.

And truth be told, she didn't mind the cursing.

"Go feed the bluebirds so they stick around and chase the damn starlings off the vines," she said. "*Then* I'll taste the wine."

"You mean like the damn starling that just pooped in your hair?"

"Stumpy has an injured foot and isn't a threat to our grapes. Besides, he's being picked up today by a wildlife group that handles nonnative species."

"You'd rescue a goddamn piranha if you found it swimming in the alpaca trough."

Reese ignored him as she picked up the glass. She took a slow sip, swishing it over her tongue. She sucked in a little air and tilted her head to the side, contemplating the wine as she watched Eric walk to the bird feeder. He had one eye on her, which was probably why he didn't see the alpaca until it head-butted him.

"Goddammit, Leon—not in the nuts again!" Eric doubled over.

Beside him, the shaggy, cream-colored beast with random patches of caramel fur made a *wark-wark* sound and twitched his ears. Reese tasted the wine once more before she set the glass on the table. Eric limped back over with Leon ambling cheerfully behind.

"Why can't you have a dog like normal women?" Eric muttered.

"At what point did you mistake me for a normal woman?" Reese reached up to scratch the alpaca behind the ears. The starling chirped and fluttered away to perch on Leon's back. Reese took another sip from the glass. "The wine's great. Seductive. Is this the one you blended with Muscat?"

Eric nodded, looking pained but pleased as he dropped onto the bench beside her. Leon rested his head on Reese's shoulder, and she reached for her cereal spoon.

"I've got most of the Viognier in steel like usual," Eric said, "but I added the Muscat to this one and kept it in oak for a little while just to experiment."

"Not bad. Maybe another week or so, but I think you're on to something."

Eric took the glass back, sipping in thought. "You know what this wine reminds me of?"

"What?" she said around a mouthful of cereal. Leon hummed softly while Reese chewed.

"The Grüner Veltliner we served at the wedding."

"That wasn't a Grüner. That was a late-harvest Sauvignon Blanc."

"No, not *our* wedding—and that was a late-harvest Gewürztraminer anyway—my wedding to Sheila. The *good* wedding."

Reese rolled her eyes, not insulted by the wedding slight or the reminder he'd moved on to a new wife, but damn sure she knew her wines. "That was *not* a Gewürztraminer at our wedding, it was a Sauv Blanc—a nice one."

"It was not a Sauv Blanc. Remember? You wanted a late-harvest Gewürz because your parents ordered that pork dish."

"We were not serving Gewürztraminer—we changed that at the last minute because your mother wanted that crappy chicken."

"Right, but we kept the Gewürztraminer because it went with the lemon buttercream cake you just had to have." He frowned. "I never did get a piece of that cake."

"*No one* got a piece of that cake. Your best man passed out on it, remember?"

Eric grinned. "Clay didn't pass out at my wedding to Sheila," he pointed out.

Reese dug into her Cocoa Puffs. "One of seven hundred and eighty-three signs that your present union is a vast improvement over our ridiculous excuse for a marriage."

"Are you going to read that magazine? Because there's an article about winemaking in Rioja and—"

"Go away, Eric."

He didn't budge. Instead, he looked up at Leon.

Leon spit on him.

"Damn animal," Eric muttered, wiping his arm on his T-shirt. Reese resisted the urge to remark that now it looked like SpongeBob was drooling.

Eric picked up the wineglass and stuck his nose in again, pondering the aromas. Or pondering something. Reese watched him as she took another bite of cereal, wondering what was bothering him.

"You worried about the expansion?" she asked. "It's a lot of pressure on you as the winemaker, and I know the jerk at Larchwood says it's too much to take on, but—"

"Worried? No, it's great. This place is about to hit it big time."

"That's the hope," Reese agreed as she shoved cereal into her mouth and studied her ex-husband. "You and Sheila doing something fun for your anniversary?"

"We're having dinner at Subterra, and I got her a jacket she's been wanting."

"The purple suede? Excellent, she said I could borrow it for the Memorial Day event."

"And I got her this cool lacy thing at Victoria's Secret."

"I won't be borrowing that."

He grinned. "You know, you could be happy again, too."

"I wasn't happy the first time I was married," she pointed out. "No offense. But you were there, and you hated it, too. We're excellent friends but lousy spouses."

"No offense taken. Clearly I ruined you for other men."

She laughed, spilling milk on the table. "Yes, Eric, that's exactly it." Leon leaned down to sniff the milk.

"Seriously, you should get over your issues," he said.

"My *issues?*"

"Issues," Eric repeated. "Your parents have the most perfect marriage on the planet, so you got this idea love was easy. When you realized it wasn't—"

"Gee, this therapy session is fun. Weren't you leaving?"

He shrugged. "Look, I'm just saying you seem sort of miserable lately. All you've done since college is work at the vineyard and fix broken animals—there's been no excitement, no change, no passion, no—"

"Drama? I hate drama, in case you've forgotten."

Eric sighed. "You just seem stuck. Stagnant. That's all. It wouldn't kill you to date or something."

Reese bit her tongue and reminded herself not to be bitchy. He was trying to help. She reached up and scratched Leon again, earning a contented cluck from her pet.

"As much as I enjoy having my ex-husband advise me on my love life, I'm fine. Really. I'm happy."

"Whatever you say, boss."

Eric buried his nose back in the wineglass and Reese watched him warily. So it wasn't the expansion, and it wasn't anything with Sheila.

But something was definitely on his mind. She'd known Eric for fifteen years, and with the exception of the year they'd been married, they'd always been good friends. People were always surprised when Reese told them her ex-husband was the winemaker for her family's vineyard—a vineyard she'd been managing for almost a decade. Truthfully, the arrangement had never bothered either of them.

But something was definitely bothering Eric now.

"What's wrong?" she blurted.

Eric sighed. "Look, there's something I've gotta tell you."

Reese felt a slither of something cold run down her spine. Dew from the overhanging tree, but still, it didn't seem like a good omen.

"What?"

He looked at her, his hair flopping over the bandana and his expression somewhere between beaten puppy and morose hippie. Behind them, Leon hummed again.

"It's something big," Eric said.

Reese set her spoon down and braced herself. "Let's hear it."

◆　◆　◆

Ten miles away, "something big" was eating an omelet at Crescent Café.

"Clay? Clay Henderson, is that you?"

Clay looked up to see June and Jed Clark headed toward his table. Jed had his hand in the back pocket of June's jeans, while June had her arm slung around her husband's waist like a beaming cheerleader laying claim to the quarterback.

They'd been married—what?—thirty-five years? Clay watched with a mixture of admiration and nostalgia as Jed paused to kiss June's temple en route to Clay's side of the restaurant.

"Haven't seen you for ages, son," Jed said once they arrived at the table. "Eric said you'd moved to Idaho."

Clay nodded, swallowing a bite of omelet. "Boise. I've been there more than three years."

"You still doing that environmental building stuff?"

"Yes, sir. Still with Dorrington Construction. They've had me working out of southwest Idaho until just a couple days ago."

Clay watched their faces for a reaction, for some sign that Eric had told them the news. There was nothing.

Then again, they weren't paying much attention to him. Jed was busy trying to look like he wasn't intentionally grazing the side of his wife's breast with his arm, while June brushed a strand of salt-and-pepper hair from his temple.

Some things don't change, Clay thought, trying to decide if that was a good or a bad thing.

"So we hear you, uh—made some changes in your life," Jed said.

June shot an uncomfortable grimace at Jed. Jed met his wife's expression with an apologetic eyebrow lift, and Clay watched as June's frown softened. It dawned on Clay that he'd just watched an entire conversation between two people who didn't require a single word to communicate, and he wondered what it would be like to have that connection with another human being.

He also wondered whether he should just go ahead and address the elephant in the room. "Yes, sir," he said. "I went to rehab. I've been clean and sober almost four years now."

Jed smiled. "*Sir?* I'm not used to hearing you be so polite, son. Is that the sobriety talking?"

"Something like that," Clay agreed, fighting the familiar sensation of feeling awkward in his own skin.

"Congratulations, honey," June said, touching Clay's shoulder. "That's great news. So how long are you in the area? I'm sure Eric and Reese would love to catch up."

Clay took a sip of coffee, then cleared his throat. "Well, actually, I'll be here awhile. Dorrington won the bid to build your new tasting room and event pavilion out at the vineyard."

"Oh," June said, surprise registering across features that didn't look a day over forty, though Clay knew her daughter was thirty-four.

Reese, he thought, and felt an unexpected flood of warmth.

"We knew Dorrington won the bid, of course," June was saying. "They did such a nice job with the new cellar for our neighbors at Larchwood Vineyards last summer. It's just that Jed and I have been gone for two weeks on the most *romantic* Caribbean cruise, so we've been a little out of the loop. I didn't realize—"

"Does Reese know?" Jed asked, never one to beat around the bush.

"I'm not sure," Clay admitted. "I told Eric last night when I had dinner with him and Sheila. He was planning to tell Reese this morning."

June and Jed exchanged a look, though Clay couldn't know for sure what it meant. Might have been concern. Then again, they might have been telepathically communicating plans for a quickie in the restroom.

"Will you boys excuse me a minute?" June said. "I need to visit the restroom."

Clay choked on his coffee. Jed smiled at his wife and squeezed her hand. "Want me to order the usual?"

"Thanks, honey. Blueberry this time?"

"Perfect. I call dibs on the crust."

"I call dibs on the orange coffee mug."

"All yours, baby." He kissed her temple, then turned and sat down in the seat across from Clay. As Jed picked up the saltshaker, he studied Clay from across the table. "You've seen the plans for the new building, then?"

"Looked them over last week with the branch manager," Clay replied. "That's great you guys are going green, doing the LEED certification and all. Environmentally conscious building is the hot ticket in Oregon wine country right now."

"That's why they sent you."

"That's why they sent me," Clay agreed.

He paused, waiting to see if Jed would add anything else. Jed seemed content just fiddling with the condiments, spinning the pepper shaker around in lazy circles. Clay remembered a joke he'd heard about a woman with a medical condition that caused her to have an orgasm each time she sneezed.

What are you taking for it? the joke went.

Pepper.

Clay opened his mouth but shut it again fast.

You're a sober adult now. No more dirty jokes.

"So are you still leading wine country bike tours, sir?" Clay asked.

Jed laughed. "Sir," he repeated, shaking his head. "I can't get over that. Yeah, the bike tours have gotten pretty big these days. We'll have three dozen people out with us at the height of summer."

"No kidding?"

"Nope. Business is booming. June's still managing the business end, of course, and Eric's still making great wine for us. Larissa's doing marketing, and we've got Reese running the vineyard full-time now." He grinned. "She's got plans to make Sunridge the next big thing in Oregon wine country."

"And she's succeeding?"

Jed nodded with fondness and leaned back in his seat. "Ever known Reese not to succeed at something she put her mind to?"

"No, sir," Clay said, though he knew damn well Reese would disagree. After all, her marriage to Eric hadn't gone according to plan.

A marriage you never should have let happen, dumbass.

Clay cleared his throat, forcing his brain not to venture down that path. "How's Grandpa Albert doing?" he asked, hoping like hell the old man was still alive.

"He goes by Axl now."

"Axl?"

"It's his street name. He got it in prison a few years ago."

"Prison?"

Jed shrugged. "He only did a few weeks. Got caught trafficking drugs, but they let him off easy since he was just selling counterfeit Viagra to a rival biker gang."

"Isn't he in his late seventies?"

"Just turned eighty last week, but that hasn't slowed him down much. Actually, would you mind keeping an eye out for him and flagging him down when he gets here?"

"Uh—sure."

"Thanks," Jed said, standing up and clapping Clay on the shoulder. "I need to chat with the chef about the catering for a wine event in a few weeks. You'll recognize Axl when you see him."

"No problem."

Jed hurried away, and Clay directed his attention to the front of the restaurant. The instant he turned, the door burst open to reveal an old man in aviator sunglasses and a black leather jacket. Spotting Clay, Grandpa Albert gave a start of surprise, then swaggered over to the table and eyeballed him.

"Well, well, well," he said, dropping into the seat beside Clay and running a hand through his wispy white hair. "If it isn't the guy who face-planted in my granddaughter's wedding cake."

"Hello, sir."

"And got arrested for pissing in the ashtray at Finnigan's."

"Good to see you again, sir."

"And plowed down a row of Reese's thirty-year-old Zin vines on a riding mower."

"You're really looking good, sir."

Albert pulled off the aviator sunglasses—bifocals, Clay realized— and looked at him. "I always liked you."

Clay hadn't seen that coming. He swallowed, wondering when the lump had formed in his throat. "Thank you. I always liked you, too."

"Of course you did. Everyone does. So where the hell you been? I thought you and Eric and Reese were the Three Musketeers for life, and then you up and left."

Clay cleared his throat. "I had some things to straighten out."

"Damn right you did. Where'd you go for rehab, Hazelden?"

"Good guess."

"It's the best. A couple guys I ride with had to go last year. Started building model airplanes with their grandkids and got hooked on sniffing glue. You know how it is."

Clay wasn't sure he did, but he nodded anyway and took a sip of his coffee.

Albert leaned close and lowered his voice to a conspiratorial level. "If the rehab doesn't take, I might have a business proposition for you. I'm not at liberty to say too much just yet, but it has to do with a special little harvesting operation and—"

"Actually, sir," Clay interrupted, "I'm pretty committed to sobriety. And I'm going to be working at the vineyard awhile building your new event pavilion and tasting room."

"Is that so?" Albert sat back and studied him. "Well, Eric'll be glad to have you back."

"Eric," Clay repeated. "Not Reese." He didn't phrase it as a question but still left room for Albert to object.

There was no objection. Instead, Albert just studied him with a look so intense, Clay had to fight not to drop his gaze. "Reese always got screwed when it came to you," Albert said at last. "And not in the good way."

He gave Clay a pointed look, and Clay felt his neck grow hot. Albert was right, of course. Reese had bailed him out of jail more times than he could count. She'd not only endured his lame excuses but the ones Eric had made on his behalf. Then there was that awful night at Finnigan's. The bar fight that had killed any chance he'd ever had of—

"I know," Clay said, interrupting his own dangerous train of thought. "I'm sorry about that. About all of it. I plan to apologize as soon as I head out there tomorrow. I'm a different person now."

The old man looked at him. "You'd better prove it. Girl's got ambition. She's making something big out of that vineyard with a new pavilion and the wine club and media attention and shit. Doesn't need you making a mess of things again."

"Yes, sir."

Albert slugged him in the shoulder. "What's with the *sir* bullshit? You think you're talking to an old man or something?"

"No, si—no, that's not it at all."

"The name's Axl now, dammit."

"Axl," Clay repeated, trying it out. "Okay."

Axl picked up Clay's mug, downing the rest of his coffee without comment. "So you're not a drunk anymore," he said, thunking the mug down on the table.

Clay cleared his throat again. "I prefer the term 'recovering alcoholic.'"

"And you're going to be working at a winery."

"Yes, s—*yes*. That's right."

"With your best buddy making wine."

"Yep."

"And my granddaughter giving you orders."

"Right."

Axl studied him for a moment, then shook his head. "Don't fuck it up."

CHAPTER TWO

"I don't see why I have to change my shirt," Larissa argued.

Reese stared at her cousin for two beats, wondering which would emerge first—smoke from her own ears or Larissa's boobs from the purple push-up bra thrusting them to terrifying heights.

"Because I've seen prostitutes dressed more conservatively," Reese said. "This is a wine tasting room, not a strip club."

"This is a *barn*," Larissa said.

She did have a point. Since Sunridge Vineyards didn't have an official tasting room yet, they'd been holding tastings in the winery itself. With barrels stacked everywhere, a drain running the length of the concrete floor, and the scent of fermenting grapes saturating the air, it was hardly the ambiance Reese wanted to create. Still, the hordes of wine tourists appearing each week assured Reese she was on the right track.

Mostly on the right track, she amended, looking at her cousin in the purple lace bra and sheer yellow blouse. Reese flipped the end of her own gold-brown ponytail over one shoulder and tried to keep her voice calm.

"Look, Larissa—we're trying to build a professional reputation for Sunridge Vineyards, and part of that is looking like professionals. *Not* professional streetwalkers."

Larissa folded her arms over her chest. "Is the baby opossum in your pocket part of our professional image?"

"I'm not working with the public right now. You are." Reese touched the front of her flannel overshirt and felt the tiny creature stir. "I ran out of incubator space and he needed lunch."

"You're breastfeeding?"

"His bottle's in my office. Come on, Larissa. Work with me here."

"Fine." Larissa sighed. "Do you need me to go raid your closet for a knee-length flannel shirt, or can I use my own wardrobe?"

"Your own clothes are fine."

"Damn right they are. I just wore that kick-ass blue dress when I convinced the buyer for Anthony's HomePort Restaurants to start carrying our '12 Pinot Noir and the '14 Pinot Gris. That's nearly thirty restaurants in the whole chain."

Reese stared at her, stunned. "Wow. Larissa, that's—great job."

Larissa beamed, her cheeks pinkening. "Some of us just have what it takes to market wine."

"You slept with him." Reese's tone flattened.

"So?"

Reese sighed. "Just change your top. Please? For me."

"Fine. But only because you're my third-favorite cousin." With that, she sashayed out of the room.

It was best not to dwell on the fact that she was, in fact, Larissa's only cousin. Larissa's parents had run off to Bali when Larissa was fifteen and Reese was ready to graduate from high school. Larissa had stayed behind in the care of Reese's parents, eventually following Reese to college and sticking around the vineyard to handle sales and marketing.

A knock on the door signaled the arrival of more wine-tasting visitors. Reese straightened her crewneck T-shirt and dusted some cracker crumbs off the bar. Larissa must've closed the door on her way out, so Reese strode over and opened it.

"Hello, welcome to—"

The words died in her throat.

She recognized the face, of course, but this wasn't the same man she remembered trying to fill her livestock water trough with beer six years ago.

His face had thinned, with angles and planes replacing the mottled puffiness of his cheeks the last time she'd seen him.

The shoulders were still broad and his hair was still the same caramel shade, but it was shorter now—almost a buzz cut. And what was that tattoo peeking out from beneath his T-shirt sleeve—

"Hello, Reese."

The warmth in his voice made her stomach flip like it always used to. She would have known that voice anywhere. She was more familiar with the sound of it phoning from jail at two a.m., but still. She gripped the edge of the door harder and took a deep breath.

"Hello, Clay," she said as levelly as she could manage. "Eric said you were back in town."

"So you know I'm the foreman on the project?"

She nodded. "And I know you got sober. Congratulations on that."

"Thank you."

His eyes dropped to her breasts, and Reese felt an unexpected flutter of desire. It was a pleasant tingle that started under her sternum and sent a pulse of heat all the way to her nipples.

Then she remembered her passenger.

"It's a baby opossum I rescued," she said, touching a finger to her shirt pocket. "I didn't grow a mutant nipple, in case that's what you're thinking."

She saw his Adam's apple bob as he swallowed. "I wasn't thinking about your nipple. Or anyone's nipples."

"That's a first."

He blinked. "I've changed, Reese."

Something about his words knifed straight through her core. Maybe it was Eric's accusation that *she* hadn't changed. Maybe it was the question of how much Clay had. Maybe it was something else entirely.

She weighed her next words carefully, not sure how to bring up the subject. "Aren't you worried that—um—well, working at a winery—"

"I'll climb into a barrel of Pinot and drink my way to the bottom?"

"Something like that."

"No."

"You sound pretty confident."

He gave her a small smile. "I am."

"You always were."

"True," he said, shifting his weight to lean against the doorframe. "But I've been sober almost four years now. I've earned it."

Reese nodded, still taking him in. He was the same, but different. They'd been buddies in college—her, Eric, Clay. The Three Musketeers. Back then, he'd been Eric's roommate and one of her best pals. That was before she and Eric got married and Clay dropped out of college to work construction and drink himself into oblivion. He'd been crazy even then, was probably still crazy now.

But had his eyes changed color? They'd always been brown, of course, but usually more bloodshot than anything. They were clear now, and the most remarkable shade of root-beer brown with tiny flecks of—

"I suppose you'll want to see the area where you'll be working," Reese said, stepping back a bit to put a few feet of distance between them.

"Reese—before we get started, I want to say something."

"Oh?"

She felt the baby opossum wriggle in her pocket and saw Clay's eyes drop to her chest again. She touched her fingers to the flannel, and Clay didn't look away this time.

"You were always so soft," he murmured. His eyes widened the second the words left his lips. "A *softie*," he clarified. "A softie with the animals."

He shook his head and took a deep breath. Reese waited, not sure what to expect.

"I'm sorry," he said at last. "Really, I know I wasn't a very nice guy those last few years, and you bailed me out more times than I deserved. It couldn't have been easy on you or on your marriage to Eric, and I want to apologize for—"

"You didn't wreck my marriage to Eric," she interrupted. "That was a mistake from the start."

"Of course it was, but I know my behavior—" He stopped, probably sensing from her expression that he'd misspoken. "I didn't mean to imply your marriage was a terrible idea."

"It doesn't matter; it was." She swallowed, not sure why she felt so flustered. She'd never been heartbroken about the divorce, not even when the wounds were fresh and she and Eric were fighting all the time. Now it was more a dull emptiness. Mourning for what was *supposed* to be, instead of what was.

She cleared her throat. "Eric and I were meant to be great friends, but nothing more. Didn't take long to figure that out."

"Right," Clay said, and Reese could see him regrouping. "My point is that even after you two split, I hung around for years and made life miserable for both of you. And then there was that business at Finnigan's, the night you got hurt—"

"You already apologized for that," she said. "You called from rehab four years ago, remember?"

"Right. I'm sorry. I'm sorry about all of it, Reese."

She nodded. "Okay."

Clay shifted awkwardly, and Reese wondered what to do next. Hug him? Slug him in the shoulder like an old friend? She tried to imagine what his shoulder might feel like under her hand and then realized she knew *exactly* what it felt like. She remembered it well, hard and solid and bare beneath her clutching palm . . .

"Let's look at the construction site, shall we?" she blurted, her cheeks burning.

Clay nodded and started to reply. He stopped, turning as a trio of middle-aged women came giggling up the walk behind him in a cloud of perfume so thick Reese could see it.

"Is this where the wine tastings are?" called a heavyset blonde woman in a pink cashmere sweater and a diamond ring that could double as a paperweight.

"Yes," Reese said, moving to one side as Clay stepped to the other and held the door open for the women to pass. A second woman wore designer boots and clutched a dog-eared copy of *Wine Trails of Oregon*. The third woman toted a handbag Reese knew cost more than her car. All three were flushed with wine and the exertion of climbing up the walkway. Reese was glad the new tasting room would be on lower ground with a parking lot and a picnic area and—

"Aren't you a gentleman, holding the door for us?" giggled one of the women as she beamed up at Clay. "Very sweet."

"Ma'am," Clay said, and pulled the door closed behind them.

"Welcome to Sunridge Vineyards, ladies," Reese said as she moved toward the wine bar. "Are you here to do some tasting?"

"We are," agreed Pink Cashmere. "The guy in the tasting room at Larchwood Vineyards said you weren't open, but I knew you would be."

Reese gritted her teeth, silently cursing the neighboring vineyard owner. "He does that sometimes, but I can assure you, we're open. Seven days a week, eleven to six. Will you pardon me for just a moment?"

She scrambled into her office and tucked the baby opossum into a small pouch she'd placed on a heat pad in the cage. Latching the cage door, she turned to scrub her hands at the sink before hustling back to the tasting area. Clay was standing at one end of the bar smiling his old familiar smile at the customers, and Reese felt her heart twist.

"So were you ladies hoping to do our full tasting menu, or just some select wines?" she called.

"The full thing," piped the woman toting the wine book. "We hear your Pinot Blanc is just to die for."

"It hasn't killed anyone yet, but the day is still early," Reese said with deliberate cheer.

She reached up and grabbed three wineglasses from the overhead rack, tugging the hem of her shirt as it rode up. She glanced at Clay, wondering whether he'd stick around or wait outside.

He was watching her with an expression that gave Reese the peculiar sense he could see right through her clothes. She ordered herself not to think too much about it as the women sidled up to the bar. It wasn't really a bar so much as a large piece of plywood over two retired wine barrels. The linen cloth Reese had covered it with added a small touch of class, but still.

"So what's your name, dear?" asked one of the women as she rested her hip on the makeshift bar. "Are you with the family that owns the place?"

Reese smiled and placed the glasses down in front of them. "I'm Reese Clark. My grandparents started the vineyard in 1974 growing grapes for other wineries. It wasn't until 1992 that my parents opened the winery, and then I stepped in after college as vineyard manager and viticulturist."

"Viti-what?" asked the second woman as she plunked her massive handbag on the bar and leaned against one of the barrels.

Reese winced as the wood wobbled, but everything seemed to be holding. She gave it a wary glance as she began uncorking a bottle of Pinot Gris. From the corner of her eye, she saw Clay move to the opposite end of the bar.

"Viticulture is the science of grape production," Reese explained. "We look out for pests and diseases in the vineyards, deal with things like fertilization and irrigation, tend to fruit management and pruning and harvest and—"

"Oh, my, that sounds interesting," said the third woman with a tone that suggested she found it as interesting as pocket lint. She placed her palms down on the bar and leaned forward to peer at the bottles lined up on the shelf behind Reese.

The plywood gave a faint creak, and Reese sucked in a breath, the chilled bottle poised above the glasses as she waited for the whole bar to come crashing down.

She glanced at Clay. He was gripping the edges of the plywood with both hands, trying to look casual, but Reese could see what he was doing. He was holding up her bar.

Ironic, considering how many bars had propped *him* up over the years.

Ignoring the way his biceps flexed under the thin T-shirt, Reese turned back to her guests. They were all staring at Clay.

"Pardon my reach, ladies," Clay said.

All three fluttered their lashes at him. The woman with her palms on the bar turned toward him, leaning down in a blatant effort to give Clay a glimpse down the front of her shirt. Clay looked at Reese and gave an almost imperceptible shrug.

The woman in the pink cashmere licked her lips. "Are you a viticulturist, too?" she asked, shooting a pointed look at Clay.

Clay didn't loosen his grip on the bar. "No, ma'am, just a carpenter."

"Oh, join us for a drink, then!" piped the woman with the expensive handbag. "We could use a little male companionship."

"Please?" pleaded Pink Cashmere, leaning sideways on the bar and causing it to sway as she patted the empty stool beside her. "Just one drink. It's a girls' getaway, but we'll make an exception for *you*."

Clay smiled, his expression nearly as tight as his grip on the bar. "Thanks, but I'm doing great right here. You ladies enjoy."

Reese waited for one of them to wrestle him to the floor and pour wine down his throat, but they backed off and turned their attention back to her.

"This is our 2014 Reserve Pinot Gris," Reese announced as she tipped it into the stemware. "As you can see from the tasting notes in front of you, it was a gold-medal winner at the Northwest Food and Wine Festival last year. We age this in steel for six months before we filter and bottle it right here on site."

"Only six months?"

"That's common for a lot of white wines like Pinot Gris," Reese explained. "Others—like our Chardonnay, which we'll be tasting next—are aged in oak, so they take a little longer. And many of our red wines spend years in the barrel."

There was much chatting and sipping, with the women commenting on notes of pear and apple. Reese shot a glance at Clay, who was still holding the end of the plywood steady. He smiled and Reese gave a small nod of thanks before reaching for the Chardonnay.

She cycled through the white wines and moved on to reds, pointing out a bronze-medal Pinot Noir and explaining that most of their wines were estate grown.

"What does that mean?" one of the women asked. "Estate grown?"

"It means we grow all the grapes right here in our vineyards. Except for the dessert wine we're sampling at the end—that's a blend of some grapes from Southern Oregon."

She bent to retrieve a small brass bucket from under the wine rack, conscious of Clay's eyes on her as she plunked it down on the bar.

"This is a rather long tasting list, so it's perfectly okay to expel the wine. I'm sure you ladies know, but it's not mandatory that you swallow wine to taste it. Go ahead and spit if you like."

She shot a quick look at Clay, though if he'd seen the opening for a dirty joke about swallowing versus spitting, he hadn't taken it. The old Clay would have at least smirked, but this one just stood there stone-faced, hands gripping the edge of the bar. Reese uncorked a Maréchal Foch and started pouring, wondering what the hell was taking Larissa so long.

The ladies chattered among themselves, one of them taking only a small sip of each wine before passing it off to the woman in the pink cashmere, who obligingly polished it off.

Reese continued to move through the list, her lips forming the words while her mind was a thousand miles away—well, more like three feet away at the other end of the bar. She kept stealing glances at his shoulders, those beautiful, chiseled arms, the way his narrow waist tapered into worn jeans that fit snugly over his—

"That's it for the tasting list," Reese said as they sipped the last drops of specialty Vin Glacé dessert wine. "Did you have any questions or want to sample anything not on the list?"

"I'd like to buy a case of this one," announced the woman with the expensive handbag, jabbing a finger at the Reserve Pinot Noir. She fished for a wallet with her free hand and peeled out a credit card.

"Excellent choice," Reese said, accepting the card as the woman leaned across the bar, making it sway again. "Let me just run this, and then I'll help you carry it out to your car."

"I can get it," Clay said. Every female eye shifted toward him. "Which box is it?"

"Oh," Reese said. "It's right over there in that stack against the wall, but you don't have to—"

"I insist," he said, waiting until the women pried themselves away from the bar before loosening his grip on it. Reese watched as he ambled over to the cases and hoisted one like it was filled with cotton balls.

"Ladies," he said. "Would you mind pointing the way to the car?"

"Oh, it's the gray Lexus right out here," chirped the woman as Reese handed her credit card back. "Let me get the door for you."

Clay smiled and followed after them. "If you're not okay to drive, I'd be happy to give you a lift wherever you're headed."

"Aren't you the sweetest," one of them twittered. "Don't worry, though, I only took tiny sips of everything since we all agreed ahead of time that—"

The door closed behind them before Reese got to hear the end of the sentence. *Was that really Clay Henderson giving a lecture on sober driving?*

"Was that really Clay Henderson giving a lecture on sober driving?" called Larissa, bursting into the winery wearing a V-neck sweater that— thankfully—only showed the top quarter inch of her bra.

Startled, Reese began gathering up the glasses as Larissa tucked the white wines back in the chiller. "Yes, it was."

"God, he's still hot. Hotter than he was five years ago, and he was damn hot then. What's he doing here?"

"Working, believe it or not." Reese moved toward the kitchenette with Larissa on her heels, eager for details.

"No joke? He's working here? Better lock up the good stuff."

"He's not working in the winery, he's building the tasting room. And he's not drinking, either. He went to rehab."

Larissa blinked. "Wow, that's hard to believe. He used to be wild. I remember one time—"

"Larissa, could you hold down the fort in the tasting room for the rest of the afternoon?" Reese interrupted. "I told Clay I'd show him around, give him the lay of the land."

Her cousin gave a wicked grin. "Considering the way those women were sizing him up, you won't be the only one offering him a lay."

"God, that's just what he needs. Sexual harassment from our customers while he tries to get his life back on track."

"Clay's a big boy. I'm sure he can handle it."

Reese nodded, annoyed with herself for feeling irritated at the thought of Clay handling anyone. "So you've got the tasting room covered?"

"No problem."

"Oh, and FYI—Dick Smart at Larchwood is back to telling people our tasting room is never open. We need to have another talk with him."

"Asshole."

"Pretty much."

"I'll pay him a visit. He likes staring at my legs. Maybe if I distract him, he won't notice when I hit him over the head with a bottle of Chardonnay."

"Thank you." Reese paused, her hands frozen in the soapy water clutching a wineglass. "Hey, Larissa?"

"Yeah?"

"Do you think I'm miserable?"

Larissa looked surprised, then studied Reese long enough to assure her the answer wasn't a simple *no*.

"Miserable how? I mean, you could add some highlights so your hair isn't so brown and blah, and you've got those great boobs no one ever sees since you're always wearing those baggy shirts—"

"I don't think he meant miserable *looking*, but thank you for that."

"He who?"

"He Eric," Reese said as she toweled off the glasses and avoided her cousin's eyes. "He said I work too much and my life has stagnated and I need to find passion and excitement and start dating again so I can be ridiculously happy like he and Sheila are."

"He got the ridiculous part right." Larissa paused. "I thought you never wanted to get married again."

"I don't."

Much, Reese amended silently, thinking about the scene she'd witnessed behind the barn after breakfast. Her mother had been teaching her father to play smashball with the wooden paddles they'd bought for family events at the vineyard. Her dad had said something that made her mom throw her head back and laugh before Jed grabbed her around the waist, swooping her in circles until they both toppled laughing into the grass.

I'd only get married again if I could do it like that.

"Can't say I blame you," Larissa mused, still tracking with the original conversation. "Tying and untying the knot within a twelve-month span before you hit twenty-five would make anyone swear off marriage."

"It seemed like a good idea at the time." Reese set down a wineglass, not sure if she meant the marriage or the divorce.

"Did it? Getting married, I mean. I'll never understand why you did it. You and Eric had zero chemistry."

"You might have pointed that out *before* we walked down the aisle."

Larissa shrugged and began to wipe down the counter with a rag. "I figured you knew. If you wanted to pledge eternal devotion to a guy who seemed more like your brother than your lover, who was I to tell you not to go through with it?"

Reese toweled off another glass and wondered for the millionth time why she *had* gone through with it.

Because you thought marriage was the ticket to happily ever after.

Because your parents made it look easy.

Because you needed to forget about him.

"Anyway, why do you care what your stupid ex says?" Larissa asked, jolting her back to the present.

"I don't, I guess. I just thought if I was giving off a miserable vibe, I'd want to know."

"I wouldn't say *miserable*," Larissa said, setting aside her rag to reach for the dried glasses. "But you haven't changed much in the last decade. You should probably get laid more."

Just then, Clay pushed through the door. He nodded at them. "Ladies."

"Hey, Clay," Larissa said, shooting Reese a knowing look before turning to walk the glasses back to the bar. "You're looking good."

"Thanks, Larissa—you, too. Reese, did you want to go over to the building site now?"

Reese nodded as she dried her hands and folded the towel over the edge of the counter. "Sure thing. Let me just—"

The door burst open again, cutting off the rest of her sentence. Her mother stood there with flushed cheeks and a wild look in her eyes.

"Reese—come quickly! It's your grandfather."

CHAPTER THREE

At the panicked sound in June's voice, Clay yanked his cell phone from his back pocket. "Should I call 911?"

"No!" shouted the three women.

Clay froze, phone in hand, wondering if they'd all lost their minds.

June took a step forward, shaking her head. "No police. Please don't make this worse than it is."

"But if Albert—um, Axl—needs help—"

"No one's hurt," June said. "Not yet anyway. Reese, come on, hurry."

Reese moved to follow her mother out the door, and Larissa scurried after them, clearly not wanting to miss anything. Clay hesitated. No one seemed distressed in the way he might have expected if Axl were having a heart attack. Still, maybe they'd need help lifting him or something.

The whole family helped you out when you were at your worst. The least you can do is lend a hand now.

He fell into step behind them, though it was obvious they'd forgotten he was there.

They trudged up a grassy slope past several rows of spindly vines just beginning to sprout for the season. At the end of the rows was a thick forest buzzing with insects. Clay remembered Eric telling him Reese nurtured certain bugs to keep the less desirable ones off the vines, and he wondered if that's what he was hearing.

Between the forest and the vines stood Axl, with a shovel in one hand and a tape measure in the other.

"Gramp—dammit, Axl!" Reese yelled. "Stop right now. What are you doing?"

The old man whirled around and frowned. "What does it look like I'm doing? Planting. Been doing it on this land since before you were born, and I can still—"

"What are you doing to the goddamn vines?"

The heat in Reese's words was enough to halt even Axl in his tracks.

"Figuring out where to put my plants, that's what," he huffed.

"*What* plants?"

June touched her daughter's elbow, looking grim. "That's what I was trying to tell you. Your grandfather wants to grow marijuana next to the Muscat vines."

"Not all of them," Axl protested, looking like a defiant teenager. "Just this section right here. It's an experiment."

"An experiment," Reese repeated, looking incredulous.

"An experiment," Larissa said, looking eager.

"Hell, yes," the old man said. "Don't you remember back when June planted lavender beside the Riesling vines, and for a few years after that, all the wine reviewers went on and on about the 'delectable hints of lavender in the bouquet'?"

Reese stared at her grandfather. Even from three feet away, Clay could see the muscles in her jaw clenching and unclenching.

"Okay, Axl, not to split hairs or anything," Reese said slowly, "but last time I checked, it was *legal* to grow lavender."

"It's legal to grow weed, too!" Axl insisted. "This is Oregon, remember?"

"I'm aware of that, but I also know you need special permits to grow large amounts. It's regulated by the government, and there are all kinds of rules for growing it. You can't just start a pot plantation in your backyard."

"I got that covered, sweet pea." The old man grinned and reached into the back pocket of his pants, pulling out a folded piece of paper. He held it out triumphantly, shaking it in front of his granddaughter.

Reese just stared at it like he held used toilet paper. She finally took it, and Clay watched as her eyes traveled back and forth over the page.

"Medical marijuana?" she said.

"That's right," Axl said. "It's big business these days."

Larissa tried to peer over her cousin's shoulder at the words on the page. "Why is 'medical' spelled with two *Ls*?"

"Because it's a forged form," Reese said, handing it back to Axl, who scowled as he took it. "And even if it were legit, there are limits on how much you can grow and where you can grow it. I really don't think a vineyard is the best place, and right here next to the forest and my Muscat vines—"

"Well, where am I supposed to do it, then?" Axl snapped. "I thought you'd be happy about infusing your wines with a little extra somethin'-somethin', if you know what I mean."

The old man tried to wink, but the gesture seemed to throw him off balance, and he started to tip. Clay caught him by the arm before he could go toppling down the hill.

"Hands off the goodies, son," Albert said, stepping back and brushing off the arm of his jacket. "But thanks."

"No problem, sir—uh, Axl."

The old man sighed. "All right, then, where am I going to put my doobage?"

The cracking of twigs snapped everyone's attention to the edge of the woods. A man was standing there with his arms folded over his chest and an expression Clay would've called a "shit-eating grin" before he gave up swearing.

Reese's jaw clenched. "Dick," she snarled.

Clay looked at her, a little surprised at the curse until he realized it was probably the guy's name.

"Reese," the guy replied. "Planting a new crop?"

"No," Reese said. "Just checking the progress on the Muscat this season."

"Hmm," Dick replied. "You've never had much luck with Muscat here, have you? Such a shame, seeing how it seems to grow so well in my vineyard."

Larissa snorted and took a step closer to her cousin. "Too bad your Pinot comes up short." She sent a pointed glance at the guy's crotch, effectively doubling the insult.

"My Pinot is none of your concern," Dick snapped. "What *is* my concern is what you're planting in this area, seeing how my property abuts yours right along that ridge over there."

"Abuts," Axl grunted. "That's definitely the first word that comes to mind when I think of you, Dick."

June put a hand on her father's shoulder as Dick glared at them. Reese folded her arms and matched the glare with one of her own.

"I'm aware of the property lines between Sunridge and Larchwood, Dick," Reese said. "As you can see, we're safely on our side."

"And at the moment, you're on *our* property," Axl added. "Those woods are ours—always fuckin' have been, always fuckin' will be, and if you're here to badger me about selling again, the answer is no. 'Scuse me, the answer is *fuck no*."

Dick ignored him and sneered at Reese. "I'm watching you. Don't think I don't know about that little event you're hosting out here later this month."

Larissa rolled her eyes. "*Everyone* knows about the event. We sent out a press release. It was on the front page of the newspaper."

"Well, I certainly hope you know how to contain your guests. *And* your plantings, whatever they may be."

He cast a dubious look at Axl, who spat on the ground at his feet. Then he turned on his heel and stomped back into the forest.

"Asshole," Larissa muttered before the guy was out of earshot.

Reese sighed and waited a few more seconds for Dick's footsteps to retreat before turning back to her grandfather. "Look, you're not planting medical marijuana here. No way. Not with Dick watching and questionable paperwork. It's too close to the property line."

Axl was glaring into the woods after Dick. "Asshole better not step on my 'shrooms," he muttered before turning back to Reese. "So where the hell do I put my weed?"

Reese waved an arm down the hill. "There's the pole barn where we used to do the grafting. I think I've even got some old grow lights down there. Why don't you go do some research on indoor grow operations? And find out exactly how much you can have and where you can put it and—"

"I've got all that, Peanut Butter Cup. I've been doing my research on the interspace."

"Internet," June said with a sigh.

"That's great, Grandpa," Reese said. "I'll do some research, too, okay? Just to make sure everything's legal."

Axl frowned a little at that but didn't say anything else. June reached out and took the shovel from him. "Come on, Dad—I've got some brownies in the oven down at the house. What do you say we have a few of those with some milk?"

"Brownies?" Axl seemed to perk up at the suggestion. "I was just reading up on a new recipe for brownies with a *special ingredient*, if you know what I mean."

Clay braced himself to catch the old man if he tried to wink again, but Axl was apparently done. He allowed June to take him by the elbow and steer him down the hill. Reese and Larissa and Clay stood staring after the pair as they headed into the house that had stood at the edge of the vineyard property for more than forty years.

The sound of an approaching car drew their attention to the gravel road beyond the house. They all watched as a blue hybrid SUV crunched its way toward the winery.

"Someone's here for wine tasting," Reese said. "Larissa, could you—"

"I'm on it," she said, already wobbling down the hill in a pair of ridiculously high heels.

Clay's mind flashed back to the first time he met Larissa, fresh-faced and eighteen and teetering in the same sort of silly shoes. She'd been a new freshman, while he'd been gearing up to drop out of school, already hell-bent on fucking up his life with booze and bad decisions. Larissa had stood there smiling and earnest, gripping her cousin's arm like her whole world revolved around Reese.

Clay could relate. Both then and now.

"See you at dinner later, Reesey?" Larissa called over her shoulder as she moved down the hill.

"Maybe," Reese said. "I might be working late on some contracts. Don't forget to top the bottles with the argon gas when you close up, okay?"

"I know, I know."

Larissa made her way toward the winery, and Reese stared after her for a moment. When she turned and looked at him, Clay felt the full force of those blazing green eyes like an electric jolt to the spleen.

"Still sure you can handle this?" she asked.

It took him two beats to realize what she meant. "You mean being surrounded by alcohol, drugs, and possible illegal activity conducted by members of your crazy family?"

"Right."

"I think I'm safe."

Reese smiled, not a huge smile, but enough to make Clay want to make her do it again.

Dude, get a grip, he reminded himself. *Your best buddy's ex, remember?*

As if hearing his thoughts, Reese cleared her throat. "Shall we get down to business?"

◆ ◆ ◆

As they strolled the site of the new tasting room and event pavilion, Reese watched the careful way Clay jotted notes and took measurements. Several times they stopped so he could ask a question or pace off an area. She studied him as he bent down to rub the red clay soil between his fingers. The sleeve of his T-shirt rode up, exposing the tattoo she'd glimpsed earlier. She leaned closer, trying to make out what it said.

"You read Latin?"

Reese jumped at the sound of his voice. "What?"

He smiled. "The tattoo. It's Latin."

"Oh. No. I mean—what does it say?"

He looked at her for a moment, then stood up. "Come on, let's go review that materials estimate."

Flushing a little, Reese turned and headed back toward the winery. She led him to the back door where the tiny office held all the paperwork and blueprints for the new facilities.

"Coffee?" she offered, clearing a stack of books off one chair so he could sit down. "Or there's juice or water or—"

"How about two shots of Irish whiskey and a beer chaser?"

She frowned. "Can you really—?"

"I was kidding."

"Right. Well, I have Cran-Apple juice and—"

"I'm fine, Reese. Let's sit. Please."

He hesitated, and she realized he was waiting for her to take a seat first. *How gentlemanly.* She sat, feeling like a moron, not sure why she was so rattled. It was just Clay. It's not like she hadn't seen him on the floor in his boxer shorts hugging the toilet in her guest room.

Needing a distraction, Reese retrieved the bottle of formula in the small warmer on the corner of her desk. "Give me just a second to screw on the nipple," she told Clay.

Reese winced as the words left her mouth.

Screw? Nipple? Seriously, Reese?

She waited for the dirty joke, but Clay just cleared his throat. "Need help?"

"Would you mind grabbing Oscar out of the cage there?"

Clay nodded and gently unlatched the wire door. She watched his work-roughened hand scoop the warm bundle from inside. The baby opossum wiggled as Clay handed it to her, and Reese brought the bottle to the tiny creature's mouth.

"So you're still saving the world's wayward creatures," he said.

Reese nodded. "It's a little different now than in college. I got licensed through the Department of Fish and Wildlife to rehabilitate small animals a few years ago, so I'm all certified."

"Oh, good. I'll phone the police and let them know they don't need to send the SWAT team after all."

Reese laughed and tilted the bottle to get a better angle. "I still have that raccoon you brought me. The one you found on the side of the road that spring?"

"He's still alive?"

Reese nodded, keeping her eyes on the baby opossum as he greedily emptied the bottle. "He mostly lives in the woods now. Axl taught him to fetch."

"Fetch what, his bong?"

"Don't give him any ideas."

Clay grinned. "Your family's looking good. June and Jed haven't aged a bit, and Larissa's really grown up."

"Yeah, she's become quite the PR whiz. She does a lot for us around here."

Clay was still smiling as Reese focused on the baby opossum so she wouldn't be tempted to look back at him and blurt something stupid about how she missed him or felt proud of him. What did you say to a recovering alcoholic, anyway? Especially one whose gaze made you lightheaded and stupid and tingly all over.

She scratched the tiny animal and commanded herself not to think about that damn tingle. She'd been trying for years, and she'd even succeeded for a while.

Despite what Larissa said about the lack of chemistry between her and Eric, she'd been determined to make that marriage work. She'd shoved aside all her doubts and fears and unwelcome feelings about Clay, and she'd flung herself headfirst down that aisle with the absolute certainty she was doing the right thing in marrying her best friend. She'd been brimming with hope and determination and a love that sure as hell seemed like the right sort of love at the time.

How was she supposed to know there were so many kinds?

She could still feel Clay's eyes on her as she set the empty bottle on her desk and stroked the opossum under the chin. When he spoke, his voice was low and soft.

"I'm proud of you, Reese," he said. "Not just for the animal rescue stuff, but everything you've done with the vineyard."

She looked up at him and nodded. "Thank you." She felt warmth pool in her belly. It was possible the opossum had just peed on her, but more likely it was the effect Clay had on her. She turned and tucked Oscar in his cage before facing Clay again.

He was sitting with his hands folded on the desk in front of him, just watching her. She nodded at his clipboard. "Ready to talk business?"

"Absolutely." He smiled. "This is a pretty ambitious project you're taking on. The wine tourism thing?"

Reese shrugged. "We've gotten flak from some of the other wineries—especially Dick, the guy you just met from Larchwood Vineyards. It's the whole 'we're not in this to make money, we're in this to make wine' thing a lot of vineyard owners like to say."

"And what's your take on that?"

Reese shrugged and picked up her letter opener. "We already make great wines. Doesn't do us much good if no one knows that."

"Good point," Clay said, leaning back in his chair in a way that pulled his T-shirt snugly across his chest. Reese tried not to stare. "So how does the rest of the family feel about the big expansion?"

Reese began to roll the letter opener between her palms. "They're all really supportive—Mom, Dad, Axl. We've been taking it slowly, starting up a wine club that's been really successful, holding events and tastings. This event pavilion is sort of the next big step."

She shut up as she realized Clay's eyes were fixed on her hands. She stopped rolling the letter opener between her palms and waited.

Clay gave a nod that seemed to signal a change in tone, and Reese braced herself for whatever was coming next.

"Let's talk numbers, shall we?" he said.

"Yes, let's," Reese agreed, annoyed by the formality in her own voice. She began to roll the letter opener again, comforted by the curve of it against her palms.

"You want the good news or the bad news first?"

"Good."

"Okay. The area you've staked out looks great. I don't anticipate problems with excess rock or anything like that, and the permits should be pushed through by the end of today. We could break ground as soon as tomorrow."

"What's the bad news?"

Clay sighed. "As we spelled out in the bid, the materials estimates were based on market conditions and prices at the time of the bid. We gave that to you two months ago."

"Has something changed?"

Clay nodded. "For starters, you'd planned to use wood certified by the Forest Stewardship Council for green building—that gives you the points you need for LEED certification."

"Right. So what's the problem?"

"FSC-certified wood just doubled in price in the last month."

Reese stopped rolling the letter opener between her palms. "Oh."

"It gets worse. The plan was to use recycled fly ash in the concrete so you get LEED points for that. But there's been a recall after significant amounts of arsenic were found in a large shipment of fly ash from several big mines in Virginia. It's tougher to get now, which means—"

"Let me guess—the price has gone up?"

Clay nodded and handed her the stack of papers he'd been holding. Reese took them from him and studied the figures in silence, feeling sick. She looked back at Clay. "Why didn't Dorrington Construction plan for this?"

Clay cleared his throat. "We did. There's a contingency in the bid for shifts in market price. If you'd signed off on the estimate two months ago, we might have been able to purchase materials sooner, but—"

"Things don't move that quickly in a family-owned operation like this," she said, swallowing back a surge of panic. "You know that. It took a lot of time to get our finances together, and then the whole family had to agree."

The tension in her own voice made her cringe, and Reese wasn't sure if it was the result of grim news or how unsettled she felt having him so close after this many years. She was almost sure she could feel the heat of him from across the desk, could smell the wood shavings on his skin. The thought made her cheeks grow warmer.

"Look, we can alter the plans here," Clay said. "If you want to change tracks and not go the green-building route, there are a lot of less expensive things we can do."

Reese closed her eyes, feeling her head start to throb. "Not an option. *Wine Spectator* is doing a huge spread on Gold LEED certification. It's been all over our website for months, and we're holding a special Memorial Day event where we'll be unveiling the model."

"Right."

"Environmental stewardship is the backbone of our branding on this whole project. This is Oregon—this is what wineries hang their hats on here."

Clay nodded. "So you're committed."

Reese looked at him, gritting her teeth. "You mean I'm screwed."

"I wouldn't say that, exactly."

"Clay Henderson, missing the opportunity to say *screwed* in any context? That's a first." She grimaced at the waspish sound of her own voice and forced herself to take a few deep breaths before speaking again. "So now what? I don't spearhead multimillion-dollar construction projects on a daily basis. What do I do now?"

He gave her a small smile, one that seemed to warm the brown pools of his eyes, and Reese felt her belly begin to liquefy. "The other pages I gave you outline different options," he said. "Review the numbers, let us know if you want to change course."

Reese frowned. "What if I want to ditch Dorrington Construction altogether and use a different builder? What then?"

"That would be unfortunate," Clay said, stone-faced.

"That's your professional assessment?"

He sighed, folding his hands on the desk. "That could get ugly. You've already signed the contracts, and I'm certain my employer will hold you to that."

"Thank you for your candor."

"No problem."

She looked down at her hands, surprised to see they were shaking. She clenched the letter opener more tightly.

"Look, this is all a little overwhelming," she said. "First you show up out of nowhere, claiming you're clean and sober. Now you're not only going to be working here, but you're telling me this bid is so far off the mark that I can't even see the fucking mark."

"Your frustration is understandable."

Reese dropped the letter opener, something inside her bubbling over the top now. "Frustration? You make it sound like I'm sexually deprived, not in danger of losing this whole construction project. *Frustration* is putting it mildly."

She saw his jaw clench, and he opened his mouth to say something. He hesitated, then closed it. The old Clay would have jumped all over the *sexually deprived* comment, but this one sighed.

"Are we talking about the numbers or about me being here?"

Reese picked up the letter opener again, not meeting his eyes. "I don't know. Look, I'm sorry. The bid thing isn't your fault. I know that. I'm just upset, okay? I should have pushed the family to move faster or—well, whatever. It's done now. The ball is rolling and you're here now." She bit her lip. "*God*, you're really here? It's all so—so—"

Clay cleared his throat. "Look, if it helps, let me say this. Wine was never my poison. You know that. I was a beer man, and this isn't a brewery."

"It's still alcohol, and you're an alcoholic." She flinched at her own words. "I'm proud of you for getting sober and everything, but well— aren't alcoholics always alcoholics, even after rehab?"

"That's true."

Her throat felt tight with emotion, and she was pretty sure it had nothing to do with the bid anymore. "So to be surrounded by temptation like this—"

"I can handle temptation," Clay said, his voice so steely Reese sat back a little in her chair. "I'm well acquainted with temptation."

Reese didn't say anything. She couldn't even blink as Clay's eyes held hers, warm and a little dangerous. He reached across the desk as if to touch her, then stopped, drawing his hand back.

"I take it one day at a time, just like I've been doing for the last four years."

Reese took a shaky breath, her mind not entirely occupied by thoughts of Clay swilling from barrels of Reserve Pinot. That wasn't the temptation that worried her. She looked up to see those root-beer-brown eyes studying her with an intensity that made her stomach clench.

Her mind flashed again to those muscular shoulders, the sheen of sweat on bare skin, the feel of—

The letter opener fell from her palms.

Clay reached over and picked it up, handing it back to her without a word. His fingers brushed hers as she reached out to take it. Before Reese could draw back, he wrapped his fingers around her fist and held tight.

"I can handle this if you can," he murmured.

Reese took a deep breath and looked down at his hand engulfing hers. "I can handle it."

◆　◆　◆

That evening, Clay leaned back from the dinner table and grinned at Eric and Sheila. "You guys have to stop feeding me like this. You'll never get rid of me."

Sheila beamed and passed him a plate of homemade chocolate chip cookies. "It's so wonderful having you here for a little while."

Clay helped himself to a cookie, taking note of the gentle warning: *A little while.* Translation: *Don't get too comfortable, buddy.*

Hell, he deserved that. Clay had still been hanging around when Sheila and Eric started dating a few years after Eric split with Reese. They'd all seen him at his worst, so how could he blame them for thinking he might drag them all through it again?

He'd just have to work harder to prove that wouldn't happen.

"Eric's thrilled to have his oldest friend back in town," Sheila continued as she took a cookie for herself and set it on a little white plate.

Eric squeezed his wife's hand as he tipped his chair onto its back legs and took a bite of cookie. "You hear that?" he said to Clay through a mouthful. "She just called us old."

"Actually, she just called *me* old," Clay pointed out as he grabbed another cookie. "Which makes no sense, since I'm eight months younger than you and brimming with youthful vigor."

Eric snorted. "You're brimming with something, all right."

Sheila stood and began to stack the empty plates, tucking her blonde hair behind one ear as she leaned across the table. Clay got to his feet, setting his cookie aside and reaching out to take them from her. "Let me get those. I'll do the dishes while you guys relax."

"Absolutely not," Sheila said, giving his hand a light swat. "You're a guest. You boys sit here and catch up. There's some of that nonalcoholic beer in the fridge, or I could get you some more water or—"

"I'm fine, really," Clay insisted. "Just let me help with the dishes—"

"Sit!" she commanded.

Clay sat. "Thank you for dinner, Sheila. It was delicious."

"No problem, honey. I'm heading out to watch *The Bachelor* with Reese and Larissa, but you boys stay here and get comfortable."

Eric and Clay began to stack plates as Sheila maneuvered around the table and headed for the kitchen. Clay glanced at Eric, noticing the way his friend watched his wife with undisguised fondness. He tried to remember if Eric had ever looked at Reese that way.

Stop thinking about Reese, he commanded himself. He grabbed another cookie and took a bite.

Eric dropped his chair back to all four legs with a thud. "I think we're grounded."

"Huh?"

"The cookies, the fake beer—my lovely wife is terrified we're going to sneak out for a wild night on the town."

"Ah, I see—she's afraid I'll be a bad influence?"

"Something like that."

Clay wasn't sure what to say to that, so he took another bite of cookie and chewed hard. It wasn't the first time someone from his past showed skepticism about his sobriety, but this time stung a little more for some reason. He sipped his water—recently topped off by Sheila—and ignored the frosty microbrew in the glass beside his friend's plate.

"So things went okay at the vineyard today?" Eric asked.

"Not bad," Clay said, picking at the corner of his cookie. "Reese was pretty upset about some changes in the material costs, but hopefully we'll get it ironed out."

"She seem worried about you being out there with your history and everything?"

"A little," Clay admitted.

"She'll get over it."

"Hope so. We'll be spending a lot of time together."

"Yeah?"

Clay shrugged. "This LEED-certified building process is pretty intense. I'll practically be living out there for some phases of construction. And since Reese *does* live there, I imagine we'll be seeing a lot of each other."

"So you've swapped out alcoholism for workaholism now?"

"Is that even a word?"

"Sure it is," Eric said. "So is douche bag, which is what I'm going to call you if you eat that last cookie."

Clay broke the cookie in two and handed half to Eric. When they were both munching in silence, Clay spoke again. "So is she seeing anyone?"

Eric's eyes narrowed a little. "Reese?"

"Yeah," Clay said, picking at his cookie and trying to look nonchalant.

"Not really. Sheila and I have been trying to get her to date again. Sheila wants to set her up with this guy she knows from work, but Reese keeps canceling."

Clay broke off a piece of cookie, not sure why he couldn't just drop the issue and talk about the Trail Blazers or *Breaking Bad* reruns or something. "I'm surprised she never remarried like you did. Her parents have always been so crazy about each other. Seems like with that sort of example—"

"With that sort of example, Reese is a fucking basket case about marriage," Eric said. "Her parents made it look too easy. Sorta like growing up with a dad who's a tennis pro or a mom who's a supermodel. All you can do is notice how far you fall short."

Clay raised an eyebrow. "Does the doctorate in psychology just come with the enology degree, or did you pay extra for that?"

Eric gave him a look like he was an exceptionally dense child. "Jed and June have the world's most perfect marriage. There's no way Reese can match it, so she doesn't bother trying."

Clay nodded, not sure he followed the logic, but pretty sure Eric knew Reese better than he did. They both picked at the last of the cookie crumbs in silence.

"Why are you asking about Reese?" Eric said at last.

"No reason," Clay said, determined to keep his tone light. "Just curious."

"Because if you're thinking of asking her out—"

"Dude," Clay said, looking up with an expression he hoped conveyed the right amount of horror. "Your ex-wife? Isn't that like the number one rule in the guy code of ethics?"

Eric grinned. "It's the one between not talking at the urinal and never sharing an umbrella with another guy."

"No, I think it's the one just before never watching men's gymnastics on TV."

"After the requirement that you be able to quote at least three lines from *Rocky*, though, right?"

"Yeah, but I think it's before the one about making sure every guy hug is preceded by a bro handshake."

"And never using the term YOLO."

"Or setting your Facebook profile photo to a picture of your pets or kids."

"And never making eye contact while eating a banana."

"Exactly," Clay said, relieved the familiar pattern of their banter had defused the awkwardness of the conversation.

But Eric wasn't ready to drop it just yet. "It would be weird. You and Reese, I mean. It's not just the man code. We're friends. All three of us. You don't shit where you eat, you know what I'm saying?"

"Your wife ever tell you you've got a real romantic way with words?"

"No."

"Can't imagine why."

Eric fell silent a moment. He cleared his throat. "You're not still sore about college, are you?"

Clay looked up. "What do you mean?"

"I know you kind of had the hots for Reese first, but then she and I got together and then—"

"No," Clay said, shaking his head for emphasis. "No."

"Because I don't want things to be weird."

"Don't be an idiot. We never even dated."

Clay felt his gut twist on that comment, but he forced himself to hold Eric's gaze, not to look away or even blink.

Eric was studying him with an interest that made Clay uncomfortable. "Still—"

"Dude, it was a long time ago," Clay said, brushing cookie crumbs off the front of his shirt. "Vodka under the bridge and all that."

Eric nodded. "Whatever you say."

CHAPTER FOUR

Reese drained her wineglass and took aim at the TV with the remote. "Well, that was a stupid choice."

Sheila laughed as she stood up and reached for Reese's empty glass. "Since when do women on reality TV dating shows make smart decisions about men?"

Larissa handed her glass over with a snort. "Since when do *any* of us make smart decisions about men?"

"Speak for yourself," Sheila called as she set the stemware on Reese's counter before trooping back to the sofa. "I happen to think I picked a pretty good guy, myself."

"I'd raise a toast to that if you hadn't just taken my glass," Reese agreed.

"You want it back?" Sheila asked. "The glass, not the man. I'm keeping him."

Larissa rolled her eyes. "Okay, can I just say you two are my weirdest friends? In what world can two women be BFFs after tying the knot with the same guy?"

"Reality TV," Sheila said, beaming. "Is *Sister Wives* still on the air?"

Reese shrugged. "No idea. But I like our arrangement better anyway. She has the guy, I have my sanity. It's a win-win for everyone."

"Amen," Sheila said. "Not everyone finds their soul mate on the first try. There's no shame in a starter marriage."

Reese nodded, though she felt a dark wave roll through her. She didn't think it was shame, exactly, but something made her want to change the subject in a hurry. "What's Eric up to tonight?"

"Hanging out with Clay at the house."

The dark wave was replaced by a swirly little flip in Reese's gut at the mention of Clay's name, but she kept her expression neutral. "Drinking beer and farting like old times?"

"Not that I could tell," Sheila said as she plunked back down on the sofa beside Reese. "Well, not Clay anyway. Eric's probably doing both, but Clay's too busy trying to be a model citizen."

There was a sharp note in Sheila's voice that made Reese look up. "Not a Clay fan?"

Sheila shrugged. "Clay's fine. I'm glad he got sober and all. I just don't know that Eric needs that energy in his life right now."

"*Energy.*" Larissa laughed. "Is that another way of saying women throw their panties at Clay and you'd rather not have Eric catching a pair?"

Sheila was spared having to answer as the doorbell chimed. Reese glanced at her watch, annoyed at whoever felt the need to drop by at nine p.m. on a weeknight.

She flung open the door. "Dick," she said.

"Yes!" Larissa called from the couch. "I've been wishing there was a delivery service for dick."

Reese ignored her and raised an eyebrow at her disgruntled-looking neighbor standing on the front porch. "Can I help you?"

"That animal is a menace!"

Reese resisted the urge to smile as Dick cupped a protective hand over his groin. Beside the house, Leon the alpaca gave a proud chortle and twitched the ear with the heart-shaped splotch. "Was he on your property?"

Dick glowered at her. "That doesn't matter. I needed to come over to discuss official business, and that *thing*—"

"Why are you here, Dick?"

"Well, for starters, would you mind informing me just where you plan to put all the cars that will be coming out for your little Memorial

Day weekend event? If you think they're going to be parking on my property—"

"We've hired a horse-drawn carriage service," Reese interrupted. "Guests will be able to park in the lower acreage, and we'll bring them up in groups in the carriage."

"I included that in the press release," Larissa said, leaping off the couch and moving to the doorway so she stood shoulder to shoulder with Reese. "I sent a copy to all the other wineries we're on friendly terms with. Oh, wait—that wouldn't be you, would it?"

"Dick, go home," Reese said. "We've got everything under control here."

"Oh, really?"

"Really. I know you're still pissed about my grandpa not selling you the east acreage and the fact that we won those three medals, and—"

"And the fact that your wife ran off with your hottie winemaker," Larissa added cheerfully. "Sorry about that."

Dick flushed crimson, and for a moment Reese worried he might take a swing at Larissa. Instead, he tried another tack.

"You'd better make sure you have those event permits in order," he snapped. "I have a friend who works for the county. I'm having lunch with him tomorrow, and it would be a shame if you held an event out here without having the proper permits."

"Goodnight, Dick," Reese said, and shut the door in his face. She turned to Larissa. "You did get the permits, right?"

Larissa rolled her eyes. "Of course. He's just being a—well, I was going to say *dick*, but that's an insult to penises everywhere. Hey, speaking of penises—"

"We were not speaking of penises," Reese said.

"We could start," Sheila called from the sofa.

Reese's cell phone rang, and for the second time in five minutes, she was grateful that the sound of ringing had saved her from an awkward conversation. She snatched the phone off the end table as Sheila and Larissa got down to the business of discussing genitals.

"Hello?" she said as she stepped into the hallway.

"Hi, Reese."

The voice made her throat clench. Not an unpleasant sensation, and not unfamiliar, either. She hadn't realized she'd stopped breathing until she felt herself grow dizzy.

"Clay. Um, hello. Hi. Good evening."

"Just wanted to make sure Sheila's okay to drive," he said. "I'm heading past there on my way back to the hotel. Eric said you guys were drinking wine, and if she's had too much, I'm happy to pick her up."

"Oh," Reese said, gathering her bearings. "I'm pretty sure she's fine. One bottle split three ways over the course of two hours—" She held the phone away from her ear. "Sheila, you okay to drive?"

"Is that my dashing and considerate husband? He's *so* getting lucky tonight."

"Um, no. No, it's Clay."

Sheila looked up from her station on the sofa. "Clay?"

"Offering a ride."

Larissa grinned. "I can think of a lot of women who'd take him up on that."

Reese rolled her eyes and put the phone back to her ear. "We're all fine, but thanks for the offer." She hesitated, not ready to end the call, though she wasn't sure why. "Everything okay there?"

Clay cleared his throat. "Yeah, sure. Just catching up on old times—college, girls, jail terms, stuff like that."

Reese turned her back to the sofa so her cousin and friend wouldn't see her face. "Good. That's good. Reconnecting with old friends is always, um—"

"Reese?"

"Yes?"

There was a long pause, and Reese pictured him running his fingers through his hair, his frown making little creases between his eyebrows. She waited, wondering why the hell her heart felt like someone was cinching a piece of twine around it.

"It was good to see you again today."

"Right," she said. "Good to see you, too."

There was a long pause, and Reese could hear Clay's breathing, low and shallow and almost warm in her ear.

"I missed you," he said.

Reese bit her lip, not sure what to say to that. There were a lot of things she'd missed about him—the easy conversation, the wicked sense of humor, the smile that made her stomach flutter no matter how hard she tried to pretend it didn't.

There were a lot of things she *hadn't* missed—the constant worry, the calls from jail, the promises that this time, *this time*, he'd stay sober.

But had she missed *him*?

She took a breath, started to speak, then stopped. On the other end of the line, Clay cleared his throat.

"Look, about that night at Finnigan's five years ago—"

"You've already apologized, Clay."

"I know. I know I apologized that you got hurt, but—"

"You weren't the one who threw the punch."

"No, but if you hadn't been trying to pull me out of a bar fight, you wouldn't have gotten hit at all. Look, I just wanted to say I'm sorry I didn't come see you in the hospital."

Reese bit her lip. "You were in jail. And I was only there a few hours. It was just a broken nose." She hesitated, wondering why he'd brought it up at all. "You kinda disappeared after that. Just left without telling any of us where you were going."

"I know. I'm sorry about that, too. And I'm sorry you guys couldn't visit. I had to get my life together, and I needed to distance myself to do that."

"I understand. I appreciated the call from rehab so at least I didn't worry."

"Step nine," he said softly. "That's the one about making amends. I owed you a lot more of those than I could fit into one phone call."

Reese nodded, remembering the call. Remembering the stupid, traitorous way her heart had leapt into her throat, fluttering like a drunken butterfly. She and Eric had been divorced for a few years by then, but they'd still been best friends. She'd never asked him if he heard from Clay, too. If he got the same sort of phone call late on a winter evening with Clay's voice echoing down the line like it came from another planet. Maybe she hadn't wanted to know. Maybe she'd wanted to believe the call was something special, something only she and Clay shared.

Reese bit her lip. "You never told me what the fight at Finnigan's was about."

It wasn't exactly a question, but she held her breath anyway as she waited for a response. On the other end of the line, Clay was quiet. When he finally spoke, his voice sounded a few octaves lower.

"Just another drunken bar fight. You know how it was. How *I* was."

"That one seemed different."

"It's what finally landed me in rehab, if that's what you meant."

That wasn't what she'd meant, but she wasn't sure what she *did* mean. All she knew was that the night at Finnigan's had been the final straw. The only time she hadn't tried to bail him out of jail. The moment she'd really, truly given up on him.

She cleared her throat. "It's okay, Clay. My nose healed up just fine. It's not even crooked."

"I noticed," he said. "You're still beautiful. Maybe more now than you were then."

Reese felt tears sting the back of her eyes, and she balled her hand into a fist, willing herself not to cry. "Thank you," she whispered. Her voice came out so quiet she wasn't sure he heard her.

On the other end of the line, she could hear his breath in her ear, the scrape of his chin against the phone's receiver. At last, he sighed.

"Goodnight, Reese."

"Goodnight, Clay," she repeated, and closed her eyes as fifteen years' worth of stupid longing came surging back.

♦ ♦ ♦

A few hours later, Clay stared at the glowing green numbers on the hotel clock radio and wondered how hard he'd have to squint to rearrange them in an order that would let him get more than a few hours of sleep.

Midnight.

Back in his drinking days, the party would just be getting started, even if there was no party. Even if it was just him sitting alone in his kitchen with a half rack of beer vanishing before it had a chance to grow warm and bitter on the table.

Not that he was bitter now. About anything. He'd made bad choices, and he was making better ones now.

If only you'd done that fifteen years ago, Reese might not have married Eric, and you might have—

"No."

He startled himself by saying the word aloud, but it felt right, so he said it again. "No!"

He didn't turn to drinking because he lost out on the girl of his dreams, though maybe he lost out on the girl of his dreams because of the drinking. He'd been aimed down that path long before college. Long before Reese came into his life.

Once upon a time, he might have had a shot at her. Back when he was young and hopeful and just a guy who liked to knock back a few beers after class. There was that tiny window of time when he'd first met her, a fleeting instant of new friendship and blossoming attraction. A week or two?

He hadn't done anything to win her over. He didn't blame Eric for making a move.

He blamed himself for not making one.

He rolled over again and closed his eyes, willing himself to go to sleep.

◆　◆　◆

The sun wasn't even up at five a.m. the next morning, but Reese had been out in the vineyard working on the tractor for thirty minutes already. She jumped down and nodded at one of the field hands.

"Okay, I just recalibrated the sprayer," she said as she tucked the wrench in her back pocket. "You should get a little better coverage now."

The field hand—a new guy she'd just hired from a vineyard in Washington—gave her a dubious look. "This organic stuff kills powdery mildew?"

Reese nodded and pulled off her work gloves. "Sonata and Serenade are both bacterial fermentations, plus a couple of potassium bicarbonates and a little pine resin extract to help it stick—"

She stopped talking when she saw the man's eyes glaze over. "Just spray," she said. "Nice job so far."

She headed back to the winery barn with her gloves tucked in her pocket and a peaceful feeling in her soul. She wasn't a morning person, but she loved mornings like this. The soothing hum of tractors vibrated the low-slung clouds in the still and cool air, with the chirp of the birds rising above the background noise.

She pushed open the door to the winery barn and made a beeline for the coffeemaker.

She didn't see Clay until she tripped over his legs.

"Clay?" she gasped, recovering her balance as she looked down to see him sprawled on the floor. "What are you doing?"

He looked up from where he was lying on the floor beside a wine barrel and gave her a funny smile. His eyes were too bright for so early in the morning and, *oh, God*—what was he drinking?

"Morning, Reese," he said. He swayed a little as he sat up and grabbed an orange sippy cup. Reese watched his Adam's apple move as he drank. She closed her eyes. When she opened them again, he was still there, looking scruffy and wild in the same shirt he'd been wearing the day before.

He's fallen off the wagon.

Again.

He smiled at her then, and Reese wanted to kick her traitorous libido for responding when he was obviously so—so—

"Clay." She stared at the sippy cup.

Seeing her eyes on it, he lifted it in a mock toast to her. "Couldn't find any mugs, but I made coffee. You still like it black?"

"Coffee," she repeated like a very dense toddler learning to talk. He was drinking coffee? On the floor? From a sippy cup? She tried to regroup. "What are you—Why are you—"

"Couldn't sleep," he said, standing up slowly. He braced himself on the edge of the wine barrel and lifted himself to his full height—which, frankly, was pretty impressive. Reese took a step back, trying not to stare at his hands.

"There wasn't anything good on TV," Clay said. "I figured I might as well come here and take care of your wine bar before someone breaks an arm and sues you."

He sipped from the cup again. He hadn't shaved yet, and a faint sheen of sawdust and sweat clung to his arms.

Reese swallowed. When she finally found her voice, her words came out in a croak. "You fixed my wine bar?"

"Built a new one, actually," he said, thumping a fist on the large wooden shape Reese had somehow failed to notice in her panic over finding him drunk on the floor. "I hope you don't mind—I found some scrap wood out behind the barn, and I had my toolbox in the truck and—"

"You built me a new wine bar?" Her voice came out shriller than she intended, but she suddenly had very little control over her vocal cords. Or any other parts, judging from the way her body was responding to the sight of his arms in that snug T-shirt.

"Thank you," she finally stammered. "I can't believe you did this. How long did it take?"

Clay shrugged and set his cup down on the rough-hewn plywood. "Couple hours, give or take."

"You've been here since three a.m.?"

"More like two a.m., I guess. Took me awhile to find the wood in the dark."

The old Clay would have made a joke about finding wood in the dark, but this Clay just pulled out a wrench and began tightening bolts. Then he gripped the edges of the bar and gave it a firm shake. Everything held steady, a vast improvement on the old bar.

He looked back up at her and smiled. "It's a little rough, but it's sturdy. You can throw that tablecloth thing over it like you did the other one."

"I can't believe you did this," Reese stammered. "Let me get my checkbook—What do I owe you?"

Clay frowned. "Reese, cut it out. We're still friends, right? You don't have to pay me for work you didn't ask me to do."

"But—"

"I did it because I wanted to. And because I didn't want you to maim anyone with that other bar."

Reese pressed her lips together, unsure how to handle this. "At least let me give you something. Can I make you breakfast?"

"That depends. Do you still make scrambled eggs that taste like mortar paste?"

She smiled a little, not sure if it was the joke or the fact that she finally had evidence that she *had* changed at least a little in the past few years. "For your information, I took a bunch of continuing ed classes last year—mostly on wine pairings, but I did a cooking one, too. I'm now a perfectly adequate cook."

"In that case, I'd love breakfast."

"Good," she said, moving toward the door. "My house is the little place right next door."

"That tiny building? I didn't know that was a house."

"What did you think it was?"

He shrugged. "I saw all the signs that said it was private property and not open to the public. Figured it was Axl's bomb shelter or something."

Reese laughed. "No, this company called Idea Box makes these superefficient prefab homes that are really environmentally friendly. Perfect for someone living alone."

"Huh," he said. "That's not what I pictured you in."

The thought that Clay had pictured her at all over the last few years was enough to make her pulse kick up a notch, and she wondered what he'd imagined, exactly. "I'm reducing my carbon footprint. It's eight hundred and fifty square feet, has bamboo flooring, energy-efficient appliances, contemporary cabinets, a built-in wine cooler, the whole package. Why? Are you going to pick on the construction?"

"Not at all. I might pick on you for putting your home forty feet from your job."

Reese shrugged. "I like it. It's a beautiful place, and it's convenient."

"That it is," he agreed as she opened the door and led the way inside.

The home was designed to be tiny, but it looked even smaller with Clay planted in the center of her living room. Even her furniture looked miniscule.

Reese stepped away from him, moving toward the kitchen. "The bathroom is over there if you want to wash up. I've got pesto and tomatoes—how about an omelet?"

"Perfect."

"Do you like chicken apple sausage?"

He grinned. "Remind me to build things for you more often."

He brushed past her as he headed for the bathroom, and Reese shivered at the heat radiating from his bare arms.

She retreated toward the kitchen and began pulling things out of the refrigerator—cheese, eggs, orange juice. She opened the little container of pesto and frowned. Did pesto have alcohol in it? She couldn't remember if this one had white wine as an ingredient, but did that make it unsafe to serve an alcoholic? She studied the product information on the back of the container. No mention of wine. She sniffed it.

"Why does it seem like a bad sign that you're sniffing the food?" Clay asked as he returned to the kitchen and leaned against the counter.

Reese jumped and set the pesto down. "It's fine," she stammered. "I was just checking—just making sure it's okay to serve you."

He gave her a funny look but didn't comment. Reese opened the egg carton and reached for her skillet.

"Let me dice the tomatoes," he said, moving around her to grab the cutting board from beside the fridge. "Where's your knife?"

"I've got it—You don't have to do that."

"You can trust me with sharp objects, Reese. This drawer?"

"No, that one over there." She reached past him, her arm brushing his chest as she moved to hand it to him. She almost dropped it on the floor. She turned and reached into the cupboard above the stove, pulling out a plate.

"Here, you can put them on this," she said.

"Thank you."

He was quiet as he began dicing, the knife making squishy noises as it sliced through the tomato flesh. "I don't remember you being this jumpy," he said finally.

"I'm just a little off, I guess. Mornings aren't really my thing, you know."

The second the words were out of her mouth, she felt her cheeks heat up. She opened her mouth to stammer an apology, then shut it.

He's probably not even thinking about that. And even if he is, you were gone before morning came—

"Is this a good size?"

Reese whirled and looked at him, half expecting a penis joke. He was standing with the knife in one hand and a pile of perfectly diced Roma tomatoes in front of him.

"That's great. Thank you."

"My pleasure. Want me to shred cheese?"

"I've got it. Really, just sit down. Please."

He grinned. "I'm making you nervous?"

She sighed. "Look, this is just—it's a little weird for me, okay? Having you here, having you sober, having you suddenly turn up this totally changed person with impeccable manners and this constant urge to be helpful."

He nodded and set the knife down, moving toward the table without another word. He pulled out a chair and sat. "Got it."

Reese bit her lip as she picked up the container of pesto, trying to gauge his mood. Had she offended him? He didn't look angry, but she really couldn't tell. The old Clay had been simpler, with emotions amplified by alcohol and a missing social filter. But this Clay—

"I want us to be friends, Reese," he said at last. "I know it's a little odd—a former drunk and a vineyard manager. I ruined a lot of friendships when I was a drunk, so the ones I have left—" He swallowed. "You and Eric are really important to me."

She waited to see if he'd say anything else. If he'd mention what had been flitting at the edge of her memory since he'd appeared in her doorway the day before.

"Friends," she repeated. "I think I can do that."

"Good. I just don't want—" He stopped, seeming to consider his words. "I don't want things to be awkward between us. You know?"

Reese nodded, not sure she *did* know but certain she didn't want to have this conversation right now when she hadn't finished sorting through her own feelings.

"Right," she said. "I don't want things to be awkward, either."

"Good. I'm glad."

Reese looked down at the omelet, her hands shaking as she nudged it with her spatula. "So we're friends. I can do this."

He stood up again, unfolding his long legs from underneath the table. Reese gripped the handle of her omelet pan hard as Clay closed the distance between them in three slow strides.

He stopped in front of her, so close—closer than he'd been in years. She could feel his breath ruffling her hair. She stared straight at the center of his chest, afraid that if she looked up she wouldn't be able to stop herself from—what?

"Reese?"

"Yes?"

She looked up and met his eyes. Something hot and dizzying knifed through her belly. He didn't blink. She didn't breathe. They were frozen in the moment, locked in each other's gazes.

She lifted her hand to touch him. She stopped herself, bit her lip, lowered her hand.

Clay closed his eyes, his expression somewhere between pain and the dizzy euphoria he'd always glowed with after twelve too many beers. Was he holding his breath?

He opened his eyes and looked away, his face flushed. "Your plates." He swallowed. "You pulled them out of that cupboard, right?" He nodded over her shoulder. "May I set the table?"

Reese took a breath and nodded. "Table. Yes."

She started to step away, to break the force field, but he reached for her. His fingertips grazed her cheekbone, lingering there for a second as his eyes held hers. Reese didn't stop to think. She turned her face into his palm, not sure what was happening but also not sure she wanted to stop it. She stood there for a few heartbeats, his calloused hand solid against her cheekbone, her own breath warm against his palm.

She looked up to see Clay watching her. She saw his jaw clench and unclench as he took a breath. Then he drew his hand away and reached for the cupboard door.

"Plates," he murmured.

"Right," Reese agreed, and stepped back. She flipped the omelet with a shaky grip, her cheek burning where he'd touched her.

♦　♦　♦

Clay held the door open for Reese as they entered the winery barn together. She was laughing at something he'd just said—a beautiful, melodic kind of laughter that made him want to take up juggling or mime or anything that might keep her laughing like that forever—so he didn't notice Eric until they were standing right in front of him.

"Morning," Eric said with a glance at his watch. He was smiling, but he raised an eyebrow at Clay before shooting Reese a pointed look.

Clay caught a glimpse of his own reflection in the office window and felt a wave of dread. Same shirt he'd worn last night at Eric's, uncombed hair and beard stubble, and now here he was at seven in the morning with Reese laughing up at him—

"Nothing happened," Clay blurted.

Reese gave him a startled look. From the corner of his eye, Clay saw Eric shake his head.

"Dude," Eric said. "I didn't say a word."

Clay wanted to climb into an empty wine barrel and stay there until Sunday, but Eric turned away from them as a corner door swung open and Sheila came hustling through.

"Morning, everyone," she called as she beamed at them. "Reese, honey, where's the extra TP? I just used the last of it and I don't want to leave anyone hanging."

"I'll get it in a sec, don't worry about it," Reese said, stepping forward to give her a hug. "Great shoes!"

Sheila hugged back while Clay stole a glance at Eric, wondering if it was awkward to have his ex-wife and his new wife hugging and chatting about toilet paper. Eric didn't seem to notice.

"You like?" Sheila asked, tipping her shoe up to give everyone a better view. "I got them at a half-price sale in Portland last week. Aren't the little flowers just the cutest?"

"I bet they'd go great with your pink sweater," Reese said.

"Oh, you're right! I'll have to try that."

Reese stepped away and moved toward the wine bar. Clay tried not to watch, hoping like hell Eric and Sheila hadn't noticed he was having a tough time keeping his eyes off her.

Don't shit where you eat. Eric's words echoed in Clay's head, making him wince at the crudeness.

"Did you guys see this?" Reese called. "Clay made us a new wine bar."

Everyone watched as Reese ran her hand over the top of it. Clay resisted the urge to beam with pride as Reese fingered the knots in the bar's surface.

Jesus, dude—get a grip. She's just rubbing the wood.

He also resisted the urge to make that comment aloud.

"Pretty," Sheila cooed.

"We won't have to use the wine barrels and the board for tastings anymore," Reese continued. "This one's bigger, too—we can probably hold half a dozen people now."

Eric set down the wine case he was carrying and nodded at her. "That's great." He turned to Clay. "When did you find time to do that?"

Clay shrugged. "Couldn't sleep. Had to do something with my hands."

"Don't you get porn on pay-per-view at the motel?"

Clay thought about commenting that he didn't watch X-rated movies, that it was part of his quest to be a better guy after rehab. Then he felt like a jerk for even *thinking* about porn with Reese standing right there. He wasn't that kind of guy anymore.

Reese rolled her eyes at them, oblivious to Clay's inner turmoil. "You guys are such twelve-year-olds. Check it out, see how much sturdier the new bar is?"

She gripped the edges of it and pushed on it the way Clay had done earlier.

But something happened.

One second, she was smiling as she leaned into the bar.

The next, she was toppling forward as the wood gave way.

Clay didn't think. He just lunged for her, grabbing her hard around the waist as the board came loose and hit the concrete with an angry clatter. She felt warm and soft and dizzyingly perfect in his arms, and he held her tightly, not wanting to let go until he was sure she was safe.

Reese's mouth opened, then closed without a word.

He slid his hands over her, trying to be professional as he inspected her for damage, but the feeling of her body beneath his palms just made him want to keep touching her.

"Are you okay?" he asked.

She blinked up at him, her chest rising and falling fast as she opened her mouth again.

No words came out. She looked down at his arm around her waist. Clay released her, feeling embarrassed and aroused at the same time.

Eric stepped between them and put a hand on the bar. "What the hell happened? Was that board not bolted down or something?"

Clay shook his head, still too rattled to form a coherent thought. "No," Clay said. "No, I'm sure—"

He stopped. Hell, was he sure? He'd been distracted by Reese when he was finishing up. Maybe he hadn't tightened them all the way. Or maybe the booze really had pickled his brain all those years.

Sheila bent down and picked up a splintered piece of wood. She studied it for a second, then held it up for them to see. "Looks like termites," she said. "Where'd you get this?"

"Behind the barn," Clay said. "I didn't realize—" He stopped as he saw Reese rubbing her elbow. "Are you hurt?"

Again, his conscience screamed. *She's hurt* again *because of you.*

"I'm fine," she said. "Just a little bruised. Can the bar be fixed?"

"Termites?" Eric asked, turning to stare at Reese. "There are termites here?"

She sighed. "I've got it under control, Eric."

"You knew about this?" He rolled his eyes. "Were you going to tell me? Jesus, we can't have a termite-infested winery barn. Are you kidding me?"

"I said I've got it under control," she snapped.

"What, with all-natural pest control again? You're going to feed them bad tofu or something?"

She folded her arms over her chest and glared at him. "Well, would you rather I have an exterminator spraying God-knows-what chemicals around your precious wine barrels? Besides, once we've got the new facility built, it won't be a problem."

"When the hell is that going to be?" Eric snapped. "With the bid all fucked up, we could be waiting a long time."

"Guys, cool it," Sheila said, stepping between them and resting her hand on her husband's arm. "Give Reese a break, honey. She just got the stuffing knocked out of her."

"My fault," Clay said. "Really, I'm sorry."

"Forget it," Reese said. "I'm fine, you're fine, the bar's fine. Can it be fixed?"

Clay clenched his jaw and nodded. "Sure, no problem. I can replace that board in just a few minutes."

Eric grabbed the wrench Clay had left sitting on top of a wine barrel and handed it over. Hell, had he really walked out earlier with his tools lying around like that? He'd been more distracted than he'd realized. He should have noticed the termite damage, should have realized someone—*Reese*—could get hurt.

"You sure you're okay, Reese?" Eric grumbled. "Looks like you scratched your arm."

Clay looked up and saw the angry red mark near her elbow. He felt like a jerk all over again.

"I'm fine, really," Reese insisted. "I'll just get a Band-Aid."

Clay picked up the board and thought about kicking something, but figured he'd already done enough damage. The front door of the winery swung open, and Clay looked up to see Jed holding the door open for June. She breezed through with a quick kiss on her husband's cheek. Jed followed, smiling at his wife as he limped along behind her. When he paused to adjust his junk through his bike shorts, Clay had to look away.

"I fed Leon," Jed said. "Damn animal butted me in the nuts again."

"He got me yesterday," Eric muttered.

"Who's Leon?" Clay asked.

Eric shook his head. "Asshole alpaca. Reese's pet. Doesn't like to hang out with the rest of his herd, so he just stands there by Reese's place and waits to head-butt men who come near. Does it to every guy he meets except for Axl."

"Right in the gonads," Jed added. "Hard."

June gazed up at him with a look of concern. "Are you sure you're okay, sweetheart? That one was a pretty hard hit."

"It's fine," he said, kissing his wife on the forehead. "You're a nice distraction."

"Maybe a bubble bath later would help," she murmured.

"That sounds nice." He nuzzled her neck. "I call dibs on choosing the music."

"I call dibs on picking the candles. How about those ginger ones you like?"

"Guys!" Reese interrupted. "Come on, cut it out! I'm right here."

June laughed and gave her daughter a fond smile. "Oh, Reese. Are you going to do that thing where you put your fingers in your ears and hum?"

"I might if you and dad don't stop the sexy talk in the middle of the damn barn."

June's smile deepened, but she let go of her husband's arm, grabbing Reese's arm instead. "Come on, dear. You said you wanted to go over the numbers for the materials to see if we can figure out how to make this LEED thing work. You ready?"

Reese flinched and looked down at the spot her mother clutched just below the elbow. Clay felt guilt pooling in his gut as June held up her daughter's arm and frowned.

"What did you do, sweetie? That scratch looks awful."

Reese shrugged. "It's fine. Just cut it on our new bar."

"A new bar?" Jed said. He stepped up to admire it, running his hand over one of the wood planks still in place.

Somehow, watching Jed stroke the wood didn't have the same effect on Clay as when Reese had done it.

"Did you build this, son?" he asked Clay.

"Yes, sir."

"Nice work. We've needed something like this."

"My pleasure," Clay said, his mind more on Jed's daughter than on Jed. "Reese, I have a first-aid kit in my truck. Let me—"

"It's okay, really," Reese said. "I've got Band-Aids in the office."

"Let's get some ointment on it, too, sweetie," June said as she led her daughter away. "You don't want it to get infected."

He watched them walk away, trying hard not to stare at Reese's ass. He looked back at Jed, who, thankfully, was not a mind reader. Jed was more interested in adjusting his bike cleats than recognizing the fact that Clay was having impure thoughts about his daughter.

"I have to run, guys," Sheila said as she stood on tiptoe to kiss Eric. "Have a good day, okay?"

"Sure," Eric mumbled. "You mean assuming the damn termite-infested building doesn't collapse around us?"

"Be nice," she scolded. Then she squeezed his arm and went clicking across the concrete floor to the door. Eric watched her go, smiling a little as she turned and blew him a kiss.

"Anyone seen Axl this morning?" Jed asked.

"He was out back working on his motorcycle earlier," Eric said. "When did he get the T-shirt that says 'If you can read this, the bitch fell off'?"

"That was a gift from Larissa," Jed said. "We tried to hide it from him so he wouldn't offend the ladies at the Senior Center, but he found it in the hamper this morning."

As if on cue, the door burst open and Axl came marching through. He wore black leather chaps over torn jeans, and something that looked like a dog chain around his neck. Behind him stood two similarly dressed senior citizens with matted facial hair and arms that looked like tattooed tree trunks.

Axl spotted Jed and flipped up his aviator bifocals. "There you are," he said, marching forward with the men on his heels. "You trying to ditch us again?"

Jed sighed. "Axl, I keep telling you—the wine country bike tours are for bicycles—not motorcycles."

"It doesn't say that anywhere in the brochure," he insisted, folding his arms over his chest. "A bike is a bike, am I right, boys?"

One of the men nodded. "You're always right, Axl."

Jed glanced at his watch. "I thought you had a Bingo tournament this morning, Axl."

"I did, but half the crew got dragged off to the pokey last night for stealing Preparation H from Walmart. That leaves my schedule free for a bike tour."

"It's not that kind of bike tour," Jed argued. "Look, I've got twenty-eight people signed up to make the loop between here and the other five vineyards in the program, and I don't need you guys on your hogs flipping off cops and mooning cars."

"It was just that once," Axl muttered. Seeming to notice the others in the room for the first time, he narrowed his eyes at Clay. "You ride?"

"'Fraid not."

"Damn shame. The gang's always looking for fresh blood. You staying nearby while you're here?"

"I'm at a hotel in town for now," Clay said. "The company offered to spring for a long-term rental, but we haven't found anything yet."

"So you don't have a place lined up?"

"I just got here. Haven't really had a chance to go house hunting."

"Hell—you can rent my old place. The one I lived in 'til I shacked up with the kids last year? It's right there on the edge of the vineyard, all convenient for you. Nice little bachelor pad, if you know what I mean. Mirrors on the ceiling—"

"That's actually not a bad idea, Axl," Jed said, then frowned. "Not the mirrors—I mean, the cabin's just sitting there empty. Clay, you're welcome to rent it if you'd like. We'd make you a deal."

At the edge of the group, Eric cleared his throat and looked at Clay. "Didn't you say something about wanting to be closer to town?"

Clay looked at his old friend, trying to read his expression. Was Eric trying to save him from stammering an awkward refusal? Or was he trying to minimize the time Clay spent at the vineyard?

Either way, Clay knew what to say. "Thanks, but I've got a line on a couple possibilities in town. I appreciate the offer, though."

Axl shrugged. "Suit yourself. The place is empty if you change your mind. All right, boys—you want to ride or you want to go dig for 'shrooms in the woods again?"

"Ride," one of the geriatric beefcakes answered. "Later on the 'shrooms."

The other guy bobbed his head on his neckless shoulders and led them back outside.

Once the door shut behind them, Jed shook his head before turning back to Eric and Clay. "Okay, kids, I'm out of here. Tell my beautiful wife I miss her already."

"Will do, sir," Clay said, shifting the wrench in his hands.

As soon as Jed was gone, Clay set the wrench down and turned to Eric. "Thanks for getting me off the hook there."

Eric nodded once, eyeing him with an expression Clay couldn't quite read. "No sweat. I've always got your back. You know that."

"I appreciate it."

Eric picked up a bottle of wine on the edge of the shelf and studied it, not looking at Clay. "You didn't really want to stay out here, did you?"

Clay shoved his hands in his pockets and cleared his throat. "No. Not at all."

"I figured the temptation might be too much."

Clay stared at him. Eric stared back.

"All the alcohol and everything," Eric added. "Why take risks with that sort of thing?"

Clay nodded. "Temptation. Right."

CHAPTER FIVE

Reese was exhausted after spending the morning crunching numbers with her mom and the afternoon negotiating prices on new wine barrels from her favorite cooperage in France.

Exhausted and hungry. She glanced at her watch as she stepped out into the overcast evening air and turned to lock the winery door.

"Calling it a day?" Eric shouted from his perch on the picnic table.

She looked over her shoulder to see him reading one of the tattered romance novels she'd left lying around. "Yup. I'm done. Why are you still here?"

"Waiting for Sheila to pick me up. You doing anything fun this evening?"

Reese shrugged and rolled her shoulders, trying to ease the tension in her neck. "Thought I'd hang out at home, feed the opossum, maybe read a book, and catch up on some of the online orders we got for that new Pinot."

"Let me guess," he said as he held up her book "You're rereading this one again?"

"I like Jennifer Crusie."

"And you prefer rereading old books to experiencing new ones. Or doing anything to meet new people and extricate yourself from your over-idealized fantasies of love and relationships."

Reese rolled her eyes. "You know, this Freud thing is getting old."

"Tell you what," Eric said, setting down the book and pulling out his cell phone. "I've got a buddy in Newberg I think you'd really click with. Let me see what he's doing this evening. If he's free, you and me and Sheila can meet up at the Vineyard Grill for a quick dinner and some drinks."

"Eric, I don't really think—"

"I'm dialing right now."

"Come on, is this really—"

"It's ringing."

"Eric, I don't want—"

"Hey, Bob—how's it going?" Eric held up his hand at Reese to silence her, so she settled for kicking him in the shin.

"Listen, man," Eric said. "A few of us are getting together at the Vineyard Grill in about an hour if you feel like meeting up for a beer."

Reese folded her arms over her chest and considered, not for the first time, how much more convenient it would be to hate an ex-husband the way most divorced women did.

Eric grinned at her, still talking into the phone.

"So we'll meet you there?" he said. "Later!"

He clicked off and gave Reese a smug look. "See? You're getting out. You can thank me later."

"*A few of us are getting together*? You make it sound like a party instead of a ridiculous attempt by my ex-husband to fix me up with his loser friend."

"Bob's not a loser. He's a financial analyst. I think you'll really like him. So you want to meet us there, or drive yourself?"

Reese sighed, resigned to her fate. "I'm driving myself, and I'm bringing Larissa. Assuming she doesn't already have a date."

"That's not a safe assumption. Doesn't she always have a date?"

"Sometimes she gives herself the night off to line up new dates."

"God help them."

"Okay, I'll go on this date, but only because I'm hungry and I really like their crab-stuffed mushroom caps. And because I wanted to talk to Sheila about the signage for next week's event."

"I'll let her know. So we'll see you there?"

"Fine."

Reese trudged back across the lawn and let herself into the house. She spotted the breakfast plates in the sink and remembered yanking the dishrag out of Clay's hand and insisting she'd wash them later.

At the thought of Clay, Reese's mind veered into dangerous territory.

The feel of Clay's arm around her waist as he'd saved her from toppling over the bar.

The heat of his fingertips against her cheek.

The way his muscles rippled under her palms as he touched and stroked and drove her mindless with his—

She grabbed her phone off the counter and dialed Larissa's cell.

"Hello, my third-favorite cousin," Larissa answered.

"Hey, 'Riss—look, I need a favor."

"You need help doing something different with your hair?"

"No, I—"

"You want to borrow a top that shows off your rack?"

"No, I—"

"You want seduction tips for sales reps? Come on, we're reaching the end of my skills list here."

Reese rolled her eyes. "Why do I bother?"

"Because you love me. And also because I make you smile."

"This is true."

"So what do you really need?"

"Can you come with me to the Vineyard Grill to meet up with Eric and Sheila and some Bob guy they're trying to fix me up with?"

Larissa was quiet for a moment. "Let me get this straight—you haven't had a date in forever, and you're bringing your cousin, your ex-husband, and his wife along on your first?"

"It's not a date. I just didn't know how to get out of it."

"So you want me to be your wingman?"

"Pretty much. Come on, you know I'd do it for you."

"Okay. But only if you let me do your hair. And dress you."

Reese sighed. "Fine. Whatever. But I'm not dressing as a hooker."

"Define hooker. Would a high-class escort be okay?"

"Just be here in ten minutes. Please?"

"You'll owe me."

Larissa clicked off and Reese went to take a shower. Twenty minutes later, she was sitting on a stool in front of her bedroom mirror while Larissa tortured her with a blow-dryer.

"Ouch," Reese said.

"If you'd just hold still—"

"How long is this going to take?"

"A few minutes more with the hair, and then I brought you something cute to put on."

"Cute like pink bows, or cute like 'I charge by the minute for a hand job'?"

Larissa turned off the dryer and smiled into the mirror. "I didn't know you knew the word *hand job*."

"Isn't it technically two words?"

"It might be hyphenated. I'm not sure. I think *blowjob* is one word. Which are you planning to give Bob?"

"Neither, thanks. Are your clothes even going to fit me?"

"The shirt might be tight on you, but that's the point. You could even stuff your bra if you really wanted to show off the girls."

"I'm not showing off the girls. The girls are perfectly happy staying low key this evening."

Larissa shrugged. "Suit yourself. Just thought you might like a little extra oomph."

"Is there something about me that suggests I like oomph?"

"Get dressed," Larissa said as she shoved a pile of clothes at her.

Reese dropped the bundle on the bed and shucked her top. As she peeled off her jeans, Larissa clucked her disapproval. "No. Just no."

Reese looked up. "What?"

"You don't wear a white cotton bra and gray satin panties on a date."

"It's dinner, not an orgy."

"Don't you have anything that matches?" Larissa marched over to Reese's bureau and began rummaging around. "Here. Black lace bra, black lace panties. This works."

Reese frowned at them. "I haven't worn those for years. I think they're itchy."

"They're sexy. And they'll go great under the top I brought. Come on, hurry up."

Knowing there was no use arguing, Reese wriggled the panties over her hips and fastened the front clasp on the bra.

"The jeans might be a little snug, but they'll make your ass look great," Larissa encouraged. "Careful not to mess up your hair."

Reese finished buttoning and snapping and then turned to survey herself in the full-length mirror.

"Wow. I don't look like a total tramp."

Larissa grinned. "We can fix that. Just let me undo a couple buttons here—"

"No," Reese said, swatting her hand away. "I actually look pretty good. You think?"

"You're beautiful." Larissa folded her arms over her chest and gave a decisive nod. "It's about damn time you let someone appreciate that. Someone besides your ex-husband, his wife, and your cousin. Are you sure we all need to be there?"

"Positive. I'm going to need moral support."

Larissa laughed. "I'm much better with the immoral support."

"Let's go," Reese said, grabbing her purse off the chair and flipping it open to make sure she had her house key. She frowned. "Did you stick a condom in here?"

"Just looking out for you, cuz." Larissa linked her arm through Reese's and tugged her toward the door. "Come on. Let's go meet your new boyfriend."

◆ ◆ ◆

Clay shifted on the bench seat at Vineyard Grill, trying hard to listen to every word his new AA sponsor was saying, but he wasn't having much luck.

It wasn't that he didn't appreciate the guy's insights. Patrick was a general contractor who'd been sober eight years. He had shaggy brown hair, huge biceps, and a demeanor that suggested he'd been around the block a few times and bench-pressed several cars en route.

The local AA group had put Clay in touch with Patrick when he'd called to find out about meetings in the area. He was a fellow Hazelden alum, and they'd talked on the phone a few times before Clay had moved back to Oregon. It was clear Patrick had a great grasp on AA and the recovery process.

His grasp on grammar was a bit shakier. Clay couldn't stop staring at the blue tattoo on his forearm. A prison tat, from the look of it. The words read: *Your stronger than you think you are.*

Clay shook his head and tried to focus on what Patrick was saying. "That's really cool you haven't been experiencing a lot of cravings."

"Cravings?" Clay said, his mind veering in an unexpected direction before he caught up with the conversation. "Oh, at the winery?"

Patrick nodded and picked up his soda. "Well, yes—at the winery or anywhere else there might be temptation."

Clay nodded and looked at his hands. "The temptation at the winery is nothing I can't handle."

"Careful with the confidence. Remember that you can't prevent relapse alone."

Alone. The word hit him funny in the gut, but he knew what Patrick meant.

"You're right," Clay said. "I plan to hit all the AA meetings while I'm here."

"That's smart." Patrick gave an affirmative grunt and shifted in his seat, revealing another tattoo on his bicep that read: *Strength threw sobriety*.

Clay looked away and glanced toward the door of the restaurant. As if on cue, Reese walked through it. Clay blinked. It was Reese, wasn't it?

But this was a different Reese. Her hair was down and fluffed around her shoulders in a way that made Clay wonder what it would feel like to grab a handful at the nape of her neck and tug it to make her back arch. She was wearing some sort of slinky black top and jeans that hugged her—

"Clay?"

Clay swung his eyes back to Patrick. "I'm sorry, what?"

"Did you hear a word I just said?"

"Um—"

"That's okay," Patrick said with a laugh. "Those girls are beautiful, that's for damn sure."

"Girls?" Clay asked, confused by the plural. He looked back at the doorway and noticed Reese wasn't alone. "Oh. Larissa. I didn't see her."

"You know them?"

"Old friends from a past life," Clay said. "Want me to introduce you?"

"Nah, that's okay. Looks like they might be heading into the bar."

Clay nodded. "Right. And you probably want to maintain some privacy with the whole AA thing."

"Not really an issue for me," Patrick said, leaning back against the bench seat. "Everyone in town knows I'm in recovery. I try to tell as many people as possible, just to get the word out I'm available to help. If you know anyone else who needs me, feel free to pass my card along."

"I appreciate that," Clay said, trying not to make it too obvious he was sneaking glimpses at Reese. She hadn't seen him yet, which gave him a chance to watch her from afar, studying the way her hair moved, the way those green eyes flitted around the room.

Patrick cleared his throat. "Speaking of girls, have you dated much since you got sober?"

Clay shrugged and folded his hands on the Formica table. "A few dates here and there. Nothing serious."

"In four years? That's a long time."

Clay shrugged. "I've been busy with work, busy getting my life back together, busy attending meetings. You know how it is."

Busy fantasizing about my best friend's ex-wife, he didn't add.

"I took it pretty slow myself. You'll figure it out."

Clay nodded and took a sip of his Coke as he stole another look at Reese. She still hadn't seen him. In fact, she didn't seem to know anyone was watching her. He gazed in fascination as she lifted her hand, hesitated, and glanced around. Then she stuck her hand down the front of her shirt.

Clay choked on his drink.

He was still choking as he forced himself to turn back to Patrick, trying not to look back at Reese and whatever the hell she was doing with her hand in her shirt.

"I'll figure it out," Clay said, his voice strained. "You're right about that."

"It does get easier. Never easy, but *easier*."

"That's what I keep hearing."

"Well, Clay—it's been really great meeting you. I'll see you at the next meeting?"

"Looking forward to it. Thanks, Patrick—I really appreciate it."

"No sweat. Call anytime you need me. And keep on keepin' on, man."

"You, too."

They shook hands, and Patrick stood up. The second he was out the door, Clay scanned the restaurant again for Reese. Dammit, where had she gone? And why did he care?

He spotted her then, seated in the bar where he'd been extra cautious not to go. He studied her, still a little awestruck at her appearance. She occupied a booth with Larissa, Eric, Sheila, and some guy who was staring down the front of Reese's shirt so intently Clay wondered if she had a television broadcasting the NBA finals hidden away in there.

A waitress appeared at Clay's table and he tore his eyes away from Reese to watch the perky blonde deposit his check on the table with a little smiley face drawn at the top.

"Refill on the Coke?"

Clay hesitated. He was leaving, right? Staying would be stupid, and going into that bar would be more stupid. Stupid for a lot of reasons, not the least of which was that it was a bar. The flashing Deschutes Brewery sign caught his eye, but it didn't hold his attention. He looked back at Reese.

"No, thanks," Clay told the waitress as he stuck twenty bucks in the little wallet with the bill. "I was just about to leave. Keep the change."

She smiled down at him. "You new in town?"

"Sort of. I spent a lot of time around here a few years back."

"My name's Emily. And I get off at nine, if you want to hang out or something."

She slipped a piece of paper across the table at him, and Clay stared dumbly at the numbers. Before he could say anything, she swished away with her tray in hand and a wiggle in her walk he knew was for him.

Clay put the phone number in his pocket and stood up. He looked back at the bar. He wasn't going in there. He was going to leave out the side door and—

Before he could complete the thought, Reese looked up. Their gazes locked for three beats, neither of them blinking. Clay swallowed.

Suddenly, Larissa's gaze swung his direction.

"Hey—it's Clay!" she shouted across the bar. "Come join us. We've missed you!"

Clay gripped the edge of his table, considering it. There were two pitchers of beer on their table, but he hardly noticed. It was Reese who made his pulse kick into overdrive. Reese looked away first, touching Sheila's wrist and making a point of admiring her bracelet.

"Come on, Clay," Larissa shouted loudly enough that other patrons turned to stare. "Don't be shy. We've got plenty of room here."

Clay let go of the table and put one foot in front of the other, trying to look cool and probably just looking like a guy trying to look cool.

Eric grinned, the same, familiar expression Clay had seen a million times since college. Sheila smiled, too, tossing her blonde hair as she put her hand on her husband's arm.

The guy next to Reese tore his eyes away from her breasts to see what the fuss was about.

Reese was the last to turn and smile at him, a move that seemed almost calculated. The smile was worth the wait—warm and real enough to light up her eyes.

"Hello, Clay," she said. "What brings you here?"

"I just had a meeting with someone. I'm heading home now."

"Ooooh—a girl?" Sheila asked with hope. "It'd be great for you to have a girlfriend, Clay."

"Not a girl," Clay said. "My new sponsor."

"Sponsor?" Larissa asked. "Is that like the commercials you see on TV where you pay thirty dollars a month so a starving kid can eat?"

Everyone else at the table shifted uncomfortably, and Clay couldn't tell if Larissa was drunk, joking, or playing the ditz like she sometimes did in a bar full of men. Probably all three, he thought as he watched her drain her glass.

"No," Clay said. "I got connected with Patrick through the local Alcoholics Anonymous group. I contacted them last week to get a support network in place before I came out here."

"Working the steps, huh?" the guy next to Reese said. Actually, he said it to Reese's breasts, but Clay assumed the words were meant for him. "Had a brother do AA," the guy continued. "Relapsed six times."

Clay wasn't sure what to say to that, so he offered his hand. "Clay Henderson. Good to meet you."

"Bob Wilson," he grunted, looking up to extend his hand. "I'm a financial analyst. I'm with Reese."

Clay saw Reese's expression go from uncomfortable to annoyed and back to uncomfortable in a span of three seconds. He wondered if anyone else noticed.

Then he watched her lift her hand and adjust something between her breasts.

What the hell?

On the other side of the table, Eric cleared his throat. "Clay and I were college roommates, Bob. Me and Reese and Clay, we've been friends a long time." He looked back at Clay and gestured toward an empty chair sitting off to the side of the booth. "You gonna join us, buddy?"

Clay hesitated. Larissa snaked out a stiletto-clad foot and dragged the chair closer. "Come on, Clay—it's been too long. At least help us with the nachos and catch up on old times."

Clay hesitated again, hoping no one expected him to be the life of the party the way he might have been in college. Then again, people had stopped inviting him to parties within a few years of college, back when he'd gone from being the fun guy with a beer in his hand to the pathetic guy with twelve empty cans at his feet.

He could change all that.

Clay sat down and signaled a passing waiter to ask for another Coke.

He looked back at Reese. She looked away. Then she reached between her breasts and fiddled with something again.

Seriously? Was he the only one noticing this?

He glanced at Bob. Okay, so he wasn't the only one noticing. But Bob seemed more interested in the breasts themselves than in whatever was troubling them. Or troubling Reese—he wasn't really sure what was going on.

"So, Bob," Clay said. "How's the financial analyst business going?"

"Good, good," Bob said, peeling his eyes off Reese's cleavage. "What is it you do, Clay?"

"I'm in construction."

"I see," said Bob in a tone that suggested his opinion of Clay had just dropped three levels. Based on the way Bob was ogling Reese,

Clay's opinion of him had already hit rock bottom and was starting to dig lower.

Reese reached between her breasts again and squirmed. Beside her, Larissa was having an animated conversation with Sheila. Clay had missed most of the details, but Larissa shrieked with laughter. She flailed her arm to the side, bumping Reese with her elbow. Reese flinched, and Clay watched as her eyes flew wide.

Reese looked down the front of her shirt, joining Bob in what was apparently the preferred pastime for the evening.

What the hell?

◆ ◆ ◆

Reese remembered too late why she hadn't worn the damn black lace bra for years. As she stared down the front of her shirt where the broken front clasp had come unhooked, she wondered if there was any tactful way to remedy the situation.

It wasn't enough she was sandwiched between her shrieking cousin and Bob the Boob-man. Could she even make it across the restaurant like this?

If she were smaller busted, sure, and if this top weren't so tight. But the bra was now gaping open in the middle, with the underwire cups flung out to the sides like mutant wings at the edges of her boobs.

She felt her cheeks heat up as she folded her arms over her chest.

Shit, that made it worse. Bob's eyes were wide now as her arms squashed her unleashed cleavage up around her collarbones. She unfolded her arms and looked around the table to see if anyone else had noticed.

Someone kicked her under the table. Reese glanced down to see Clay's steel-toed work boot. She looked up to see him eyeing her curiously.

You okay? he mouthed.

Reese grimaced and folded her arms over her chest again, this time trying to squash her cleavage down instead of up. Beside her, she felt

Bob lean closer. She watched Clay's eyes narrow. On her other side, Larissa squealed again.

She shook her head at Clay and looked at Larissa. Screw it, she just had to make a run for the bathroom. She unfolded her arms and nudged her cousin.

"Larissa—I need to get out," Reese whispered.

"Give me just a sec—I've gotta hear how Sheila's story ends!"

Reese started to argue but changed her mind. Did she really want to march across the restaurant with her boobs flapping in the wind and the unhooked bra making funny lumps under the too-snug shirt?

She looked back at Clay.

An image flashed through her mind, one so old she'd forgotten it was there. Beautiful, long fingers on her bra clasp, flicking it open with one hand as his lips moved down her throat and his other hand cupped her—

Shit. Shit shit shit!

Now her nipples were hard.

Reese folded her arms again. Bob shifted beside her and put an arm around her shoulders. "You cold?"

She felt Clay's foot shift beside hers. "Here, Reese," he said, standing up. She watched him peel off the black wool zip-up jacket he'd been wearing, revealing the snug gray T-shirt beneath. "Take my coat."

Relief pulsed through her, sending a few gratuitous pulses to several other parts she was trying not to think about. She started to stand up to grab the jacket, but Clay leaned down and placed it around her shoulders.

"Better?"

She nodded. "Thank you."

"Don't mention it."

His gaze locked with hers. Bob's gaze locked with her breasts.

Reese pulled the jacket tight around her chest and gave Larissa a shove. "Move it—I'm going to the restroom."

She stood and zipped the jacket, then crossed her arms over her chest and made a beeline for the other side of the room. She ducked into the narrow hallway and had her hand on the door to the ladies' room when she heard Clay's voice behind her.

"Here. You might need this."

She turned to see him holding out a safety pin. She smiled and reached out to take it. "How did you—?"

"Borrowed it from the waitress."

"I meant, how'd you know my bra broke?"

He shrugged and leaned against the wall. "It was kinda obvious. Besides, didn't you have something like that happen once in college?"

Reese almost gasped out loud, stunned by the memory. "Right—at that party over in McMinnville sophomore year. How the hell did you remember that?"

He grinned. "Some things stick in a guy's mind. Can't say I recall every drunken detail of my youth, but that image is burned into my brain."

Reese bit her lip as she pulled the jacket tighter around her. She looked away, feigning interest in a spot on the wall. "I guess so."

"You need any help?"

She laughed, startling a passing waitress. "Are you offering to fix my bra clasp? Don't tell me that's within the realm of your contractor training."

"Sure, I've got my welding tools out in the truck. If you hold really still, it shouldn't melt much skin."

"I'm fine, but thank you. The safety pin should be enough."

She put her hand on the ladies' room door again, then hesitated. "Thank you, Clay. I mean it. I don't think anyone else figured out what was going on."

"Not even your date?"

"My *date*." She spit out the word like a burnt peanut. "Eric picked me a real winner there."

Clay studied her, quiet for a moment. "He means well."

"That he does." She was staring into his eyes now, those pools of root-beer-hued light pulling her in. "Thank you, Clay. Really, you're a lifesaver."

Before she could think about what she was doing, she leaned up to give him a quick kiss on the cheek.

The cheek. That really was what she aimed for.

She wasn't sure if he turned, or if some instinct drew her a few inches to the right. Her lips found his and she kissed him, part of her expecting him to draw away.

Instead, he put his hands on her waist and pulled her closer. His lips moved against hers as she swayed and felt her shoulder bump the wall beside the restroom—surely the least romantic venue for a first kiss.

It's not your first kiss with Clay, Reese's subconscious whispered as her libido screamed something else entirely. *Not by a long shot.*

She deepened the kiss, desperate to block out the voices in her head and just feel him against her. Clay responded, kissing her back as his heart pounded against his chest. Reese could feel it through her shirt, her bare breasts pressing against the thin fabric as Clay's hands slid up her back and made her shiver with desire.

"Oh, pardon me!"

Reese jumped back and turned to see a startled-looking woman at the edge of the hallway.

"Whoopsie," the woman said with a giggle. "I can come back—"

"No, it's okay," Clay said, taking a step away from Reese. "We were just—"

"Fixing my bra," Reese supplied.

"Right," Clay agreed.

The woman nodded, then gave them a knowing smile as she edged around them and pushed through the restroom door. "That's how I'd do it."

CHAPTER SIX

Reese kept an eye out for Clay the next day, telling herself she just needed to return his jacket and thank him for rescuing her.

She wasn't going to address the kiss. Maybe if he brought it up first, but it was probably best to forget the whole thing. Neither of them needed this sort of complication right now. It was best to pretend it hadn't happened at all.

Wasn't it?

But she only spotted Clay from a distance a few times, out there in his hardhat and work boots and a snug black T-shirt as he directed a backhoe and gave orders to well-muscled men with shovels. They'd been able to start some of the preliminary excavation, even with the rest of the project still in limbo. Reese and her mother had crunched numbers all morning, trying to find a way to make things work.

"Your father and I will stop by the bank on our way to ballroom dancing class tonight," June had said as they'd closed the ledgers. "The loan officer wasn't in earlier, but we'll make an appointment for you and me to meet with her next week. Is your schedule open?"

"Pretty much," Reese said. "What about that venture capitalist you and Dad met on the cruise?"

"I've got a call in to him." She patted Reese's hand. "Try not to worry, baby. We'll figure something out."

Reese gave a weak smile. "Okay. Have a good time at dance class."

Feeling distracted, she trudged up the hill toward the deserted pole barn around four p.m. with Leon on her heels. She had some old wine barrels stored there and was pretty sure they could be cleaned up and used as rustic cocktail tables for the upcoming event.

She yanked open the door and was greeted by a gust of fragrant blue smoke.

Reese coughed and covered her face with her hand. The barn was not on fire—that much she knew.

"Dammit, Grandpa!"

"Don't Grandpa me, young lady!" came a voice from somewhere in the haze.

Reese waved her hand in front of her face to clear the air. She spotted her grandfather sitting on a wine barrel about ten feet away.

"Dammit, Axl," she said, coughing. "What are you doing?"

"What does it look like I'm doing?"

Reese squinted through the smoke and funny blue light. "It looks like you're making a bong out of a Coke can while a bunch of delinquents plant marijuana in the goddamn barn."

Axl looked at the four tattooed men stringing grow lights over rows of tiny green plants. He shrugged. "Can't fault your observation skills."

Reese shook her head, dread making her gut go sour. "I thought we agreed to talk about this. You were going to research what's legal, and I was going to research what's *really* legal before you got started."

Axl set down his Coke can and sighed. "Time's a-wastin', we've gotta jump on the medical marijuana market while it's hot. Besides, I know what I'm doing."

"You can't even grow legally while you're still on probation," Reese argued. "I checked it out online. And definitely not in the sort of quantities you've got here."

"One of my girlfriends—Dolly, you know, the one with the tongue stud?—she got all the permits and shit. I'm just providing the land. It's a business partnership."

"One that's got to be illegal. Come on, Axl, if anyone finds out this is here—"

"If anyone finds out this is here, we show them the paperwork and everything's okay. Hey, boys—don't forget you've still got to plant the 'shrooms over there."

Reese rolled her eyes. "'Shrooms? I thought those were outside."

"Working on a few different angles, here. It's all perfectly legal, Peanut Butter Cup."

"Why do I doubt that? And why do I think Dick over at Larchwood Vineyards would have a field day with this?"

"Trust me, darlin'—I know what I'm doing."

"That's not reassuring."

"It's just like the time I told you I'd get you tickets to see the Dave Matthews Band up at the Gorge and I did."

"You got busted selling drug-laced brownies in the parking lot, and we had to bail you out of jail."

Axl waved a dismissive hand. "They let me go when they realized it was only Metamucil. And you got to see the concert, remember?"

"Hey," shouted one of the men behind them. "I think the camel just ate a plant."

The other three men chortled with machine-gun laughter. Reese wheeled around to see Leon standing beside a row of little green leaves, his furry jaws munching rhythmically.

"Leon!"

She stumbled over and tried to pry the alpaca's mouth open, but Leon clamped his teeth together and swallowed.

"Leon, no!" Reese pried harder at his jaws, yanking them open at last and earning herself a belch in the face.

There was a faint trace of green on his tongue.

"God, can this stuff kill him?" Reese shrieked. "How many plants did he get?"

"Just the one," volunteered one of Axl's men. "Maybe two. They're little bitty."

"Shit, I need to call the vet," Reese said, scanning Leon for any signs of duress. Leon twitched his ears and hummed. "Does anyone know if marijuana is toxic to alpacas?"

"Toxic?"

"Yes, toxic!" she snapped. "Tons of things can be toxic to alpacas— acorns, azaleas, carnations, hyacinth—"

"She said *high*," chortled one of the men as he blew out a fragrant puff of smoke. "*High*acinth."

Reese gritted her teeth. "What the hell do I tell the vet?"

"That your camel likes the wacky weed?" offered one of the men, stepping closer to pet Leon's neck.

Leon lowered his head and nailed the guy in the groin. The man doubled over and sat down in the dirt.

"He's not a camel," Reese snapped. "And that's not funny."

Another man snorted and pointed at his fallen comrade. "No, but *that* was funny. How much does the camel weigh? About one fifty?"

"He's not a camel! Do you see any humps?"

At that, the men dissolved into stoner laughter.

Axl stood up and ambled over, stopping to nudge the man in the dirt with the toe of his Doc Marten. When he reached Reese's side, he gave her hand a squeeze before scratching Leon's neck.

"He'll be fine," Axl insisted. "He's more like one seventy-five, isn't he? He didn't eat that much. Come on, I know a vet who'll check him out under the table—all hush-hush, you know?"

Reese shook her head. "Why am I not surprised you know a shady veterinarian?"

"It pays to know people in *high* places, Peanut Butter Cup."

"Right," Reese muttered, but she raced out the door after her grandfather anyway.

The two of them scurried down the hill side by side, with Leon ambling behind them, tooting a little as they passed another cluster of alpacas in the pasture. Reese glanced at him, trying to determine whether his eyes were bloodshot or if he was stumbling at all. She knew how to tend to the basic medical needs of small wildlife, but large mammals weren't her specialty.

Large *stoned* mammals were way beyond her training.

"Is that Clay down there?" Axl asked.

Reese looked away from Leon and stared down the hill to where Axl was pointing. "Yes. They're breaking ground today."

"Thought the bid came in too high and you're stalling."

"We're stalling the construction. We already have the permits, so they can start the excavation while we figure out where the hell to get the extra money."

"Hmph," Axl said. "I know a guy who made good money stealing cars. If you want, I could—"

"No. We're not stealing cars to fund the expansion."

Axl shrugged. "Suit yourself." He was quiet a moment, eyes on the construction site as they hustled down the hill. "Seems like he's done well for himself."

"Who?"

Axl snorted. "You know exactly who I mean. Don't play dumb with me. *Clay.*"

"Mmm," Reese replied, turning her attention back to Leon. Was he staggering? She couldn't tell. She picked up the pace, pulling Leon behind her as they approached the winery.

"The boy finally got his shit together," Axl said.

"Clay? I guess."

"Always thought you'd end up with him."

Reese stumbled on a molehill. She caught herself with a hand on Leon's back, causing the alpaca to chortle softly.

Axl kept moving, not missing a step.

"Me?" Reese stammered. "And Clay? Why would you say that?"

He shrugged. "The yin and the yang. Twin spirits. All that bullshit, plus he used to drive a kick-ass Mustang."

"Right, a kick-ass car—the basis for all good relationships."

Axl looked at her. "You know something better?"

"Obviously not. I'm divorced, right? "

"That's horseshit," Axl growled. "You married the wrong guy and you know it."

"Maybe I was the wrong woman."

"Of course you were. For *Eric*. Jesus Christ, girl—you didn't really think that would work, did you?"

Reese didn't answer right away. They were approaching the winery barn, and the sound of heavy equipment rumbling through the dirt was vibrating her brain.

"Eric and I had a great friendship," Reese said. "Our love life was pretty good, and we got along well. Isn't that what my parents would say is the basis of a great marriage?"

Axl hooted loudly, prompting Leon to echo the sound with a high-pitched tooting noise of his own. Reese looked at her pet, then at her grandfather, wondering who was more stoned.

"*Friendship* and *pretty good sex* are not enough to make a relation-ship last," Axl barked.

"Is this going to be another one of those lectures about how rela-tionships take work?"

Axl rolled his eyes. "Don't be an idiot, girl. Work isn't the secret. The key to any good relationship is keeping your expectations low."

"I think I saw that on a Hallmark card."

"I'm serious. You think your grandma and I lasted as long as we did because we sat around swapping roses and dining by candlelight every night?"

Reese frowned. "Grandma ran off with a plumber."

Axl patted her lightly on the shoulder and nodded. "Good talk, girl. Now let's get the damn camel off the doobie."

◆ ◆ ◆

Clay had spent his whole day trying his damnedest to stay focused on the job. He was working with a lot of heavy equipment and shouting orders left and right at the crew. Hardly the time to lose focus.

Even so, he couldn't help but notice when Reese and Axl came hurrying down the hill toward the winery bar. Reese looked worried. Axl looked high. Leon the alpaca was right on their heels, his fuzzy ears twitching each time the backhoe went in reverse.

Clay watched from the corner of his eye as Axl banged through the door of the winery while Reese stood outside, her hand on Leon's neck.

Clay shifted the shovel in his hands, determined to keep his distance.

Seconds later, Axl was back outside shouting something at Reese and waving a telephone around. When Reese started to cry, Clay dropped the shovel. Reese wasn't a crier. If she was in tears, something was very wrong.

Screw distance.

"I've got the vet on the line," Axl was yelling to Reese as Clay approached. "Is he experiencing ataxia, bradycardia, or conjunctival hyperemia?"

"I don't know what any of that means!" Reese shouted back with tears spilling down her cheeks. "Find out what's on the list of things that are poisonous to alpacas. Don't you remember the one that died over at the Beezlers' place last year when it ate foxglove?"

Clay moved into place beside her, hesitating only a moment before placing a hand on her arm.

"What's wrong?" he asked. "Can I help?"

"Leon ate pot," Reese sniffed. "It was only a little, but I don't know if it's toxic to him and—"

"The vet wants to know if he's experiencing urinary incontinence," Axl demanded, holding the phone away from his ear.

Reese looked at Leon. Leon made a funny humming noise. Axl shrugged and knelt down to peer at the shaggy animal's underbelly. "Wow, he's pretty well hung. You seen this thing?"

"Stop sexually harassing my alpaca!" Reese snapped. "You're not going to be able to tell if he's incontinent from staring at his—his—"

"My vet friend can't get here until Sunday," Axl said, straightening up and gesturing with the phone. "He's at a motorcycle rally in Nevada, but he says it shouldn't be toxic, as long as Leon didn't eat too much. You should keep him calm and feed him something to get things moving through his system."

Clay cleared his throat. "Is there something I can do?"

Reese looked at him. "Do you know anything about stoned livestock?"

Clay shrugged. "I've been around a lot of stoned people."

Another tear slipped down Reese's cheek as she stroked Leon's neck. The alpaca made a purring sound and looked at Clay. Clay reached out and scratched behind its ear.

"I don't know what alpacas usually act like," Clay said. "Is he behaving oddly?"

Reese nodded. "He isn't head-butting you in the crotch. That's odd."

"Thank you, Leon," Clay said. "Look, I just hooked up with the local AA group. It's a long shot, but you want me to see if there are any members who might be veterinarians? AA is always a supportive group when it comes to—well, delicate situations. It might be worth a try."

"Shit, yeah," Axl said as he switched off the cordless phone. "Your drunk-ass friends will know all about camels eating pot."

"He's an alpaca!" Reese shouted before looking back at Clay. "If you wouldn't mind—"

"No problem. Just let me make a call."

Clay grabbed his cell from his belt and hit the speed-dial number for Patrick, his new sponsor. He'd programmed the guy's number into the phone the other day, knowing it might be handy at some point.

He hadn't envisioned using it to summon help for a stoned alpaca.

The phone rang once. Twice. Three times. Patrick picked up, his voice fretful.

"Clay? Is that you? Is everything okay?"

"Hey, Patrick—yeah, it's me. Look, there's been a drug-related incident here, and I was just wondering—"

"Oh, God. Clay, where are you? I can get there in a few minutes, wherever you are. Just hold tight and—"

"No, dude—it's not me. Really, I have this friend—"

"Sure, sure, a friend—whatever you say. The important thing is that your *friend* deals with this head-on, right now, before things spiral and—"

"Patrick, stop. It's an alpaca."

Patrick was quiet a moment. "That's that new street drug, right? The one that gives you an erection for four days?"

"What? No. It's kind of like a camel. A really small, shaggy camel with no hump."

There was more silence on Patrick's end. "I don't understand."

"Look, I just need to know if there's a vet in the local AA group—a veterinarian, not a war veteran. We want to find out if there's anything we should do for my friend's alpaca."

Patrick didn't respond right away, so Clay pulled the phone away from his ear and looked at Reese. "Any idea how much he ate?"

"Just one small plant, I think. Maybe two. I can't be sure," she said. "I didn't see it before he ate it, but all the plants were really little."

"Okay, Patrick?" Clay said, speaking into the phone again. "It sounds like he ingested a fairly small amount of marijuana. Is there anyone you can think of who I could talk to?"

"Um, well, there's Wally. He owns a vet clinic in Newberg. He's just a friend of mine, not an AA guy, but I trust him. You want me to give him a call?"

"That'd be great. You can have him call me on this number, or if it's not too much trouble, maybe he could come out here to the winery?"

"You're at a winery with a stoned camel?"

Clay watched as Reese scratched Leon behind the ears. "He's not a camel. Just let me know what Wally says, okay? Thanks, man."

He clicked off the phone and looked at Reese, who was still stroking Leon's neck with a shaky hand.

"Thank you," she said. "I just didn't want to call Leon's regular vet to explain this. He got mad last Halloween when Axl tried to dye Leon orange. I don't want him to think we're completely irresponsible alpaca owners."

"Not a problem. Just hang in there. Should we try feeding him something like Axl's guy said?"

Reese nodded. "I'll go get some of his food. Can you keep an eye on him?"

"Sure."

Clay watched as Reese hurried off in the direction of her little house. Once she was gone, Clay turned to Axl.

"Do I want to know how this happened?"

"Probably not," he said. "He's going to be okay, right? It's not gonna kill him like those other plants Reese was talking about?"

"I have no idea. He looks fine to me, but this is the first alpaca I've ever seen up close. Is he always like this?"

"Pretty much. He actually looks happy, don't you think?"

Clay looked at the animal. Happy? He wasn't sure what a happy alpaca looked like, but as the beast stooped to pull a mouthful of grass from the tufts at the edge of the barn, Clay had to admit he seemed content.

"Is it okay if he eats grass?"

"Huh?" Axl asked. "Oh, you mean like hair of the dog? Sure, I left my bong back at the pole barn, but I think Reese might get pissed if we gave him another hit."

"No, not—never mind. Here comes Reese."

He watched her jogging across the lawn, trying not to let his eyes linger too long on her chest. That would be a caveman thing to do. He wasn't a caveman.

Still, the way everything moved under that shirt as she ran—

"Got it," Reese called, holding out a small canvas bag. "C'mere, Leon—get some oats."

The alpaca lifted his head and pricked his ears. He leaned out, snuffling at the edge of the bag.

"Good boy," Reese crooned. "That's a good, good boy."

Leon stuck his head in the bag and began munching.

Clay scratched him behind the ears again, earning a contented hum that sounded funny in the rhythm of chewing.

"Alpacas have three stomachs," Reese explained softly, as though Leon might be offended at being discussed thusly. "I guess we just want to get everything moving through him."

"Makes sense," Clay said. "Had a few benders like that myself."

"He seems to have the munchies," Axl pointed out.

Reese held up the feed bag and peered inside. "All gone. Feeling better, Leon?"

Leon chortled a little and snuffled at the edge of the bag.

"So is Leon a pet, or does he serve a useful vineyard function?" Clay asked, trying to keep Reese's mind off the animal's condition. "Hauling grapes or something?"

Reese shrugged. "They keep the pasture mowed down, but it's more about the fleece. Mom and Gramp—*Axl* got a whole herd of alpacas a few years ago after reading about how the fiber made from their fleece is worth a lot of money. We shear them every spring."

"What's the difference between a llama and an alpaca?"

"Llamas are bigger, and you use them more for packing and hauling," Reese said. "We have a few of those over in the east pasture. Alpacas are a lot smaller, and people keep them more for their fleece than anything."

"So what's the deal with Leon? Why isn't he with other alpacas?"

She gave Leon a fond smile and stroked the side of his neck, and Clay kicked himself for feeling jealous of a farm animal. "He got kind of attached to me after I bottle-fed him as a baby when he got sick," she said. "He hangs out with the other alpacas sometimes when I'm not around, but most of the time, he'd rather be near me."

Clay could relate, but he didn't say so.

The sound of tires crunching over gravel drew their attention toward the driveway. They watched as a blue Subaru pulled into the circular parking area at the front of the winery barn and eased to a halt in front of them. The brake lights flickered and a dark-haired, thirty-something man in a green fleece jacket hopped out and extended his right hand, gripping a medical bag in the left.

"You must be Clay," he said. "Patrick called just as I was leaving a sheep farm five miles down the road. I'm Wallace O'Brien—you can call me Wally. Is this our patient?"

Clay nodded. "Thanks so much for coming out like this. Leon here ate some, uh—"

"Medical marijuana," piped Axl. "Perfectly legal. We've got the permits and everything."

"Er, right," Clay said. "This is Axl, and Reese here is Leon's owner. She's understandably worried."

"Reese," the man repeated, his eyes coming to rest on her face. He studied her with undisguised appreciation, and Clay stood up a little straighter.

"It's a pleasure to meet you," said Dr. Wally. "Tell me, have you noticed any disorientation or behavioral changes?"

"Well, his normal behavior whenever a man is around is to—"

Leon chose that moment to display his normal behavior. He lowered his head and nailed Wally squarely in the groin.

"Ooof!" said Wally and doubled over.

"Oh no! I'm so sorry," Reese said. "Are you okay?"

Wally nodded but didn't say anything beyond a squeak as he clutched his groin with one hand. Reese winced and rested a hand on Leon's back, while Clay did his best to feel sympathetic.

"I can't believe he just did that," Reese said. "I should have warned you that's what he always does, but I thought after he didn't hit Clay in the—um—the—"

"Nutsack," Axl supplied.

"Right," Reese said. "I thought maybe the marijuana made him not want to do that, but I guess I'm glad he's being his normal self. I mean, I'm not glad you got hit, but—I mean—can I get you some ice?"

"I'm fine, fine," groaned Dr. Wally, straightening up and pasting on a strained smile. "Let me just do a quick exam here, if you don't mind."

"Absolutely," Reese said, stepping aside as Dr. Wally opened his medical bag and pulled out a stethoscope.

Clay watched as the vet tucked the earpieces into place and held the flat metal end against Leon's furry chest, listening intently. The name had left Clay expecting a much older man, but Dr. Wally couldn't be more than a year or two older than he was.

The vet nodded to himself after a minute, then put the stethoscope away and pulled out a little penlight. He put a hand on the side of Leon's face and shined it in the animal's eyes.

Leon curled his lips back and spat.

Clay tried not to laugh. "At least his aim isn't affected."

Dr. Wally grimaced and wiped the alpaca slime off his cheek. "No worries. He does seem to be in high spirits, doesn't he?"

Axl snorted. "*High.* You could say that."

Dr. Wally gave a faint smile and pulled out a thermometer. "Um, would one of you mind holding him steady?"

"Of course," said Reese, and wrapped her arms around the alpaca's neck.

Dr. Wally moved around in back and tried to lift Leon's tail. Leon hooted with alarm and pulled his tail down.

"Come on, buddy," the vet murmured. "Just cooperate."

Clay scratched one of Leon's fuzzy ears, the one with a heart-shaped splotch on it, and tried to think of something comforting to say. "Sorry, man," he murmured to Leon, trying not to notice the heat coming from

Reese's hand as she stroked the alpaca's neck. "He didn't even buy you a beer first."

At last, the vet released Leon's tail and returned to pull an alcohol wipe from his medical bag. He nodded at Reese as he began wiping down the thermometer.

"His temperature is normal, heart rate pretty steady," he informed her. "His pupils are a little dilated, and he's clearly a bit agitated, but that's to be expected under the circumstances."

"So is he going to be okay?" Reese asked. "There are so many plants that are poisonous to alpacas, so I just worried—"

"He should be fine. The best thing you can do right now is just keep him calm."

"Anything else?" Reese asked, stroking Leon's neck.

"Give him plenty of water, and watch for anything unusual—vomiting, malaise, diarrhea, depression."

They all turned to Leon, looking for signs of depression. Leon hummed.

"Right," said Dr. Wally. "Here's my card. Call me if anything changes. Or—you know—if you want to go out sometime?"

Reese stared at him for a second before reaching out to take the card. Clay felt dizzy, and realized he was holding his breath.

It was Axl who broke the silence, smacking Reese on the arm.

"Jesus, girl—the man just asked you on a goddamn date. You've gotta give him an answer, unless you want me to kick his ass?"

Reese flushed, then smiled at Dr. Wally. "No, that's fine. I mean—no ass kicking will be necessary. Thank you, Wally. I'll hold on to your number. Um, here's mine," she said, fishing a business card out of her pocket. "You can mail the bill to the address there."

He glanced at the card, then smiled up at Reese. "Why don't we just call it a favor for a friend?"

"Oh, no, I couldn't—"

"I insist. It was a pleasure to meet you."

Reese bit her lip. "Thank you. Really, I appreciate you coming out here on short notice like this."

Clay cleared his throat and extended his hand. "Thanks again, man. Great to be able to connect with people through AA like this."

Wally looked at Clay, stole one more glance at Reese, then looked back at Clay. "You can call me anytime, too."

Somehow, Clay doubted Wally would be as excited to get a midnight call from him as he would from Reese.

"Okay, then," Clay said. "Have a good night."

They watched the good doctor climb into his car and fire up the engine. He turned the car around in the wide gravel circle of the driveway and beeped the horn twice as he drove away.

Leon made a *wark-wark* noise and pawed the ground.

When the car disappeared, Clay looked at Reese. She was studying the card. She looked up and met his eyes.

"He seemed like a nice guy," Reese said. "Thanks for getting him to come out, Clay."

"Not a problem."

"No, really—it's a big deal. Calling Leon's regular vet would have been embarrassing, so I don't know what I would have done without you."

"Really, I'm glad to help."

"I feel like I owe you something," she said. "Can I make you dinner?"

"Um—I, uh—"

The door to the winery burst open. Eric stormed out, his face pale and his eyebrows cinched together. When he spotted Reese, he snarled and kicked the dirt.

"Get in here," he said. "We have a problem."

CHAPTER SEVEN

Reese stared dumbfounded at the giant, sticky red lake on the floor.

It wasn't blood, but that would have been preferable.

She gripped the edge of a wine barrel to keep herself steady. "What the hell happened?" she asked, bracing herself as a wave of nausea rolled through her.

Her ex-husband's face revealed the same shell-shocked expression he'd worn the day Clay had stolen a milk truck in college and backed over his car.

"I have no idea," Eric said. "I went out for a late lunch and then met with the wine distributor for Whole Foods, and when I came back—"

"Holy hell," Reese breathed.

"No kidding."

"The Wine Club Pinot." She thought saying it out loud might take some of the sting out, but that wasn't true. She stared at the pool on the floor, blinking hard with the faint hope that when she opened her eyes again, the wine would be back in the barrel where it belonged.

Nope. Still there.

Beside her, Axl was uncharacteristically subdued. Even he understood what this meant. "Son of a bitch," he muttered.

Clay cleared his throat. "I'm sorry, what is Wine Club Pinot?"

Reese shook her head slowly, not trusting her voice yet. "For the last five years, we've had this wine club. It didn't start out very big, but we're up to over five hundred members this year. On top of their dues, they can pay to get a Reserve Pinot Noir bottled in limited quantities and only available to them."

"It's a special blend," Eric said. "We only make one barrel of it, just to create hype and demand. I've had it in the barrel for three years. We did a small tasting last month to build up orders. Only wine club members get it."

"There's a waiting list," Reese continued. "All the bottles have been presold."

Clay frowned. "Do you mind if I ask how much?"

"A hundred and eighty macaroons per bottle," Axl grunted.

"Smackaroos," Reese muttered, her eyes still fixed on the floor.

Eric shook his head. "And at three hundred bottles per barrel—"

"We're fucked," Axl finished.

Reese shook her head. "It's not just the money—it's the hype we've had over this particular wine, this special, limited-edition wine available to a select group, and now—"

She couldn't finish the sentence. This couldn't be real. Not when they'd been doing such a good job building their reputation as a premier winery. Not when people were really starting to take an interest in their wines.

"What happened?" she asked Eric.

Eric grunted and knelt on the floor beside the barrel. He pointed to a spot on the underside. "Take a look at this."

Reese crouched down beside him. "It's cracked."

"Yup. A big crack, too."

She bit her lip, afraid to say it. "Termites?"

"I doubt it. Doesn't look like that kind of damage, and I don't think termites would go after a wine barrel anyway."

"But you were so worried—"

"About the building. I don't want termites eating the building where we make wine, but I don't think that's what caused this."

She nodded, still uneasy. "I don't understand—you check these barrels every day. So do I. How could we not notice something like this? A little leakage or something?"

Eric stood up and held out his hand, and Reese let him pull her to her feet.

"It can happen suddenly sometimes," he said. "I saw it once when I was interning in France. This is one of our older barrels—I don't know, maybe it just gave."

Reese shook her head. "What are we going to do?"

"Where's Larissa?" Axl asked. "She's gotta be able to put a good PR spin on this."

"On three hundred bottles of spilled wine?" Reese shook her head. "I doubt that."

Axl grunted. "Unless you're planning to get a turkey baster and suck it up off the floor, I can't think of another option."

She gritted her teeth and looked up at Eric. "Okay, you've got that other barrel of Reserve, right? The one we were planning to roll out for the Memorial Day event next week? That's the same vintage."

"Right, but it's not the exact same wine. The members will know the difference."

"We'll have to tell them, obviously."

"So what do we serve the VIP guests at the event?" Eric asked. "It's going to cut into our profits for that."

"What choice do we have?" Reese asked. "We'll write a letter to the club members explaining what happened, and offering to substitute the other Pinot. We can use one of the younger wines for the event. The 2013 has been aging nicely, right?"

"Sure, but that's gonna leave us with that much less next year."

Reese sighed. "I don't know what else to do, Eric. That's the best I've got."

He grunted and shook his head but didn't say anything else for a while. "Dick over at Larchwood is going to love this," he muttered at last. "A hundred bucks says he hears about it and makes it a point to tell everyone who comes through his tasting room for the next month."

Reese grimaced. It really wasn't the money—though in light of the added cost for materials in the new building project, the money hurt.

No, the worst of it was the loss of the reputation she'd worked so hard to build. "We'll look like hacks," she said with a heavy sigh.

"Get out of here, Peanut Butter Cup," Axl finally said. "You've already had a rough day with Leon. Eric and I can stay here and clean this up."

"No, it's my responsibility," Reese argued. "I should have been here."

"What for?" Axl snapped. "You think you should sit here twenty-four hours a day with your ass parked on a wine barrel waiting to stick your thumb in a crack?"

"I don't—"

"Go!" Axl insisted. "Go take care of the damn camel."

Reese hesitated, then nodded. "Thank you, Axl. I'll talk with Larissa when she comes in tomorrow. She can work her PR magic, figure out the best way to explain this to the members."

She started to turn around, then realized Clay was still standing there looking lost. Or looking forlorn over the wasted wine, she really couldn't tell.

"Clay—I offered you dinner earlier, didn't I?"

He tore his eyes away from the wine and shook his head. "Don't worry about it. You've got enough on your mind. If someone could show me where the mop is, I'd be happy to help clean this up."

"No, really," Reese insisted. "I feel like I owe you for your help with Leon. I don't know what I would have done if you hadn't gotten Dr. Wally out here."

Clay shook his head. "Really, Reese, you don't have to feed me."

"I insist. My place, one hour. Be there. I'll throw something simple together."

Eric looked up sharply. "You're cooking? Count me in. Sheila's working late tonight. What do you have?"

Reese blinked, then regrouped. "Sure. I can do that. I think I've got frozen shrimp and some angel hair pasta. Shrimp scampi okay with everyone?"

"Perfect," Eric said. "I just picked up a great little Pinot Gris from Sokol Blosser that'll go great with that."

Reese felt Clay go still beside her. She looked at him, trying to read his expression. "I have water," she offered. "Or soda. Or juice. Or—"

"I'm fine," he said, his eyes fixed on Eric. "Really, I don't want to impose."

"I insist," Reese said. "So dinner at my place in an hour. Axl? Want to join us?"

"Nah, I've got a hot date. Don't tell Francie, okay? I've got a little somethin' on the side with this other lady, if you know what I mean."

Axl tried to wink, and Clay reached out to steady him before he started to tip.

"Okay," Reese said with an eye roll. "Well, then. I'll see the rest of you at my place in just a little bit."

Reese marched out of the room, feeling eyes on her back. She wasn't sure whose they were, but she didn't dare turn around to look.

As she got outside, she breathed in the smell of wet grass and spring onion. Leon spotted her and came trotting up, his shaggy ears pricked. She surveyed him for any wobbly movements or odd behavior, but he looked pretty much the same.

"Quite a day, Leon," she told him. "First you get stoned, then I lose a whole barrel of one-of-a-kind Pinot Noir. Not sure which is worse."

Leon hummed and fell into step beside her as she marched across the lawn toward her house. The phone was ringing when she walked in, and Reese scrambled to grab it, leaving the front door ajar so she could keep an eye on Leon.

"Hello?"

"Hey, cuz," Larissa chirped. "What are you doing tonight?"

"Making dinner for Clay and Eric, apparently. Why?"

"I just got stood up by this guy I've been seeing. Wanna get together and play with makeup and have pillow fights in our underwear?"

"Did you miss the part where I said Clay and Eric are coming over for dinner?"

"No, I got that part," Larissa said. "I thought they'd like to watch."

Reese snorted. "No. No pillow fights, no makeup. But if you want to come over, I'm making shrimp scampi. Bring salad."

"I'll be there in a few. Love you!"

Reese hung up the phone and went to her refrigerator to make sure she had everything she needed. She hadn't planned on an impromptu dinner party, but she was surprised to see she had plenty of shrimp and a big bunch of asparagus. Maybe an easy hollandaise sauce? Plenty of butter for the scampi, plus a couple loaves of French bread in the freezer.

She pulled out the ingredients and was about to check on Leon when the phone rang again.

"Hello?"

"Hi, honey, it's Mom—listen, Grandpa's got other plans for dinner tonight, and I thought maybe you'd like to come over and join us? I made huckleberry cobbler for dessert."

"Actually, I'm having Eric and Clay and Larissa over here." She hesitated, not sure if having her parents there would make the dynamic more or less awkward.

Could it really get more awkward?

"Why don't you two join us for dinner?" Reese suggested.

"We wouldn't want to impose—"

"Don't worry about it. Just bring chairs. And bring the cobbler, too."

"You're sure?"

"No problem. Come whenever you're ready."

She hung up the phone and carried two asparagus spears outside to where Leon was standing beside her house sniffing a patch of grass.

"How are you feeling, buddy?" she asked, offering him a piece of asparagus.

While Leon munched, she scratched his ears. As soon as he stopped chewing, he burrowed his face in her cleavage and nuzzled hard.

"Slut," she muttered, massaging his long, fuzzy neck.

"First you get him stoned, then you call him a slut?"

Reese looked up to see Clay approaching from the side of the house. Her stomach did a loopy somersault and her skin began to tingle. She glanced at her watch, then back up at him. "You're early."

He stopped just a few inches from her, so close she could feel the heat radiating from his bare forearms. Her skin prickled with desire, and she resisted the urge to take a step back.

Clay cleared his throat. "I wanted a chance to talk to you for a sec before everyone showed up. I just didn't want this to be weird."

"Weird? What could possibly be weird about having dinner with a stoned alpaca, my ex-husband, my over-amorous parents, my nympho-maniac cousin, and a recovering alcoholic?"

"Larissa's coming?"

"How many nymphomaniac cousins do you think I have?"

"Right. Look, I just wanted to make sure you're okay with every-thing. I know this is a little weird for you and all, and then there was that kiss the other night—"

"It's fine," Reese said with a shrug, not wanting to dwell on it. Spot-ting a paper bag under his arm, Reese nodded at it. "You brought your own drink?"

"It's seltzer."

"There's going to be wine at dinner. I'm sure you've been around that before, but I figured I should warn you."

"I'm okay. That's why I brought my own drink."

She bit her lip. "Clay, if this is too hard on you at this stage—"

"If what's too hard on me?"

Reese watched his eyes, waiting for the hard-on joke. There wasn't one, except in her mind. Reese bit her lip. "Look, I've been wanting to ask you about something."

"Yes?"

She closed her eyes for a second. She took one deep breath, then another. Sooner or later, they had to talk about this. It had been fifteen years. Might as well get it out in the open now. "Clay, do you remember—"

"Hey, kids—what's shakin'?"

Reese opened her eyes to see Larissa shimmying up the walkway with a board game under one arm, a bag of salad clasped in one hand, and a bottle of white wine in the other. "It's Sauvignon Blanc," she said, lifting the bottle. "You said shrimp, right?"

"Right," Reese said, casting a look at Clay before reaching out to take the bottle from Larissa. "Thank you for thinking of it. Eric's got a Pinot Gris, so we're all set."

"My pleasure," she said, pausing to kiss Leon on the lips before sashaying through the front door.

Reese looked at Clay. "We'll talk later."

"Sure," Clay agreed, giving her a wary look. "Everything okay?"

"Absolutely," Reese said. "Never better."

◆　◆　◆

Clay was surprised to discover six people could fit comfortably in Reese's tiny dining room.

Space-wise, anyway. The meal wasn't exactly comfortable. The dining surface was glass, which meant every time he reached for the bread-basket, he was treated to a view of June caressing Jed's knee under the table. Not that there was anything inappropriate about it, but he could tell it was making Reese uncomfortable.

Among other things.

Reaching for the bread, Clay grazed Reese's arm with his and watched her bolt right out of her chair.

"More scampi, anyone?" she asked in a shout.

Clay drew his arm back, not sure if it was the kiss the other night or something else making things so tense between them. He settled for smiling and holding out his plate.

"Sure, I'll take more—unless anyone else wants it?"

"There's plenty," Reese said. "Stop being so polite."

Larissa snorted. "Bet that's not something you ever thought you'd say to Clay."

Clay forced his smile to stay in place and tried to keep his eyes on his food. The sound of ice sloshing drew his attention to the chill bucket at the center of the table, where Reese was replacing the empty Pinot Gris bottle with the Sauvignon Blanc Larissa had brought.

"More wine, anyone?" she asked.

Eric hoisted his glass, putting it right at eye level for Clay. Clay looked at it and swallowed hard as the pale liquid sloshed onto the table. He stared at the droplets for a second, then forked a shrimp into his mouth.

"How's Leon holding up?" he asked Reese.

"Good," she said. "I just checked on him. He seems pretty much like his normal self."

Jed nodded and wiped his mouth with a napkin. "Went right for my nuts when I came up the walk. I blocked him with the cobbler."

Clay grimaced and made a mental note to avoid the cobbler.

"I'm glad Leon is okay," June said. "I don't know what we're going to do with your grandfather."

"Um, how about dismantling his medical marijuana operation?" Reese suggested.

"He insists it's legal. There's no arguing with him. As long as it doesn't get out of hand—"

"Out of hand?" Reese asked. "Have you ever known anything with Axl *not* to get out of hand?"

"Could you pass the bread, Clay?" Eric said.

Clay nodded and handed it over. He studied his old pal for a moment, curious why he seemed so quiet.

"You okay?" Clay asked.

"Sure, why?"

"You're not talking much."

Eric shrugged. "It's nothing. Just got into it with Sheila on the phone earlier, no big deal."

Reese frowned. "Everything's okay, right?"

"Of course," Eric grumbled. "She's just been nagging about moving back to New York to be closer to her family. She got a job offer from some big ad agency out there, says she has a lead on a job for me."

Everyone stopped talking at once.

"What?" Larissa snapped. "You might be moving?"

"Of course not," Eric said around a mouthful of bread. "It's just this wild hair Sheila had. She'll get over it."

June dabbed the corner of her mouth with a napkin and pushed her plate aside. "Even so, honey, make sure you give us plenty of notice if you're considering it at all. Without you as our winemaker, I don't know what we'd do."

"I'm not going anywhere," Eric said. "Really, there's no chance of it. It's just Sheila being—well, Sheila. Who's ready for huckleberry cobbler?"

Clay set his fork down and stood up. "Let me help clear some of these plates."

"I can get it, Clay," Reese said. "Let me."

"No, sit down. Really. You've hardly touched your food, you've been so busy serving everyone else."

Reese frowned at him but sat down and forked up the last of her salad. Clay began gathering plates, and Larissa stood to help.

"Hey!" she said as she grabbed Reese's salad plate out from under her. "Anyone want to play a game over dessert?"

"What sort of game?" Eric asked.

"I brought a board game," she suggested.

Eric grunted. "*Bored* being the operative word?"

Larissa rolled her eyes. "Fine, something else, then. Something fun." She trudged to the kitchen sink looking more wobbly than normal on her high heels, and Clay made a mental note to keep an eye on her. The line between social drinking and a genuine problem could be squiggly and blurred, which he knew damn well from experience.

Clay set the plates beside the sink and turned back to the table to gather another batch while Larissa got to work running the sink full of soapy water.

"I think we're out for the games," June said as she stood up and piled her plate on top of Jed's, smiling as she grazed her husband's hand. "There's a meteor shower tonight, so we're taking a blanket out to the north pasture to see if we can spot any shooting stars."

"Should be a great night for it," Jed said.

June grabbed another plate and nodded. "I call dibs on picking the spot this time."

"Deal," Jed said. "I call dibs on making the cocoa."

Clay watched the private smile that flashed between Reese's parents, marveling at the intimacy simmering in that small exchange. He slid his gaze to Reese, wondering if she noticed it, too, but Reese had already glanced away.

"Let us help with the dishes before we go," June said, brushing her daughter's shoulder as she moved past her into the kitchen. "That way you kids can get started on your game."

"Don't worry about it, Mom. I've got it."

"You sure?"

"Positive." Reese swallowed her last bite of scampi and reached for her water glass. "Don't you want dessert before you go?"

June slid her arm around Jed's waist as the two turned toward the door. "I have all the sweet stuff I need right here."

Jed beamed and pulled his wife closer, and Clay wondered if they'd be able to fit through the doorway linked like Siamese twins. Something like longing flickered in Reese's eyes, but it was gone so quickly, Clay decided he'd imagined it.

"Goodnight, sweetie," Jed called. "Thanks for dinner."

As the door shut behind them, Larissa pulled her hands out of a sinkful of soapy water and rinsed them beneath the tap. "Okay, then," she said. "Screw the board games. Let's play something fun like 'I Never.'"

"What's 'I Never'?" Clay asked.

"A drinking game," Eric muttered.

"A *sexy* drinking game," Larissa amended.

Clay shrugged. "Can't say I remember it. Of course, I was probably too blitzed to play."

"Don't worry," Larissa assured him. "It's more about sharing secrets than getting drunk. You can have water."

Reese stood up and started gathering her dishes with a clatter. "We don't have any secrets. We've all known each other forever. Let's play something else."

"Come on, you guys!" Larissa pleaded. "We haven't done anything fun together since Clay came back. It'll be like old times."

Eric grunted and glanced at Clay. "Aren't we all supposed to be doing supportive shit so we avoid things being like 'old times'? Doesn't seem like a drinking game would be the best idea."

Clay felt a sharp pang in the center of his gut. He knew Eric was aiming for helpful, not accusatory, but the words still stung. "Actually, admitting past failures is part of the recovery process," Clay said. "I haven't played 'I Never,' but it sounds like the same idea."

"Sure!" Larissa said. "I mean, you kinda want to avoid words like 'failure' if you want it to be fun, but it's all about revealing salacious things you've done."

Clay shrugged. "I'm game."

Reese bit her lip but didn't meet Clay's eyes. "It just seems like a bad idea. Isn't this—what's the word I'm looking for?"

"Dumb?" Eric offered.

"No, that's not what I meant." Reese waved a hand in Clay's direction, flinging soap on Larissa's shirt. "A *trigger*. Something that wouldn't be good for Clay."

Larissa rolled her eyes. "You guys, he's been sober four years. Don't you think he's capable of deciding for himself what's good for him?"

All three pairs of eyes shifted to him, and Clay stood frozen in the space between the kitchen and the living room, the space between the fun guy they remembered and the responsible guy he knew he could be. He hesitated, not knowing what the right move was here, but knowing he wanted to prove to all of them that he could do this. He could be fun and spontaneous and still be a responsible adult who didn't end up ruining everyone's evening either by passing out or passing up a chance to do something enjoyable.

He folded his arms over his chest and met their gazes one by one. Larissa, Eric, Reese. "Let's play."

Eric shrugged. "Fine by me. I've got nothing better to do."

Larissa looked at Reese, who had started ladling huckleberry cobbler into bowls. "Reese?"

She sighed. "This all seems a little awkward. Come on, Eric and I used to be married. Don't you think that's weird?"

"No weirder than you being BFFs with his second wife," Larissa pointed out.

Eric refilled his wineglass and stood up with a shrug. "Isn't awkwardness the whole point of the game? I'm not endorsing it, just saying."

Reese sighed, looking defeated. Larissa gave her a one-armed hug, then grabbed a bowl of cobbler and a glass of wine before flouncing into the living room. Eric shrugged, then picked up a bowl of cobbler and followed. Clay watched him sink into the center of a leather sofa the color of an old saddle, while Larissa curled up in a bright-orange armchair lined with flowery turquoise pillows. Clay stared at them for a moment, his throat welling with a flood of nostalgia for his lost college years. If only he hadn't fucked everything up—

"You don't have to do this, you know," Reese murmured.

Clay turned to look at her and felt the wistful pang grip him tighter. He cleared his throat. "It's fine. I'm fine."

"I'm not talking about the alcohol." She shot a nervous glance toward the living room, then lowered her voice. "I'm just thinking about that time in college when—"

"Come on, you guys," Larissa yelled. "Hurry up!"

Clay looked at Reese, still wondering what the right move was. She stared at him, her expression unreadable. He turned back to the living room. "Why don't you guys play and I'll finish up the dishes?"

"No way," Eric said. "I'm not going to be the only guy playing. Get your ass in here. You, too, Reese. Come on, we'll get the dishes later."

Clay looked at Reese. He took a step closer, making his voice low. "I promise I'm okay with this," he said. "You don't have to worry about it being a trigger."

He watched her throat move as she swallowed, and she took a shaky breath. "Okay. That's fine, I mean. I just—how do you want to handle—"

She broke off there, not finishing the question, but Clay watched her gaze flit to her wineglass on the counter. Right, the alcohol. This was a drinking game, after all.

"It's not a big deal," he said. "I'll drink water. 'Riss seems drunk enough not to notice who's drinking what anyway."

She seemed to think about that for a moment, her gaze drifting out to the living room. Part of him ached to reach out and touch her the way he had in the kitchen or at Vineyard Grill. He glanced at Eric, who frowned at him.

Right. Touching Reese would be bad.

At last, Reese nodded. "Let's play."

She marched past him into the living room and Clay stared after her, admiring the sway of her hips. She chose a spot on a comfortable-looking love seat that matched the couch, and Clay watched her tuck her delicate bare feet up under her as her caramel-colored braid slipped over her shoulder. He saw Eric watching him and quickly feigned interest in a potted fern on the edge of the counter.

"You coming, Clay?" Larissa yelled.

Not anytime soon, dammit.

Kicking his inner pig in the head, he cleared his throat and headed for the living room. "Yeah, sure."

He picked a seat as far away from Reese as he could get, settling on the end of the sofa near Eric while he ordered himself to grow the fuck up and stop ogling Reese. He could do this. He could renew friendships and revisit old memories and go home with no regrets. This is the way normal people functioned, right?

Across from him, Larissa began to explain the rules, though Clay suspected he was the only one who required a refresher. "Okay, so someone starts and they have to make a statement that starts *I never*. It has to be true, and it's always best if it's a little bit dirty. Like I could say, *I never had sex on an airplane*, and anyone in the room who's done that would have to drink."

Clay shifted his water glass in one hand. "So how do we know who wins?"

"There's no winner or loser," Larissa explained with exaggerated patience. "It's just about learning people's deepest, darkest secrets. The more you drink, the less inhibited you become, the more you cough up the dirt."

Eric nodded at Clay's glass. "Probably good the guy with the most dirt is drinking water."

"Come on," Larissa said. "Let's just play."

Reese sighed and settled back onto her love seat with a glass of wine beside her on an end table. Clay watched, wondering what she was thinking. This was awkward for all of them, but probably more for Reese, who tended to be a private person. Maybe he still had time to put a stop to it. Maybe—

"Why don't you start, 'Riss?" Reese suggested. "Show us how it's done."

"Okay, fine—I never had sex with two people at once," Larissa declared.

"Oh, come on," Reese said. "That hardly seems—" She stopped and stared at Clay as he took a slow sip of water.

Everyone's attention swung to him, and Clay froze mid-sip, pretty sure he'd just started things off on the wrong foot. He set his glass down and frowned at Eric. "What?"

"Stud!" Eric slapped him on the shoulder.

Larissa laughed. "There's a story I'd love to hear."

Clay grimaced, feeling like an idiot just thirty seconds into the game. Everyone was staring at him, which was the last thing he wanted. He felt awkward in his own skin, and remembered how easy it used to be to grab a beer at a party to make that feeling go away.

"I thought that's how the game worked," he said, wondering if it was okay to take another sip of water. His mouth felt dry all of a sudden. "That's how we're supposed to play, right?"

"Right," Larissa said. "And no one is allowed to judge, so quit looking at him like that, Reese."

"I wasn't," she said. "Just surprised, that's all."

Clay scuffed his toe across the rug. "Alcohol may have been a factor."

Reese bit her lip. "It often is."

"You're up, Reese," Eric said. "We go in a circle, right?"

"Right," Larissa agreed. "Come on, Reese—lay it on us."

"Oh, fine." She grabbed her own wineglass, not meeting Clay's eyes. "I never had sex in the winery barn."

Eric and Larissa both lifted their glasses and drank. Reese snorted. "Larissa doesn't surprise me, but Eric? I wouldn't think Sheila would agree to that."

"Wasn't Sheila," he said. "This was after you, before Sheila. Remember that intern six years ago? The one with the big—"

"Okay, moving on," Reese said. "Eric, you go."

He shrugged. "I never had anyone spank me in the bedroom."

Larissa and Reese both lifted their glasses. Larissa giggled. Clay felt lightheaded.

"Reese—kinky!" Larissa said.

"You said no judging," Reese said, and Clay watched her cheeks flush crimson. "But if you must know, it was that horse trainer I dated three years ago. He thought a whip would be a nice thing to bring on a third date."

Eric laughed. "You sure can pick 'em."

"Hey, I'm proud of you, cuz," Larissa said, giving Reese a reassuring squeeze. "I didn't know you had it in you to be so experimental."

"I didn't say I liked it," Reese said, her cheeks still beautifully pink. She looked at the ceiling and gave a funny little smile. "Then again, I didn't say I *didn't* like it."

Larissa laughed and turned back to Clay. "Okay, gorgeous, your turn."

Clay gripped his water glass, not sure what to say. Hell, there was plenty he *could* say. Plenty he remembered, plenty he didn't, plenty he wished he could forget. He opened his mouth to say something. Then closed it. Then opened it again.

The sound of the doorbell dragged everyone's eyes off him and onto the door.

Reese frowned. "What the—"

"Uh-oh," said Larissa. "I know who it is."

Before anyone could ask, a voice outside started shouting. "Goddammit, Larissa—I know you're there. Open the door!"

CHAPTER EIGHT

From her perch on the love seat, Reese frowned at the front door, then at her cousin. She had a sick feeling in her gut, which made this the second time today she'd been pretty sure she was about to toss her cookies.

"Larissa? Who's that? And how did he know where you'd be?"

"It's Joey—the dude I was supposed to go out with tonight?"

"Right," Reese said. "You said he stood you up?"

"Kinda. Or maybe it was the other way around, I can't remember now."

"You mean you stood *him* up?" Reese said, feeling the same sense of dread she always did when she ended up in the middle of one of Larissa's romance dramas. "And then you told him where you'd be this evening?"

"Hey, a girl's gotta play hard to get, but you gotta let 'em know where to find you."

The doorbell rang again, and a man's voice shouted from the other side. "Come on, Larissa. We need to talk about this. I know you're there."

"I don't feel like talking," Larissa shouted back. "I'm tired of talking. Talk, talk, talk—what about action?"

"I'll give you action, I will. Come on, just let me explain."

Eric lifted an eyebrow. "What did she do now?"

Reese sighed and glanced from the door to her cousin. "'Riss, you want me to call the cops, or you want to let the guy in?"

Larissa rolled her eyes. "I'll let him in. But only so I can tell him to his face that the way to woo a woman is not by falling asleep when she's giving you a hand job."

Reese closed her eyes and tried to remember why she'd agreed to host this dinner party in the first place. She opened her eyes again to see Eric sitting up straighter on the couch and grinning at Clay.

"And you wanted to go home early," Eric said, nudging Clay in the ribs with his elbow. "See? Things are just starting to get interesting."

"Cheaper than hotel pay-per-view," Clay agreed.

Larissa flung the door open to reveal a man whose size suggested a fondness for lifting small automobiles. He looked more sad than dangerous, but Reese watched Clay and Eric bristle anyway.

"Come on, Larissa, I said I was sorry," the guy pleaded. "Just let me explain."

"You don't need to explain. I got the message loud and clear last night. Obviously I wasn't interesting enough for you to bother staying awake."

"But it wasn't my fault, baby. I was just so tired. I loved what you were doing with your hands, and then when you did that twisty thing with your thumb and—"

"Hi, I'm Reese," she said, bolting off the sofa and hustling to the door before things got more awkward. She extended her hand to the guy, not sure if she should be defending her cousin or locking her in a bedroom. "And you are?"

"Joey," he said, and stepped inside to shake her hand. "I just want to talk to Larissa."

"We're busy right now," Larissa huffed, turning to march back to the living room. She plunked down on the love seat this time, then turned back to face them with her arms folded over her chest. "We're playing 'I Never.' Here's one: *I never had a guy fall asleep during a hand job until last night.*"

Reese winced, wondering if there were normal families somewhere that didn't feel the need to overshare. She looked at Clay and Eric, who were staring at Joey with expressions of male sympathy.

"Dude," Eric said.

"Ouch," Clay agreed.

Larissa's date gave an exasperated sigh and followed her into the living room. "Well, *I never been so tired as I was last night*. Come on, I worked late and—"

"Are we supposed to drink to that?" Eric asked Clay. "Because I've been pretty tired, and there was this one time a few years ago with Sheila where I just didn't feel like it."

"I think we're still playing," Clay said. "You should probably drink."

Reese shook her head, pretty sure the time had come for the game to be over. "Can we just call it a night?"

"We're still playing," Larissa insisted as Joey sat down beside her on the love seat. Reese couldn't help noticing her cousin didn't move away.

"Clay hasn't even gone yet," Larissa pointed out. "Everyone sit down and let's keep going. I haven't decided what to do with *you* yet," she said, directing her ire back at Joey. "But we're not done here. Clay, go. It's your turn."

Clay lifted his water glass, considering. "I never had sex on an airplane."

Larissa rolled her eyes. "No fair, I already did that one."

"You just did it as an example, not as a real *I never*," Clay pointed out.

"No dice, go again."

Clay sighed. "I've never been in love with anyone I've dated."

Reese bit the inside of her lip. Larissa's eyes widened. Everyone was quiet for a second.

Joey was the first to speak. "Wow, man. That's kinda depressing."

"Yeah," Eric agreed. "Not exactly sexy."

Clay rolled his eyes. "You didn't say it had to be sexy. Just that it had to be the truth. I'm making amends for past wrongs here, remember?"

"And we're not judging, *remember*?" Larissa said, shooting a pointed look at Reese.

"I'm not judging," she said. "That's just the first time I've ever heard someone say something like that when playing 'I Never.'"

"It still counts," Clay said. "Come on, I've gone twice, someone else go."

"I'll go," Joey said. "I've never slept with anyone in this room, but I'd really, really like to. Um, I mean Larissa. I'm talking about Larissa. Because she's so smart and pretty."

Larissa beamed, and Reese resisted the urge to roll her eyes. Clearly, Joey had homed in on her cousin's fondness for flattery.

"That's sweet," Larissa said, edging closer to him on the sofa. "Fine, you're forgiven. You can take me to dinner next week."

Joey put an arm around her. "That's great, baby. I won't let you down, I swear."

Reese felt someone kick her shin and looked over to see Eric holding up his glass of wine. "I guess we have to drink to what he said— the *I never slept with anyone in this room?* We were married. I think we might've had sex once or twice."

Reese shrugged and felt her face start to flood with heat. She wanted to blame it on the public spectacle of the whole thing, but she knew damn well she was avoiding looking at Clay. "Fine," she said, and took a sip of wine.

From the corner of her eye, she saw Clay shift in his seat. She set down her glass and kept her expression neutral and her gaze trained on a throw pillow for what seemed like an eternity.

Finally, she couldn't stand the suspense. She stole a glance at Clay. He was looking at his water glass and frowning, but he must have felt the weight of Reese's stare. He looked up and gave a shrug so small, she might have imagined it. Then he set his glass down without taking a sip.

"I think that does it for me, guys," he said as he stood up. "I have to get up early in the morning."

Reese stood, too, wiping her palms on her jeans as twin surges of relief and disappointment coursed through her. "Thanks for coming," she said. "And for the help with Leon earlier."

"No sweat," Clay said. "Good seeing you guys."

"Later," Joey said, his eyes focused on Larissa. "I think I'm gonna take off. You want to go grab a drink?"

"A drink, huh?" She grinned at him. "Yeah, that's what I'd like to grab."

The two of them stood up, and Joey put his arm around Larissa. Reese stepped aside as they moved toward the door in a cloud of sexual energy Reese could hear crackling in the air.

"Be safe," she called, then felt like kicking herself for sounding like a schoolmarm. She walked them all to the door and flipped on her porch light to make sure they made it to their cars.

As soon as the door shut, Eric stood up. "Thanks for dinner, Riesling."

"Don't call me Riesling."

He grinned and carried his wineglass and empty cobbler bowl to the kitchen. When he turned back around, the grin had vanished.

"Look, Reese—promise me something, okay?"

"To love, honor, and cherish?" Reese leaned back against the counter. "Sorry, been there, done that, outgrew the T-shirt."

Eric shook his head. "I'm being serious for once. Just promise me you'll be careful with Clay."

Reese felt the words like a punch to the gut. Her pulse sped up, but she forced herself not to blink. "What do you mean?"

"I think you know."

"I really don't." She swallowed hard, hoping he didn't see her tight grip on the counter behind her. "Are you worried about me or him?"

"Yes." Eric frowned. "I love you guys, but you're totally wrong for each other. A recovering addict and someone with an unrealistic concept of relationships? I just don't want to see either of you mess up each other's lives."

"Bite me, Eric."

He managed a small smile at that. "You mentioned the spanking, but I didn't realize biting was your thing, too."

She shook her head, not willing to loosen her grip on her irritation in exchange for his dumb jokes this time. She folded her arms over her chest, hoping he couldn't tell how much his words had gotten to her. "Were you always this charming? I can't remember if this is why I married you or divorced you."

"Both." He gave her a smile she knew was meant to soften his words, but they still sliced through her like little bits of hot wire. "Just promise you'll listen to me. Clay's rebuilding his life here, and we're the only friends he still has. You guys can't let something stupid like libido screw that up."

She shook her head, determined not to let him see the way her hands were shaking. "I'm not promising anything because there's no need," she insisted. "I'm not hot for Clay, and he's not hot for me. We couldn't be more wrong for each other, and we both know it."

He stared at her, an expression she recognized as his best effort to bite back the word *bullshit*. Reese stared back, unflinching.

"Nothing's going to happen between Clay and me," she insisted, as much to reassure herself as Eric.

"Whatever you say."

"Go home, Eric. Say hello to Sheila."

"You want help with the dishes?"

"I've got it, thanks."

"Goodnight, Riesling."

"Goodnight, bastard."

Eric gave her a chaste peck on the forehead, which she answered with a soft punch to his gut.

"Ow," he muttered, grinning as he headed toward the door. "See you tomorrow."

"Sure."

As soon as he was gone, Reese closed her eyes and leaned her head back against the cupboard.

She didn't love Clay. She *couldn't* love Clay.

She thumped her head on the cupboard a few times, willing it to be true.

◆ ◆ ◆

Clay put off going into Reese's office for as long as he could the next day. Finally, there was no avoiding it.

She looked up the instant he knocked on the doorframe, her green eyes flashing under the fluorescent lights. Her hair slid back over her shoulders, framing her face in a cinnamon-gold halo, and Clay felt his breath catch in his throat.

"Hey," she said. "Thanks for coming over last night."

He nodded, trying not to think about what her hair would feel like sliding through his fingers. He didn't see it down too often, and he ached to reach out and touch it. He pushed the thought out of his mind and cleared his throat. "Thank *you* for dinner. It was great."

Reese smiled. "Even when things got a little weird with Larissa?"

"I've known Larissa since she was a teenager," he said, returning her smile. "When do things not get weird with her?"

"It's part of her charm. What's up?"

Clay hesitated a moment at the threshold, then came in and shut the door behind him. He dropped into the chair in front of her desk and rested his clipboard on his lap.

"We're reaching a point where you're going to need to make some decisions," he said. Seeing her face register alarm, he gripped the edge of his clipboard tighter. "About the building. Decisions about the building project, I mean."

"I know what you meant," Reese said. "I've got an appointment with the bank tomorrow to discuss additional financing in light of your increased estimate."

"Technically, it's not our estimate that increased," Clay pointed out. "It's the price of materials."

Reese rolled her eyes. "What's the point in having an estimate if the numbers are completely arbitrary?"

"They weren't arbitrary. They were based on market conditions at the time, and it's not our fault material costs went up."

Reese gritted her teeth. "I'm not going to argue with you. I'm too tired, and the bottom line is that we can't do anything about the price of the stupid fly ass."

"Fly ash."

"What?"

"It's fly ash, not fly ass."

"Whatever," she said, beautiful in her flustered state. "Just give me a few days to work things out with the bank. Do you and your crew have enough you can do in the meantime?"

Clay gave a small nod. "We've got several more days of clearing and grading, but we can't stall too long."

Reese gritted her teeth. "We should know something by then."

"Okay, then. I'll get back to work."

Reese nodded. She opened her mouth to say something, then closed it. She picked up her letter opener. Clay watched for a moment as she rolled it between her palms.

"You've done that for as long as I've known you," Clay said.

"Done what?"

"Fidgeted with something when you're uncomfortable. Rolled it around between your palms like that. It always used to be a pen—back when we were in college, I mean. The letter opener is a change."

Reese stared at him for a second, then set the letter opener down. "So moving from the pen to the letter opener is a sign that I'm growing and maturing?"

Clay raised an eyebrow. "What?"

Reese shook her head. "Nothing. Just seems like I've been hearing a lot lately about how I haven't changed."

"Is that a bad thing?"

She shrugged. "Being stagnant isn't a good thing, is it?"

"I wouldn't say stagnant. Just consistent. Consistently charming."

"Or lacking growth and maturity, one or the other."

"Growth and maturity aren't all they're cracked up to be. Neither is change. Take it from a guy who's had to do a whole lot of that."

She gave him a look that was somewhere between sympathy and uncertainty, and Clay felt his chest tighten. He kicked himself for driving the conversation down a dark path and tried to think of a good way to steer them back on course.

"For what it's worth, I think your rolling habit is endearing."

"Thanks. I think." She stayed quiet a moment before picking up the letter opener again, this time rolling it more slowly in her palms. "You know, the old Clay would have made a dirty joke about my palm-rolling habit being a sign of my fixation with hand jobs."

Clay gripped the clipboard tighter, willing himself to keep breathing so he wouldn't pass out or lunge across the desk to kiss her. He honestly wasn't sure which would be worse.

"I wasn't aware you had that fixation," he replied evenly.

Reese laughed. "That's not what I meant. I guess I just meant that's one of the ways you've changed—you no longer seize every opportunity to make dirty jokes."

"Pretty sure that *is* a sign of growth and maturity."

"Mmhmm," Reese said.

Clay sat still for a few more seconds. There was something on her mind. Was it the kiss at Vineyard Grill the other night? That had been dumb. *Really dumb.* Talk about a stupid risk. With only a handful of friendships left, should he really be jeopardizing the two most important ones in his life?

Or maybe Reese wasn't thinking about that at all. Maybe it was the other thing. The issue they'd been avoiding.

"Thanks for last night," Reese blurted. "For not drinking during the whole *I've never slept with anyone in this room* thing."

Clay swallowed hard, not sure what to say now that the words were out there on the table. "It seemed like the respectful thing to do, under the circumstances."

She laughed. "Like things weren't awkward enough last night."

"Exactly."

She nodded. "Right. It was. Look—"

The phone rang, and Reese glanced down at the caller ID. She frowned. "Shit, it's the bank. I've gotta take this. So we'll talk again later?"

"Absolutely," Clay said. "Enjoy the rest of your day."

He stood up, part of him wishing they'd had a chance to finish the conversation.

But most of him damn glad they hadn't.

◆　◆　◆

Reese was reviewing a draft of the Sunridge Vineyards e-newsletter with Larissa late that afternoon when her phone rang for the millionth time that day. Larissa leaned across the desk, spilling cleavage as she peered at the readout.

"Who's Wallace O'Brien?"

Reese looked down at the phone. "That's Dr. Wally. He's the vet who took care of Leon yesterday."

"A vet, huh? Cute? Single?"

"These are the criteria I should use when selecting a veterinarian now?"

"What do you mean *now?*" Larissa grinned. "They've always been the criteria."

Reese rolled her eyes and picked up the phone. "Sunridge Vineyards, this is Reese speaking."

"Reese, this is Wallace O'Brien. We met yesterday after your alpaca ate—"

"Right, right—I remember," she said, leaning back in her chair as

Larissa leaned forward to eavesdrop. "Thanks again for everything. For coming out on short notice and all."

"Of course. How's he doing?"

"Perfect. He seemed a little hungrier than normal last night, but other than that, he seems fine."

"Good. That's good." Wally cleared his throat. "Look, I won't keep you long. I just wanted to say that I'm going to the Friday Art Walk tonight in Newberg. I was wondering if you might like to join me?"

"Tonight?"

"I'm sure you've been before—it's the first Friday every month, and all the shops and galleries have art and wine and cheese."

"Oh—well—"

Dr. Wally laughed. "Sorry, is that dumb to invite a wine pro on a date where wine will be served? Too much mixing business with pleasure?"

"No, actually, it's great," Reese said, her brain sticking a little on the word *date* as she tried to decide how she felt about that. "Um, I think I'm free tonight."

Across the desk, Larissa perked up. She mouthed the word *date?* and made a kissy face while Reese tried to ignore her.

Dr. Wally rattled off details about the artists and galleries and shops, and Reese wondered if she should be writing down the information or feeling her heart go pitty-pat in her chest. She couldn't seem to muster up the enthusiasm for either one, so she settled for grabbing her letter opener.

"So can I pick you up around seven?" he asked.

"I was thinking I'd just meet you there, but—"

Larissa shook her head vehemently. She grabbed a piece of paper out of Reese's recycle box, then snatched a pen and scrawled something in big, block letters. She shoved it across the desk at Reese, who was still trying to focus on the conversation with Wally.

Let him drive! Car sex is fun!

Reese rolled her eyes and shoved the note back at Larissa.

"Sure, go ahead and pick me up," Reese said. "Not for car sex, but—"

"What?"

Reese squeezed her eyes shut and gritted her teeth. "I was talking to my cousin. I mean—never mind. I'll see you at seven."

Reese hung up the phone and set down her letter opener, not sure whether to kill her cousin or herself.

"You have a date!" Larissa squealed.

Reese shook her head. "No. You don't get to dress me this time."

"Please? No front-clasp bras, I promise."

"Larissa—"

"I'll be good, I swear. Pretty please?"

Reese sighed. "Fine. But nothing slutty, okay?"

"Your version of slutty or mine?"

Reese stared at her.

"Fine," Larissa said, rolling her eyes. "Nothing slutty. I can do that. I can do your hair, too, right?"

Reese smiled in spite of herself. "Sure. You can do my hair. You want to come to my place, or should I come to yours?"

"Yours," she said. "I have a date tonight with this new guy, but I'm afraid Joey might try to stop by my place to see me again."

"How the hell do you manage this?" Reese asked. "Seriously, I get hives just thinking about the one date."

Larissa beamed. "It's talent."

"It's something, all right."

"This will be fun," Larissa said. "Don't you feel better now that you're dating again?"

"I'd hardly call the thing with Bob the Boob-man a date. More like a visual assault."

"Good point." Larissa shrugged. "Okay, so Bob is out. Really, you can't rely on your ex-husband to set you up with a quality man. I have a good feeling about this vet guy, though."

"You've never met him."

"No, but he came to rescue Leon, didn't he? Must be a nice guy."

"He's a recovering drunk." The second the words left her mouth, Reese felt a rush of shame. Still, it was something she couldn't overlook. "I mean, I assume he's an alcoholic. Clay found him through AA."

Larissa stared, her smile fading into something a bit darker. She folded her arms over her chest. "Since when did you get to be a judgmental snob about that?"

Reese reached for her letter opener, then stopped. She pressed her palms against the desk, weighing her words. "Look, I just think it would be irresponsible for someone who makes a living hawking alcohol to get involved with someone who nearly ruined his own life drinking it."

"We still talking about the vet here?"

Reese looked down at her hands. "I need to get out in the field to check the nitrate levels. You okay with coming over around five?"

"Sure," Larissa said, standing up and striding toward the door. "But don't think I didn't notice you failed to answer that question."

Reese sighed but couldn't think of a clever comeback before Larissa had disappeared down the hall. She finished editing the newsletter and printed a copy while she dialed her mom's cell phone.

"Hey, honey," June answered in a chirpy voice. "What's up?"

"Larissa and I just finished up the e-newsletter. She also put together a little direct-mail piece for the wine club to explain the whole wine-down-the-drain thing."

"Did we lose any more members?"

Reese looked at the spreadsheet on her laptop and tried not to feel grim. "Three more today. They were all really pissed about the Pinot."

"Well, these things happen."

Her voice was upbeat, but Reese could hear the tension. They were all worried—about money, about the vineyard's reputation, about the event coming up next week. She sighed and forced herself to adopt a business-as-usual tone. "Do you want to see the newsletter and the direct-mail piece before they go out?"

"You know I trust you, sweetie."

"I know you do," Reese said. "You still want to see it, though, right?"

"If it's not too much trouble. We're down at your grandfather's old house right now doing some cleaning. Could you bring it over here?"

"I'll be there in five."

Reese hung up the phone and shoved the papers in a file. She closed her office door and passed Eric as she made her way past the stacks of barrels in the winery. "I'm heading out," she called. "Can you lock up when you leave?"

"No sweat. So you've got a hot date?"

Reese rolled her eyes. "Are there families where relatives don't inform ex-husbands about every detail of the ex-wife's love life? Because if there are, I'd like to join one."

"I think it's great," he said as he clapped her on the shoulder. "It's about time you got out of your rut and got serious about dating again."

"Have you always sounded like a self-help book or is this a new thing?"

"You know you love me."

"Not especially, but that didn't stop me from marrying you." She grinned to show she was teasing but stopped grinning when Eric regarded her with a serious expression.

"It's not just about love, you know."

Reese stopped walking. "What isn't?"

"Marriage."

She snorted. "Since I don't ever plan to do that again, I don't see why it matters."

"I'm just saying. Relationships are a lot of work. Look at me and Sheila. Not a day goes by that we don't work at it."

"Please don't feel you need to share the details of how you work at it."

Eric laughed. "Have a good date, Riesling."

"Piss off," she replied without venom. She headed out the door and down the hill toward Axl's old place.

The front door stood wide open, and Reese could hear voices near the back of the house. The smell of popcorn drifted from the kitchen, and Reese hesitated in the doorway.

"Mom? Dad?"

"We're back here, honey! You'll never guess what we found in a box in Grandpa's old linen closet."

"I'm afraid to ask," she muttered, moving through the entryway past a long row of photographs. There were several shots of Axl as a young man working at a vineyard in Italy, followed by one of her grandparents on their honeymoon in Mexico sporting matching tattoos. She kept walking, her gaze drifting past images of Larissa's parents in Bali and some shots of June as a young girl.

Toward the end of the hall her mom had grouped another set of images, these more recent—one of her parents on a beach in Maui, arms wrapped around each other as the sun set over the ocean; another of her mom perched on her dad's shoulders plucking apples from the orchard; another shot showed June and Jed beaming at each other as they twirled jump ropes in double-Dutch fashion while Larissa and Reese spun in giddy circles between them.

Reese ran a finger over the frames, wondering what it would be like to collect a lifetime of memories with the person you knew with absolute certainty had been put on the Earth just for you.

"We're in the family room, honey," her mom called, and Reese tore her gaze off the photos.

She moved toward the back of the house where the scent of fresh popcorn and citrus furniture polish was heavy in the air. Stumbling over something in the hall, she looked down to see her old tricycle there. She toed the front wheel, remembering her parents walking hand in hand behind her as she pedaled as fast as her chubby legs could go trying to keep up with Axl on his motorcycle.

She stepped around the trike and halted in the doorway to the family room. Her parents were curled up on Axl's old sofa, a shared blanket and a bowl of popcorn between them. The flicker of the TV drew her attention to a grainy video that was all too familiar.

"Look, sweetie," her mom said, smiling up at her from the couch. "It's our wedding video. Have you seen this since we had the old film reels digitized?"

Reese leaned against the doorframe and smiled back. "Only about two hundred times, but I think it's been a few months."

"Smart aleck," her mom replied, tossing a piece of popcorn at her. "Want some of this?"

"I'm good, thanks." Reese held out the folder she'd brought with her, and her mom reached out to take it. "We've got a printout of the e-newsletter, a direct-mail postcard, and a second press release about the Memorial Day event."

June flipped open the cover of the folder and whistled low between her teeth. "Wow, this looks nice. I like the font you used here."

"That's all Larissa. She's got a real eye for the branding stuff."

"Hmm, I see that. Gimme a sec to read this."

"No problem." Reese's gaze drifted to her dad as he sat riveted to the television screen, so Reese turned her attention there, too. She watched as her youthful father lifted her mom's veil and kissed her with an intensity that made Reese want to look away.

She didn't, though. She might have seen this a million times, but she could never stop staring, or stop wondering about a union with such absolute certainty, such devotion, such love.

"My favorite part is coming up," her father said.

Reese bit her lip, disgusted with herself for feeling envious of her own parents. "You mean the part where Axl uses the unity candle to light farts at the reception?"

Her dad laughed. "No, that's not for a few more minutes. It's the part where your mom sees the inscription on her wedding band for the first time."

Reese nodded, picturing the words in her mind and remembering the way she used to trace her finger over them as a little girl.

I call dibs.

Her parents' private joke. She'd heard it before, the way June had called dibs on the cherry on Jed's banana split during their very first date. Jed had spooned up the cherry, offering it in exchange for dibs on June's evening plans the next night. And the night after that.

They'd laid claim to each other again and again, drifting into the blissful ease of knowing they belonged to one another. With each shared breath, they radiated it. *I am yours and you are mine for as long as we both live.*

Reese watched the screen as her mother's gaze slid over the words, then filled with tears. As Reese looked on, newlywed June looked up at her new husband with an adoration that took Reese's breath away.

They make it look so easy, she thought as she gripped the back of the sofa. *Then and now.*

Her mom patted her hand, and Reese looked down to see June watching the screen, her finger resting on the newsletter to hold her place. "Aren't you a handsome thing!" June exclaimed, moving her hand from the page to squeeze her husband's knee. "Honey, isn't your father a handsome thing?"

"My father is a handsome thing," Reese parroted, earning herself a good-natured swat from her mom. She kept her gaze on the TV, watching as the scene shifted to the reception and to her father dropping to one knee and hitching up the hem of her mom's wedding dress.

"I still have that garter in my cedar chest somewhere," June mused. "The guy who caught it gave it back to me after the reception. Said he felt awkward about having it."

Reese snorted. "What could possibly be awkward about pocketing the undergarments of another man's new wife?"

"Oh, stop," June said, laughing. "You never were very sentimental."

"Maybe that's why I'm divorced, huh?" Reese said, struggling to keep her tone light. "I never got schmoopy over garters."

"Honey—"

"You always had the best legs," Jed said, oblivious to the conversation going on around him. "Still do."

June beamed at him and planted a kiss on his temple before returning her gaze to the paperwork. Reese kept her eyes on the screen, unable to look away. Her mom, barefoot in the grass, wore a ring of daisies in her hair and a white dress that barely concealed the fact that she was already three months pregnant with Reese.

God, they were young. So young, so in love.

On the sofa, her dad shifted the popcorn bowl so he could put his arm around her mom. Her mom snuggled into the embrace and kept reading.

"Hmm," June said, still flipping through the folder of printouts. She tapped the edge of the newsletter and smiled up at Reese. "This looks great. Did you do this part?"

"Nope, that's Larissa. She's turning into a pretty serious copywriter."

"That's great," June said. "Speaking of getting serious, we hear you have a date."

Reese sighed. "For crying out loud, did Larissa call you?"

"No, Axl. He ran into Eric in the winery barn."

She shook her head, not sure whether to feel irritated or loved. Funny how often the two sentiments intertwined when it came to her family. "Did you already call it in to the newspaper, or should I do that in the morning?"

"We think it's great, honey," June said. "We just want you to be happy. Love is such a wonderful human experience."

"I *am* happy," Reese said, trying not to notice the on-screen image of her father scooping her mother into his arms and twirling her around so her wedding dress fluttered in the breeze. She looked away, hating the rawness in her throat. "Mom, are you worried about our meeting with the bank?"

Two frown lines appeared between her mother's eyebrows. "A little. I think we've got our ducks in a row, but—"

"It's a lot of money," Reese said softly. "And if they won't lend it to us, I don't know what we'll do."

Her father shook his head and looked away from the TV. "We could always delay the expansion. Maybe in a few years—"

"No!" Reese snapped, panic rising in her chest. "We've already been shouting about it for months on our website and in the press. We'll look like idiots if we cancel now. Like idiots who don't know how to run a business."

"She's right, hon," June said. "Besides that, we've already got a ton of special events booked for the new space. Most of them have already put down deposits."

Reese shook her head. "God, can you even imagine having to give all those back?"

"Or call couples to tell them their dream-wedding venue won't be ready in time," June said, her gaze drifting back to the TV screen.

"Okay, okay," Jed said, holding up his hands. "It was just a suggestion. I'm sure things will go fine tomorrow."

He turned back to the TV and squeezed June's knee. "We should make that chicken dish tonight. The one we served at the wedding?"

"Oooh, with the mushrooms and that little hint of—"

"Rosemary, yes! You know, our '14 Pinot Gris would be perfect with it. Do we have any—"

"—artichoke hearts? Yes, I just grabbed some the other day." June leaned forward and kissed him on the temple while Reese took a step back, then another.

"So, guys—I need to head out to the field to check the nitrate levels before I get ready for my date. Everything look okay with the communication pieces?"

"They look great, sweetie," her mom said, closing the folder and setting it on the coffee table. "You're doing such a nice job with everything. Oh, look—I love this part!"

Reese watched as the video cut to a scene of her parents slow dancing to "Unchained Melody." She stared for a few beats, wondering if she'd ever stop feeling like she forgot to get in line when the universe handed out soul mates. She turned away, letting the notes of the love song fade behind her as she crept down the hallway and out the front door.

It had started to drizzle, and she thought about heading back to the winery barn for rain gear but decided against it. Not like she wasn't used to working in soggy conditions.

Out in the fields, she lost track of time as she gathered soil samples and snipped small pieces of the vines. She breathed in the heady smell of damp earth and crushed grass, aware that her hair and clothes were getting drenched but not minding much.

By the time she returned to the winery barn with the samples, her clothes were soaked through. The pale-pink T-shirt beneath her flannel overshirt had turned transparent.

Dripping as she went, she moved into the tiny kitchen where she kept her test kit. The barn was silent, except for the distant tinny sound of NPR on the radio Eric must've forgotten to switch off when he left.

Reese was straddling a puddle of muddy rainwater bent low over her test tubes when she heard a voice behind her.

"You're still here."

She whirled to see Clay in the doorway. For the briefest instant, his gaze fell to where the wet T-shirt hugged her breasts. It returned quickly to her face.

"Sorry," he said. "I didn't mean to scare you. I didn't know anyone was here."

"I just came back to finish some testing," she said, blaming her shortness of breath on the startle instead of the magnificent, muscular sight of him. "I thought you were gone already."

"I left some paperwork on the counter there. Can I sneak by you and grab it?"

Reese nodded and stepped to one side. Clay seemed to hesitate. Then he edged past, his bare forearm brushing the damp front of her T-shirt. Reese felt her nipples contract.

The papers fluttered to the floor.

"Oh, shit," Reese said, kneeling down. "The ground's all wet. I hope these aren't your only copies."

"It's okay, really, you don't have to—"

"No, let me get them."

He crouched down beside her, scrambling to grab the mud-speckled sheets of paper. Reese's hand trembled as she grabbed one piece, then another. They both reached for a page at the same time, and Clay's hand closed over hers.

A surge of heat pulsed up her arm and her heart slammed hard against her rib cage. Reese stared at his hand, transfixed by the sight of those long fingers engulfing hers. Then she looked at his face. He was watching her, pupils dilated in those root-beer-brown depths. He didn't blink.

Clay looked down at her hand. "God, you're freezing."

"My hands are always cold."

"I remember."

He didn't let go of her hand. Reese swallowed as her stomach clenched in a tight, fizzy ball.

They stayed frozen like that for what seemed like minutes, Clay's huge palm warm against the ridges of her knuckles. The smell of rainwater and wine and damp earth hung heavy in the air between them, along with something else Reese couldn't name. His breath ruffled the damp hair pasted to her cheek. Outside, the rain drummed the roof in a slow, heavy beat.

"You're getting wet," he murmured.

Reese blinked. "What?"

"The floor. You're kneeling in a puddle."

She looked down, her face warming. "Right. I was already wet. I mean, I was out there in the rain and—"

She stopped talking, her cheeks flaming despite the chill in the room. She looked up in time to see Clay close his eyes for just an instant. When he reopened them, they locked on hers. He moved his hand and Reese felt a pang of disappointment at the loss of his warmth.

Then he reached up and grazed her cheek with his fingertips. He pushed a few strands of damp hair from her face, his gaze holding hers. Reese held her breath as her pulse pounded in her ears.

Before she could register what was happening, Clay leaned forward and brushed his lips over hers, tentative at first, testing.

Reese clutched the front of his shirt and pulled him to her. He kissed her harder then, his palms cupping her face as his mouth explored hers. He tasted cool, like he'd been nibbling the rain-soaked mint leaves beside the barn.

The heavy spatter of droplets on the roof and the soft rush of their breath filled Reese's ears, fighting for space with the pounding of blood in her head.

Clay deepened the kiss, his lips warm and soft and so very, very good at what they were doing. Reese gasped at the delicious scrape of his stubbled cheek against her chilled one.

She wanted to devour him, to explore every inch of his mouth, of his body. Clay kissed her harder, responding to her need or maybe his own. His hand cupped her face, holding her against him while his other hand slid up her side. She felt his fingertips graze the side of her breast and she pressed into him, craving more. He slid his thumb over her nipple as the rest of the fingers cupped her breast, testing the weight. His lips moved from hers and down her jaw, planting a trail of kisses in the hollow of her throat. His thumb stroked her nipple again and Reese cried out, wanting all of him at once.

At the sound of her whimper, Clay drew back. His eyes flashed from desire to alarm, like she'd bitten him.

He dropped his hands to his sides and pulled away. "Reese, I'm so sorry. I didn't mean to do that."

She blinked at him, her breath still coming fast. "It's okay. Really—"

"No, it's not okay. God, my best friend's wife—"

"*Ex*-wife."

"And my employer—"

"I haven't actually paid you."

"And right before you're going out on a date—"

"Date?" Reese sat back on her heels, breathless, as reality slithered into her consciousness like a drizzle of rainwater down her neck. "Right. A date."

She dropped her hands from Clay's chest and looked down at her watch. It was almost five. She took a breath. "Dammit."

He jumped to his feet and reached down to help her up. Reese took his hand, dizzy for reasons that had nothing to do with standing up too fast.

Clay wouldn't meet her eyes. "Here, let me find you a towel or something. You must be freezing."

"Clay, really—it's fine." She took another breath. "These things happen. Lord knows we've both learned that."

He nodded and stepped back, still holding her hand. He took a breath and let go. "Have a good date, okay?"

He stood there for two more pulse beats. Then he turned and walked away, leaving her standing there with a puddle of rainwater at her feet and her heart lodged firmly in her throat.

CHAPTER NINE

Clay wasn't surprised when his sponsor called that evening to check in. He was only surprised it had taken so long.

"Hey, Patrick," Clay said when he grabbed his cell phone off the nightstand in his hotel room. "Thanks again for sending the vet out. I owe you for that."

"No problem. Everything's okay with the camel?"

"Alpaca. He's doing great. Dr. Wally's a great guy, really helpful."

Clay bit back the urge to feel bitter about the kindly young vet and his date with Reese. It wasn't his place to judge, and God knows he had no claim on Reese himself.

But that kiss—

Patrick cleared his throat. "Is everything okay, Clay? You seemed a little shaky when you called yesterday."

"I'm doing great. Really, everything's *fine*."

Patrick seemed to hesitate. "I hope you don't mind me saying so, but the situation you're in seems risky. Spending every day working at a facility that produces alcohol—it just seems like a lot of temptation to face."

"You could say that," Clay muttered, then regretted his words. He hadn't been thinking about alcohol at all. He'd been thinking about Reese in his arms, Reese with her damp clothes and warm lips, Reese with her body pressed against his—

He cleared his throat and tried again. "I really appreciate the concern, Patrick. I do. I'm glad to have a support system out here."

"Good. That's good. You know you can call if you need me, right?"

"Absolutely."

Clay hesitated. He knew he should be more forthcoming with his sponsor, maybe sharing the history of his connection to Reese and the feelings he was having now. But something stopped him. Something made him bite off the words before they could form in his throat.

He'd never told Eric. He'd never told Reese. If he couldn't be honest with his two best friends, how could he tell someone he'd known less than a week?

On the other end of the line, Patrick was quiet. Clay wondered if he was waiting for him to fill the silence, to share what was on his mind. Hell, maybe he *should* do that.

A phone call didn't seem like the right way to handle it, so Clay cleared his throat. "Actually, what are you up to tonight?"

"Nothing much," Patrick said. "Working on some bills, maybe reheating leftovers."

"Maybe we could meet up at Finnigan's for a couple Cokes and their halibut fish-n-chips."

"That sounds great," Patrick said. "Seven thirtyish?"

"I'll see you there."

Clay hung up the phone and set it back on the nightstand. He surveyed the room, taking in the bleak walls and neutral gray comforter on the bed. Was it just him or was the place looking smaller?

His HR contact at Dorrington Construction had called earlier that morning, apologizing for the delay in finding a temporary rental for Clay.

"It's the damn college kids," the guy had lamented. "They've rented up everything within thirty miles of Linfield and George Fox. Probably not a coincidence they've got a bunch of colleges right in the middle of wine country, huh?"

Clay was trying hard to remember why he didn't want to rent Axl's place out at the vineyard. There were plenty of reasons, good ones. Patrick was right—working at a vineyard was risky enough for a recovering drunk. Living at one? Bad idea. Very bad idea.

It's not the wine you're worried about, said a voice in the back of his head.

He heard Eric's words again. *Don't shit where you eat.*

"Shut up," Clay said aloud, and went to take a shower.

But once he was naked and soapy, thoughts of Reese just intensified.

He drifted back to college, to the first time he'd met her their sophomore year. He'd been sitting there alone in the back row on the first day of class that fall, wondering if he should have bought pens instead of pencils to demonstrate his status as a mature, confident college student.

"Someone sitting here?"

He'd looked up to see her with the fluorescent lights of the classroom making a halo around her head. She wore her light-brown hair gathered in a low ponytail beneath her right ear, cinched with a red elastic that sent a cascade of sun-streaked waves over her shoulder and into the hollow between her breasts. She hadn't been wearing anything memorable—not to anyone else, though Clay recalled she wore a flannel shirt over a yellow T-shirt that hugged her curves. But there was something in the way she carried herself that made him sit up and take notice. Her cheeks were flushed and lovely, and she wore a tatty canvas shoulder bag with a romance novel peeking over the top.

He tried to get a closer look at it, but she nudged the bag back over her shoulder, obscuring the book from his view. Then she extended her hand.

"I'm Reese. I'm studying viticulture. How about you?"

Clay had just stared at her for a few beats, barely registering her words. He was mesmerized by those green, green eyes, the flush in her cheeks, the roundness beneath her T-shirt.

"Clay," he finally stammered. "Clay Henderson. Horticulture."

"Yeah? Do you like wine, Clay?"

He was startled by the question and started to stammer some inane reply, but she cut him off.

"My family owns Sunridge Vineyards over in Dundee. You should check it out sometime."

He'd nodded, so enchanted by her that he almost forgot she'd asked him a question.

"I like beer," he'd blurted lamely. "You, um—you asked if I like wine, but I'm really more of a beer man."

It was a stupid thing to say, but she'd grinned at him as she dropped into the seat beside him. "It takes a lot of beer to make good wine."

"What?"

"It's an expression in the wine industry. Come harvest time, everyone's putting in long hours and the last thing they want to drink is wine. It's a pretty intense few weeks. There's a lot of beer flowing then. Keeps everyone fueled."

"Sounds like a good party."

"It can be," she'd told him, tucking her hair behind one ear. "We're always looking for volunteers. Harvest is coming up in October if you want to join us. We could always use help running the de-stemmer or scrubbing mildew off pipes—stuff like that."

Clay nodded, not sure if she was asking him out or just looking for free labor but not caring much either way. He would have walked on his knuckles through broken glass to scrub mildew off her pipes.

The professor had stepped to the front of the room then and launched into a monotone explanation of the syllabus. Clay didn't hear a word of it. The only sounds he was aware of were the scratch of Reese's pencil on her notepad, the soft rustle of her hair against the flannel of her shirt, the steady rhythm of her breathing.

Even now, Reese was the only thing he really remembered from his college days.

His years as a stumbling drunk may have stolen a lot of his memories, but he'd never forget the curve of her cheek against her palm as she tapped her pencil on her teeth and looked toward the front of the lecture hall.

Idiot, Clay told himself as he shut off the shower. *Why didn't you make a move then? You're the king of botched opportunities.*

He shook off the memory as he shook the water out of his hair, then stepped out of the shower. He toweled off quickly and dressed in clean jeans and a T-shirt. Grabbing his jacket off the hook by the door, he stopped and inhaled.

It smelled like Reese.

He'd never known her to wear perfume, not even in college. It must be her shampoo, or maybe just Reese—something grassy and sweet, clinging to the wool of his jacket. He pulled it on, fighting the mental picture of Reese hugging it over her breasts after her bra malfunction the other night.

Then he thought about the kiss in the hallway, the kiss in the winery barn, the feel of Reese warm and damp in his arms—

"Knock it off," he ordered himself out loud. "You made her life hell once before, *remember?*"

Still, he couldn't stop thinking about her.

He drove slowly to Finnigan's, remembering how many times he'd gone there in his drinking days. Back then, he headed straight for the bar—no screwing around on the restaurant side ordering halibut and drinking Coke.

But now he sat in the parking lot looking at the side of the building. The paint looked the same, the neon sign flickering faintly as dusk drifted toward darkness. He could hear the blare of music inside, and he watched as a laughing couple came stumbling out, their fingers hooked in each other's belt loops. He remembered the smell of spilled beer and the crush of bodies near the bar, but those things didn't make him wistful. Not anymore.

He hadn't been inside since that night. That awful, horrible night. He still couldn't shake the memory of that guy's fist smashing into Reese's face, a punch meant for Clay. He remembered the look of betrayal on her face, the moment he knew for certain any chance he'd ever had with her was gone forever.

My fault, he thought.

So win her back, whispered the voice in his head. *Prove you've changed.*

He shook his head, pretty sure that wasn't an option.

He pushed open the door of his truck and made his way inside. He was five minutes early, which gave him a chance to check out the scene inside. Even for a Friday night, the place was packed. He sat down at one of the tables in the middle of the room where he could see both the front door and the bar. The taps rose above the edge of the bar—Bud, Bud Light, Laurelwood, Deschutes Brewery, and Boneyard all lined up in a colorful row.

He stared at them for a moment, waiting to see if temptation would grab him by the throat and squeeze. It didn't. There was a familiar tang of nostalgia, but he didn't think it was the beer calling to him.

He felt his limbs start to relax and he picked up a menu to study it. He recognized a few new dishes, but it was mostly the same. There was something comforting in that. He set down the menu and tried to catch the eye of a passing waitress. There were none to be seen, and he wished he'd thought to bring a water bottle the way a lot of guys did. It would give him something to do with his hands, something to sip so the temptation didn't creep up on him unexpectedly.

But his hands stayed steady and the scent of beer didn't send his heart racing the way it used to. *You've got this.*

Ten minutes passed. Fifteen.

"Hey, sorry I'm late," said Patrick as he slid into the seat opposite Clay wearing a T-shirt that showed his ham-size biceps and misspelled tattoos. "Did you already order?"

"I've been trying to get someone's attention, but no dice," Clay said.

"Wow, they're really packed. Guess it's Friday night, huh?"

"That it is."

Patrick grinned. "So, Clay, how have you been?"

"Good, really good. Things are really getting underway with the construction, so that feels positive."

"You're enjoying the job?"

"I am. There were some hiccups with the bid, but we're working on it."

"Good. Look, about the thing with the marijuana the other day. You know that if you need to talk about anything—"

"Thank you," Clay interrupted. "I appreciate that. But things are okay, really."

Patrick frowned. "Drugs and alcohol in the same place? I'm not sure how I'd handle that myself."

Clay swallowed and looked at the menu. "I'm handling it pretty well."

"Are you the only one there who doesn't drink?"

Clay considered that. "Probably."

"That must be hard."

"Not as hard as you'd think," he said, resisting the urge to make a hard-on joke.

"What's with the shit-eating grin?"

Clay looked up. "Nothing." He shrugged. "Just something dumb I used to say. Old joke. Ancient history."

Patrick studied him, and Clay fought the urge to look away. "You know, not everything from your past life needs to be shoved under the carpet."

Clay felt his jaw clench. "What do you mean?"

"Just that it's okay to cut out the things that were unhealthy, but keep the ones that were harmless parts of your personality. Your identity."

Clay nodded. It was on the tip of his tongue to tell Patrick about Reese. It would feel good to confide in someone, to let him know how intensely the feelings were swirling around him since his return.

Maybe after he had a beer.

No. Not a beer. A plate of nachos, and maybe a Coke.

"I think the waitress forgot us," Patrick said.

"No doubt. Why don't I just go up to the bar and see if I can place an order there?"

Patrick frowned and glanced around, clearly hoping a waitress would materialize so Clay wouldn't have to venture into the danger zone.

Clay smiled and clapped his sponsor on the shoulder as he stood. "Tell you what," he said. "If you see me guzzling straight from the beer taps, you can come rescue me."

Patrick grinned. "Deal."

Clay maneuvered through the maze of tables into the bar. The music was louder, and the smell of beer made the back of his tongue feel itchy. Clay ignored it. He leaned forward on the bar, trying to catch the eye of the guy slinging drinks.

"Stop touching me!" shrieked a female voice at the other end of the bar.

Clay squinted that direction. He couldn't see through the maze of bodies and the curve in the bar, but the voice sounded familiar. Larissa?

"Stop it!" she yelled again. "I said no."

A dark figure at the end of the bar blocked his view—broad shoulders draped in black leather, dark hair hanging forward to conceal any view Clay might've had of the woman who'd yelled. Clay glanced around, wondering why no one else was concerned. Most of the other patrons seemed numb with beer and loud noise. Clay looked back at the other end of the bar.

"C'mon, baby," the guy growled. "I just want a piece of that sweet ass."

"I mean it, Derek. Knock it off."

This time, Clay was certain it was Larissa. The guy's next words confirmed it.

"Aw, 'Rissy—you've been giving off vibes all night long. What's a little—"

"Pardon me, is there a problem?"

Clay wasn't sure how he wound up at the other end of the bar, but suddenly, there he was. Side by side with Larissa, nose to nose with her date.

The shaggy-haired guy stared him down, none too pleased by the intrusion. Clay didn't blink.

"We're just talking," the guy said. "Just a friendly conversation, that's all."

"Funny, it didn't sound too friendly to me," Clay said, trying to keep his voice light. He stole a glance at Larissa, who looked dazed and a little rumpled.

"Dude, stay out of it," the guy warned.

The smell of beer on his breath practically gave him a contact buzz, but Clay didn't step back. Larissa blinked at him and swayed a little on her feet.

"Maybe you missed that day in high school health class where they explain how *no* means *no*," Clay said slowly. "That sounded like a pretty clear *no* to me."

The guy snorted. "No never means no with this one."

Clay looked at Larissa again. "'Riss?"

She swayed a little, blinking through smeared eye makeup, and reached out for the edge of the bar to steady herself. "Hi, Clay."

"Want me to get you home?" Clay asked.

Larissa opened her mouth to say something, but her date cut her off by snaking an arm around her shoulders. "Back the fuck off, okay? I don't need your help."

"You may not," Clay said, "but she seems to. Come on, man. Just let her go and we'll get out of here. No hard feelings, no trouble."

Larissa tried to shrug off the guy's arm, but he gripped her tighter. Behind them, the bartender spoke. "There a problem here, guys?"

"No!" snapped the other guy. "It's a personal matter, between me and this douche bag."

Clay gritted his teeth, his eyes on Larissa. He was fighting hard to keep his composure, not to lose his temper the way he might have a few years ago.

The way he had the night Reese got hurt.

They could still do this civilly. "C'mon, 'Riss—let's get you home, okay?"

The guy shoved him so fast, Clay didn't see the blow coming. He staggered back one step and felt his hands clenching into fists by pure instinct. He gripped the edge of the bar and resisted the urge to push back.

"Guys—" the bartender warned.

"I'm not going to fight you," Clay told Larissa's date. "Let's be adults about this. Just let her go and we'll walk away."

Larissa finally succeeded in shrugging out from under the guy's arm and took a step toward Clay. The guy sneered and grabbed Larissa's elbow so hard her head jerked forward. She gave a little yelp of pain.

"Make me," the guy snapped. "The bitch ain't worth it and you know it."

Those were the last words Clay heard before his knuckles cracked bone.

◆　◆　◆

"This cheese really tastes amazing, don't you think?"

Reese smiled up at Wally and nodded. "It's terrific. Pairs great with the Chardonnay from Firesteed, though I think their '15 would have been an even better match than the '14."

Wally shook his head and smiled. "I'll take your word for it."

"Sorry," Reese said. "I didn't mean to tempt you or anything."

"No, it's totally fine. I do drink occasionally, just not tonight when I'm driving."

"You drink? But I thought—"

"I'm not an alcoholic," he said. "I just have a lot of acquaintances in recovery. My partner, my dad, several friends."

"Partner?"

He grinned and plucked a piece of cheese off a passing tray. "Veterinary partner, not life partner. I'm single, in case you weren't clear on that. And straight."

Reese felt her cheeks grow warm as she stopped to admire a large painting. "This one is really beautiful."

"Mmm," Wally said, popping the cheese in his mouth as he looked up at the chaotic assembly of colorful brushstrokes. "It is. So are you. Really, I thought you were attractive out at the farm the other day, but seeing you dressed up like this—"

"Thank you," Reese said, flushing again. She caught sight of herself in the mirror by the door and made a mental note to thank Larissa. The simple black dress and tall boots gave her a streamlined, elegant look, while the French twist in her hair and the smoky liner around her eyes completed the ensemble. Her cousin might have her faults, but she also had some great clothes.

"That's quite a menagerie you have out at the vineyard," Wally said. "Have you always been so interested in animals?"

"Pretty much," Reese said. "I got serious about it in college, though. Clay was always bringing me broken animals to fix, so I got certified to do the rehab thing through the Department of Fish and Wildlife."

"So Clay is someone you've known awhile?"

Reese opened her mouth to say something, not sure how much to volunteer. She was saved the trouble of figuring it out when a male voice interrupted.

"Hey, you're Axl's granddaughter!"

Reese spun around to see a buxom woman with a towering silver beehive hairdo and a streak of bright-pink lipstick somewhere in the vicinity of her mouth. She smiled and held up a tray of hors d'oeuvres.

"Um, hello—" Reese struggled to remember her name. "Frenchie?"

"Francie," she corrected. "Axl's main squeeze. Hey, how's he doing? I tried to go see him at the hospital, but they wouldn't even confirm he was there. Privacy stuff, you know how it is."

"Hospital?"

"Yeah, I thought we could have one of them conjugal visits like we did when he was in prison," she said. "Figured the surgery didn't sound too bad, and he could just lie there anyway while I did all the work."

Reese frowned, wondering what the hell she was missing. "Um, I'm sorry, I don't understand."

Francie's face darkened. "You mean Axl ain't in the hospital?"

Reese bit her lip. "You know, I haven't seen him for a while," she backpedaled. "We really aren't that close, so maybe my mom forgot to tell me—"

"Don't give me none of that, I know your family's tight. Axl is screwing around on me, right?"

Reese closed her eyes, wondering if it was weirder to have her grandfather accused of screwing around, or weirder that it was probably true.

"Um—" said Reese.

"Hi," Wally said, putting out one hand for Francie to shake as he slid the other around Reese's shoulders. "Wow, these hors d'oeuvres look really great, what are they?"

Francie frowned down at Wally's hand, then at the platter. "I dunno. Probably shrimp or something."

"Mushrooms," Reese said. "I think they're mushrooms."

Wally nodded and touched Reese's elbow. "Nothing like a good mushroom, eh?"

Francie cast a confused look down at the platter. "Guess so."

Reese reached out to take one, then hesitated. "Actually, I'm allergic to peanuts. Would you mind checking with the caterer to see if these have any peanut oil in them?"

"Peanut oil?"

"Please? My throat will swell closed, and I'll have a psychotic episode and probably end up destroying all these lovely paintings. Could you just check for me?"

Francie gave her a dubious look, then swung her eyes toward a door at the back of the room. "I guess I could find out. But then I want to talk to you about this thing with Axl, okay?"

"Right," Reese said.

Francie retreated and Reese looked up at Wally. "Any chance you'd want to grab dinner? Quickly? There's a really great Thai restaurant a few blocks away."

"Thai? Doesn't that have a lot of peanuts?"

She couldn't tell if he was joking or not, and opened her mouth to clarify that the peanut thing was just a ruse, but the ringing of her cell phone saved her. Reese reached into her handbag with an apologetic smile.

"Sorry, I should get that."

"No problem."

Reese stared at the caller ID readout. She blinked, trying to bring the words into focus. *Newberg Police Department?*

Reese looked up at Wally, hoping her shock didn't show. "I'm sorry, I'm going to take this outside. If Francie comes back—"

"I'll handle it."

The phone rang again. Reese stepped toward the door, her hands shaking.

"Is everything okay?" Wally asked.

"Fine, fine—just give me a sec."

She ducked out onto the drizzly sidewalk and hit the button to take the call.

"Hello?"

There was a sniffle, followed by a choked sob. "Reese? It's me. Oh, God, Reesey—something bad happened."

Reese felt her blood turn to ice. "Larissa? Where are you? Why does my phone say you're calling from the police department?"

"Because I am," she sobbed. "I left my cell in my purse back at the bar when the police hauled Clay away, and now they've got him in a holding cell and—"

Reese's knees buckled and she grabbed the cold brick doorframe to keep herself upright. Larissa's words slurred in her ears, and Reese leaned against the side of the building, not trusting her legs anymore.

"Clay is in jail," Reese repeated. "Are you okay? What happened? Do I need to come get you?"

"I'm sorry, I didn't know who else to call."

"Are you hurt, Larissa?"

"No," she sniffed. "But Clay might be."

Reese closed her eyes, hating the sick feeling in her gut almost as much as she hated the familiarity of it.

"I'll be right there."

CHAPTER TEN

Reese clicked off the phone and hurried back inside, cursing herself for not driving her own car. Now she was going to have to ask Wally to take her to the police station on their first date.

And this is why I'm single, she thought.

Wally was standing by the door when she walked in, a frown making deep brackets around his mouth. "Is everything okay?"

"No," Reese said. "I hate to do this, but is there any chance you could take me to the police station?"

"Police station?" He frowned, and Reese stood up a little straighter, braced for judgment.

"I don't know what's happened, but my cousin is in trouble and my friend Clay—my old friend from college? He—he—"

She stopped, not sure how much to say. Hell, she didn't know much more than that, did she? "Please?"

"Absolutely, let me get our coats. I'll head off your grandfather's friend if she comes back. Why don't you wait right here?"

Reese stood there in the doorway shivering until Wally brought the thin black trench coat she'd borrowed from Larissa. He set it over her shoulders, giving her a second to shrug her arms into it and cinch it around her waist before leading the way to his car.

Wally was quiet on the drive there. Maybe he sensed her need for silence or maybe he was second-guessing the wisdom of dating a woman who'd had two brushes with illegal activity in the first twenty-four hours he'd known her.

That was hardly Reese's biggest concern at the moment. Her mind buzzed with questions. Was Larissa okay? Had Clay been drinking? Part of her was furious—he'd slipped off the wagon, she knew it, she *knew* it.

Part of her just wanted to cry.

This isn't the first time you've bailed Clay out of jail, whispered a voice in her head.

By the time they pulled up in front of the police station, tears were pricking the back of her eyes. Reese unbuckled her seat belt and threw open her door.

"Do you want me to wait here or come in?" Wally asked.

She hesitated, not sure what etiquette called for when making jail visits on a first date.

"I'll come in," he said, unbuckling his seat belt. "You might need someone who's not emotionally invested."

"Thank you," Reese said as she hustled to the door.

She pushed her way inside, blinking hard against the white walls and fluorescent lighting. A uniformed officer leaned against one wall writing something on a clipboard. Behind a glass wall, a woman spoke rapidly into a telephone receiver. The room smelled of stale coffee and unwashed bodies.

On a bench across the room sat Larissa. She had mascara streaks running down her face, and her shirt was rumpled and beer stained.

Reese hurried toward her and dropped to her knees in front of her cousin, brushing her hair back off her face. "Larissa, my God, are you okay?"

"Oh, Reesey—thanks for coming." She sniffed, looking up with red-rimmed eyes. "I'm so sorry."

"What happened? Are you hurt?"

Larissa shook her head and a tear slid down her cheek. "He tried to grab me and he wouldn't stop and I said no, but he kept coming at me and—"

"Clay? Clay tried to grab you?"

Larissa reeled back as though struck. She blinked hard, then shook her head. "What are you talking about?"

"You said he tried to grab you. Clay, you mean?"

Larissa shook her head, a bewildered expression on her face. "Of course Clay didn't hurt me. Clay's the one who saved me."

"Saved you?"

Larissa stared at her, confusion giving way to something darker. "Is that really how you see him?"

The door beside the cop flew open and Clay walked through with another man behind him. They both froze when they saw Reese kneeling on the floor.

"Reese," Clay said flatly. "What are you doing here?"

Reese blinked up at him, still trying to figure out what was happening. "Larissa called me. I heard there was trouble."

Clay nodded once, his expression steely. "It's over."

"You're not in jail?"

"No." He glanced at the other man, then back at her. "They brought me in for questioning because of my past arrest history and the alcohol clause in my probation, but no. I'm not in trouble."

"And he wasn't drinking," added the guy at Clay's side, folding his tattooed arms over his chest. "I can vouch for that."

Clay nodded at the guy, then at Reese. "Patrick, this is Reese. Reese, this is Patrick. My sponsor."

She bit her lip and held out her hand, a little taken aback Clay was bothering with pleasantries like introductions.

"Where's Derek?" Larissa sniffed.

Reese saw a muscle clench in Clay's jaw. "Derek may be tied up awhile."

Patrick snorted. "They're hauling his ass to the county jail in McMinnville. Guy already had an outstanding warrant for his arrest."

"Good!" Larissa snapped. "God, Clay, I didn't mean for you to get dragged into that, and I'm sorry—"

"Stop it," Clay interrupted. "It's not your fault he hurt you."

Reese felt her heart constrict and she grabbed Larissa's knee. "Your date hurt you?"

Larissa bit her lip. "Clay stopped him. It's okay now."

Reese looked up at Clay, noticing for the first time that he had a tiny, flesh-colored butterfly bandage over one eye. She glanced at his hands, noticing the tightly clenched fists at his sides. His knuckles looked red and raw on his right hand, and he had another bandage there, too. She looked back up at his face. Her heart squeezed tighter in her chest, and she felt tears gathering at the edges of her eyes.

"Did you get hurt?" she whispered.

Clay shook his head and moved his hands behind his back. "No. I'm fine. The bartender jumped in before it got bad."

"Finnigan's?" she asked, trying not to think about that night.

He nodded but said nothing.

"Derek had already been kicked out of the place twice before for fighting," Larissa added, slurring her words enough to give Reese an idea of how much she'd probably had to drink. "I'm done with bad boys. I mean it. I'm dating chess players from now on."

Reese squeezed Larissa's knee and stood up. "Come on. Let's get you home."

Behind her, Wally cleared his throat. "There should be room for all three of you in the backseat if you give me a second to get some of the stuff out."

Wally. Hell. Somehow, Reese had forgotten all about him. She gave him a weak smile as she offered Larissa a hand up. "Thank you. I know the evening hasn't gone the way we'd planned."

"It's fine, really," he said, smiling a little. "It's definitely one of the more interesting dates I've had."

"You're on a date," Clay said, his voice hollow. "That's right. Reese, I'm sorry you got dragged down here. Look, I can take Larissa home.

Patrick can run me back to Finnigan's for my truck, and I'll drive 'Riss from there. We don't need to ruin anyone else's evening with this mess."

Reese shook her head. "It's okay," she told him before turning back to Wally. "I've had a great time so far, but maybe we can do a rain check on dinner?"

"Absolutely."

"No, really," Clay insisted. "I've got my truck back at Finnigan's. I need to get it anyway and I can take Larissa home from there. Go on, Reese—don't give up your date on account of us."

Reese shook her head. "Larissa called me, I want to be here for her. 'Riss, you ready to go?"

Larissa blinked up at Clay, then looked to Reese. "No, Clay's right—I'm sorry I dragged you down here, Reesey. I wasn't thinking when I called you. I knew about your date, but I got so worked up and forgot and—"

"It's fine, sweetie," Reese insisted. "I don't mind. I want to be here for you."

Larissa shook her head. "I'll go with Clay. Really, I'm sorry. I just didn't want to go home alone and I panicked."

"Tell you what," Wally said, reaching out to give Reese's shoulder a small squeeze. "Why don't I run Reese home right now, Patrick can take Clay and Larissa back to get Clay's truck, and Clay can drive Larissa back to your place so she's not alone tonight?"

Reese looked up at him as the relief flooded through her body. "You're sure you don't mind?"

"Positive. You need to be with your family right now."

She nodded and turned back to her cousin. "That sound okay to you?"

Larissa bit her lip, then nodded. "That would work," she said, brightening a little. "That way you and Wally can be alone in the car to make out, and when I get to Reese's, she can tell me all about it."

Reese rolled her eyes and pretended not to notice the way Wally's face also brightened at that idea. "She's drunk," Reese told him. "But I like your idea about the driving. Clay? Is that okay with you?"

Clay nodded, then looked at the cop. "We're all free to go, right?"

"Right." The cop nodded at Larissa. "As long as that one's not driving."

"Definitely not," she said, reaching down to help her cousin to her feet. "You sure you're okay, 'Riss?"

"I'm fine. I'll see you back at the house."

Reese nodded and looked at Clay. He held her gaze for a moment, his eyes flashing beneath the fluorescent lights. "I'll get her home safely."

"I know you will." She swallowed. "Thank you for everything."

He held her gaze a few beats longer, then turned to Wally. "Sorry to kill your date, man."

"No sweat," he said, reaching out to shake Clay's hand. "Sounds like you did a good thing there."

Reese saw Clay grimace—from the words or the pressure of the grip on his hurt hand, she wasn't sure.

She turned and followed Wally out to the car. They buckled their seat belts in silence, neither of them saying a word until they were safely out on the road.

"That really wasn't how I pictured this date going," Reese said.

"It's fine, it made for an interesting evening." He laughed. "Why do I have a feeling there's never a dull moment when you're around?"

Reese folded her hands in her lap and frowned down at them. "Actually, I am pretty dull. It's my family that generates drama."

Wally touched the back of her hand. "I definitely don't think you're dull."

"Thanks, but trust me, I'm very dull. So dull I reread the same romance novels over and over again."

"Nothing wrong with liking a good story."

"So dull I've worn my hair the same since middle school."

"I like your hair."

"So dull the last serious relationship I had was my ex-husband."

Wally was quiet for a second. "I didn't know you'd been married."

Reese shrugged. "I thought I'd slip that in there while we were being jovial."

"Good plan," he said. "I don't mind. I'm just surprised, that's all. Did it end badly?"

"No, we're still good friends." She settled back in the seat, feeling a little warmer now that she was out of the rain and basking in the comfort of the car heater. "That was the problem, really. The friendship was terrific, so we thought the marriage thing would just come naturally. Turned out we're lousy spouses."

"How so?"

Reese looked out the window, trying to come up with the words to describe what had gone wrong between her and Eric. "It wasn't anything dramatic like adultery or abuse. I think we just mixed up the kind of love you have for a friend with the kind of love you should feel for the person you spend your life with."

"Interesting," Wally said. "You always hear people talking about the importance of marrying your best friend."

"That's just it," Reese said. "He's still one of my best friends. But there has to be more than that. Passion. Affection. The desire to have each other's back no matter what. That soul-deep connection that seems to come naturally for so many happily married couples."

Her tone had turned wistful, and Reese kicked herself for going so far down that path on a first date. Not that there was any way of turning it into a normal first date at this point.

"I'm sorry," Wally said. "About your divorce, I mean."

"It's fine," she said, shaking her head. "He's remarried to a great woman, so everything worked out okay."

"Not everything. You're still single."

Reese frowned. "Why does everyone always assume that's a bad thing? Maybe I like being single."

"Do you?"

She thought about that a second. "I'm not sure. I've thought so for a long time, but maybe I'm just kidding myself. Marriage was so much harder than I thought it would be. I'm not looking to try again anytime soon. Maybe ever."

"Really? You've given up on marriage?"

Reese shrugged. "I don't know. I know it can be good. Lord knows my parents are still disgustingly in love. I just don't think I'm cut out for it."

"Maybe you just haven't met the right person."

"Maybe I'm just not the right person myself."

Wally arced a turn down the gravel road leading toward the vineyard. "Kind of a weighty conversation for a first date, huh?"

"Yeah, sorry. Maybe we should save abortion and physician-assisted suicide for the second date?"

He grinned. "Are you offering a second date?"

Reese felt her face grow warm again, and she was thankful for the car's dim interior. "If you're interested, sure. If nothing else, it'll give me a chance to prove that stoned alpacas, confrontations with my grandfather's jealous lover, and trips to the police station aren't part of my everyday routine."

"That's too bad."

He pulled up in front of her little house, and Reese held her breath for a second, wondering if he'd kill the engine or just bid her a quick farewell. Which did she want?

Wally put the car in park and kept the engine running. "Thank you for coming out with me, Reese. I had a nice time. Did you?"

"Yes," said Reese, a little taken aback. "Yes, I guess I did."

He smiled and took her hand. "Good. I'm glad."

He lifted her hand to his lips and planted a chaste kiss on her knuckles. Then he set her hand back in her lap and smiled.

Hardly the make-out session Larissa was hoping to hear about, but Reese knew she wasn't really the sort of woman who inspired men to pounce on her in the front seat of a Subaru.

"Goodnight, Reese."

"Goodnight, Wally. Thanks again for everything."

"My pleasure."

Reese climbed out of the car and trudged up the walkway to her house. She never locked her front door, so she pushed it open and flicked her porch light off and on a couple times to let Wally know she was safely inside. She closed the door behind her and leaned against it, basking in the few moments of solitude she had before Larissa arrived.

Instead of peace, she felt a wave of guilt.

She'd been so certain Clay had fallen off the wagon. So sure he'd been the one to do something wrong, to end up in jail for fighting or public drunkenness or God knows what else.

Judgmental bitch, she muttered to herself as she pulled off her boots and wriggled her toes on the sisal mat at her front door.

Well, hell, how many times had she gotten calls just like that one? Calls when the worst thing really did turn out to be true.

She'd lost count of the drunken messages, the trips to the police station, the rowdy bar fights, the times she'd had to scrub puke out of her car.

Why wouldn't I think the worst?

Still. Maybe she owed him an apology.

The headlights of Clay's truck swung down the driveway, and Reese turned to the window to watch him move slowly along the gravel. The old Clay would have come blazing up the road at twice that speed, heedless of small rodents or dust flying up behind him to coat her grapes. The new Clay was certainly more cautious.

Reese reached for the door.

An apology. She could give him that much.

◆ ◆ ◆

Clay killed the engine in front of Reese's house and stepped out of his truck. Larissa was sound asleep in the passenger seat, so Clay walked around to the other side and opened her door.

"'Riss?"

Nothing. Just a small snore and a thin ribbon of drool connecting her bottom lip to the hem of her skirt. He hesitated, feeling a small pang of sadness for her. It seemed a shame to wake her.

Hell, she couldn't weigh that much. He unbuckled her seat belt and reached under the seat to grab a blanket. Wrapping the soft wool around her, he hoisted her out, pausing to kick his truck door shut as he headed up the walk with her in his arms.

Larissa moaned softly in her sleep but didn't stir. Clay was trying to figure out how to knock on Reese's door without waking Larissa when the door swung open and Reese stood there in her bare feet looking up at him.

"She's asleep?" Reese whispered.

"No, I clubbed her over the head and wanted to bury her dead body in your backyard." Clay stepped around her into the warmth of the living room. "I'd actually say *passed out* is a better description than *asleep*. I think she had a lot to drink."

"Not the first time," she said, biting her lip. "We can put her in the guest room. I keep a bed made up for her."

Clay raised an eyebrow. "You have a guest room in this place? Doesn't seem big enough for an extra dish towel."

"I like my house. It's plenty of room for me, my rescue animals, and the occasional drunken guest," Reese said. "Right in here."

Reese held open a door, and Clay carried Larissa through it. Reese bent forward to pull the covers back so Clay could set her down on the bed. He reached for the sheet, ready to pull it up to Larissa's chin.

"Hold on, let me take her shoes off," Reese said. "Er, *shoe*. She's missing one."

"Probably left it in my truck. I'll go get it."

"We can grab it later. Let's just get her tucked in."

"We don't have to undress her, do we?"

Reese laughed. "You may be the first man who didn't jump at the chance to remove Larissa's clothes."

Clay shrugged and said nothing.

Once they had Larissa tucked in, they moved silently out of the room. Reese shut the door behind her and padded barefoot into the kitchen, her black dress brushing the soft hollow at the back of her knees.

Clay followed, intending to make a hasty retreat. He just needed to grab 'Riss's shoe and get out of here. Lingering with Reese would be bad, especially now that he'd slipped up twice and kissed her. Jesus, it was like he was *trying* to screw up all his friendships.

Then Reese reached up to pull two glasses out of a cupboard, and Clay promptly forgot his exit strategy. Instead, he watched her dress ride up the back of her thighs, exposing a pale swath of skin that looked so soft he itched to run his finger over it. The dress was some sort of silky material, and it hugged her curves without being obscene. He watched her calf muscles flex, watched her bare arm as she—

"Don't you think so?" Reese asked.

Clay's mind came crashing back to the present. *Shit.* What had she just asked him? He tried to think of a tactful way to recover.

"That's an interesting question," he said. "Maybe if you rephrased it, I could give you a broader answer."

Reese blinked at him. "Okay," she said. "The ice we get from the well out here always tastes better than the crap we get in restaurants, wouldn't you agree?"

Dammit.

"Right," Clay said, and rested his elbows on the serving bar as Reese set a glass in front of him and poured cola over the large chunks of ice.

He watched her for a moment as she lifted her own glass to her lips to take a sip. Clay picked up his glass and drained half of it in one gulp. He set it down and looked up to see her studying him. He cleared his throat.

"How are all your animals?"

"Good. Leon's recovered from his bender, Oscar the orphaned opossum is almost ready for solid food, and Axl taught Earwax the raccoon to sit up and beg."

"That's everyone?"

"No, just the ones you've met. There's a skunk with an injured foot, a kestrel with a broken wing, a couple fawns I'm bottle feeding—"

"Wow. You have your hands full."

"I like it. You're part of the reason I got serious about animal rehab in the first place."

Clay looked down at his hands, not sure how to take that. Reese certainly had a soft spot for lost souls. Is that what he was to her? The thought reminded him of the drunk girl snoozing in the guest room. He cleared his throat. "So, Reese. Does Larissa get wasted like that a lot?"

Reese twisted her glass in her hands, considering. "Occasionally. More than I wish she did, but not like—"

She stopped and bit her lip. Clay knew why.

"Not like I was? A drunk, you mean?" He saw Reese flinch. "Not yet, but she could be headed that way. I remember her doing that a lot in college, and the fact that she's still at it is a red flag."

"I appreciate your concern," she said, her crisp tone suggesting she definitely didn't.

Clay sighed and wrapped his fingers around the glass again. "I'd be a jerk if I didn't say something, Reese. I know what it's like. And I know you think it's your job to take care of all the living creatures in need. I'm just saying, keep an eye on her."

She looked up at him, tears brimming in her eyes. "I know," she murmured. "I'm sorry. I don't know why I'm still being a bitch to you."

"It's fine, Reese. It's fine." Clay shook his head, trying not to notice the glitter of her tears. It felt like a sucker punch to the spleen knowing he was responsible for making her cry.

Again.

He drew in a breath, struggling to do even that. Suddenly, the room felt very small.

"Don't cry, Reese," he said.

A stupid thing to say. She turned her face away from him, and he saw the first tear slide down her cheek.

Shit.

"Just give me a second, okay?" she whispered. "It's just—Larissa, and all this stuff with you and—"

He stood up, feeling awkward and stiff in his own body. The room seemed too hot. She wouldn't look at him.

"Reese."

He reached for her, pulling her to his chest for a comforting hug. He was surprised when she came willingly, more surprised when she molded her body to his.

His breath caught in his throat as the grassy-sweet smell of her engulfed him, making his head spin like he'd just downed a fifth of Jack.

She's so soft.

His arms circled her torso, and his hands came to rest beneath the sharp points of her shoulder blades. He slid them down a little, just a few inches, to rest in the curve of her lower back.

It's a friendly hug, just that. Just comforting a crying woman. A friend.

Reese moved against him and the word *friend* ran screaming from his brain, replaced by something else. *Lust,* maybe.

Urgency.

Get out!

He felt himself responding to her, though his brain was still yelling at him to move away from her, to get the hell out of this kitchen.

Your best friend's ex.

Don't shit where you eat.

Off limits.

Reese tilted her head to look up at him, and Clay's head spun as he looked down into those wild green eyes. His hands seemed to move on their own, sliding down her back, cupping the curve of her ass as his mouth descended and found hers.

Then he was kissing her, kissing her hard as her fingers twined in his hair and her breath pressed her breasts against his chest. Her lips were soft and tasted like cola and something else, maybe wine—he couldn't remember, it had been so long.

He tried to pull back, but he couldn't. Somehow, his fingers found their way into her hair, tugging it free from its knot so he could feel it cool and slippery between his fingers. He slid his lips from her mouth and began kissing his way down her chin, her throat, her chest—

Reese gasped and drew back.

Clay swallowed, his hands stilled in her hair.

"I'm sorry," he said. "I shouldn't have—"

"Stop." She blinked at him, and he could have sworn her eyes were darker than before. Evergreen, almost. She licked her lips, and Clay felt himself grow dizzy again.

"Stop apologizing, I mean. My room," she whispered. "Okay?"

And with his mind reeling with lust and desire and the warm, sweet smell of her, he could only manage one word: "Okay."

CHAPTER ELEVEN

Reese had no idea what came over her. One minute she was attempting a sincere apology, steeped in worry about how she'd been treating Clay and whether Larissa's drinking was something to fret about.

The next minute she was so dizzy with lust she tripped over her own bare feet as she dragged him toward her bedroom. She locked the door behind them and turned to face Clay.

Her body buzzed with desire, and a million crazy justifications whirled through her head.

It's okay, he's a friend.

It doesn't mean anything, it's just sex.

It's not like we haven't done this before.

"What?" Clay murmured, and Reese realized she'd spoken her last thought aloud.

"Nothing," she said, and tugged at the hem of his T-shirt, trying to pull it over his head. He let go of her long enough to yank his arms free of the warm cotton, and then he was standing there in front of her, naked to the waist.

"My God," she whispered and dragged her fingers down his chest.

Clay groaned low in the back of his throat, but his hands stayed at his sides. It was like he was suddenly afraid to touch her now that they were in a dark room with a bed and desire so thick she could see it in the air between them. Reese hooked her fingers under his belt and looked up at him. He wasn't meeting her eyes.

"What?" she asked.

He looked down at her. "You—I'm just—It's just—" He took a breath. "If you need to stop, now's the time."

She tilted her head to the side, a little incredulous. "Stop? Why would I want to stop?"

Clay closed his eyes for a second, and Reese watched his hands ball into fists at his sides. She saw him clench and unclench his jaw.

"Do *you* want to stop?" she asked. "I didn't mean to drag you in here like—"

"No!" he said, his eyes wide as his hands came up to cup her arms just above the elbows. "No, I don't want to stop. But once we cross that line—"

Reese stood on tiptoe to kiss him, stopping his words with her lips. She pressed her body harder against him, her tongue finding his, her fingers sliding up and over the taut muscles of his back to pull him closer. His hands stayed on her elbows for a few more beats, then slowly slid down her rib cage and nestled around her waist.

Reese stopped kissing him long enough to look him in the eyes. "The line's already been crossed, wouldn't you say?"

Clay blinked down at her, seeming not to hear her words. He held her like that for a second, his breath coming fast, his pupils dilated. Then he slid his hands down over her ass and touched the hem of her dress. He hesitated there, his eyes fixed on hers.

"Want me to take it off?" Reese asked, not bothering to wait for a response. She let go of him and reached down to tug the dress over her head, trying to remember the sexiest way to do this. It had been so long. She crossed her arms and grabbed the hem, her arms making a natural *X*, crossing and uncrossing beneath the fabric.

Then she was standing there in just her bra and panties, suddenly self-conscious. She shivered.

Hell, it's not like he hasn't seen it before.

True, everything was a decade older, and gravity had had its way with a few things, but overall, she knew she still looked pretty good.

She stood up a little straighter, wondering if she should have left her high-heeled boots on.

"Beautiful," he said in a strangled voice, one hand coming up to brush the strap of her bra. "You're so beautiful."

Reese smiled a little shyly. "Blue satin," she said. "Not like the black lace the other night. The front clasp that wasn't meant to be, but—"

She didn't get a chance to finish whatever inane thing she'd been about to say. His mouth found hers again, and then there was no talking at all. Reese went up on tiptoe, wishing again she'd kept the boots on. He was so tall, so big. Her hands slid over his biceps, marveling at the size of him. She remembered something, drew back. In the dimness of her night-light, she peered at his skin.

"Your tattoo," she whispered. "What does it say?"

"Not important," he said, and kissed her again.

Reese forgot about the words—all words—as she felt herself dissolving into him, devouring him, touching him everywhere. He smelled like sawdust and sunshine, and Reese wondered if it was cologne or just Clay.

He was harder everywhere than last time—leaner, more solid. His hands made slow circles on her back, still tentative. There was a hesitance in him that hadn't been there the last time.

The only time.

"You won't break me," she whispered against his chest.

"It's not that. It's just—"

"What?"

"I want you so much."

The words made her dizzy all over. She caught him by the belt buckle again and pulled him toward the bed, glad she'd had the foresight to put on clean sheets that morning. Not that she'd been planning on doing anything illicit, and certainly not with Clay.

Clay, her brain murmured, and Reese waited for that to seem strange. It didn't.

Reese shoved her down comforter aside, then knelt on the bed and pulled him closer. He was standing in front of her now in the faint glow of moonlight seeping through the window. She slid her hands up his sides and felt him shiver beneath her palms.

"Cold?" she asked.

"No," he said, his hands drifting down her shoulders and coming to rest against her collarbones, just above her breasts. He left them there, his fingertips warm on her flesh. "Not cold at all."

He leaned forward and his lips found hers in the semidarkness. Then his hands slid down, finally cupping her breasts, testing their weight in his palms. Reese moaned aloud, trying to remember if it had felt this damn good the last time.

His thumbs stroked her nipples through the satin, and Reese arched her back, pressing herself into all that sensation. She slid her hands down his back and over his jeans, thrilling herself with the hardness there that she couldn't quite touch.

Clay let go of her breasts, and Reese made a small whimper of protest. His hands moved around her back, tracing the wings of her shoulder blades before his fingers found the clasp of her bra.

"Oh," she gasped as he unhooked it in one deft move, then reached up to slide the straps from her shoulders. Reese sighed as the bra fell free and his hands curved around once more to cup her. He bent forward and slid his tongue over one nipple, then the other, taking his time, making slow circles until Reese was sure she'd topple off the bed.

She trailed her hands down his chest and fumbled with his belt buckle. Clay sucked in a breath and drew back, moving his fingers over her shoulders to hold her away from him for just a moment. He looked at her, just looked at her.

Reese shivered, her hand frozen on his belt buckle.

"Reese," he whispered, his lips forming a small smile. "Reese."

"Yes?"

"I can't believe this."

He stopped, and Reese smiled back as she fumbled with his belt buckle. "Is this okay?"

He laughed then, the first time she hadn't feared he was still considering fleeing the room.

"It's okay," he said. "Want help?"

She nodded and sat back on her heels to watch as he slowly unhooked the belt and tugged open the button fly on his jeans. She tried not to stare, but hell, wasn't that the point? Admiring the evidence that she was able to arouse him like this, seeing the swell of him straining against his black boxer briefs.

He bent down to untie his boots, then toed them off before sliding off his jeans and underwear until he stood there naked in front of her.

Reese stared. "My God."

He smiled and slid one finger from the edge of her chin down her collarbone and over the swell of her breast. "I can say the same for you."

She smiled back, still drinking in the sight of him in all his naked glory. "Sobriety's been good to you."

Reese drew herself back up to her knees, eager to feel him against her bare breasts. She kissed him hard, felt him respond by reaching down to cup her ass. She should probably take off her panties, that last layer between them, but the teasing was ecstasy. So close, but not quite there. She ground against him, enjoying the slide of damp satin.

Clay drew back again, his breath coming hard. "I didn't bring any—"

"Condoms," Reese murmured. "Bedside drawer, right beside you. God, I hope they aren't expired."

She wondered if that was a dumb thing to say but decided it wasn't. It was better than suggesting she regularly bedded strange men she brought home from the bar.

Which was exactly why this was okay. This was Clay—not some stranger. *Clay.*

He pulled out the foil packet and drew it toward his chest, fumbling.

"Want help?" Reese asked.

"I've got it."

"I want to touch you," she said, reaching for the condom, surprised by her own boldness.

She took it from him and tore open the wrapper, then slid the condom on slowly, enjoying the way he moaned as her hand traveled the length of him. Then she released him and reached down to peel off her panties. She knelt there for a second, panties in one hand, and reached for him again.

Clay shook his head—wonderment or dismay, Reese wasn't certain, but she was pretty sure she knew. "Last chance to stop before things change forever," he whispered.

Reese gave him a curious smile. "Forever? It's sex. I'm not going to make you marry me in the morning."

Clay smiled. "Okay."

She kissed him again. Then she twined her fingers around his neck and pulled him down to her, letting herself fall back on the bed. He moved with her, coming to rest with his hands on either side of her head, his weight braced on his arms. Reese arched up, wanting to feel more of him.

A lot more.

She reached down between them. "Remember that joke you used to tell? What's the definition of a nice girl?"

Clay grimaced. "God, what a jerk."

She laughed and wrapped her fingers around him, guiding him toward her. She waited for him to add the punch line to the joke, but he only made a soft strangled sound in the back of his throat.

"A nice girl," she whispered. "One who puts it in for you."

Then she did.

They both gasped at the same moment, she from the sudden shock of penetration, he—well, probably from the same thing. Just a different sensation, Reese thought as she began to move with him.

He stroked deep inside her and she moaned, feeling her legs come up off the bed to wrap around him. He was still holding himself up with his arms, trying to keep his weight off her chest. Afraid to crush her, probably, but God, she wanted to feel him against her.

"Come down here," she whispered. "Come closer."

Clay slid deeper and Reese cried out. He smiled. "I don't think it's possible to get much closer."

"Your arms," she gasped, dizzy with the next thrust. "I want to feel your chest against—oh God!"

Clay quickened his pace and Reese forgot for a moment how much she wanted to feel the weight of him pressing her down into the mattress. The heat was building inside her, too soon—way too soon—but God, it had been so long.

Reese arched her back and gripped a pillow with one hand, the other hand coming up to clutch the side of his waist. He stroked into her again, and Reese felt something snap inside her.

"Oh, Jesus," she shrieked, then remembered Larissa and fought to stifle her screams as stars burst behind her eyes and everything inside her exploded with pleasure.

She was still gasping for breath when she opened her eyes to see Clay smiling down at her. "You okay?"

Reese nodded, not sure she could speak.

"I was worried about crushing you," he murmured.

Reese smiled and reached up to grab his shoulders. She pulled him down to her, forcing his weight on top of her.

"Stop being so damn polite," she said.

Clay laughed and Reese felt the vibration of it deep in her chest. "That might be the strangest thing anyone's ever said to me in bed."

He was still hard inside her, still ready for his turn. Reese grinned.

"I'm honored," she said, and flipped him on his back.

♦ ♦ ♦

Clay lay there in silence after Reese drifted off to sleep. His head was swimming, even though his body was so saturated with pleasure that his nerve endings ached.

What the hell did you just do?

Not that he regretted it. Not exactly. Hell, it had been amazing. *Reese* was amazing. He couldn't regret that, but still.

Your best friend's ex.

One of the only friendships you have left.

Clay eased away from her reluctantly, trying not to wake her. He pulled the covers up around her, feeling his heart twist as she smiled in her sleep and made a soft whimpering sound.

God, she's perfect.

He stood there watching her sleep for a few breaths, not quite ready to go. But hell, he had to. Larissa was sleeping in the same house, and the last thing he needed was to have her wake up and discover them twined around each other. The whole family would hear about it, and Reese would never live it down.

Still, he hesitated. He didn't want to just leave without a word. That would be rude, something the old Clay might've done. Maybe if he slept on the couch?

No, still too close. Even worse, her family would see his truck there in the morning, would know he'd spent the night.

Okay, so he'd go.

The thought of driving back to his cold hotel room wasn't appealing, either, but it was his only option. He looked at Reese again, her hair spread out on the pillow and her hand curled against one cheek.

So beautiful.

He shook his head, thinking this is what perverts did. Stand there naked watching a woman sleep. He dressed in silence, figuring he could shower when he got back to the hotel.

He opened the bedroom door and crept into the living room.

There, he looked around for some paper and something to write with. He found a notepad on the kitchen counter with a pen tucked into the spiral and sat down to write her a note.

What the hell should he say?

The old Clay wouldn't have left a note at all, or maybe he would have. Something gauche—*thanks for the great lay* or an asinine thing like that. Clay looked down at the blank paper, not wanting to blow it.

Reese, he wrote. *I had a great time.*

He stopped, stared at the words on the page. Stupid. It sounded like bathroom graffiti. *For a good time, call Reese.*

He tore off the page and tried again.

Reese, I wish I could stay, but—

But what?

"Dammit," he muttered, and tore off the page again.

"Whatcha writing?"

Clay jumped. He looked up to see Larissa padding barefoot into the kitchen. Her hair was rumpled, but she'd changed into a pair of shorts and a T-shirt that must've belonged to Reese. Or maybe she kept a stash of her own clothes here for occasions just like this. Her still-smeared eye makeup made her look like a hungover raccoon.

"Nothing," he said.

She rolled her eyes and reached up to grab a water glass out of the cupboard. Her shorts stretched tight over her butt, and Clay was surprised to realize he wasn't at all interested in staring. Not the way he'd done an hour ago when Reese had stretched and reached the same way.

Larissa said nothing as she filled her glass at the sink and downed it in a few quick gulps. She refilled it and did the same thing again. Then she set the glass on the counter and looked at him.

"Here's what you say in your note," she told him. "*Reese. You are amazing.* Period. That's it."

Clay stared at her, not sure how to respond. "We didn't—"

"Of course you did. I know you're a gentleman these days, but there's no protecting Reese's virtue when she moans that loud. Nice job, by the way."

Larissa turned and filled her glass again. Clay swallowed and looked down at the notepad. "I don't want to blow this."

"Funny, I said that to Derek earlier."

Clay laughed in spite of himself. "I'm serious. I've screwed up with her before. A lot."

Larissa shook her head. "You'll do fine. You're a different guy now, aren't you?"

"Yes."

"So prove it. Write your damn note and get out of here before Grandpa Axl shows up and starts giving you sex tips."

Clay winced and looked back down at the page. Finally, he scrawled a few words. Not what Larissa had suggested, exactly, but the sentiment felt right.

"Want me to give it to her?" Larissa asked.

"No, I don't want you to give it to her. I want you to go back to bed and pretend you have no idea anything happened here tonight, got it?"

Larissa grinned. "So this is a secret love affair?"

"I don't know what it is. But I do know your family thinks of Reese's love life as public domain, and it really shouldn't be anyone else's business. I'm asking you to keep this one quiet for now, okay?"

Larissa sipped her water and shrugged. "Is that because you care about her or because you're worried what Eric will think?"

"Does it matter?"

"To me or to Reese?"

Clay looked down at the page, then back up at Larissa. "Either, I guess."

"Yes. On both counts."

"Okay, then. I'm asking you, as a friend, to keep this quiet. I care about her a lot. A whole lot."

Larissa studied him for a moment, so intently Clay was tempted to look away. She took a few small sips of her water, then shrugged. "Thank you for bailing me out earlier."

"Not a problem."

"I don't know what I saw in him."

"Beer goggles," Clay said. "Happens to the best of us."

Larissa snorted. "Guess so."

"Be careful, okay?"

"With boys or with beer?"

"Yes."

Larissa nodded. "Thank you. For caring, I mean. And for rescuing me."

Clay nodded and stood up. "I'm sticking this on her nightstand now. Please don't sneak in there and read it, okay?"

"You take away all my fun."

"I doubt that."

Clay crept back into Reese's room, glad to see she hadn't stirred. He stood there for a few seconds, watching her chest rise and fall. One edge of the sheet had slipped beneath her left breast, and he reached down to pull it up for her. His fingers grazed her warm flesh and he nearly lost his mind as she stirred and smiled in sleep.

It was all he could do not to bend down and kiss her. He knew this was better, that they needed to protect whatever was happening between them until they had time to sit down with their clothes on and talk things through. He set the note on her nightstand and backed out of the room, still reluctant to take his eyes off her.

At last, he closed the bedroom door behind him. Larissa had gone back to bed or to the bathroom or something, so Clay didn't have anyone to say goodbye to as he opened the front door and stepped out into the damp night air. The frogs and crickets conducted a noisy symphony in the darkness, and somewhere Clay heard a train whistle. He breathed in the scent of wet earth and fermented fruit and the grassy scent of Reese still clinging to his skin.

He pulled the front door shut behind him, and crept quietly across the gravel driveway to his truck. He opened the door, wincing a little at the squeak, and climbed in, pulling it closed as softly as he could. Reese's window was only a few feet away, not to mention her parents' house just across the vineyard. Sound carried out here.

He eyed the slope of the driveway and decided to coast to the flat spot before cranking the engine. He stuck the key in the ignition and flicked the lights, releasing the emergency brake. The truck began a slow roll down the driveway, gravel popping under the tires.

Clay was so focused on making a silent exit that he almost didn't see it. He wasn't sure what caught his eye exactly—a moving shape? A person? A car?

Or just the thick plume of gray smoke curling slowly up from the side of the winery barn.

"Oh, shit," he said, and slammed on the brakes.

CHAPTER TWELVE

Reese was still mostly asleep when she patted the mattress beside her and found it empty. She frowned. The sheets were damp, and the room still smelled like sex, but the space next to her was cold.

She opened her eyes, blinked in the darkness, then closed her eyes again.

She hadn't expected Clay to still be there, but still. Even in her sleep-addled state, it was tough not to be a little disappointed.

Weren't you the one who left before he woke up fifteen years ago?

Reese thought about that for a moment, trying to remember the details. They'd only known each other a few weeks at that point, and she'd felt daring and grownup having her first tipsy fling. She'd crept out while he was sleeping, that was true. And they'd really never talked about it after that. She and Eric had started dating seriously within a few weeks, and the engagement and marriage just sort of snowballed from there.

Eric's a safe choice, she'd assured herself back then. *A good friend and a dependable husband. Not the kind of guy who'd get wasted and walk into chemistry class holding a banana like a gun while pretending to be a Stormtrooper.*

So her only night with Clay had remained a secret. They'd never even acknowledged it until a few days ago.

A wailing in the distance jerked Reese's mind from her memories and back into the present. She sat up in bed, listening.

Sirens?

She craned her neck, trying to peer out the window. The flicker of red-and-white lights pulsed back at her, coming up the gravel driveway with alarming speed.

Shit.

She scrambled out of bed, her feet tangling briefly in her discarded bra. She fumbled in the dark for clothing, coming up with the black dress she'd peeled off earlier when Clay was watching. Her arms tingled at the memory, but she tossed the dress aside and reached for the light switch.

She started grabbing clothes from a pile in the corner. Yoga pants, dirty T-shirt—where did she throw that bra? She cursed as she wriggled it on, wishing she were one of those women who could dash out the door without one. She shoved her feet into her clogs and grabbed a fleece sweatshirt off the hook on the back of her door.

"Reesey?" Larissa's voice echoed high and panicked from the living room. "Something's happening."

"Can you see what it is?"

"I'm trying."

Reese yanked open her bedroom door and hustled into the living room. Larissa was standing there in a pair of Reese's old gym shorts and a T-shirt that once belonged to Eric.

"Do you smell smoke?" Larissa called over her shoulder as she peered out the front window.

Reese sniffed the air, panic hitting her like a punch in the gut as she threw open the front door. The smoke smell expanded outside. "Shit."

She could see the flames from her front porch, licking at the side of the winery barn as smoke slithered up into the night sky. The pulse of lights from the fire engines cast an eerie glow on the nearby grapevines, making them look like twisted old men.

"'Riss—go put Leon in his pen and stay with him," she yelled. "Check on all the other animals and make sure they're safe. Take your cell phone and call my mom and dad."

"Be careful!"

Reese took off running. Her feet slipped on the damp grass as the smoke stung her nostrils, but she recovered her balance and kept running.

"Honey! Stay back!"

"Dad?" Reese squinted between the darkened rows of grapevines, trying to see him. "What's going on?"

"The fire department has it, hon," he called. "They said it looks worse than it probably is. Stay put for now, let them do their jobs."

"Where are you?"

"Hold on just a sec. Don't move, I'll come to you."

Reese turned back toward the fire, watching through ashy darkness as her eyes adjusted to the haze. Burning orange streaks slashed the sky, but she could see streams of water gushing from the end of the hose as fire crews attacked the flames. She watched, horrified, from the safety of her front lawn.

The winery barn still stood, and now that she could see more clearly, she realized the fire was contained to the east end of the building. Not where the wine was stored, not where the expensive equipment was kept.

She felt her father's hand on her shoulder and turned.

"What happened?" she asked.

"I don't know."

She glanced down, then wished she hadn't. "Why are you in your underwear?"

"Your mom and I were making love in the moonlight when—"

"Never mind," Reese said, yanking off her fleece and handing it to him. Once it was safely tied around his waist, she continued the conversation. "So you saw the fire and called 911?"

"Not me, Clay."

"Clay?"

"Your mom texted me a second ago with the details. Guess he was dropping Larissa off at your place when he saw the flames. He tried to get it put out with the hose on the side of the building but called the fire department to be safe."

Reese bit her lip as she watched the crews hose down the end of the building. "Is he okay?"

"I think he got a little burn on his arm, nothing too bad."

"Where is he?"

"Down there with the ambulance crew getting checked out."

Reese nodded, not sure whether to rush down there or play it cool. "How did it start?"

"No one knows yet. Looks like it's close to where the de-stemmer was, so maybe some wiring?"

"There's no reason it would even be hooked up this time of year, is there?"

"Probably not. Maybe something overheated?"

Reese bit her lip. "I'm going down there to talk to the crew. Where's Mom?"

"She went back down to the house to get me some replacement pants and make sure Axl was okay."

"Where are your pants?"

"Mom got carried away and tossed them in Leon's trough."

Larissa would pull them out. Reese sighed and headed across the lawn to where the lights from the fire trucks were still pulsing. Off to one side, several people from the neighboring cattle ranch were gawking at the scene. Beside the winery barn, the crews were coiling up their hoses and speaking in jovial tones. Reese said a quiet prayer of thanks, realizing the damage didn't look too bad.

"Excuse me," she said as she caught the arm of a passing fireman. "I'm Reese Clark—this is my family's vineyard. Any idea what happened?"

The man nodded and touched the edge of his helmet. "Can't really say. Looks like the fire started over there, but we won't know anything for sure 'til the fire marshal gets out here."

"Can I go look?"

He shook his head. "Not yet. It wasn't a bad fire, but we can't say for sure how stable things are."

"How bad is the damage?"

The guy shrugged. "I don't really know how much that stuff costs, but I'd say you got lucky. The fire was pretty contained. Most of the big equipment didn't get hit. You'll probably have a few bucks tied up in building repairs, but it's mostly just smoke. You owe a lot to that dude down there in the ambulance."

Reese bit her lip. "Is he okay?"

"He's fine. A little shook up, maybe. Go see him if you want."

"Thanks."

Reese trudged off toward the ambulance, which wasn't screaming off into the night with sirens blaring. That seemed like a good sign.

"Clay?" she called as she approached.

A medic looked up at her. "Give him a sec, honey. We've got him on oxygen right now."

"Oxygen?"

"Just a precaution. He's fine."

Reese reached the side of the ambulance and looked down. Clay was sitting up, but there was a mask covering his nose and mouth. He had some sort of monitor hooked to one finger, and there was a bandage on his right forearm. Other than missing his shirt, he looked normal.

Well, aside from the clearly defined fingernail marks on his right shoulder. Reese flushed, remembering how they got there.

He looked up at her. She couldn't see his mouth, but she could see his eyes and was pretty sure he smiled.

"Hey," she said. "I heard what happened. Thank you. Can you nod if you're okay?"

Clay nodded, then glanced at the medic.

"Go ahead and take it off," the guy said. "Just put it back on if you feel dizzy."

Clay drew the mask back and gave her a small smile.

"Hey."

Reese felt her eyes start to well up, and she knew it wasn't just the smoke. "You got hurt."

"I'm fine. The burn is pretty small, and I sucked in some smoke, but I'll be okay."

One of the medics laughed. "Someone owes this guy a beer."

Reese bit her lip. "Thank you. I don't know what to say, really. If you hadn't been driving by right then—" She stopped, struck by a realization. "I never thought I'd be so grateful to have a man run out on me after sex."

Clay grimaced, and the medic gave a choked laugh. "You two want a minute alone?"

Reese shook her head. "No—it's okay. Just take care of him, please."

Clay shook his head, his expression somewhere between amusement and embarrassment. "I left a note."

"I believe you," she said. "I didn't see it, what with my barn catching on fire and all, but I'm not mad. Really, it's okay."

Clay nodded. "Not quite the exit I envisioned."

"It's fine, don't worry about it. I'm just glad you were here."

"My pleasure."

"Do you need to put that mask thing back on?"

He gave her a funny little half smile. "I am feeling a bit lightheaded."

He pulled the plastic mask back over his nose and mouth, and Reese glanced back at the winery barn. Firefighters had the blaze extinguished at last, and crews were stringing yellow crime-scene tape around the charred outer edge. She knew it was just to keep people out but couldn't help but feel violated at the sight of it.

She looked back down at Clay. "I'm going to go see if they'll let me have a closer look at things. You okay here?"

Clay nodded and gave her a thumbs-up.

"Thanks again," she said. "For everything."

Reese turned and took two steps toward the winery barn before her mother's voice stopped her in her tracks.

"I brought brownies," she called. "Just a little something to say thank you to all of you for saving our place."

Reese turned to watch her mother weaving through the crowd of gawking neighbors and firefighting personnel, a large tray of chocolaty treats balanced in her arms. She was wearing yoga pants and a button-down shirt that displayed the small heart she'd had tattooed above her left breast with *Jed* spelled out in curlicue letters.

Reese felt her phone vibrate and glanced down to see a text from Larissa.

All OK w/ your zoo. 2 squirrels in outside cage humping. You?

Reese texted back. *Everyone safe. Too soon to tell damage.*

"Hey, honey," her mother said. "Did you get a chance to get a look at things yet?"

"Not yet. I was just headed that way."

"I'll go with you!" announced Axl, pushing his way through the crowd. "I saw a good-lookin' lady firefighter down there, and I'd like to ask her to uncoil my hose."

"Dad, stop it!" June hissed. "That's our neighbor, not a lady fire-fighter."

Reese rolled her eyes. "So it's okay if he sexually harasses firefighters but not the neighbors?" She grabbed Axl by the arm and pulled him away from the crowd. "Come on, Axl. Come with me to check out the winery barn, okay?"

"Yeah, maybe they need some muscle down there," he said, flexing one arm.

"Wait, sweetie," her mom called. "You want a brownie?"

"No, thanks, Mom. Clay, how about you?"

Clay pulled off the oxygen mask again and shook his head. "I'm good, thanks."

Reese's mom smiled down at him. "Thank you so much for everything you did, honey. We owe you a lot more than a brownie."

Axl snickered and looked at Reese. Reese ignored him.

"It was nothing."

Reese's mom shook her head and began rearranging the brownies on her tray. "We sure got lucky tonight, didn't we, Reese?"

Axl snorted, still looking at Reese. "Sure did. Got lucky, all right."

Reese glared at him. "Come on, *Grandpa*—let's check out the winery barn."

She grabbed Axl by the arm and dragged him away, ignoring the neighbor who made a snide comment about manhandling an old man.

As soon as they were out of earshot, Reese stopped walking and glared at Axl.

"What the hell was that about?"

Axl grinned. "Nice beard burn on your cheek."

Reese raised a hand to her face, feeling herself flush. "So? I had a date tonight. With that hot vet, the one from yesterday."

"It wasn't the vet who left you grinning like a cat who got porked with a Q-tip," Axl said. "Looked like Clay hadn't shaved this evening, you notice that? That five o'clock shadow sure can chafe sensitive skin, eh?"

Reese closed her eyes and shook her head. "Axl—"

"And then there's the claw marks on his shoulder," Axl continued. "Oh, and the lipstick on his earlobe. Same shade you were wearing earlier, wasn't it?"

Reese sighed. "What do you want?"

"You to admit it."

"Admit what?"

"That you scratched your itch with that boy. That you two stroked the lamb's head, got hay for your donkey, did the wild monkey dance, tickled the—"

"Okay, fine!" Reese snapped. "Stop! We did, okay? Is that what you want? It wasn't a big deal."

Axl grinned. "The hell it wasn't. You two have been hot for each other for years. 'Bout damn time you did something about it."

"Can we just drop it?"

"Sure, sure," he said, waving a hand as he glanced over at the barn. "Whatever you want, Peanut Butter Cup."

Reese gritted her teeth. "I want something to cover the beard burn. Give me your scarf."

"Nah. There's no beard burn. I just wanted you to admit it. I can die happy now."

Reese glared at him and wondered about the penalties for elder abuse. "Keep that up, you'll be dying a lot sooner. Come on. Let's go look at the damage."

"You go ahead," Axl said, turning back the direction they'd just come from. "I gotta go check the woods, make sure nothing damaged my 'shrooms, you know what I'm sayin'?"

"No, I really don't. That's usually best, isn't it?"

Axl shrugged and trudged off up the hill, leaving Reese staring after him.

"Rough night, Reese?"

She turned and saw Dick Smart from Larchwood Vineyards. He wore the same smug expression he always wore and was immaculately dressed for a guy who'd been roused from bed at one a.m.

"What are you doing here?" she snapped.

"Came to see if you needed any help. Being neighborly."

"You're not being neighborly. You're being nosy."

He ignored her snide tone and nodded toward the winery barn. "You lose anything in the fire?"

"I don't know yet. I've been trying to find someone to talk to, but I keep getting pulled away."

"Hmmm. Well, I do hope it all turns out okay for you. Be a damn shame if you lost any of your wines."

Reese looked at him, narrowing her eyes a little. Dick stared back, his expression unblinking.

"What?" he demanded.

Reese shook her head, suppressing a shiver. "Nothing. Nothing at all."

♦　♦　♦

Clay got to the vineyard early the next morning. Early by construction standards, anyway, which were pretty damn early. But he was learning that was nothing compared to winery hours.

From the looks of things, the vineyard crew had been there awhile. They were standing next to the winery barn, frowning at the blackened hole in the side of the building. Yellow police tape fluttered in the breeze, and everyone wore matching grim expressions.

Clay approached quietly and kept his distance, not wanting to interrupt.

"Look, at least we didn't lose any equipment," Reese's dad was saying. "We can count our blessings for that. The structural damage was minimal. All in all, we got lucky."

"What about the wine?" Reese asked. "How's the smoke going to affect what we've got in the barrels here?"

Eric scratched his chin. "We're lucky we moved all the Reserve down to the other cellar a couple days ago, but I'll have to go through and check everything else for smoke damage."

"Can we move all the barrels out of here?" Reese asked. "I don't want any of the wines getting worse just sitting in this smoky building."

"Already on it," Eric said. "I've got a couple guys coming in to help run the forklift and get everything moved to the other cellar."

"What about the white wines?" June asked. "Everything we have stored in the tanks—the smoke can't be good for those."

Eric sighed. "There's the Sauvignon Blanc in steel over there. It's pretty delicate. We might lose that one."

"The whole tank?" June asked. "What about the Chardonnay?"

Eric shook his head. "We can taste it and see, but—"

He trailed off, looking grim. Reese closed her eyes. What did that leave them with? How many of those white wines were presold? How much money would they lose?

"Most of those are sold to restaurants already," Larissa whispered. "Without the white wines—" She bit her lip.

Reese sighed. "Let's just move what we can and hope for the best."

"No one was hurt," June said. "That's the important thing. It was a pretty small fire all in all."

Clay felt a pang in his chest as he watched Jed put his arm around his daughter. "It'll be okay. I've got a meeting in an hour with our insurance guy. This is what we have the policy for."

"But we're already thin on whites for this season," Larissa said. "Our buyers have all been demanding more. What do I tell them now?"

Sheila—who must've driven Eric—squeezed her husband's hand. "I don't like this. Any of it. This whole thing seems dangerous to me."

"Accidents happen, hon," Eric said.

"Are we sure it was an accident?" Larissa asked.

Reese frowned at her cousin. "What are you suggesting?"

"I don't know. Just speculating if anyone would want to do this on purpose."

Jed sighed. "Let's not jump to any conclusions yet. The guys from the fire department will be checking everything out. It doesn't do us any good to speculate right now."

June linked her arm through his and gave a weak smile. "The damage could have been worse. Someone could have been injured or even killed."

Sheila shot a worried look at Eric. "Is it safe to be in there? Did the fire marshal clear it yet for you guys to work?"

"We can get our work done," Reese said, "but it can't be open to the public."

"What about the event next week?" Larissa asked.

Reese shook her head. "It doesn't look good for holding it inside. Not unless the guests want to smell like a bonfire."

"The invitations went out last week," Larissa moaned. "We've already got more than a hundred RSVPs. After that thing with the Reserve Pinot, the wine club already hates us. If we have to cancel—"

"Not an option," Reese snapped, and Clay watched her straighten like a rod had speared her spine. "Our reputation is already tanking. Did you see that article from that online news site?"

Sheila sighed. "The article wasn't so bad, but the headline—"

"'Local Vineyard Suffers String of Misfortunes,'" Eric muttered. "They might as well have kicked us in the nuts while we're already on the ground."

"How the hell did they get all that information anyway?" Larissa asked. "The fire stuff I get—they listen to the scanner—but the things about the broken barrel and the construction—"

"Reporters are assholes," Reese muttered. "Let's deal with one thing at a time. What are we going to do about the event?"

Clay cleared his throat, not wanting to intrude, but figuring he might be able to help. "Could you hold the event outside?"

Reese gave him a sad smile. "In the Willamette Valley? In May? There's pretty much a ninety-nine percent chance of rain."

"What if you had tents?"

"Tents?"

"Sure," Clay said, thinking fast. "Dorrington Construction has some of those big tents. They're for the company picnics and some of the trade shows we go to. You could probably get a couple hundred people under them and I think we've got two."

Larissa brightened. "Do they rent them out?"

Reese shook her head. "'Riss, we can't afford that."

"Let me see what I can do," Clay said. "I might be able to get them for free, or at least for a really discounted price."

All of them stared at Clay. Jed was the first to speak.

"That's mighty kind of you, son. We appreciate the help."

"Yes, sir," Clay said. "I know things haven't gone the way you wanted with the bid and construction is moving a little slowly. It seems like the least I can do."

Reese caught his eye and looked away quickly, her cheeks flushing. Larissa gave him a knowing look, but said nothing.

It was Sheila who finally broke the silence. "I need to get to work," she said to Eric. "Call me if anything else happens?"

"Will do."

"Do you want to meet for lunch?"

Eric shook his head. "Gotta work straight through."

"Be careful, okay? I'm really worried."

He nodded and pulled her close. "Have a good day."

"You too, sweetie."

They kissed, and everyone averted their eyes except June and Jed, who exchanged knowing smiles and laced their fingers together.

Jed kissed his wife's temple and whispered something Clay couldn't make out. The two embraced, and Reese looked away, suddenly very interested in inspecting the charred edges of the building. Clay wanted to touch her hand, to do something to let her know he realized how awkward it probably felt to have parents whose affection for each other was so overwhelming.

But he didn't want to draw attention to anything unusual between them.

"I'm gonna taste a few of the wines before I start moving barrels," Eric said to the group as Sheila disappeared down the driveway.

"I'll join you in a minute," Reese called to his retreating back.

"I have to do some damage control with the media," Larissa muttered. "Ten bucks says our asshole neighbor makes it on the morning news saying something about unsafe practices or subpar wines or some bullshit like that."

"Fix it," Reese said. "We can't keep taking hits like this. How many wine club members have we lost?"

Larissa shook her head. "I'm not sure, but the *LA Times* called yesterday. Said they're not going to include us in that feature on eco-friendly wineries unless we can guarantee by the end of the week that we'll be LEED certified with the new building."

Reese closed her eyes. "I've got an appointment with the bank today. We'll get the money somehow."

Larissa nodded. "I'm going to get a press release ready to go. I'll e-mail you a draft."

Everyone drifted away in opposite directions, leaving Clay and Reese standing alone on the hillside above the vineyard. Farm equipment whirred, birds chattered, and the tension between them was so thick, Clay wanted to shove it away like a low-hanging branch. He glanced around, making sure none of her crazy relatives was hiding in a barrel somewhere.

Then he looked back at Reese, who fingered the soft edge of a grape leaf and looked more than a little lost. He touched her hand.

"You okay?" he asked.

Reese nodded and looked up at him. "Everything will be fine."

"I'm sure it will. If there's anything I can do to help—"

"Thanks. I appreciate that."

They stood there in awkward silence for a few moments longer. Reese shuffled her feet in the grass.

Clay cleared his throat. "Look, Reese. Last night was—"

He faltered, looking for the right adjective. *Beautiful. Amazing. Moving. Mind-blowing.*

Reese looked up at him, a smile tugging at the corners of her mouth. "A nice surprise?"

Clay nodded, feeling a sharp surge of relief. He'd half expected her to be regretful or angry or embarrassed.

"Exactly," he breathed. "A very nice surprise."

Reese let go of the grape leaf and turned to him. She stood on tiptoe, sliding her fingers up the back of his neck. She planted a soft kiss at the edge of his jaw, and for the briefest moment, Clay forgot to worry about Eric or anyone else seeing them.

"This is one of the lousiest mornings of my life, but I'm glad you're here," she murmured.

"Me, too."

"I know we need to talk about what happened last night, and that we might have just done something really dumb, but right now—" She shrugged. "I don't regret it."

"I don't, either," Clay said, pulling her into an embrace and not caring if the whole damn family showed up and applauded. "I don't regret anything at all."

Even then, with Reese snug in his arms and the scent of her hair in his lungs, he knew that wasn't entirely true.

CHAPTER THIRTEEN

Eric dipped the wine thief into the bunghole and withdrew it, depositing a bit of the amber liquid into Reese's glass before filling his own.

Reese leaned against the barrel as she stuck her nose in her glass. From the corner of her eye, she studied the grim set of her ex-husband's jaw.

"That's the first time in fifteen years you haven't made a bunghole joke," she observed. "You're taking this fire pretty hard."

"You said *hard*."

"There you go."

Eric shook his head. "I worked my ass off on this wine. We *all* worked our asses off on this wine. I take that pretty fucking seriously."

Reese nodded and took a sip. There was just the faintest hint of smokiness in the bouquet, which wasn't the worst thing in a Chardonnay. It actually complemented the oaky undertones and added an interesting depth. She swirled the wine in the glass, checking clarity. Eric did the same, pausing to spit a mouthful into the drain at their feet. He took another sip, considering.

"We should bottle it now," he said.

"You sure?"

"I just don't want to risk moving it down below or exposing it to smoke for even another day."

Reese nodded. "We weren't planning to bottle for a while yet. I don't think we have enough bottles."

"I've got a few pallets at my place. Why don't you go over with your dad and bring them back up here?"

"Dad's got a meeting with the insurance guy, and everyone else is busy." Reese glanced toward the side of the building where she'd left Clay stringing plastic over the charred side of the building to keep the rain out. "Clay wants to help. He's got a truck. I can ask him to help move bottles."

Something dark passed over Eric's face, but he nodded and reached into his pocket to hand her his keys. "You know where everything is. Just be careful."

Reese rolled her eyes, knowing full well he wasn't worried about her breaking bottles or exceeding the speed limit.

"Yes, Daddy."

Eric snorted. "Daddy issues. That's just what we need to make this whole thing weirder."

◆　◆　◆

Twenty minutes later, Reese pushed open the door to Eric's barn. She felt Clay tense beside her and turned to look at him. With his hands in his pockets, the tattoo on his left bicep peeked out from beneath the sleeve of his black T-shirt. He hesitated, then followed her inside.

"You okay?" Reese asked.

"Yeah. Absolutely. Happy to help."

"But?"

He gave her a small smile and touched the inside of her wrist. "I don't know. It feels funny, I guess. Being here with you at Eric's place after what happened last night."

Reese laughed. "We're picking up wine bottles, not having an orgy on his bed. Besides, it's not like Eric and I ever lived here when we were married."

"I know, I know. It's just this hang-up I have, okay? You're his ex-wife, this is his house."

"You make me sound like a car or a jockstrap. Besides, you and I were friends first, remember?"

"I remember," he said. "I definitely remember. I guess it's just a weird guy thing."

She grinned and laced her fingers behind his neck, pulling him down to her. "I'm rather fond of your guy thing, so I guess I can deal." She pressed her lips to his for what was supposed to be a quick, playful kiss.

Clay responded with unexpected eagerness, drawing her tighter against him, deepening the kiss. His hand slid into the small of her back, and Reese felt her whole body surge with lust as Clay pressed the hard length of his body up against hers. He kissed her harder and Reese swayed, bumping her hip against an old barrel.

They were both breathless by the time they drew apart. Reese smiled up at him again. "Wow. You're pretty good at that."

He grinned back. "Always easier to be good at something you enjoy."

"In that case, keep enjoying me."

"Come on," he said, giving her a light tap on the butt. "Let's get the bottles."

They worked in companionable silence for a while, shuffling the heavy cases out to the truck. Clay did most of the lifting, while Reese opened box after box, making sure they grabbed the right kind of bottles and had enough of them to handle all the Chardonnay.

"He's got a ton of these," Clay mused as he hefted another box.

"Eric does a lot of Chardonnay. Good thing, or he wouldn't have enough bottles for us to use now."

"Do most guys make wine on their own like this? Seems like it would be a conflict of interest for a winemaker."

"Not at all. Eric sources most of his grapes from other places—a lot from the Columbia River Gorge, while we grow our own. They're totally different wines. He actually travels to New Zealand to do his Sauv Blanc."

"I remember him being over there last winter. He sent me a postcard with a filthy joke about sheep."

Reese laughed and peered inside a dusty box. "That sounds like Eric. He missed you, you know. He acts like a jerk sometimes, but he really cares about you."

"I know," Clay answered, turning away to grab more bottles. "That's why I couldn't come back until I got my life straightened out. Until I'd stood on my own two feet for a few years and had gotten used to the way that felt." He turned and looked at her, his hands frozen above the boxes. "I do, you know. Have my life straightened out. Do you believe that?"

Reese swallowed. "Yes. I do. I want to, anyway."

He nodded and reached for the box. "Last night's bar fight notwithstanding."

Reese bit her lip and watched as he hefted the heavy box, admiring the muscled line of his shoulders. She was dusty and tired and still numb from the devastation of the fire, and she'd never wanted him more.

Focus, she told herself, and tore her eyes off his back. She bent down to shift a case of empty Cab bottles to one side.

"Ouch!" she yelped, yanking her finger back and sticking it in her mouth.

Clay spun around. "You okay?"

"Staple," she muttered around her finger. "Damn, that hurts."

"Let me see."

"It's fine, I'm just being a wimp."

"You've had a tetanus shot lately?"

"Yeah, I'm okay."

"Come on, let me see it."

Reese withdrew her finger and held it up. Blood welled from the tiny puncture like a little red bead.

"That looks bad," Clay said. "Do you think you need stitches?"

Reese shook her head and turned to the small sink along one wall. She turned on the tap and ran her hands under the water, wincing as it stung the fresh cut. She grabbed a bar of soap and scrubbed for a moment before turning off the tap and shaking the water from her hands. She studied the wound again.

"I think I just need a Band-Aid. Eric's probably got a first-aid kit in the office."

She moved around him to the musty little room. Flicking on a light switch, she began rummaging through desk drawers. "God, he's got a lot of crap in here," she muttered.

"Let me," Clay said. When Reese didn't move right away, he circled his hands around her waist and hoisted her onto the counter, maneuvering her out of the way.

Reese squeaked, not minding one bit. It was kind of sexy having him take charge.

"Let me dig for it," he muttered. "You're getting blood all over."

"It's not even bleeding anymore," she said as she kicked her heels against the front of the cabinet and watched the back of his head. He was hunched over the drawer, pawing through paperclips and old corks and a pair of plastic lips. Finally, he produced a small red pouch with a white cross on the front. Unzipping it, he dumped the contents on the counter.

Reese reached for a Band-Aid. "I can get it, Clay."

He caught her wrist and locked his fingers around it. "No. You take care of every other living creature on the planet. It's my turn to take care of you."

She saluted with her uninjured hand. "Yes, sir."

Clay stepped into the space in front of her, nudging her knees apart as he tore open a packet of something. Reese grinned and opened her legs, giving him easier access. She could feel the heat of him through the worn denim of her jeans, and her body screamed at her to get closer.

Clay raised her hand to eye level, frowning as he studied the tiny wound. Then he began to dab her finger with an alcohol wipe.

"Ow," she said, though it didn't really hurt.

"Want me to kiss it better?"

"Kind of."

He grinned and lowered his lips to her palm, skipping her finger altogether as he moved his mouth over the fleshy pads at the base of her fingers. He nipped at the delicate ribbon of flesh between her thumb and forefinger, and Reese wrapped her legs around him, locking her ankles at the back of his thighs to draw him closer.

Clay released the injured hand and moved on to the other one, drawing her index finger into his mouth. Reese gasped, savoring the warm wetness of his tongue against the pad of her fingertip. He withdrew her finger and kissed his way down the side of it, his tongue lingering in the sensitive hollow between her middle and ring finger. Reese moaned as he licked gently there for an instant before slipping up to dab kisses along her knuckles.

He plunged her finger into his mouth again and Reese whimpered. "I never get this treatment at the doctor's office."

"That's probably a good thing."

"Want to take my temperature?"

"That's the worst pickup line I've ever heard."

"Stick around, I've got more."

Clay grinned and drew back, reaching for a Band-Aid. "Come on, now. This is serious medical business. Hold still."

He held her wrist again as he dabbed a bit of ointment onto the injured finger. Reaching for a Band-Aid, he fumbled with the wrapper before securing it in place. He planted a kiss on the tip of her finger and smiled at her again.

"All better?"

"Almost," she whispered as he bent to kiss her.

Clay's hands slid up under her flannel shirt, finding her breasts through the thin fabric of the T-shirt she wore beneath. Reese gasped as his thumbs circled her nipples, her throbbing finger all but forgotten.

She felt the slightest prick of guilt for feeling so good right now with everything going to hell back at the vineyard, but she promptly pushed the thought from her mind.

I deserve to feel good, just for a minute.

She kissed him harder and pressed her fingers into his back, feeling the firm flex of muscle through his shirt.

The humid chill of the room settled over them, with the faint smell of damp soil and old grapes. Reese breathed it in, savoring the sawdust smell of Clay, too. His hands were hot and eager as they slid under her T-shirt and Reese moved against them, loving the deftness of his fingers against her bare skin. He slid his palms up, and Reese went dizzy as he stroked her breasts through the thin lace of her bra.

She tightened her legs around him, pinning him against her. His hardness strained against the fly of his jeans.

"God, Reese," he murmured against her throat. "You feel so good."

"Don't stop."

"Never."

His mouth traveled over the warm flesh of her throat, and Reese went dizzy as she tilted her head back to give him better access. Her eyes focused for a split second on the wedding photo of Sheila and Eric atop a file cabinet, and Reese wondered if Clay had noticed.

"Hello?"

Somewhere in the barn, a door creaked. They jerked apart like they'd been doused by cold water. Clay's watch caught on Reese's shirt, and he fought like a trapped animal to free it.

"Hello?" the voice called again.

Clay moved away from her, his hand free, his face frozen in terror. *Eric?* he mouthed.

Reese shook her head and jumped off the counter, tugging her shirt down as she moved toward the door.

"Dad? Hey, we're back here."

She stepped into the open area of the barn, daring a glance over her shoulder at Clay. He wasn't looking at her. His eyes were fixed on the wedding photo, a guilty look shadowing his face.

Reese grabbed his hand and jerked him forward just as her dad rounded the corner.

"Hey, honey," he called. "I finished with the insurance guy, and Eric said you might need help out here. What'd you do to your finger?"

Reese held up the bandaged digit and shrugged. "Just a little cut, it's no big deal. Clay got me fixed up."

Her dad smiled at Clay, his expression suggesting he knew damn well they'd been doing more than playing doctor. "Good job, son."

"Sir," Clay said stiffly. "We've got most of the bottles loaded, but there are a few more boxes on those pallets over there."

"Let's get to them, then."

Reese watched as the two of them retreated to the other side of the barn. She flicked the light off in the office, not taking her eyes off the pair as they chatted about bicycle tours and the new brewery opening in Newberg. Clay's cheeks were still flushed, but he seemed to have regained his composure.

As if sensing her eyes on him, Clay looked up and caught her eye. She smiled.

He smiled back and winked at her, then bent to grab the next box.

◆　◆　◆

Clay drove the truck back to the vineyard, conscious of Reese warm and round and beautiful in the cab beside him. God, he'd almost lost his mind back there in that office. What was it about her that made him so crazy, so thirsty for her? It was a little like being a drunk, but without the hangover.

"So tell me about your recovery," Reese said, and Clay wondered for a moment if she'd read his mind. He glanced over at her, surprised to see her biting her lip. Was she nervous? "It's okay," she said quickly. "You don't have to talk about it if you don't want to, but I just thought—"

"No, it's great," he said, and gave her a reassuring smile. "I want to talk about it. I'll tell you anything you want to know."

"You've mentioned the steps, but I don't know that much about them. Can you tell me more?"

"Sure. Examining past behaviors and trying to figure out how you got there is one of the big ones," Clay said. He kept his grip loose on the steering wheel, relieved to feel like he could talk to her about his. That he didn't have to pretend it never happened.

"And what did you figure out?"

"I wasn't such a great guy when I was drinking," he said. "I did some pretty dumb things."

"Like what?"

"There was the time I stole that scooter from the old folks' home and challenged Axl to a race."

"You would have won if he hadn't cheated."

"Or the time I got on the PA system at the school library and told everyone there was a faculty orgy happening in the rec hall."

"Half the students believed you."

"Or the time I forgot to wear pants when I went out to buy Cheetos."

"I think Eric still has that video somewhere."

Clay grimaced, wishing she hadn't been a witness to so many of his worst moments. He took a shaky breath, wondering if he should apologize again. He was still deciding when she asked her next question.

"So what made you an alcoholic? I mean—how does it happen, exactly?"

"Well, genetics are a factor," he said. "My grandpa was an alcoholic, and so was my dad."

"That's right, I remember," she said softly. "It seemed like things got worse for you after he died."

"They did, I guess. That's not an excuse, but it was definitely a trigger."

He glanced at her in the mirror again, expecting to see pity in her eyes. Instead, he saw a mix of curiosity and determination that made his heart feel like it might burst. "So what's left?" she asked. "Are there still more steps left?"

He nodded. "Learning to live a new life with a new code of behavior," he said. "I'm working on that one now."

"You're doing a good job."

It was the simplest nugget of praise, but his whole body surged with pride. "Thanks. I'm trying."

She reached over and put her hand on his knee, and the warmth in his belly grew. "Let me know if there's anything I can do to help."

"Thank you. I will."

"And thank *you* for your help just now—with the bottles, I mean. I don't know what I would have done without you."

"My pleasure."

They rode in silence for a moment, but it didn't feel as awkward as it had earlier in the day. He wanted to reach over and brush his fingers over her cheek, but wasn't sure about the rules in this relationship. Everything was so new.

Finally, he cleared his throat. "Look. I want you to know last night was special. I don't do that sort of thing all the time. I mean—maybe I had a reputation in college, and obviously I did some dumb stuff when I was drinking and slept around more than I should have, but since I got sober—"

She turned and smiled at him. "Not so much?"

"Not at all." Clay downshifted as they turned onto the gravel driveway, then glanced over to watch her face. "Not since rehab, anyway."

Reese's eyes widened. "Really?"

"Really."

"Huh," Reese said, grinning up at him with those green eyes flashing. "In that case, I've gotta say that while you were pretty terrific in bed when you were drunk, you're phenomenal now that you're sober."

A faint roar began to surge in Clay's ears, and it wasn't just the sound of gravel under the tires. He felt himself growing dizzy, regretted the words even before they left his mouth.

"What do you mean?"

He glanced at Reese in time to see her eyebrow quirk. "I mean that night fifteen years ago—" She stopped, her eyes fixed on his face. On what Clay knew was a very blank expression.

She frowned. "Are you kidding?"

Clay brought the truck to a halt in front of the winery barn and turned to face her. "I'm sorry, I didn't—I don't understand."

Reese's eyes narrowed. "I'm talking about the time we slept together in college." The words were slow, clipped.

Clay stared at her. He watched her face for a few seconds, trying to buy himself some time to find the right words. Maybe he could just pretend he knew what the hell she was talking about—

"You don't know what the hell I'm talking about, do you?" Reese demanded.

For a second, Clay considered lying. *Of course I remember. It was amazing.* You *were amazing.*

But hell, what if she was teasing him? What if this was all some kind of bizarre joke?

Stick with honesty, his old sponsor used to say. *Hurts sometimes, but it's easier to remember later.*

"Um," said Clay. "No. No, I don't. There are so many blank spots in those years I was a drunk and—"

"So what did you mean the other night?" Reese snapped, folding her arms over her chest as the truck engine ticked nervously. "You didn't drink when we played '*I Never*'—when there was that whole thing about not sleeping with anyone in the room? I guess that makes sense now that I think of it—but the next day when I asked you, you said it seemed like the respectful thing to do. To pretend nothing happened. Isn't that what you said?"

Clay closed his eyes and nodded, not liking where this was headed. "Yes."

"So what the hell were you talking about?"

Clay gritted his teeth, knowing there was no possible right answer here. There was no way this was going to be okay, no matter what he said next.

The truth. Just tell the truth. Own your mistakes.

"Larissa," he said. "I was talking about Larissa."

CHAPTER FOURTEEN

Reese stared at Clay, his words echoing in her ears.

Larissa. I was talking about Larissa.

She swallowed hard and stared at him. "You fucked my cousin."

Clay winced like he'd been slapped. "It was eight or nine years ago at a Halloween party. I was stupid and drunk and possibly dressed in a bear costume and a tutu—"

"You were drunk with me, too. The first time, I mean."

Clay closed his eyes, looking pained. Reese would have felt sorry for him if she weren't so damn mad. Mad and confused. She clenched her hands into fists, wishing she had something to grip.

Or to throw at his head.

"Let me get this straight," she said, struggling to keep her voice even. "You have no recollection of drunkenly sleeping with me fifteen years ago, but you remember boning my cousin under the same circumstances?"

Clay winced and shook his head. "I thought maybe I kissed you once—that party over in McMinnville? But I—"

"Don't recall fucking me?"

Clay cringed again, then let out a slow, shaky breath. "Please don't call it that."

"What should I call it then? Burping the worm? Batter-dipping the corndog? Riding the baloney pony? Putting the candle in the pumpkin? What is the correct term when one of the participants can't even remember taking part in it?"

She hated the sound of her own voice, the shrill echo of it in the tiny, damp cab of the truck. But she was too damn hurt to figure out how else to speak.

"Reese, I'm sorry," Clay said.

He reached for her, but Reese yanked her arm away, too stung for comfort now.

Clay drew his hand back. "I'm so sorry. I can't explain which things I remember and which things I don't. There are big chunks of my memory just blacked out. Things I did, things I said—important things. Things I can't remember at all because I was too drunk—"

"It doesn't matter," she snapped. She tried to meet his eyes but found she couldn't do it. She looked at the side of the winery barn instead, hoping like hell she wouldn't cry. Then she wanted to cry anyway, looking at the charred mess of wood and spilled wine. "It doesn't matter at all, Clay. It really doesn't."

"It does matter," Clay said, and reached out to touch her arm. Reese pulled away.

"Look," she said, "what happened last night shouldn't have happened."

Clay shook his head. "I disagree."

She ignored him. "And what happened fifteen years ago *really* shouldn't have happened. I never should have brought it up."

"Reese, I wish I could remember—"

"Don't," she said, meeting his eyes at last. She blinked hard against the glare of sun-streaked raindrops on the windshield and something she hoped wasn't the beginning of tears. "Just don't, okay? This is awkward enough."

Clay sighed, then looked down at his boots. "Does Eric know?"

Reese bit her lip, wondering if that was really what he cared about. "About last night or fifteen years ago?"

"Either."

"No. Your secret is safe. Hell, it was safe from you until I shot off my mouth, wasn't it?"

She couldn't believe how stupid she felt. *Jesus.* She'd thought it had meant something. It sure as hell had meant something to her. She swallowed hard, trying to force the ridiculous lump back down her throat.

"I'm sorry," Clay whispered.

"Stop apologizing!" Reese snapped. "Just stop. I need to get to work. It's not a big deal, Clay. Just forget about it, okay?"

"Reese, I—"

"I mean it, Clay. I don't want to talk about it. It was just a misunderstanding. A mistake."

"A mistake," he repeated.

"A big, stupid mistake. Both times."

She flung open the door of the truck before he could respond, oddly grateful for the giant hole in the wall of the winery barn. It meant she could walk right though the side of the building and straight to her office without fumbling at doors or feeling his eyes on her as she tried to keep her shoulders from shaking.

◆　◆　◆

Clay sat there in the truck for a few minutes, feeling like he'd just been punched in the gut by a drunken gorilla.

Should he go after her? Try to say something to make it right?

There's not a damn thing you can say to make it right.

He opened the door and stepped out into the damp dirt. He stared out over the vineyard for a moment, watching a bird flit between the wooden posts at the end of each row of grapes. Off in the distance, he heard the field hands shouting to each other in Spanish as they pruned the rows of plants.

He slammed the door of his truck. *Dammit.*

He'd screwed that one up big time. Why hadn't he figured it out earlier? Surely Reese had dropped clues, given him some hint something had happened between them in the past. It's not like this was the first time he'd been confronted with a story that began "remember when?"

and ended with him staring blankly at the storyteller, having no recollection of the events.

But it was the first time it had mattered. The first time he desperately, urgently wished he could remember.

He'd been telling the truth about the kiss. He thought he'd remembered something like that, but he'd never been sure. It had always seemed safest just to forget about it, to be thankful he'd never acted on his fondness for his buddy's wife.

She wasn't his wife then, the voice told him. *You could've done something about it then instead of pining away for her all these years. You could've had a chance.*

Not anymore. Any chance he'd had was out the window. Then and now, his fault both times.

But you've changed since then, the voice said.

Doesn't matter. Not now, not to Reese.

God, he wished he could remember. Last night had been amazing, no doubt about it.

But what he wouldn't give to remember the first time. The smell of her hair, the scrape of her nails down his back, the throaty murmur of her voice against his ear for the first time.

You can never get that back.

"Dude, you just gonna stand there with your thumb up your ass?"

He turned to see Eric approaching from the other side of the barn.

"Just enjoying the view," he offered weakly.

"Whatever. Your crew isn't here yet, and I need a hand. Help me move some of the cases out of the way so I can get the damn forklift up to the barrels."

Clay turned and followed him into the winery barn, grateful at least that his best friend was a guy, and therefore not inclined to ask questions about his buddy's sullen demeanor. Clay dared a glance at Reese's office as they trudged past, but the door was shut tight and he couldn't see inside.

"You do something to piss her off?" Eric asked.

Clay pulled his eyes off the door and looked at Eric. "Why?"

"She came stomping in here like someone spit in her Pinot. Figured you might've given her more bad news about the construction project."

Clay shook his head and dared one last glance at the door. "Nope. No bad news on the construction. The ball's in her court right now."

"You said *balls*."

Clay looked at him. "It's nice how you've matured in your old age."

"Maturity is overrated. So is politeness. You can still make dirty jokes, too, you know."

Clay shrugged and eyed the pile of boxes stacked against one wall. "Sure."

"What is it with you, anyway? You've been prancing around here like Miss Manners since you got back to town. *Please* this and *thank you* that and God help me if I ever fart or belch or have a dirty thought I happen to say out loud."

"Whatever, man. I just don't want to be a jerk anymore."

Eric frowned at him and shoved an empty barrel out of the way. "It's just us here now. The only way I'll think you're a jerk is if you tell me my Gewürztraminer sucks. Since you won't be tasting that, I think we're safe. Grab a box."

"Right." Clay moved toward the towering stack of wine cases lined up against one wall. He hefted one up and looked at Eric. "Where do you want it?"

"Over there against the wall. We just need to make room for the forklift."

Clay nodded and trudged across the concrete floor to the spot Eric had indicated. He set the box down and turned around, headed back for another. They worked like that for a few minutes, silent except for one colorful string of expletives from Eric when he scraped his knuckles on the concrete.

Clay's brain began to wander back down the dark alley toward thoughts of Reese and last night and that long-ago night he couldn't remember. Had her hair been different then? He was pretty sure she'd kept it the same. Long, with a little bit of curl at the ends. Had she trailed it over his chest that first time the way she had last night? He shivered a little at the thought, remembering how she'd smiled down at him as she teased his skin with the soft, grass-scented strands, drawing her fingers down his rib cage, along his stomach, over his—

"Way to go last night, by the way," Eric grunted as they both stooped to lift a box.

Clay froze. "What?"

"You were kind of a stud, huh?"

Clay stared at him, speechless. Had Larissa said something? Had Reese? "Um—"

"The fire?" Eric raised an eyebrow. "I heard you were the one who helped put it out, the one who called the fire department. Isn't that right?"

"Oh. Right." Clay swallowed, feeling his heartbeat return to normal. "It was nothing, really. I just happened to be driving by."

"Yeah, that's what I heard." Eric cleared his throat and hoisted his box. "So you just happened to be driving by at one a.m.?"

Clay picked up a box and avoided Eric's eyes. "Dropping off Larissa. She got into some trouble with a guy at Finnigan's. I happened to be there and helped her out."

"Sure, sure—that's what 'Riss said. Must've been pretty late?"

Clay shrugged and carried his box across the floor toward the pile. Did Eric know something, or was he just being his usual nosy self? "Beats me," Clay said. "Took us a while to finish things at the police station, and then I had to go get my truck so I could drive 'Riss back here. We were trying to give Reese a little alone time with her date, you know?"

"That's right—I almost forgot Reese had a date. Did you meet him?"

"Yeah, met him the other day. He's a veterinarian. Seems like a good guy."

"That's what Reese deserves. A good guy."

Clay set his box down, trying not to read too much into Eric's words. *A good guy,* Clay thought. *That's not me.*

"Absolutely," Clay agreed. "Nothing but the best."

"She looked good this morning," Eric said. "I mean, considering everything with the fire and the drama with Larissa. She seemed kind of glowy."

"Maybe she's getting sick," Clay suggested. He dusted his hands and trudged back across the floor toward the boxes. Behind him, Eric set his box down with a solid *thunk.*

"Maybe she got laid."

Clay stumbled. He caught himself quickly, glad he'd already set his box down. "Dude—are you sure you should be talking about your ex-wife's sex life?"

Eric just laughed. "Relax, I'm kidding. Mostly. She did have a certain look about her this morning, didn't you think?"

"I have no idea."

"Not that she's the sort of girl to jump into bed with a guy she hardly knows, but good for her if she did. She deserves to cut loose once in a while."

"Right." Clay bent down to pick up another box, still avoiding Eric's eyes. "Don't you think this is a weird topic of conversation?"

"Spend enough time around this family, you get used to weird in a hurry."

"Good point."

Eric grinned. "So maybe this guy is the one. Someone who can pull her out of her rut, shake her up a little, put some spring in her step."

"Maybe so."

"She deserves it."

"Absolutely."

"Don't fuck it up."

Clay froze, the box of wine suddenly deadweight in his arms. "What's that supposed to mean?"

"It means I've seen how you look at her. How you've *always* looked at her. And the way she looks at you. I know, I know—" He held up his hands to silence the objection Clay was too dumbfounded to raise anyway. "I know you're not planning to lay a hand on her. I know there's the whole guy code and all that shit about her being my ex-wife and you not wanting to screw up the friendship. But I also know how things can happen."

"Nothing's going to—"

"You two would be the worst thing in the world for each other." Eric picked up another box, his eyes still fixed on Clay's. "She's got all these hang-ups about marriage and her parents, and you've got your issues with addiction and recovery. Seriously, you'd be a disaster together."

Clay stared at Eric for a few seconds, then nodded. "I'm touched by your concern."

"Yeah. Well, just forget about any touching and you'll be fine."

Clay turned his back and headed toward the far wall with his box of wine. "I can pretty much guarantee there won't be any touching between Reese and me."

Not now, anyway, Clay thought. *Not after today.*

"Good. That's good."

It wasn't. Not in Clay's opinion.

But he politely refrained from saying so.

◆ ◆ ◆

Reese's mood was as gray as the Willamette Valley sky on the car ride back from the meeting with the bank. With her mother behind the wheel, Reese's mind could drift like an untethered buoy.

June sighed. "That didn't go as well as I'd hoped."

Reese looked at her mother. "They might as well have locked the front doors when they saw us coming."

"It wasn't that bad."

"Not that bad? The bank manager laughed at us. *Hard.* Did you miss the part where he choked on his danish?"

June frowned and steered the car back toward Dundee. "We'll come up with something, sweetie. Just because this bank won't loan us more money for the construction doesn't mean—"

"You heard what he said. No bank is going to loan us money with a fire under investigation and a budget so rubbery it could work as a prophylactic."

"That reminds me, Axl asked us to stop at the drugstore for a box of those ribbed condoms."

"Can it wait? I'd really like to get back and start crunching some numbers."

June nodded and kept the car pointed forward. "Maybe we could scale back on some aspects of the construction. We just got started, so we could go for smaller square footage or do away with some of the custom woodwork or—"

"That costs money, too. We'd have to have new plans drawn up, new blueprints, new permits—not to mention the fact that *Wine Spectator* just ran that article with the sketches that show our current plans."

"Right, right."

Reese closed her eyes and slouched lower in her seat. "We've made the whole damn thing so public."

June sighed again. "Let's just sleep on it, honey. Maybe something will come to us."

"Sleep. That sounds nice. I didn't get much last night."

"Right, the fire."

"The fire, the drama with Larissa—" Reese trailed off, feeling the heat creep into her cheeks. There was more than one reason for her sleepless night. One of those reasons had made her mindless with his hands stroking her hips, his mouth on her breasts, his body pressing against her, hot and hard and—

"Something on your mind, sweetie?" her mom asked.

Reese opened her eyes and bit her lip. "Just thinking about Larissa."

Which was true, in a way. Is that what Clay had been thinking about last night? In bed with Reese, had Clay been comparing her to her cousin? Remembering his night with Larissa?

"You think 'Riss is in trouble?" her mother asked. "She does go out a lot. I don't remember you being like that at her age."

"I wasn't," Reese said. "I don't know if she's in trouble, honestly. She's always been wild, but I thought she might have settled down by now."

"Maybe Clay could talk to her," June suggested. "He's been down that road, after all. The binge drinking, the irresponsible behavior. Maybe it would help Larissa to talk with someone who's learned the hard lessons."

"Hard lessons," Reese muttered, her mind wheeling down a dangerous path. "I'm sure Clay would be happy to talk to Larissa about hard lessons."

June glanced over with a worried look, and Reese realized her voice had taken on a dark tone. She softened it and tried again. "I'll mention it to him the next time I see him."

June nodded and glued her eyes back to the road. "How did your date with the veterinarian go last night?"

"Okay, I guess."

"He's a nice man?"

Reese shrugged. "He's very nice. Held the door for me, laughed at my jokes, helped subdue Grandpa's jealous girlfriend, and picked up my drunk cousin at the police station. Typical first-date stuff."

June smiled. "How about fireworks? Chemistry? That wonderful spark between two people who are just made for each other?"

"I don't even know what that means."

Yes, you do, chided the voice in her head.

Shut up.

"What's that, dear?" June asked.

Reese bit her lip. "Nothing."

They were both quiet a moment, the sound of wet pavement slosh-ing beneath the tires. Reese stared past the trees and rolling green hills and tried not to think about Clay.

She'd really thought there might be something there, which was stupid. He was the worst possible match for her. A recovering alcoholic who was best friends with her ex and fuck buddies with her cousin?

But still, she'd felt something between them. She always had. Some-thing that hadn't been there with Eric, or with any other man she'd dated in the last decade.

Her parents talked about being soul mates. It was a stupid con-cept, one Reese refused to believe in. Relationships were about hard work and solid friendship and the ability to be patient with the other person's shortcomings, and even then, there were no guarantees. There was no magical formula, no woo-woo chemistry that kept two people together. Some people just had the ability to make relationships work, and some people didn't.

Reese sure as hell didn't. It was as simple as that.

Still. Maybe she was missing something. Wouldn't be the first time. She glanced over at her mother, then down at her mom's wedding ring.

I call dibs . . .

"Mom?"

"Yes, sweetie?"

Reese turned and looked out the window, not sure what the hell she wanted to ask. *Am I doomed to fail at love? Can people ever really change? Can you screw up love the first time and still get it right someday?*

She cleared her throat. "Do you have any Popsicles at the house?"

June stayed quiet, so quiet Reese turned to look at her. Her mother's eyes watched the road, but she wore a peculiar expression as she stared straight ahead at the rain-slick road.

"Popsicles?" June asked. "That's what you want?"

Reese nodded, hating that she was too chicken to ask for advice or wisdom or anything more substantive than comfort food.

"Or cookies or donuts. I can pick some up at the store later," Reese said. "I just thought—"

"No, I think I have some. Want to come down to the house now and sit on the porch and talk for a little bit?"

Reese hesitated. "I'd better finish up some things in the office."

"I'll drop you at the winery barn, then."

"Thanks for driving."

"No problem, honey."

June wheeled the car into the circular drive, her tires spitting up bits of gravel. She turned and smiled at Reese. "You sure there's nothing you want to talk about, sweetie?"

Reese gripped the door handle and nodded. "Thanks, I'm good."

"You want to come over for dinner later?"

Reese shook her head. "I may stop by for a snack, but I'm pretty beat. Thanks for the offer. I'll probably just turn in early."

"You did great in there today."

Reese laughed and popped the door open. "For all the good it did. Thanks, you weren't so bad yourself."

"We'll figure something out, honey. Try not to worry."

Reese eased herself out of the car and patted the roof. "Love you, Mom."

"Love you, too, sweetie."

Reese shut the door and watched as her mom cranked the car around and headed the few hundred yards down the hill to their house. With a sigh, Reese turned and trudged into the winery. She forced herself not to look over at the construction site, though she could see from the corner of her eye that the heavy equipment was parked and the crews had gone home for the day. No sign of Clay, not that she was looking for him. She didn't know whether to be sad or relieved that he'd left.

She pushed her way through the winery door, breathing in the comforting scent of fermenting grapes and French oak. She glanced around the cavernous space, noticing the racks of wine barrels missing from the west side of the building. Eric and his crew had been busy moving everything down to the other cellar.

She looked over at the coat rack, at the empty, upturned barrel where Eric usually left his lunch pail. The coat and the lunch box were gone, and Reese felt relieved. She had the place to herself.

She threw open her office door and felt a sinking in the pit of her gut. "Reese. I've been waiting for you."

CHAPTER FIFTEEN

Reese offered a weak smile as she took in the view of Larissa parked in her desk chair. She wore a short skirt that showed off her legs and sent an inexplicable surge of fury through Reese. She hated herself for imagining those legs wrapped around Clay's waist, and hated herself even more for caring.

But Larissa smiled, and Reese couldn't bring herself to hate her cousin. Truth be told, she was actually the most welcome sight among her visitors.

"Axl, Sheila, Larissa," Reese said, her voice tinny with false cheer. "What are you guys doing here?"

"We wanted to hear how things went with the bank," Larissa said. "Did you get the money?"

Reese sighed and shook her head. "Long story. The short answer is no."

"Motherfucker," Axl spat.

"Pretty much," Reese agreed and leaned against the wall. "Look, I'd love to stay and talk, but I've got to go feed all the animals."

"I fed them all an hour ago—even that little opossum—so you could stay and talk," Larissa said. "Come on, we need details."

"Thank you." Reese sighed. "Do we have a bottle of Pinot open?"

Larissa stood up and headed for the wine bar. "Nothing open, but let me grab a bottle from the '09 Emerald block. We've got a lot of that left."

As Larissa scurried from the room, Sheila gave Reese a sympathetic smile. "I dropped by to pick Eric up, but he's still finishing up down at the other cellar. Larissa told me you were with the bank people, so I thought I'd stick around and offer moral support."

"Thanks," Reese said. "I suppose I need it."

"So no luck with the bank fucks?" Axl asked.

"No fuck with the—" Reese closed her eyes. "No luck with the bank fucks."

Sheila shook her head. "A friend of mine manages a credit union over in McMinnville. If you want, I could try talking to her, see if there's anything they can do."

"Thanks, but I don't think there's much use," Reese said. "Word got around fast about the fire, and we're already mortgaged to the hilt. I don't think bank loans are the answer."

"Larissa always goes to those sales pitches with those little-bitty skirts and low-cut blouses," Axl said. "Seems to work with the wine reps. Maybe we should send her in to talk to investors or bankers or something?"

"Sure," Larissa chirped, breezing back into the room with a bottle of Pinot under one arm and the stems of four wineglasses wedged between her fingers. "I'm always happy to show a little skin for the sake of the business. Who am I flashing?"

"No one!" Reese snapped. "We don't need you flashing anyone." Wincing at the waspishness in her voice, she softened it and tried again. "I don't think cleavage is the answer here."

"Depends on the question," Larissa said as she held out the wineglasses for Sheila to take. "Anyone know where all the corkscrews are? I can't find a single one."

"They're not in the drawer?"

"Nope. The drawer is empty."

Reese sighed. "What the hell kind of winery can't open a bottle of wine?"

"Gimme that," Axl said, snatching the bottle from Reese. "I'll just shove it in."

"A phrase no granddaughter ever wants to hear from her grandpa," Reese muttered.

"You're lucky I've got my hands full or I'd smack you upside the head right now," Axl said as he used his teeth to peel the foil off the top of the bottle before shoving the cork in with his thumb. Wine splashed down the neck and bits of cork floated inside, but it got the job done.

"There," Axl said, thunking the bottle on the desk. "All done. Someone pour."

Sheila lined up the glasses and took the bottle from Axl. "So what's your next course of action?" she asked. "If sex appeal isn't the answer, what is?"

Axl snatched a glass. "You want I should rough somebody up?"

"No," Reese said. "No violence, no cleavage."

"You're really not leaving us a lot of options, hon," Sheila said. "I guess there's always bribery or bank robbery."

"I'm in," Axl volunteered.

"No illegal activity," Reese interrupted. "We'll come up with something, but I don't think we're on the right track here."

Larissa shook her head and began pouring wine into the glasses. "How about your new boyfriend, Reese? He's loaded, isn't he? Maybe he'll loan us the money."

Reese froze. "Boyfriend?"

Larissa grinned, not meeting Reese's eye as she began to pour the wine. "The veterinarian? Aren't you two dating?"

"Right," Reese said, regrouping. "I hardly think one date that involved picking my cousin up at the police station is grounds for requesting a six-figure loan."

Axl shrugged. "Maybe if Larissa showed him a little leg—"

"Enough with the sexy talk about Larissa!" The second the words were out of her mouth, Reese regretted them.

Everyone was looking at her oddly, so Reese took a shaky breath and tried again. "I'm sorry, 'Riss. I didn't mean it like that."

"No, you're right." Larissa squeezed her hand. "Now's not the time to joke about it."

"I just don't know what the hell to do," Reese said, letting her head fall into her hands. "We can't get a loan, our construction project is screwed, our wine club hates us, the media is starting to figure out we're hacks, and our winery barn has a giant fucking hole in it."

"Maybe it's a sign, hon," Sheila said, touching her arm. "Maybe you've taken on too much."

Reese shook her head, but couldn't think of a snappy retort. She was just too damn tired. Sheila patted her hand and took a sip of wine. "Let's talk about something else. I want to hear about the boyfriend! Eric said you were seeing someone, Reese, but I didn't know it was serious."

"It's not serious," Reese said. "I've seen him exactly two times. The first time he stuck a thermometer up Leon's ass, and the second he took me to the police station to get my drunk cousin."

Larissa grinned. "Romantic."

"So you're bonding," Sheila said brightly.

Axl looked up from his wine. "Bondage?"

Reese sighed and stuck her nose in her Pinot glass. "I don't know where things are headed. It's complicated. And it's early. Let's talk about wine instead."

Sheila rolled her eyes. "Why would we talk about anything else?"

Reese shrugged. "You're in a winery. You married the winemaker. Our topics for conversation are a bit limited. Does Eric think we can save most of the stuff that was in the barn when the fire started?"

Larissa nodded. "The Sauvignon Blanc wasn't as bad as he thought but still not worth putting our label on. We can maybe wholesale it."

"For less money," Reese muttered.

"Not as bad as it could've been," Larissa pointed out. "We got lucky."

Axl grinned at Reese, but she cut him off before he could make a crack about getting lucky. "That reminds me, Axl, I saw your girlfriend at the First Friday Art Walk last night. Francie? She seems to be under the impression that you're in the hospital."

"Aw, fuck. What'd you tell her?"

"That my grandpa is a skanky man-whore. Not something every granddaughter gets the chance to say."

"Beats sitting around a nursing home playing pinochle," Larissa said. "Who's the other woman?"

Axl grinned, unperturbed by the insult or the prospect of having to make excuses with his girlfriend. "A stripper I met at Stars the other night. She gave me a free lap dance and I told her about my Harley."

Reese took another sip of wine. "That's a sweet story, Axl. Remind me to save it for the grandkids."

"Mmmph," Axl said. He sipped his own wine for a moment, eyeing Reese over the rim of the glass. "You're really shook up about this loan thing, aren't you?"

Reese looked up at the ceiling. "I've put everything we've got into this construction project," she said. "If we can't get the money, it's not just a matter of losing ground on the construction. It's not even about our reputation with the wine club and the rest of the public. Do you know how many special events we've got on the books for the pavilion?"

Larissa bit her lip. "Now's probably not the time to tell you we had another wedding party cancel this morning."

Reese closed her eyes, but all she saw were dollar signs swimming over the backs of her eyelids. "It's like we're taking handfuls of hundred dollar bills and flushing them down the toilet. We can't host any of the things we've booked if we don't have the pavilion done."

Axl nodded. He started to lift his wineglass, then stopped. "Let me see if I can come up with a plan, Peanut Butter Cup."

"Axl," Reese said, shaking her head. "I don't want anything illegal tied to the vineyard. Really, we can just—"

"It's not illegal!" Axl insisted. "Not much, anyway."

"Illegal?" Sheila asked. "What are we talking about here?"

"Long story," Reese said. "Suffice it to say, Axl is either growing perfectly legal medical marijuana or perfectly illegal street-worthy weed."

"Recreational pot is legal in Oregon!" Axl insisted.

"Not in quantities large enough to bail like hay," Reese retorted.

"Where?" Sheila asked, mystified. "Not here?"

Reese sighed. "Out in the pole barn. Axl says it's all on the up-and-up. The jury's still out on that. I just don't want things to get out of hand."

"Because things never get out of hand in this family," Larissa added.

Reese rolled her eyes and looked at Sheila. "We're trying to keep it kind of quiet."

"Mum's the word," Sheila said. "My aunt had cancer a few years ago. She was living in Idaho, so of course medical marijuana isn't legal there. She ended up having to get my teenage nephew to hook her up when the pain got really bad."

"See, Reese?" Larissa said. "It's a charitable thing. Axl is just acting out of the kindness of his heart."

Reese glanced over at Axl, who had taken out a switchblade and was using it to trim his fingernails. He sliced off one nail, which went flying and landed in Sheila's wineglass.

Reese shook her head and reached for the bottle. "That's Axl," she said. "A regular Pope Francis."

◆ ◆. ◆

Clay was at the carwash cleaning vineyard mud off the floor mats of his truck when he found the shoe under his seat.

He held it up, examining it. An impossibly high stiletto with silver sequins across the toes.

"Larissa," he muttered.

The old guy parked beside him frowned under the brim of a filthy baseball cap. "You one of those fellas who likes dressing up in lady clothes?"

Clay dropped the shoe on his seat. "No, sir."

"Because there's a bunch of us that get together every Friday night over in McMinnville. You look like you'd be about a size twelve, right?"

"Um—"

"Gary's been looking for someone to trade with."

"Right," Clay said, clearing his throat. "Thank you for the invite, but I'm okay. Have a nice evening."

Clay shoved his floor mats back into place and got into the truck. He sat there for a minute studying the shoe. Larissa must have dropped it last night when he'd driven her home. He had no idea where she lived now, but he knew where Reese lived.

Don't be an idiot, he told himself. *She doesn't want to see you right now. Especially not with her cousin's shoe.*

But he already had the truck in gear, pointed back toward the vineyard. He second-guessed himself the whole way there, but he didn't turn around.

Not even when he spotted the blue Subaru in the driveway. He tried to remember if it looked familiar, but there had been so many of them cycling through for wine tastings the last few days. All cars were starting to look the same.

He killed the engine, picked up the shoe, and got out of the truck. Before he could even knock, Reese opened the door.

Her face was flushed, and she studied him with mild alarm.

"Clay," she said.

He looked at her and lost his breath. She was wearing some sort of thin, sleeveless top and stretchy pants that were either for sleeping or exercising. Her feet were bare, and he was pretty sure she wasn't wearing a bra.

Before he could even kick himself for ogling her, a male voice called out behind her.

"Everything okay, Reese?"

Reese opened her mouth to speak as Dr. Wally approached and rested a hand on her shoulder. He smiled at Clay. "Hey, there. Good to see you again."

It wasn't good to see Dr. Wally. Not at all, especially not at Reese's house, but Clay didn't say so. Instead, he nodded at them both.

"Good evening."

Reese bit her lip and glanced at Wally, then back at Clay. The message was clear. Now wasn't the time to mention what had happened last night.

"What brings you here, Clay?" she asked.

He held up the shoe. "I brought this," he said lamely.

Dr. Wally gave a good-natured laugh. "I think you've got the wrong house. Cinderella lives two blocks that way."

Reese offered a stiff smile and reached out to take the shoe. "That's Larissa's."

"I know."

She met his eyes then, and Clay tried to absorb what he saw there. Hurt? Jealousy? Anger? Lust for the guy standing beside her? He honestly couldn't tell.

He cleared his throat. "Sorry to interrupt, but I happened to be passing by and thought 'Riss might need that."

"It's okay. Dr. Wally just stopped to check on me. The news did a big broadcast about the fire and he was worried."

Clay looked at Wally, trying not to notice the guy's hand on Reese's shoulder or think about how pleasant it would be to rip it off at the wrist, throw it in the gravel, and back over it with his truck. "What are they saying about the fire?"

"They made it sound pretty bad," Wally said, giving Reese's shoulder a squeeze. "They mentioned someone was injured, and I wanted to come out and be sure Reese was okay."

Clay caught sight of a vase of daisies on the coffee table behind them and felt something twist in his chest.

Wally brought her flowers. You brought her another woman's shoe.

He cleared his throat to speak but couldn't think of anything to say. Reese bit her lip again and glanced at Dr. Wally.

"It was actually Clay who got hurt," she said. "He helped put out the fire before the fire crews got here."

"That so?" Dr. Wally asked. "Lucky he happened to be here, then."

Clay looked at him, trying to assess his tone. It seemed bland enough, but something in his eyes suggested suspicion.

"Right," Clay said. "Well, I should be going."

"I'll walk you to your truck," Reese said.

Clay looked at her. "You're barefoot. And I'm pretty sure I can find my way ten feet back to the truck."

She glared at him, stuffed her feet into a pair of rubber boots beside the door, and turned to Dr. Wally. "Will you excuse me for just a moment? Family business."

Without waiting for a response, she shut the door behind her and stepped out into the drizzle. Clay looked at her bare arms. "You need a coat."

He didn't wait for her to argue. He pulled off his coat and settled it around her shoulders.

She rolled her eyes. "Now *you* need a coat."

"I have long sleeves. You don't."

She pressed her lips together, ready to disagree. Then stopped. "Thank you."

"You're welcome."

"I suppose you already heard how things went with the bank."

Clay shook his head. "I left before you got back. We've run out of prep work we can do without knowing how you want to proceed with construction."

Reese gave a thin little laugh and hugged her arms around herself. "How I *want* to proceed is not the same thing as how we're going to be able to proceed. The bank turned us down."

The words stung like salt in a paper cut. "Reese—I'm so sorry."

"Me, too. Not what I needed to hear today, on top of everything else."

"Everything else," Clay repeated. "I'm sorry about that, too."

"You've been saying that a lot lately."

"I mean it."

She shook her head. "I know. It's just—I just can't do this, Clay. Not again. Not after so many years of disappointment and hurt and complications with you and—"

She looked down at her rubber boots, not meeting his eyes. Her hair was getting wet and Clay wanted to reach up and brush the damp strands from her eyes. He wanted to crush her against his chest and just hold her. He wanted to throw her in his truck and drive away someplace he could make love to her over and over until they both dropped from fatigue. He wanted to storm inside and tell the goddamn veterinarian to stay away from her—that she was *his*.

But she wasn't.

And he didn't do any of those things.

He lifted a hand to touch her, then stopped. "Reese, about last night. About what happened today—"

"Don't," she said, looking up at him. "Just don't."

"But—"

"I have to get back inside."

Her eyelashes glittered with tears as she blinked them away, and he didn't know what to do. He took a step toward her. She took a step back.

Clay stopped moving and nodded. "Okay."

"Goodbye, Clay." Reese grasped the doorknob.

The words twisted in his chest like a corkscrew.

"Goodbye," he said, and turned away from her.

◆　◆　◆

Reese walked back inside her house, not bothering to take off the rain-slick boots.

"Everything okay?"

Reese looked up to see Dr. Wally standing in her living room. She'd forgotten he was there.

"Fine," she said, licking her lips. "Everything's fine."

"I see you've turned to thievery."

"What?"

"You stole Clay's jacket."

Reese looked down. "Oh."

She started to turn, thinking maybe she could chase him down the driveway and give back the coat, but his taillights had already faded down the gravel drive.

And she knew the jacket wasn't the reason she wanted to chase him down. She dropped onto the edge of the couch, glum with that thought.

Wally sat down beside her, his knee brushing hers. "Sorry about stopping by so unexpectedly. I just wanted to see you and make sure you're okay. I got worried when you didn't answer your phone, and then I heard about the fire."

She gave him a halfhearted smile. "Thank you for the flowers. They're lovely."

He reached out to adjust a stem in the vase, then dropped his hand to one of the picture frames adorning the coffee table.

"Who's this?"

"My grandfather, Axl. This was thirty years ago."

"No kidding? Is that his Harley?"

"Yeah. And that's a barrel of our Reserve Pinot in the sidecar."

He set the photo back down and picked up another. "This must be your parents?"

Reese took the photo from him and polished a spot off the corner with the hem of her shirt. "That's their tenth anniversary party. I was nine."

"They look so young."

"They were." Reese stared at the picture, annoyed by the stupid stab of jealousy poking her right below the breastbone. She should be proud of her parents. She *was* proud of her parents. Just because she wasn't capable of having that kind of relationship with someone didn't mean other people shouldn't get to enjoy it.

She cleared her throat. "They met in first grade, started going steady in middle school. They got married right after high school, put each other through college, have been living happily ever after since."

Wally gave her a funny look. "That's a bad thing?"

"No, why?"

Wally shrugged. "You sounded a little tense. Thought maybe I'd struck a nerve."

Reese set the photo back down on the coffee table. Her eyes settled on another photo of her parents, this one taken at the edge of the vineyard just a couple years ago. They were smiling into each other's faces, oblivious to the camera, the vineyard fanning out behind them like a postcard view.

Leon hovered ominously beside her father.

"I love my parents," Reese said finally. "My mom is my best friend in the whole world, and my dad is the ultimate great guy. They're both amazing people."

Wally nodded. "I'm waiting for the *but*."

She tucked her bare feet up under her and looked at Wally. "My parents are great. Their marriage is pretty much perfect."

"Then that's a good sign."

"For them or for me?"

"Both. For you, it means you've seen firsthand what makes a relationship work."

Reese snorted. "I'll be honest, Wally," she said. "I couldn't be more clueless about what it takes to make a relationship work than if I'd been raised by a pack of badgers."

"I don't know about that. You seem very loving. I've seen you take care of all the animals around here. Especially Leon."

"Leon's different. He's sweet and devoted and uncomplicated and appreciative and doesn't accidentally sleep with my cousin."

"What?"

"Nothing." Reese bit her lip. "Thanks again for taking care of him the other day."

There was a long silence. Reese wondered if he was working up the courage to kiss her. She tried to decide how she felt about that.

At last, Wally cleared his throat. "How long have you been in love with him?"

She looked up. "Leon?"

He smiled. "You know who I mean."

"I don't think—"

"It's not about thinking, Reese. Love never is."

"Why is everyone I know talking like a goddamn Hallmark card lately?"

He touched her knee. "Look, I'd love to have a shot with you, Reese. I think I've made that clear. But it's also clear you're spoken for. Whether you know it or he knows it, it's obvious."

"No," she said, shaking her head. "There's too much baggage there."

"For you or for him?"

"I don't know. Both."

He smiled. "Sometimes, the baggage is the best part."

He leaned down and gave her a soft, platonic kiss on the cheek. Then he stood up and walked toward the door.

"Goodnight, Reese. Good luck with everything."

CHAPTER SIXTEEN

Reese blinked at the bottle in her hands, certain she was seeing things. It was early in the morning, so fuzzy vision wasn't outside the realm of possibility.

But one look at the matched expressions of bafflement around her, and Reese knew this wasn't her imagination.

"The bottle says *pork*," she said. "We're proposing our customers drink *pork* with their dessert."

Eric shook his head and snatched the bottle from her hands. He glared at it so viciously, Reese feared he might hurl it through the wall.

Apparently reading his thoughts, Sheila took it from him. "Calm down, Eric. This isn't the end of the world."

"*Calm down*? This port is supposed to ship to the White House tomorrow. It's being served with cheese that costs more than my car stereo. The goddamn President of the United States is going to be drinking *my* port, only he'll take one look at this bottle and wonder why the fuck his culinary team decided to offer him liquefied pig."

"God, how did no one see a typo like that?" Larissa asked, reaching into the case to pull out another bottle. "I swear we proofed it a dozen times."

Sheila shook her head. "Maybe the printer did something screwy with the file or had a problem with the font."

Reese shook her head and bent to pick up a bottle. "Pork," she repeated, still too dazed to come up with anything more than that.

"We're fucked," Eric muttered. "This was such a big deal. Our big break—one of our wines served at a state dinner. Jesus."

Reese bit her lip. "They'll probably serve it in decanters so the bottle won't matter anyway—"

"The whole fucking point is that we wanted them to see the label," Eric snapped. "We wanted them to know where it came from. Willamette Valley *port*, not *pork*. Goddammit!"

He drew his foot back and Reese closed her eyes, waiting for the crash of shattering glass.

Instead, Eric snarled another string of obscenities. "This place is fucking cursed!"

With that, he turned and stormed out the door.

Sheila bit her lip and looked at Reese and Larissa. "I'd better go after him."

"He's coming unglued," Larissa said.

"I think everything's just getting to him," Sheila said. "The Wine Club Pinot, the stuff that got smoke damaged, now this." She shook her head. "He takes his craft so seriously."

"We all do," Reese said. "That's why we're here."

"Go get him," Larissa said. "Before he drives the tractor into the pond or something."

Sheila gave Reese's hand a squeeze before turning to follow her husband. Reese shook her head. "What the hell are we going to do? These are supposed to get shipped out today."

Larissa held up her phone. "Let me make some calls, okay? Maybe they can do a rush order on a reprint, and if we get everyone in here to help steam the labels off—"

The phone rang, and Larissa stopped talking. "Maybe that's them now."

Reese peered at the caller ID. "Not unless they're phoning from Larchwood Vineyards."

Larissa rolled her eyes and snatched the receiver. "Dick," she snapped.

Reese couldn't make out the words, but the tone was unmistakably furious.

Larissa rolled her eyes. "No, Dick, we're not paying for smoke damage to your grapes. We've already been over this."

Reese held out her hand for the phone, but Larissa shook her head and covered the mouthpiece. "I'll handle this dick," she whispered, nodding at the door. "You handle that one."

Reese looked up to see Clay standing in the doorway. Larissa turned and headed for the back room, her tone rising as she told Dick exactly where he could stick his bill.

Reese looked at Clay, her heart hammering hard against her rib cage. He wore a dark-gray T-shirt and a look that suggested he feared she might be armed.

"You're here," she said, then kicked herself for making such an inane observation.

"We need to talk."

The words made her gut clench and her heart lodge itself somewhere in her throat. She closed her fist around the pen she'd tucked in her back pocket and brought it up. She began to roll it in her palms, trying to keep cool.

"We need to talk *now? Now?* Don't you think the talk should have happened fifteen years ago?"

She saw his Adam's apple bob as he swallowed. "About the construction project. We need to talk about that."

"Right," Reese said, feeling her face grow hot. "That."

"And other things."

Reese shook her head and looked down at the bottles of "pork" at her feet. "I don't have the energy to deal with other things right now, Clay. There's a lot going on here, in case you hadn't noticed."

"I noticed. I heard Eric shouting about the misprinted labels. I'm sorry."

Reese squeezed her eyes shut and rolled her pen between her palms. "I don't know what to do about any of this. I'm at a total loss here."

"Look, I can draw up some work-arounds," Clay offered. "Modifications in the plan, alternate ways to approach the project, corners we can cut in the LEED certification process."

Reese blinked at him. "Is there really anything to cut? Everything was already so lean in our budget. We've already made such a big public deal about this whole project. What does it say about Sunridge Vineyards if we can't stick to our plan?"

"That you're human?"

Reese snorted. "That's no excuse."

"Sounds like a good one to me."

"Are we still talking about construction?" she asked. "Or does the 'only human' apply to everything around here?"

"I thought we weren't going to talk about the 'other things.'"

"I changed my mind."

Clay nodded. "Fair enough. Look, Reese—I'm sorry. I'm really, really sorry. I made a lot of dumb decisions when I was drinking, and I don't even remember half of them."

"Convenient," she said. "You get to make dumb decisions and forget all about them, and everyone else gets stuck cleaning up messes and getting punched in the nose."

She saw him wince, and felt bad for hurting him. But hell, she was hurting, too. Why should she be the only one?

She knew there was a flaw in that logic but didn't want to dwell on it.

"I deserve that," he said, and looked down at his lap. "I'm sorry. I'm really so sorry—"

"Don't you get tired of apologizing all the time?"

Clay blinked. "Well, it seems like there's no shortage of things for me to apologize for."

Reese took a deep breath. "Look, Clay—it was a dumb mistake. A fling, okay? A momentary lapse in judgment."

He folded his arms over his chest. "Which time?"

"Both. Either one. Especially the other night, though. Really, can you imagine anything so stupid? A vineyard manager and a recovering alcoholic? It's like an animal rights activist and a fur coat designer or a—a—" She struggled to find another analogy but couldn't come up with anything, so she settled for rolling her pen faster between her palms.

Clay shook his head. "People change, Reese."

"I haven't. Not one bit in the fifteen years you've known me. I mean, look at me, I've still got the same damn nervous habits, the same books, the same flannel shirts, the same hairstyle. I haven't changed at all. Why the hell would I believe *you* have?"

"Give me a chance to prove it. I know you can get over your hang-up about us if you just—"

"*My* hang-up? So it's all about *my* issues, is it? What about you?"

Clay frowned. "What about me?"

"You're so terrified Eric might find out about us that you won't even look at me when he's in the room. This whole stupid guy code thing you two have—like he already peed on my fire hydrant, so you won't even sniff me when he's around?" She stopped. "That sounded weirder than I meant it to."

Clay shook his head. "I'm happy to sniff your fire hydrant, Reese. The guy code thing isn't that big a deal."

"No? Then why don't we go out and find Eric right now?" She took a step toward the door and watched him flinch. "Why don't we go let Eric know you fucked me so hard the other night I still have bruises on my thighs?"

Clay looked away. He didn't say anything.

"That's what I thought," Reese said. "Look, Clay—this isn't going to work."

He looked back at her. "Is that why you had the vet over last night?"

"What?"

He shrugged. "You looked awfully cozy. Moving on pretty fast."

She rolled her eyes, feeling her blood start to boil. "Not that it's any of your business, but nothing happened. Unlike you, I don't hop from one bed to another in a span of twenty-four hours."

"It wasn't like that," he said. "That's not how it happened. With you and me and then Larissa—"

"How the hell do you know? You don't even remember being with me, so how can you be sure you didn't nail us both the same night?"

"Because I know. Because I—"

Before he could finish his sentence, the door burst open. Reese's father marched into the room, his expression grim.

"Reese, there you are."

From the look on his face, she knew he wasn't coming to challenge her to a game of Boggle. "Dad? What's wrong?"

He glanced at Clay, then back at Reese.

Clay moved toward the door. "I can leave. Give you guys some privacy."

Jed looked back at Reese. "I guess it doesn't matter. It'll be all over the news before we know it. I just got off the phone with the fire marshal. They're calling it arson."

"What?" Reese sat down hard on the edge of a wine barrel. "Why? How on earth—"

"They found some things at the scene that suggest it wasn't just a faulty wire or something like that. Accelerant of some sort, he wasn't specific on the phone. He's going to come out here in an hour to go over it with us, but he wanted to give me a heads-up beforehand."

"Accelerant? Like alcohol? It's a fucking winery, there are a few flammable things here."

Jed shook his head. "I don't think it's that simple, honey. He sounded pretty sure. I'm trying to get everyone rounded up so we can all be there when he explains it. Have you seen Larissa?"

"She's on the phone," Reese said. "I'll go find her."

"I already caught Eric outside, so he'll be here. Your mom is down at the house getting Axl."

Reese sighed. "Okay, then, right here in an hour?"

Jed nodded. "I have to hustle to get today's tour canceled."

Reese shook her head, trying not to think of the lost revenue, of the angry customers who wouldn't understand the need to cancel their much-anticipated wine country bike trip with only a few hours' notice. Even though her dad's cycling tours hit plenty of other vineyards, everyone knew they were based out of Sunridge. Their logo was all over the website and brochures.

"How many people did you have signed up?" she asked.

"Thirty-three," he said. "There's still time to let most of them know, to issue refunds or let 'em pick a different date, but—"

"The tourists. The people from out of state."

"Right." Jed sighed. "We'll figure this out. I'll see you back here in an hour, okay?"

Reese shook her head and watched her father amble out the door in his bike shorts. As soon as he was gone, she looked back at Clay. "So I'm thinking now might not be the best time for us to discuss our relationship."

Clay nodded. "I understand. But this conversation isn't over, Reese."

She shook her head, her chest feeling like someone was standing on it. "It's over. It's definitely over."

CHAPTER SEVENTEEN

Reese wasn't sure what to expect from the meeting with the fire marshal. Chaos wouldn't have been her first guess, but it also wouldn't have been her last.

Everyone assembled in a circle as though they expected to play duck-duck-goose instead of discuss who might want to burn down the winery. Jed and June held hands on one side of the circle, while Eric sat with his arms folded over his chest and scowled. Larissa wore a neon-orange halter top Reese was pretty sure she'd donned to distract the fire marshal.

Axl beat her to the punch there.

"Be a damn shame if anything happened to that pretty white car of yours," he said, glaring at the fire marshal. "Maybe you should just drop this whole thing and head on out of here."

"Um—" said the fire marshal.

"Dad!" June warned. "You promised."

"I promised not to stab him," Axl retorted. "You see a knife?"

The fire marshal took a step back and cleared his throat.

"Um, good morning, folks," he said. "Thanks for meeting me here on such short notice."

"Would you like a brownie?" June offered. "Before we get started, I mean. There are brownies on the tray behind you. Baked fresh this morning."

"We didn't even put weed in 'em this time," Axl added. "In case you need to pass a drug test."

Reese sighed. "Can we just get on with it? Please? I don't know about the rest of you, but I've got work to do."

"Right," the man agreed. "I'll just get right to it, then. I've given you each a copy of the preliminary report, which details our findings about the type of accelerant we found and some of the reasons we suspect arson in this case. Obviously, I'm not laying all our cards on the table—this is an active investigation, after all."

"So why are you telling us this?" Jed asked.

"Because I want your help putting the pieces together."

Reese picked up her copy of the report and began to skim, while the fire marshal droned on about the steps in the investigation and the time they'd need to carve out for individual interviews. Reese glanced up at that point, feeling ill as he explained how they'd all be interviewed separately immediately following the meeting, and they should expect tough questions.

The implication was clear, and it annoyed the hell out of her.

"So you think one of us did it?" Reese interrupted. "That's what you're driving at, right? You think it's for insurance money or something like that?"

The fire marshal stiffened. "We aren't suggesting anything at this point. Obviously that's one theory we'll consider, but it's just one of many."

"What else?" Eric demanded.

"Well," he began, "for starters, I'd like you all to think hard about any unusual activity you've seen around here lately. Any changes, maybe someone visiting the tasting room more than normal, any strange comings or goings—"

"Dick," Larissa volunteered. "He owns Larchwood Vineyards next door and he hates us. He's always dropping by."

"And he's an asshole," Axl added.

"What about that repair guy the other day?" Jed suggested. "The one who fixed the label machine? I've got his card here somewhere."

"I met with a new barrel distributor two weeks ago," Eric offered.

"Good, good," said the fire marshal as he jotted something in his notebook. "Keep going."

June frowned. "Sally Kreitzer brought me a dozen eggs from her farm the other day, but I hardly think she'd burn down our barn."

"You didn't give her any of the meringue cookies you made," Axl pointed out. "Maybe she took it personally."

Larissa raised her hand. "What about that religious group that showed up last week asking if we sold any nonalcoholic wine?"

"Didn't you just fire one of the field hands last month?" Eric asked. "The one you caught stealing Larissa's underwear?"

"That guy was sweet," Larissa said. "I don't think he'd light our barn on fire."

"Clay," Reese heard herself say. "Clay is new here."

Everyone stopped talking and stared at her. Reese felt her face heat up. "What?"

"Jesus, Reese," Larissa said.

"I'm not accusing him," she pointed out. "I thought we were just throwing out names of people who'd been on the premises, right? New additions, strange people, unexpected visitors, that sort of thing."

Larissa shook her head and frowned. "You really think the worst of him, don't you? That's what this all comes down to."

Reese threw her hands up. "No more than Mom thinks the worst of Shirley the egg lady or dad thinks of the repair guy or—"

"Who is this Clay character?" the fire marshal asked.

"Old buddy of mine," Eric volunteered, his gaze fixed on Reese's face. "He's heading up the construction crew on the new tasting room. Good guy."

The fire marshal nodded, scribbling in his notebook. "Last name?"

"I can't believe you," Larissa hissed, narrowing her eyes at Reese. "After everything he's done to try to get his life back together, to prove he's a decent guy, and you go throwing his name out like—"

"Cut it out, Larissa," Reese snapped. She wished like hell she'd never said anything. She didn't really think he'd done it, did she?

"This Clay," the fire marshal interrupted. "Is he the same gentleman who spotted the fire and called 911 that night?"

"You're right!" Larissa gasped in mock horror. "I'm sure that means he started the fire!"

Reese rolled her eyes. "That's not what I said. And who appointed you his defender, anyway?"

"Well, someone has to do it."

"And you're always eager to *do it*, aren't you, 'Riss?"

Larissa narrowed her eyes. "What's that supposed to mean?"

"Nothing," Reese said, hating herself for being such a bitch but unable to put a cap on the hurt and anger that had been simmering since yesterday. "Can we just move on?"

"No!" Larissa snapped. "I want to know what you meant by that. Let's get this out on the table now."

Reese gritted her teeth, knowing she should just shut up. Knowing she was going to regret whatever came out of her mouth next but somehow not finding the strength to care. She took a breath.

"Fine," she bit out. "You want to go there? We'll go there. I think you're letting the fact that you slept with Clay cloud your judgment."

"Yeah?" Larissa said. "That's funny. I was going to say the same thing to you."

Eric sat up in his chair. "Wait, what?"

"Woo-hoo!" Axl hooted. "This is getting good."

The fire marshal frowned. "Um, ladies, if we could just get back to—"

"And what the hell are you talking about anyway?" Larissa hurled at Reese. "I never slept with Clay. I might've given him a hand job once, but that was ages ago and we were both so wasted I don't even remember—"

"So, honey," June interrupted, reaching over to pat Reese's knee. "I didn't realize you and Clay had been seeing each other, but that's wonderful to hear. You know your father and I would love it if you'd find someone special. When did this happen?"

"Kinda what I'm wondering," Eric said. "Care to fill me in?"

Reese whirled on him. "No! Why the hell is it any of your business who I sleep with? We're not married anymore, in case you missed the memo. You have no claim on me."

"No, but I do have a vested interest in making sure you and my best friend don't fuck up each other's lives."

"Clay and I are adults, Eric!" she yelled. "We can make our own decisions."

"Yeah? How's that working out for you?"

Larissa frowned. "Wait, maybe I did sleep with Clay. Was this at that party over in—"

The fire marshal cupped his hands around his mouth to form a make-shift megaphone. "Can we please get to the topic of the investigation?"

"No!" Axl shouted back. "Are you kidding me? This is the most interesting thing that's happened here since Leon ate pot."

The fire marshal raised an eyebrow. "Leon?" He clicked his pen. "Does Leon have any other history of drug use or criminal activity?"

Reese put her head in her hands and wished like hell the ground would swallow her up.

◆　◆　◆

Clay worked outside for the rest of the afternoon, wishing he could be there for the fire marshal's talk with the family. He wondered what was happening, what sort of evidence they had of arson.

He was so lost in his thoughts that he didn't even hear Eric approach. "Hey, you're still here."

Clay turned to see Eric standing there with the familiar blue bandana holding back his ponytail. His expression was grim.

"Hey," Clay said. "Are you just getting out of the meeting with the fire marshal?"

Eric nodded. "Pretty brutal."

"Did they say what caused the fire?"

"Lighter fluid in a trash can. He didn't actually tell us a lot. I guess they like to keep a lid on the details when there's an investigation going."

"And when there are suspects in the room?" Clay guessed.

Eric shrugged. "Doesn't take a rocket scientist to guess they'd look at the family first, but they've gotta know that's a dumb theory. It's not like the insurance money is worth risking the whole damn vineyard."

"You don't think they had anything to do with it, do you?"

"Hell no."

"So who else? Outside the family, who else?"

"Larchwood Vineyards, maybe. Dick's been a thorn in everyone's side for a long time, and his property is right over there."

"And he's a jerk?"

"There's that."

Clay scuffed his toe in the dirt and waited. Eric had something else to say, Clay could tell. He had an idea what it was, and the thought made his gut clench. He stood quietly, holding his breath, waiting for his best friend to look him in the eye and say it.

Eric wasn't looking him in the eye. He was looking out over the vineyard, his expression somber.

"Eric?"

"Yeah?"

"Who else?" Clay asked. "Who else are they looking at for suspects?"

Eric sighed. "Let's go grab a beer."

Clay frowned. "Very funny."

"Sorry. I forget sometimes."

"No one else seems to be able to. That's why they're accusing me, isn't it?"

Eric shook his head and looked away. "I don't know."

Clay felt something in his gut sink. Part of him had been hoping Eric would deny it, would tell him it was crazy to think his name would make the list of suspects.

And part of him really wanted that beer.

"It's probably just a formality," Eric assured him. "The fact that they want to talk to you—I doubt it means anything."

Clay nodded. "What did the family say? Do they think I set the fire?"

"No," Eric said. "I don't think that's the real issue here."

"Do *you* think I did it? Do you think I'm capable of that?"

Eric hesitated, then shook his head. "You're capable of a lot, but not that. I think you're a guy who's gotten a shitty deal here. You've screwed up a lot in the past, that's for damn sure. But you're trying, and maybe you're due for a break."

Clay didn't know whether to laugh or cry. Instead, he stared down the hill as Leon came ambling toward them, ears pricked at attention.

Eric saw him coming and stepped back, covering his groin. "Shit. Not what I need right now."

Clay reached out and began to scratch behind the alpaca's ears. Leon made a rumbling sound in his throat and leaned into Clay's hand, eyes closed in bliss. Eric took a step closer and Leon opened his eyes, lowering his head to crotch level.

"Dumb animal," Eric muttered without venom as he stepped back again.

"He's just fickle," Clay said. "There's no rhyme or reason to who animals decide they like."

"Pretty much like women," Eric said, turning back to Clay. "There anything you want to tell me?"

Clay stopped scratching Leon and looked at him. "About the fire?"

"About anything."

Clay frowned and went back to scratching. "Nothing I can think of."

Eric nodded once. "Okay, then." He turned and started to walk away, giving Leon a wide berth. Then he stopped and turned back around. "I always knew you loved her."

"What?" Clay stared at his best friend, pretty sure he hadn't heard right.

"Reese." Clay watched Eric swallow, watched him breathe deeply the way he always had when he needed to say something important and didn't know how to get it out. "When we were in college. I knew you loved her first, but I didn't care. I wanted to date her, I wanted to marry her, and I didn't give much thought to anything beyond that."

Clay looked at Leon, not trusting himself to meet Eric's eyes right then. He concentrated on scratching the delicate spot right on the back of the alpaca's ear.

"Obviously, Reese wanted to marry you, too," Clay said.

"We both knew it wouldn't work. Deep down, we both knew. It was safe and friendly, and we thought that's all it took. I shouldn't have gone after her. That's part of guy code, too, you know."

Clay swallowed. "It was a long time ago."

"Not really."

"Things are different now."

Eric shook his head. "No. You're still the same guy you always were, but you've muzzled yourself now. You spend half your time trying not to offend anyone, and the other half trying to make up for past offenses, but otherwise you're still the same. So is Reese, you know. And that's not such a bad thing."

Clay shook his head and met Eric's eyes again. "Thanks, Freud."

"I'm serious. I don't know what happened with Reese or how you're going to fix it, but I do know you've got to get over this pansy-ass thing you've been doing."

"Pansy-ass?"

"That's the most important part of the guy code," Eric said, his tone softer now. "The need to tell your friend when he's being a pansy-ass."

"I appreciate it."

The weird thing was, he did.

CHAPTER EIGHTEEN

Clay knew he should stick close to the vineyard. Eric had already told him the fire marshal had questions and wanted to talk to him as soon as possible.

But here he was parked on a barstool at Finnigan's nursing a Coke and picking at a plate of French fries as he replayed the conversation with Eric.

He wasn't sure which was more upsetting—the fact that he was a suspect in an arson investigation or the fact that his best friend knew he'd slept with his ex.

He took another sip of his Coke and then picked up the ketchup, pouring a healthy dollop of it on the side of his plate. He traced a French fry through it and was just about to shove it in his mouth when he heard a familiar voice.

"Clay!"

He turned to see Patrick ambling in, his shirtsleeves rolled to display the misspelled tattoos.

"Hey, Patrick, good to see you."

"Whatcha doing?"

"Getting wasted on Coca-Cola and French fries, how about you?"

Patrick glanced at Clay's glass, looking visibly relieved. "That's just Coke?"

"Want a taste?"

"No, no—I trust you."

"That's good. I was starting to think you implanted a tracking device in my forearm so you know when I come within ten feet of a bar. Have a seat."

Patrick eased himself onto the stool and folded his hands on the bar. Clay tried not to stare at the tattoos.

Your stronger than you think you are.

Strength threw sobriety.

"So how have things been going, Clay?"

"Okay," Clay said. "I've been better."

"You want to talk about it?"

"I wouldn't know where to start."

"Try me."

"Okay. Turns out I slept with the girl of my dreams fifteen years ago and didn't remember it because I was a drunk idiot, but I do remember sleeping with her cousin, which I also did because I was a drunk idiot. Now I'm about to lose the dream girl to a veterinarian who's such a nice guy I'd probably date him if I swung that way. On top of that, I'm being accused of arson for a fire I helped extinguish, and the construction project I moved out here for is about to go belly up."

Clay picked up a fry and shoved it in his mouth, hardly noticing it was cold.

"Wow," Patrick said. "Not your best week, huh?"

"No."

"Is it your worst?"

Clay thought about that as he grabbed another fry. "Probably not. The week my dad died was pretty rough."

"When did your dad die?"

"When I was a junior in college."

"How did you handle that?"

Clay looked down at the plate. "I dropped out of college, got wasted for a week on Jack and Coke, and ended up in jail on a DUI charge."

Patrick reached over and grabbed a fry. "And look at you now."

"What do you mean?"

"I mean, you're sitting here at a bar on what is arguably the second-worst day of your life, and if you're telling me the truth, there's nothing in that glass but Coke."

Clay shoved the glass in front of him. "Taste it."

Patrick shoved the glass back. "I believe you. My point is that you're dealing with it. Your life is going to hell right now, and you're handling it like a mature, sober adult."

Clay picked up the Coke glass and took a slow sip. Then he shook his head. "I've been trying so damn hard to get it right this time. I've been working the steps, trying to be a good guy, trying to make it up to all the people I screwed over. But somehow I just keep making it worse."

"You ever think you're trying too hard to earn forgiveness from everyone else and not hard enough to forgive yourself?"

Clay looked at him. "No."

"Good you're keeping an open mind about it."

He sighed. "I don't know what to do."

"Yes, you do. Don't drink. That's the hardest part, and you've already got that down."

"That's not the hardest part," Clay said, then stifled the urge to crack a crude joke. *Hardest part.*

"What?" Patrick asked.

"What do you mean?"

"You got a funny look just then."

Clay shrugged. "It's dumb."

"Dumber than sleeping with your dream girl's cousin?"

"Good point." He sighed. "Okay, my best buddy and I used to do this thing where we'd turn everything into a dirty joke. Everything was an innuendo of some sort. It's stupid. I stopped doing it when I got sober."

"Why?"

"Same reason I stopped drinking, I guess. I wanted to show I'd grown up. That I'd changed."

"You don't think not drinking was enough?"

He shrugged. "I'm not sure it'll ever be enough."

"Tell me a dirty joke."

"What?"

"You heard me. Tell me a dirty joke."

Clay raised an eyebrow at him. "Is this one of the twelve steps I missed?"

"Come on. Do it."

Clay thought about it for a minute. "Fine. Two guys are sitting in a bar and one turns to the other and says, 'If I slept with your wife, would that make us family?' The other guy looks at him for a minute and says, 'No, but it would make us even.'"

Patrick grinned. "Nice. I like it. Tell me another."

Clay glanced over at the bartender, who was drying the same beer glass he'd been drying for the last five minutes. He was smiling just a little.

"All right. Two nuns are riding their bicycles down an alley in Rome. One turns to the other. 'I've never come this way before,' she says. The other one nods, smiles. 'It's the cobblestones.'"

Patrick hooted and smacked his hand on the bar. Clay grinned in spite of himself.

"There you go," Patrick said. "You're smiling. That can't be a bad thing, right?"

Clay raised an eyebrow. "Well, I'd also be smiling if this glass were full of Jack and Coke."

"Yeah, but you'd be puking in an hour. When was the last time you puked from a dirty joke?"

Clay grinned. "Well, I know an old guy in a biker gang who tells jokes filthy enough to make me queasy. He may have learned them in prison."

"Save 'em for later." Patrick slapped his hand on the bar again. "You're going to be okay, right? No matter what happens with this girl or the construction or the investigation—you've got this."

Clay nodded, then stuck out his hand. "Thanks, Patrick. I owe you one."

"You don't owe me anything. Pay it forward sometime. You'll have the chance eventually."

Clay nodded. "I'll do that. How'd you know I was here, anyway?"

"Dumb luck. I was meeting friends for dinner across the street and I saw your truck. Thought I'd see if you needed anything."

"So it wasn't the tracking device?"

"Not this time." Patrick stood up. "I'd better get going. Be well, okay?"

"Thanks, man. Have a good night."

Clay watched as Patrick ambled off, then looked down at his empty plate.

"You want more fries?"

He looked up to see the bartender holding a plate piled high with greasy goodness.

"This a new thing?" Clay asked. "Free French fry refills?"

"Nah, but the lady in the corner just ordered 'em and now she says she doesn't want 'em. She's a little messed up. Not drunk or nothin'— she's just drinking root beer, but still. I just called a cab to come get her, but now I got these goddamn fries to get rid of."

Clay reached up to take the steaming plate, daring a quick glance at the table in the corner to see the pitiful soul who'd given up her French fries.

He almost dropped the plate.

"Sheila?"

She looked up, swaying a little in her chair. Her eyes were red and ringed with mascara, her face streaked with dried tears and snot. The top of her table was littered with soggy tissues and a half-empty glass of root beer.

He stood up and took two steps toward her. "Sheila? What's going on?"

She dissolved into sobs, her shoulders shaking so hard Clay thought she might topple to the floor.

"Oh, Clay," she sniffed. "This is bad. This is really, really bad."

"What's bad? Are you hurt? Did something happen to Eric?"

She was sobbing too hard to answer, so Clay looked at the bartender. "How much has she had to drink?"

"Not a thing. I wouldn't serve her."

"I came here to get wasted," Sheila sobbed. "To forget. Only he thought I was already drunk because I can't stop crying, so he wouldn't let me order anything. But that's not why I can't stop crying. Oh, Clay. I don't know what to do."

He dropped into the chair beside her and touched her arm. She was ice cold. Dread clenched Clay's gut like a fist.

"Sheila? What is it?"

She looked up at him and shook her head, tears slithering down her cheeks. "There's something I've got to tell you. Something awful."

CHAPTER NINETEEN

Reese couldn't remember ever feeling worse in her life. Not even the time she'd thrown up in her underwear on the last day of eighth grade, or the time she'd failed her Advanced Rootstalks & Cultivars course in college and realized she might never make it as a vineyard manager.

You felt worse when you walked out on Clay in the middle of the night fifteen years ago, she reminded herself.

You felt worse when you left him in jail to rot after you got punched at Finnigan's that night.

That didn't help.

She wasn't sure how she made it back to her house after the meeting with the fire marshal, but she knew the only thing she wanted to do was curl up in her bed and cry. She had just pulled on her pajamas and yanked the elastic off her ponytail to let her hair down when she heard a knock at the door.

Stifling a groan, she peeled back the bedroom curtain to peer out, thinking seriously about not answering it.

When she saw her mother standing on the front porch holding a tray of brownies, a box of Popsicles, and a bottle of Pinot, she reconsidered. Padding into the living room, she dragged the door open and offered a weak smile.

"Hi, Mom."

"Hey there, sweetie," June said, her voice tinged with worry. "I wanted to see if you're doing okay."

"You brought me comfort food," Reese said, feeling guilty for not confiding in her mother sooner.

But June just walked inside and thrust the brownies in front of her. "Here, have one. Or would you rather have a Popsicle?"

"Popsicle, please."

"Here you go."

Her mom handed her the whole box, and Reese opened it slowly. She took a Popsicle and peeled back the wrapper, biting into the sweet iciness. June set down the wine and brownies on the coffee table and trooped to the kitchen to throw the rest of the Popsicles in the freezer. She returned to the living room and sat down on the sofa beside Reese, giving her daughter's arm a squeeze.

"So the meeting with the fire marshal was interesting," June said. "How are you holding up, sweetie?"

Reese raised one shoulder, lacking the energy to perform a full shrug. "I feel like an idiot."

"Oh, Reesey." Her mom leaned over and wrapped her in a hug that smelled like brownies and grapes and Oil of Olay and everything good in the world.

Reese started to cry.

Then she choked on a chunk of Popsicle.

"Hold still, honey," June said as Reese wheezed and coughed and spit purple slush on the floor.

June whacked her on the back a few times.

"I can't even cry right," Reese choked, dodging her mother's blows as she regained her breath. "I screw everything up."

"That's not true—"

"My marriage, the construction project, my relationship with Larissa, any potential I might've had to enjoy any sort of relationship with—"

Her voice broke. She couldn't even say Clay's name.

"Oh, honey, no, you didn't." June stopped hitting her and tried hugging again. "This vineyard has been running strong for more than forty years. So what if we lose a little ground? We're still hanging in there. And Larissa will get over it. I saw her not thirty minutes ago and she was getting ready for a date. She's fine, honey. You two will kiss and make up."

Reese sniffled and shook her head, noticing her mom had deliberately dodged the issue of romance. She wasn't surprised. She'd already proven she was beyond hope.

As if reading her mind, June put a finger under Reese's chin and nudged it up. "Hey, look at me. You'll find love, too."

Reese just shook her head. "I don't think so."

"Of course you will."

"I don't think I'm cut out for it, Mom."

"Nonsense!" June said, her eyes taking on a rabid glow. "You *will* find love. And when you do, it'll be special and wonderful and just like your father and I have enjoyed. Don't you want that, honey? What Daddy and I have?"

Reese felt a sharp pain beneath her ribs. "Of course."

"It's out there for you, too, honey. Just wait and see. When it's right—"

"I know." Her voice came out harsher than she intended, so Reese forced a smile to make up for it. "Thanks, Mom. I feel better already."

June nodded and grabbed a brownie. "Everything will be fine, sweetie. You'll see."

"Okay, Mom. Thanks." She was trying to think of a tactful way to tell her mother she wanted time alone when her father came limping up the walkway.

"Damn Leon," he muttered as he stepped up beside June and put an arm around her. "Ambushed me that time."

June touched his leg. "Oh, honey—are you okay?"

"Fine, fine," he said. "Just wanted to come find you and see how Reese is doing. You holding up all right, baby?"

Reese shrugged. "Fine, I guess. I think I'll just take a bath and read a book or something."

"That's good. Give yourself a nice, quiet night at home to let things settle. Your mom and I will be at the house if you need to talk or anything."

"We're here for you, sweetie," June said.

Jed planted a kiss on his wife's forehead before turning back to Reese. "You sure you're okay? It's kind of a big deal, the whole arson thing and all."

"Right," Reese said. She bit her lip. "Look, about Clay—"

"Always liked that boy," Jed said, nodding once. "Good to see he's getting his life back together."

Reese sighed. "Being investigated for arson will really help with that."

Her father reached out and patted her arm. "I'm sure it'll all work out. He's a tough kid, and I'm sure he's got a good support system at St. Peter's. They take care of their own over there."

Reese frowned at her father. "The Catholic church? What are you talking about? Clay isn't religious. At least not that I know."

Hell, *did* she know? Maybe he really was a stranger to her.

Her father shrugged. "Guess I figured from his tattoo he must be Catholic. *Res firma mitescere nescit.* Latin. I think I remember it from Mass when I was a kid, or maybe I've just seen it around the cycling scene forever."

"What does it mean?"

"Depends on how you translate it, I guess. 'A firm resolve doesn't weaken,' might be one way to read it," Jed said. "'A rigid thing doesn't soften' or 'When you've got it up, keep it up,' is another, though I'm not sure that makes much sense."

"It makes perfect sense," Reese said, realization dawning. "For crying out loud, he has a dirty joke tattooed on his arm. No wonder he wouldn't tell me what it said."

"Oh, honey," June said. "I don't think he meant it that way."

Reese snorted. "I think that's exactly how he meant it. Clay was always all about the dirty double entendre. Now he doesn't even say *fuck* when he hits his finger with a hammer. No wonder he's embarrassed about the tattoo."

She shook her head, not sure whether to be annoyed at Clay for always dodging the subject of the tattoo, or for putting her in a position to find out from her father what it said.

Like it mattered.

"Sweetie, you sure you don't want to come down to the house for dinner?" June asked. "Oysters and asparagus?"

Reese shook her head, not at all interested in sharing an aphrodisiac dinner with her parents. "I appreciate that, Mom, but I really need to be by myself for a bit."

"Okay, honey. Whatever you need."

"Thanks for the Popsicles and brownies. Love you."

"Love you, too, sweetie."

Both parents kissed her on the cheek before heading out the door hand in hand. Reese watched them walk into the crisp spring evening, their heads bent close together as they made their way toward the house.

Then she closed the door, not feeling much better but not feeling a whole lot worse.

She picked up the wine in one hand and the brownies in the other and stashed both in the kitchen. Returning to the living room, she stared at her bookshelf and tried to decide between rereading her favorite Kristan Higgins romance or her favorite Jennifer Crusie.

She was still staring at the book spines when Axl burst through the front door. His frizzed white hair made him look like a big Q-tip. He yanked off a tattered leather biker bag, knocking his aviator glasses crooked.

"There you are," Axl barked. "Your mom said you were up here feeling sorry for yourself. You and me, we gotta talk, girlie."

Reese sighed. "Axl, I don't really feel like—"

"Shut up."

Reese shut up.

"I got a couple things to discuss," her grandfather continued. "Move over, make room for me on the sofa. I gotta show you something."

"Axl, if you're going to show me your nipple piercing again, I'm not interested," Reese said. "If it's infected, call your doctor."

"That's not it. Gimme one of those brownies. They got anything good in 'em?"

"If you mean eggs, sugar, vanilla, flour, and cocoa powder, yes."

"Go get me a glass of wine, then."

Reese sighed, knowing it was futile to argue. She got up to open the Pinot her mother had just brought. Retrieving a good Riedel wineglass from the cupboard, she poured a slosh of Pinot into the glass. Then she returned to the living room, setting it down in front of her grandfather.

Axl grinned and took a sip, then belched.

"Nice," he said. "It's the 2011 Resonance Vineyard Pinot Noir from Sineann, right?"

Reese raised an eyebrow as she dropped back onto the couch. "Good call."

"Yeah, I'm full of surprises," he muttered. "Like this one."

He reached into his leather satchel and pulled out a picture frame that was tarnished around the edges. He looked at it for a moment before passing it to Reese with uncharacteristic reverence.

"See that?" Axl said, stabbing at the photo with one finger. "That's me and your grandma at our twentieth anniversary party."

Reese looked at the photograph, pretty sure it was illegal in most states for a granddaughter to see her grandparents in such a state.

"You had your twentieth anniversary party at a nudist resort?" she asked at last.

"Happiest time of my life," Axl said. "She was a good woman, your grandma."

Reese frowned. "I thought you called her a no-good, cheating, skanky excuse for a—"

"I was just mad," Axl interrupted, waving a dismissive hand. "That was after she ran off with Floyd and things were a little rocky, you know what I'm saying?"

"Sure."

"But up until then, we had it pretty good. Man, we had such good times when we were first married. The date nights and the swingers clubs and the—"

"Um, Axl? I don't know that I need to hear all this."

Axl glared. "My point is this, Peanut Butter Cup—your grandma and me, we had a damn good marriage."

Reese couldn't help it. She felt her eyebrow rise with a skepticism she couldn't disguise. She half expected Axl to curse her out, but he just shook his head.

"People's marriages aren't always what you think they are," he said. "Sometimes the ones that look shitty on the surface have a lot of good stuff underneath. Nice stuff. Stuff that keeps you together and happy and doing the dirty every day for thirty-three years."

"Axl, I don't—"

"Shut up. Let me finish."

He folded his arms over his chest, looking unusually serious. Reese sat up a little straighter, the photo still gripped in her hand.

"Sometimes the marriages that seem perfect—well, they're not," Axl said. "That doesn't mean they're bad, or that they won't work out. It just means some folks are better at hiding stuff than others. Some people have to work harder than others, you feel me?"

Reese frowned and handed the photo back. "I guess so."

Axl took the photo and brought it up to his mouth, huffing a steamy breath on it and polishing the glass with his sleeve before shoving it back into the knapsack.

Then he looked at Reese again. "I'm just trying to tell you that no one really knows what goes on in other people's houses, so they sure as shit can't judge themselves by their goddamn standards."

Reese frowned. "Fine, but I'm not sure what this has to do with me."

Axl shook his head and smacked Reese on the knee. "For a smart girl, you can be pretty dense."

"This outpouring of grandfatherly affection is unsettling."

Axl ignored her, intent on digging in his knapsack again. This time, he pulled out a green folder. He held it on his lap for a moment, studying it before turning to Reese.

"This is the other thing I've gotta show you." He pushed it toward her, and Reese found herself taking it, not sure what she was being offered. "Careful with this, now. Your mom would shit a brick if she ever knew I borrowed it, so don't crease it or anything."

Something in her grandfather's voice made Reese's pulse kick up a notch. She studied the folder, the kind with little hooks on the ends to hang in a file cabinet. Frowning, she touched the edge of it, still not daring to crack it open. "Where did you get this?"

"Picked the lock on your parents' file cabinet. I always knew it was in there but never had a reason to go looking before now."

"Axl, I don't know if we should—"

"Open the fucking thing!"

Reese shut her mouth and flipped open the file.

A single sheet of paper rested there. Reese stared at it, not understanding the words at first. The instant it began to make sense, Reese felt her skin go cold.

"Divorce decree," she read aloud. She peered closer, the words tumbling at her in a confusing succession of dark ink and legal language. Her stomach began to twist itself into a knot. She stared at the date, at the names on the paper, at the stamp in the corner.

Then she shut the folder and set it on the coffee table, her hand shaking as she drew it back.

"I don't understand," she said. She couldn't bring herself to look her grandfather in the eye. "When did my parents get divorced?"

"About six months after you were born," Axl replied. "Things were pretty rough around here, what with the vineyard just getting up and running and your parents being newlyweds and all, and with a brand-new baby to take care of—well, they just sort of cracked."

Reese nodded, not even sure what she should be asking. "How long—I mean, are they still—"

"No," he said. "They got back together about a year later. You were too little to remember. They both dated a couple other people, and then they went through a bunch of marriage counseling crap. After a while, they figured out a way to make things work. Been going strong ever since, but you know that."

Reese swallowed and looked down at her hands. "I don't understand."

"Why I showed it to you or why it happened in the first place?"

"Both, I guess. I just thought—"

"You thought your folks had the perfect marriage from the get-go. Perfect soul mates forever, with no effort required," Axl said. "And that's not true. And you thought your grandma and me were a train wreck."

Reese nodded and looked up, finally willing to meet her grandfather's eye. "That's not true, either."

"No."

Reese nodded. "So what *is* true?"

Axl snorted. "Lookie here, you're turning to me for the truth now? Let me tell you, Peanut Butter Cup—relationships aren't as simple as you think they are. You've spent your whole life trying not to end up like me and your grandma, or thinking there's no way you could have what your parents do. And the thing is, you're right on both counts. No matter who the hell you end up with, it'll never be just like what someone else got."

Reese opened her mouth to speak, then shut it again. She had no earthly idea what to say. She was saved from saying anything by a familiar quacking sound from the end of the coffee table. She glanced at her iPhone, not sure she wanted to answer.

"My cell," she said. "I'll ignore it."

Axl scowled and nudged the phone with the toe of his Doc Marten. "Ain't you gonna see who it is?"

Reese picked up the phone and glanced at the readout. "Idaho number."

"Clay," he said with a nod. "Answer it."

"I don't think—"

"Answer the fucking thing. Haven't you heard anything I've been saying, girlie?"

"Axl, I'm not ready—"

"Answer the goddamn phone!"

Reese hesitated, her hand shaking a little. She hit the button and held the phone to her ear. "Clay, I'm sorry, now isn't a good time to talk about—"

"Reese, stop talking," he said. "Right now, I have something to tell you."

CHAPTER TWENTY

Considering how much effort he'd invested in walking the straight and narrow, Clay was surprised to realize it was the second time in a week he'd found himself at the police station in the presence of a scowling detective.

He had to admit he was proud neither visit had added anything to his prior police record. For the first time in his life, he was innocent.

Well, pretty much.

The same could not be said for Sheila.

"So let me make sure I've got all this," said Police Detective Austin Evans, tapping his pen against the desk. Evans had agreed to meet with them an hour ago after Sheila insisted she wanted to talk to the police immediately. Clay had tried to talk her out of it, but Sheila was adamant.

"I just want this over with," she said for the hundredth time as she mopped her eyes with a tissue.

"We're working on that, ma'am," said Detective Evans. He flipped back a few pages of his notebook and frowned. "You're confessing to destroying a wine barrel and its contents, setting a trash can on fire in a winery barn, stealing all the corkscrews, and deliberately failing to correct a typo on a wine label?"

"I also ran a red light on the way here," Sheila sniffed. "I was nervous."

Clay squeezed her hand, not sure whether to hate her for what she'd done or admire her for trying to do the right thing now. Though he'd tried to convince her to wait until Eric and a lawyer could be present, Sheila hadn't been willing. Once she decided to confess, there was no stopping her.

Beside him, Sheila looked up and sniffed. "When does it get easier, Clay?"

"When does what get easier?"

"This screwing up so badly and trying to make it right—how long will I feel like hell?"

Clay shook his head, not sure how to answer. "I'll let you know when I get there."

The detective cleared his throat. "So, ma'am, as I told you before, you're welcome to have an attorney present—"

"No," Sheila said. "I did this, I want to face the consequences."

Clay tightened his grip on her hand. "I wish you'd let me call someone—Eric or a lawyer or—"

"I let you call Reese," Sheila interrupted. "That's who I want to talk to first. I need to apologize, to try to make this right. Until I've talked to her, I don't want anyone else hearing about it."

Clay nodded. The whole story would get out soon enough, probably before the day was over. For a few hours at least, he could let her feel like she had some control.

When she'd started confessing at the bar, he'd known right away it was bad. She wasn't drinking anything stronger than root beer, but the words still came flooding out of her. He'd wanted to call Eric, to ask her to wait until she was calm before rushing to the police.

But Sheila wanted to come clean, and she wasn't willing to wait.

Clay felt his cell phone vibrate against his hip and he glanced down at the number.

"It's Eric," he said. "Look, Sheila—he's going to know sooner or later. You sure you don't want to talk to him now?"

"Not yet. That's going to be the worst part, and I'm not ready yet. I just need to talk to Reese first."

Clay nodded and hit the ignore button on his phone. "Fair enough."

Detective Evans cleared his throat again. "So, ma'am, just to be clear, this was all an attempt to get your husband—Mr. Eric Mortenson—to leave his position as winemaker at Sunridge Vineyards and move with you to New York to be closer to your family?"

Sheila looked down at her lap and began shredding a soggy tissue. "I guess. It started innocently. When I saw him get upset about the winery having a termite problem, I got the idea to poke a few holes in the barrel so he'd think his work was compromised. Things just spiraled from there when I saw he wasn't budging, and—"

She broke down in sobs again, and Clay felt his heart twist. God, he knew all too well how it felt to screw up this badly. To know he'd done something horrible and destructive to people he cared about.

There was a shrill beep from the desk phone in front of the cop.

"Detective Evans?" called a female voice. "There's a Reese Clark here for you. You asked me to call when she arrived?"

"Right, I'll be right out to get her. Just give me a sec."

He hit a button on the phone and stood up, eyeing Clay and Sheila. "I'll be right back. You two stay here."

Clay nodded and gave Sheila's hand another squeeze as the detective moved past them into the hallway.

Sheila looked up at him, eyes still shimmering with tears. "I blamed you, you know."

"For what?"

"For being the reason he wouldn't even consider moving. He was so excited when he heard you were coming back. So proud of you and the fact that you got your life back together. Did he tell you that?"

Clay blinked and looked away. "Not in so many words."

"That sounds like Eric. All dirty jokes and grunts and not a lot of sentimental talk. You thought the only thing he cared about with you is whether you'd end up with Reese?"

Clay looked back at her, a little surprised. "How'd you know?"

"I know my husband. He's protective of you both. He thought you'd be a bad combination. Personally, I thought you were perfect for each other."

Clay shook his head. "I think I already proved that wrong. Things are kind of a disaster right now."

Sheila shook her head. "I don't think so."

"I do. I screwed up, and it's too late to fix things."

"No it's not." She clenched the soggy tissue in her fist, her eyes taking on a rabid look that made Clay sit back a little. "Promise me something—promise me you won't give up on this thing with Reese."

"It's not my choice to make."

"Yes, it is. Fight for her. Convince her you want her. Tell her you won't take no for an answer."

"What am I supposed to do, club her over the head and drag her back to my cave by the hair?"

"Yes!"

Clay shook his head. "You're nuts. No offense. Though maybe you should consider that as a defense?"

Sheila squeezed his hand. "Promise me you'll try."

"Why don't you just worry about yourself for right now—"

"Promise me!"

"Okay," Clay said, holding up his hands in mock surrender. "Fine. Why don't you promise me you'll get a lawyer? Someone who'll make sure you're not screwing yourself here."

"I already screwed myself," she said, turning as the sound of footsteps came trudging down the hall. "Now I'm trying to make it right."

Clay nodded and felt his heart constrict as Reese walked into the room looking confused and nervous and so damn beautiful he had to look down at his hands to keep from jumping up and wrapping his arms around her.

He turned back to Sheila. "I can relate."

◆　◆　◆

As soon as Sheila finished telling her story, Reese asked her to repeat it.

It still didn't make sense.

Reese frowned at the cop, then at Sheila. She deliberately avoided meeting Clay's eyes. "So you did these things on purpose?" she asked Sheila. "The wine, the fire—"

"I'm so sorry, Reese."

"I thought we were friends."

"We were. We *are*. You have to believe I didn't mean to hurt you. I wasn't trying to damage the winery. I just wanted Eric to question things and wonder whether he belonged there, and it all sort of snowballed. When one thing didn't work, I tried another. I just wasn't thinking."

"No kidding."

"Reese, I'm sorry. Truly, truly sorry."

Reese nodded, not sure what to say to that. *You're forgiven* wasn't right. Not yet, not even close. She looked at Clay. He reached over and squeezed her hand, and Reese felt a small surge of strength.

Sheila sniffed and looked up at the cop. "How long will I be in prison?"

"Look," Reese said. "Let's not get ahead of ourselves. I'm sure the cops and lawyers will want to work through the details, figure out the charges, all that complicated legal stuff. Talk of prison might be a little premature."

"It doesn't matter right now," Sheila said, waving a manicured hand. "I just wanted to apologize."

Reese nodded. "Okay. Can I ask you why? I mean, I understand the whole thing about wanting Eric to move with you, but our friendship—yours and mine, I mean. That was always separate."

Fresh tears pooled in Sheila's eyes, and Reese couldn't help but feel a little sorry for her.

"You have to believe I didn't mean to hurt you," Sheila started. "I thought it would be harmless, you know? I just wanted Eric to start questioning his future at the vineyard—the lost wine would make him worry about the value of his work, and the thing with the typo on the wine label—that really was a printer error, but I saw it and I just didn't correct it."

"But the fire—you could have hurt someone."

Sheila shook her head, and Reese sat back a little for fear of being hit by flying snot. "It wasn't supposed to be that big," Sheila insisted. "It was just a little trash-can fire. It was nighttime, so I knew no one would be there to get hurt. I just thought—well, you know how superstitious Eric is. I thought if he got to thinking the place was cursed, he might not be so set on staying."

"Right," Reese said. "I guess that makes sense."

If you're completely crazy.

"Look, I know you think I'm nuts, but I did it for what seemed like good reasons at the time," Sheila said. "I want to be close to my family, and I want to be with the love of my life. You can understand that, can't you?"

Reese bit her lip and tried hard not to look at Clay. "I can understand some of it."

"I know you hate me right now, but maybe someday you can forgive me?"

Reese sighed. "I don't hate you, Sheila. I'm just shocked."

Sheila nodded and sniffed, then looked up at the detective. "Can we call my husband now? And the lawyer, I guess. I just needed to do that my way, without a bunch of people breathing down my neck about what I should and shouldn't say. Does that make sense?"

"No," the detective answered. "But most things don't in this business." He looked at Reese. "You probably want to talk things over with your family, discuss the charges, all that stuff. I understand you've already had some discussions with the fire marshal?"

Reese nodded. "Earlier today."

"You'll have more."

She nodded again, not looking forward to a drawn-out investigation but knowing this thing with Sheila probably gave them a light at the end of the tunnel. "Do you need me to do anything else right now, or am I free to go?"

"You're free to go," he said. "Ms. Mortenson will be staying with us for a while, but you two are okay to leave. Mr. Henderson, thank you for being here to—well, to smooth the waters a bit."

"No problem."

"Good to see you've gotten your life together, son," the cop added. "I remember you from years ago. Thought you'd be in prison yourself by now."

Clay nodded. "I got a second chance."

Reese felt her gut twist and she squeezed his hand. Clay turned to look at her, then offered a small smile and a hand up. His eyes didn't leave hers.

Reese shivered and looked down. She'd taken a few seconds at home to ditch the pajama pants in favor of jeans, but she was still wearing her thin cami top with an oversize flannel shirt thrown over the top like a jacket. It was unbuttoned all the way, and she pulled it closed over her chest as she felt her nipples respond to the sight of Clay standing there looking so broad and warm and dangerous.

"Are you going back to your place?" he asked.

She nodded. "That was my plan."

"I'll follow you there. We need to talk."

Reese opened her mouth to protest, then changed her mind. Between her mother, her father, and Axl, she'd had a steady stream of visitors all evening. One more wouldn't hurt.

"You're right. We do need to talk." She turned and looked at Sheila, then placed a hand on her shoulder. "You want us to wait until Eric gets here?"

"No. I think I want some time alone to compose myself, if that's okay."

"Right." Reese bit her lip. "I'm probably going to be angry with you for a long time."

"I understand."

"But I'll get over it. I know you're not a bad person. You just did some dumb things, and maybe someday we'll look back on all this and laugh."

The cop frowned. "I kind of doubt that."

"Maybe no laughing," Reese admitted. "But at some point, I might not want to take you out in the parking lot and hit you with a tire iron."

Sheila sniffed. "That's all I can hope for."

Reese turned and let Clay tow her down the hall and out into the lobby. "I need to use the restroom," she said.

"I'll wait."

"I can meet you back at the house—"

"I'll wait."

She gave him a small smile. "You think I'm going to ditch you somewhere to avoid having this conversation?"

"I'm not taking any chances."

She nodded and retreated to the ladies' room, where she splashed cold water on her face and wondered what the hell had just happened.

Sheila. Her friend. How could she?

But Reese knew. People did stupid things for love. Hadn't she proved that before?

She finished finger combing her hair and wished like hell she'd brought some lipstick. She settled for the mango lip balm she found in the bottom of her purse, along with a piece of gum with a nickel stuck to it. Finally, it was time to go back out and face the world.

The second she stepped into the lobby, she saw Clay standing there. He wasn't alone.

"Eric," she said. "How did you get here so fast?"

"I was right down the street on an errand when Sheila called," he said. "What the hell is going on?"

She took a shaky breath and grabbed his hand. "You know how you're always telling me marriage is really tough? How it's not easy, how you need to work hard at it every single day?"

He nodded, his expression wary.

Reese squeezed his hand. "Remember that, okay?"

CHAPTER TWENTY-ONE

Though Reese and Clay offered to stay at the police station with Eric and Sheila, they both declined. "We've got a lot to work through here," Eric had said in his usual gruff tone.

Reese bit her lip. "You're planning to work through it, though, right?"

"That's what marriage is, Reese," he said. "A helluva lot of work. But worth it, in the long run."

She'd nodded and retreated out to her car without another word. Clay followed at a short distance, intent on talking to her one way or another. Of course, despite his insistence they needed to talk, he wasn't entirely sure what he planned to say.

He spent the fifteen-minute drive to the vineyard contemplating it as he watched Reese's taillights flicker in front of him. Her hair slid along the nape of her neck as she glanced in the rearview mirror, her eyes catching his for a brief moment before darting back to the road.

Clay followed her up the gravel driveway, watching as row after row of grapevines fluttered past in the dark en route to Reese's little house. He hadn't set foot inside since the night they'd slept together. Since he'd held her in his arms, made her whimper, made her moan.

The thought of stepping over the threshold now made his gut seize a little.

He brought the truck to a halt and sat there for a few seconds composing himself. By the time he swung open the driver's side door and stepped out onto the gravel, Reese had disappeared inside.

The front door stood open, so Clay walked through it, his palms already beginning to sweat. He took his shoes off by the door, not wanting to track mud over her clean floor.

She stood motionless in front of the kitchen, her hands clenched awkwardly at her sides. Clay studied her face, looking for clues to her emotional state while he admired the curve of her cheek. She wore no makeup, and he couldn't remember whether she usually did or not. With her hair loose and wild around her shoulders, there was an unpredictable air about her, and it made him ache to reach out and touch her. He swallowed hard and forced himself to stop staring.

"You want something to drink?" she asked.

"No, thank you," Clay said. Then he stopped. That was an impulse response—an attempt to be polite—to not inconvenience her.

Fuck it. He *was* thirsty.

"I changed my mind," he said. "A Coke would be great."

Reese blinked, then nodded. "I'm not sure I have Coke," she said, moving into the kitchen. She didn't bother turning on the overhead lights, though the under-cabinet lighting cast a warm glow on the countertops. She pried open the refrigerator door and leaned down to peer inside. Clay felt his head spin as he watched her bend over.

Caveman, he told himself.

So what?

"There's one Coke in here," she called. "You want ice?"

She stood up and looked at him. He hesitated. A polite guy wouldn't take the last of anything in her fridge. Or he'd at least ask if she wanted it.

That seemed stupid.

"I'll take it, thanks," he said. "What are you drinking?"

"Pinot Noir, if you don't mind."

"Actually, I do mind."

"What?"

Clay folded his arms over his chest. "I don't mind if you drink around me—especially in your own home. I can handle it. But right now, for this conversation, for anything else that might happen this evening, I want to be sure you're totally, completely in control of your words and thoughts and actions."

Reese stared at him. Then she shook her head and looked down at the Coke can.

"Okay," she said finally. "I can do that. No wine, not tonight. I'll drink milk. I draw the line at pouring it in a glass, though. It's a straight-from-the-carton kinda night."

"Fair enough."

Clay reached up to grab one glass from the cupboard. He handed it to her without comment, and Reese opened the freezer and grabbed a handful of ice cubes. She dropped them one by one into the glass, the clinking sound making Clay think of Scotch. He pushed the thought from his mind and watched Reese's hands.

"Is it okay if we don't talk about Sheila?" she asked. "I'm kind of in shock, and I just—well, I just need some time to process things, okay?"

"Not a problem."

Reese kept her eyes on the glass, which gave Clay a few more seconds to study her. Her hair was the same color as the cola but bore a few streaks of caramel and a few threads of silver and cinnamon and a dozen other colors he couldn't name.

She looked up then, and Clay's gut flipped as she pinned him in place with those wild green eyes.

"You're staring," she said.

"You're beautiful."

She looked away, flushed in the dimly lit kitchen.

"Do you know what the fight was about at Finnigan's?" he asked.

She looked up, startled. "What?"

"The fight. Not the one the other night. The one five years ago. The one where you got hurt."

She swallowed and shook her head. "Do you want to tell me?"

"Yes." He balled his hands into fists, remembering every detail of that night. The smell of beer, the twang of country music over crackly speakers, the way Reese touched her hair and glanced nervously around the bar.

"I was wasted," Clay said. "What's new, right? I pulled out my wallet to buy another round, and this guy next to me catches a look at one of the pictures I've got tucked in there. He looks at you, looks at me, looks at the picture, starts going off saying all kinds of crude shit about how hot you were and what he wanted to do to you, and I just—"

"You had a picture of me?"

Clay reached into his back pocket and pulled out his wallet. He tossed it on the counter in front of her, bumping the Coke can against the glass. "I still do."

She blinked at it but didn't pick it up. She looked back at him and swallowed. "Why?"

"Because I've always been in love with you, Reese. *Always*. I still am."

"What—how—"

"I kept my distance because I thought that's what I was supposed to do. And I may not remember everything about those years I was drinking like a goddamn fish, but I never forgot that."

She looked back down at the wallet. She picked it up and opened it. She began flipping through it, past his credit cards to the photos at the back. She stopped, staring down at the wallet. "There's more than one picture of me," she said. "There are three. These are from college."

He nodded. "Back when I still had a chance with you and blew it. And don't think I didn't notice the opportunity to make a blowjob joke right there. I'm still me, Reese. I just forgot that for a little while, but I'm done holding my tongue all the time and trying to say the right thing."

She closed the wallet and set it back on the counter. She looked up at him. "Still want that Coke?"

"Yes."

She nodded and popped open the can. She began to pour—too fast. The foam bubbled up and over the rim, spilling onto her fingers. She lifted them to her mouth, but Clay stepped forward and caught her left wrist.

"Let me," he said.

He gave her a fraction of a second to resist or pull away, but she did neither. She just looked at him, those green eyes flashing in the dim light of the kitchen.

He drew her hand up and slid her fingers into his mouth.

"Oh," she said.

She tasted sweet—not just the cola but something else. Something warm and exotic and strangely familiar. He slid his tongue lightly over the pads of her fingers and felt her body shift as she angled herself closer and gasped.

Clay drew her fingers deeper into his mouth, sucking lightly, then withdrawing. His tongue found the junction of her middle and ring finger, and he tasted her there, lingering in that soft cleft.

Reese groaned, her body seeming to liquefy as she pressed closer and braced herself against the counter with her other hand.

"I thought we were going to talk," she murmured.

He pulled back, freeing his mouth but not her hand. He stroked the inside of her wrist with his index finger.

"I'm done talking," he said. "I'm done doing a lot of things."

Reese nodded, then looked at his mouth. "Not that, I hope."

"Not that," he murmured against her knuckles. "But I'm done apologizing. I've done it enough now. I'm done crawling. And I'm done not saying what I feel because I'm afraid of offending someone."

"I never wanted you to crawl," she murmured. "And what you're feeling—" She moaned as his tongue traced the ridges of her knuckles. "I always wanted you to tell me that."

Clay shook his head and slid his hand along her waist. "I told you, I'm done talking. I'd rather show you instead."

She gasped as he slid his hand down, moving along the path of her spine. He pulled her closer, his palm pressing hard into the small of her back as his mouth sipped at her knuckles.

He kissed his way along the fleshy part of her thumb and into the hollow of her wrist. She was warm there, and he could feel her pulse fluttering against his lips. He slid his other hand under her shirt, tracing the warm, bare column of her spine before slipping around to the front to cup her breast.

Reese sighed with pleasure and opened her eyes to look at him. "Two days ago you asked me at least a dozen times if I wanted to stop," she murmured. "Aren't you going to ask this time?"

"No."

"Not even once?"

Clay shook his head. "If you want to stop, I know you well enough to be sure you'll tell me."

She nodded, then whimpered as he drew her hand to his mouth once more. He moved his lips over the inside of the wrist before pressing it to his sternum. He let go, and she held it there, her fingers splaying over his chest as she blinked up at him. Her chest was rising and falling fast beneath the thin top, and the feel of her breast pressing against his palm was enough to make him dizzy. It was all he could do to resist the urge to just bend her over the sink and have his way with her.

"I want you, Reese," he murmured. "I've always wanted you. And I'm pretty sure you want me, too."

She hesitated, then nodded as she licked her lips. "Yes."

"But wanting isn't the only thing between us, is it?" he asked. "I wouldn't be here if that were the case."

He stroked his thumb over her nipple and she gasped.

Then she slid her fingers down over his abs, then around his back. Her other hand joined that one and she gripped his shoulder blades, using them to pull him closer.

Clay slid his hand out from under her shirt and moved both hands to her shoulders. He shoved the flannel aside, baring the thin straps of the tank top. He kissed her left shoulder as the flannel fell away, dropping over her hands and onto the floor. Clay kicked it aside, not caring where it landed.

He trailed both hands down her rib cage, traveling downward until he found the hem of the tank top. He gripped the fabric and, in one quick motion, pulled the shirt up over her head.

Reese lifted her arms and the top slid off, leaving her standing there in her bra. She licked her lips as her nipples strained against the pink satin. Clay tossed the tank top aside, barely registering that it landed in the sink.

Polite Clay would have worried about water stains.

Normal Clay found the clasp of her bra with both hands.

He yanked the hooks apart, releasing the tension. Then he slid his hands up and pushed the straps from her shoulders, letting the bra fall to the ground.

"Oh," she breathed as Clay nipped her bare shoulder, his teeth rough on her smooth skin. "Topless in my kitchen. This is new."

"You should always be topless in your kitchen," he said, and kissed her hard on the mouth. Reese responded, opening her mouth to him and sliding one hand up to cup his face.

He kissed her like that for what seemed like hours, moving from her lips to her throat, dragging his teeth over the rounded mounds of her shoulders. They were both breathing hard as he slid down her throat, trailing kisses until he reached the edge of her collarbone. He moved one hand beneath her breast, savoring the weight of it. He cupped it gently, moving his mouth down to kiss the edges of it. As his teeth grazed her nipple, Reese dug her fingernails into the back of his head, urging him on.

He kissed her there, savoring the soft flesh of one breast, then the other, as Reese squirmed and whimpered. She drew one hand out of his hair and found his biceps, digging her nails in lightly.

"Your tattoo," she whispered, tracing it with one fingertip. "Why wouldn't you tell me what it said?"

Clay lifted his mouth from her breast and straightened, his fingers covering her bare nipples. He swallowed.

"It was crude. I got it when I was young. After the first stint in rehab—the one that didn't take. I was embarrassed. I'll tell you now—"

"I already know," she murmured.

"I wanted you to think I'd matured. That I'd stopped making dirty jokes, stopped drinking, stopped being a jackass."

She shook her head and traced a finger over the words. "I didn't want you to stop being you."

"Me neither."

She looked up at him from under her lashes, her expression halfway between playful and dangerous. *"Res firma mitescere nescit,"* she murmured. "'A rigid thing doesn't soften.' Right?"

"Something like that."

She gave him a salacious grin. "Want to prove it?"

Clay pressed his hand into the small of her back, drawing her closer. She slid her leg between his and could feel him hard against her thigh.

"You have to ask?" he murmured.

"No, but I wanted to hear you say it."

"Say what?"

"I'm hard for *you*, Reese—I want *you*, Reese."

"I am. I do. I always have."

She smiled. "Always?"

"Longer than you know."

"Double entendre?" she murmured as she slid her hand over him, down and then back up, stroking the solid length of him through the denim.

Clay groaned and gripped her by the shoulders. In one motion, he spun her around, turning her to face the kitchen counter. She moaned as he cupped her breasts from behind, then slid one hand down to tug at her belt buckle. He yanked it open with one hand, then started on her zipper, not willing to take his other hand off her breast to speed things along.

Reese whimpered and moved her hands to her hips. She shoved her jeans down and kicked her legs free. One flip-flop went flying across the room, making a decided *flop* as it landed on the dining room table.

"Jesus," Clay said, and eased away from her—not far enough to break contact, but far enough that he could see her. She was naked and beautiful in her kitchen, bathed in dim light and pinned beneath him.

She smiled at him over her shoulder. "You planning to join me, or should I cut you out of those jeans with a butcher knife?"

Clay reached for his belt, keeping one hand on Reese's hip. He jerked his buckle free with the other hand, then tugged at the button fly. Reese wriggled her ass and squirmed against him and Clay released her for the ten seconds necessary to pull his jeans off the rest of the way.

He grabbed his wallet off the counter, fumbling for the condom he'd stuck there earlier on the slim chance Reese might be willing to give him another shot. He tore it open and slid it on, returning one hand to Reese's hip.

The other hand grabbed a fistful of hair at the nape of her neck and tugged. Her back arched, pressing her perfect ass up against him. He felt dizzy for an instant as Reese groaned and moved against him, her palms pressing hard into the counter.

"Please—" she whimpered.

"Please what?"

"I want to feel you inside me."

The urge to oblige screamed through his body, but he fought it. "Not yet."

Instead, he let go of her hair and slid both hands around to cup her breasts. He leaned forward, using his weight to press her against the counter. He nudged her hair aside with his chin as his lips found the tender skin of her neck. He kissed her there, drawing his tongue along her hairline as his palms grazed her nipples, so softly he barely touched her. Reese writhed under him and pressed her ass harder against his groin.

"Clay, please—"

He bit the nape of her neck, and she bucked against him. He leaned closer, his breath against her ear.

"You're mine," he whispered. "Only mine. You've always been mine."

"Oh, God, please!"

"For fifteen years, you're the one woman I couldn't stop thinking about. The one I've wanted, the one I've loved. Do you believe me?"

"I don't—"

"It's true. It was always you, Reese. Always you."

She bit her lip, angled her head to look up at him. She blinked, her green eyes blazing. "For me, too."

He plunged into her then, and her words turned into a startled cry. He held still for a moment, not wanting to hurt her. He slid one hand down, worried about her hip bones against the hard granite of the counter.

"Please, Clay!"

He didn't require much more prompting than that. He slid his hand away from her hip, keeping one on her breasts but drawing the other one up to grasp a fistful of her hair. He gave another gentle tug and she arched her back again.

He moved slowly at first, hoping to hold on as long as possible. But she was so warm beneath him, so soft and wet.

Baseball, he thought, running through pitching stats to keep his mind distracted enough to make this last. *Tire pressure, dog food commercials, barbecue assembly—*

He released her hair and slid his hand down, moving slowly over her rib cage and around to savor the contour of her hip before finding his way to the thatch of curls between her legs. She bucked against him as he found the spot that made her cry out.

"Oh, God," she whimpered and pressed into his fingers.

He tried to be gentle, to make slow, delicate circles with the pads of his fingertips, but Reese squirmed against him, urging him to increase the pressure. He felt her clench around him, felt her soft and wet and tight as he thrust into her over and over.

He was getting dizzy now, and he knew he only had seconds left, maybe less if she kept moving against him like that.

"Oh, God, Clay—I'm so close."

He thrust deeper, no longer afraid of hurting her. She screamed, and Clay gripped her waist, his fingers pressing into the soft flesh.

"Yes!" she screamed, and slammed against him.

Everything exploded then, the light behind his eyes, the throbbing in his eardrums, something deep inside Reese.

"I love you," he murmured against her hair. "I've always loved you."

CHAPTER TWENTY-TWO

Reese woke up blinking beneath a thin sheet of sunlight blazing through her half-open blinds. She grabbed the alarm clock, startled to realize it was after eight a.m.

She hadn't slept that late in years.

She patted the mattress beside her, hating the twinge of disappointment she felt at discovering Clay wasn't there. Sitting up, she swung her legs out of bed just as Clay swept through the doorway wearing a pair of boxer shorts and carrying a breakfast tray.

"Not so fast." He set the tray on the nightstand, picked up her legs, and lifted them back into bed. Then he crawled in beside her and grabbed the tray.

Reese reached for a cup of coffee. "Breakfast in bed?"

"We already used the kitchen for bedroom activities, might as well use the bedroom for eating."

"Very wise," she said and bit into a piece of toast.

"I am wise. That's why we're going to argue now."

She raised an eyebrow. "That's your idea of post-coital romance?"

"No, breakfast is my idea of post-coital romance. The arguing is foreplay for more romance."

She swallowed her toast and took a sip of coffee, studying Clay over the rim of her mug. He looked awfully cheerful, which made sense considering how many things they'd done last night to give each other reasons to smile.

But now it was daylight, and doubt was already trickling through her consciousness like it always did.

"You have doubts," Clay said, apparently reading her mind as he spooned eggs onto a plate and grabbed a fork. "So I'm going to shoot them down one by one. Start anywhere you like."

Reese shook her head, smiling in spite of herself. "This is all part of your new 'say what you mean, even if it's rude' agenda?"

"Pretty much."

"Fine. I run a vineyard. I *live* at a vineyard. You are a former alcoholic."

"No, I *am* an alcoholic," he pointed out. "I'll always be an alcoholic. I just happen to be in recovery."

"That's not helping your cause."

"Yes, it is, because I recognize it. You know how many drunks can't do that?"

She opened her mouth to argue, but Clay shoved in a forkful of eggs.

"Chew," he ordered. "Here's the thing, Reese—I know myself better than I ever did when I was a drunk. I know what my triggers are and how to avoid them. I know what I can and can't handle, and I know I *can* handle being at a vineyard. What I can't handle is being at *this* vineyard with you always worrying I'm going to dive headfirst into a barrel of Chardonnay." He gave a dramatic shudder. "I always hated Chardonnay."

"I love Chardonnay."

"Perfect. More for you. See how well this is working out?"

"You're asking me to trust you," she said flatly.

"No, I'm *telling* you to trust me. I'll earn it—believe me, I've been working on that. But I need you to give me a chance."

She hesitated, then nodded. "You're right. I owe you a chance."

"Damn straight. Next doubt?"

She sighed and nibbled the corner of her toast. "You slept with my cousin."

"You slept with my best friend. Actually, you *married* him. That's much worse, but I'm not dwelling on it. You know why?"

"Why?"

"Because that marriage only lasted a year. And ours is going to last a lot longer than that."

Reese choked on her toast. Clay handed her a glass of orange juice, patting her back until she stopped coughing.

She stared at him through watery eyes. "Did you just propose to me?"

"Of course not. I'll be much more romantic when I propose. I'm only informing you that I will be proposing eventually, and when I do, you will say yes and we will live happily ever after."

"You're nuts."

"That's why you love me. And also why you'll say yes to my proposal."

Reese set her toast back on the plate, and Clay grabbed her hand. He lifted it to his mouth, kissing the back of her knuckles. Reese sighed with pleasure.

"Are you going to argue?" he asked. "Tell me you don't love me? That you don't want to be with me?"

She looked up from her toast and met his eyes. Despite the cockiness in his speech, she saw real fear there. Reese swallowed as her eyes filled with tears.

"I can't," she said.

"Can't argue or can't be with me?"

"Both," she said, swallowing hard. "Clay, I'm scared. I don't think I'm cut out for long-term relationships."

"That's bullshit."

She laughed. "That's your argument?"

"No, that's just the start of it. Want to know what I think?"

"Does it matter if I do?"

"No, I'm going to tell you anyway." He took a bite of toast and chewed, while Reese wiggled her fingers inside his grip. His hand felt good—warm and solid and strong.

"I think you need to stop judging yourself by other people's relationship standards," he said. "You've been listening to Eric wax poetic about relationships being hard work and your parents spout about soul mates and Larissa yammer on about the importance of good sex and Axl tell you—actually, I'm a little afraid to guess what your grandpa's relationship advice entails."

"Nudist colonies," she said. "Also, he says I should ignore everyone else's relationships and focus on setting my own standards."

"Oh," he said. "In that case, I agree with him. The last part, not the nudist colonies. Smart grandpa."

Reese smiled. "I hate to say it, but you're right."

Clay looked at her. "Really?"

She nodded and squeezed his hand. "Really. I know I've been a bitch. I know I've been a cynic. I know I haven't given you the benefit of the doubt these last few days, but I'm going to change that. I *want* to change that. I want to be with you, Clay. I do."

He laughed. "Damn. I didn't figure you'd be this easy."

She rolled her eyes. "You had me naked three days after you got back to town. You bent me over my own kitchen counter last night. You really didn't think I'd be easy?"

He grinned and set the breakfast tray on the nightstand. Then he leaned over and kissed her. He tasted like orange juice and red peppers, and Reese was ready to drag him down on top of her and prove just how willing she was to make things work.

At least until her front door burst open.

"Reese? Reesey, where are you?"

She pulled away from Clay and sat up in bed. "Larissa?" she yelled.

Her cousin shoved through the bedroom door and dropped onto the end of the bed, cleavage bouncing under what was either a halter top or a jockstrap.

Larissa surveyed them and smiled. "Oh, good. You're doing it."

"Not at the moment," Clay said. "But give us five more minutes alone—"

"Out!" Reese commanded. A flicker of hurt flashed in Larissa's eyes, so Reese tugged the sheet up tighter around her breasts and softened her tone. "I love you more than anyone else in the world, except maybe Clay—"

"So you finally admit it?" Larissa grinned. "The part about Clay, I mean. Obviously, you love me."

"I do love you," Reese said. "And I'm sorry for what I said yesterday. But can you please get the hell out of my bedroom?"

"But I have something to tell you, and I have to do it before the others get here."

Clay raised an eyebrow. "Others?"

"Let me put some clothes on first," Reese said. "Then we can have a conversation in the living room like a normal family would."

Larissa rolled her eyes, but stood up and trudged toward the living room. "Normal families are overrated."

Clay grinned and shut the door behind her, while Reese scrambled out of bed and pulled on a rumpled pair of pajama pants and a thin tank top with no bra. She turned around to see Clay watching her and felt the warmth flood her body all over again.

"That's a good look for you," he said.

"Thanks. Maybe I'll start dressing this way in the tasting room."

"You'd certainly make my cork pop."

Reese laughed. "It's nice to see the old Clay is still in there somewhere."

"Come on," he said, taking her by the hand. "Let's see what Larissa wants."

They trudged out to the living room, where Larissa was bent over the baby opossum's cage, cooing softly to the little animal. She looked up as they entered and gave them a broad smile.

"The morning-after glow looks good on you," she said.

"Thank you," Reese said. "And in case you missed it in there, I'm sorry."

"No need," Larissa said. "I have some growing up to do. I know that. I've been playing around for too long with boys and booze, and while I'm not a degenerate lush like Clay was—"

"Thank you."

Larissa smiled. "No offense."

"None taken," he said. "I *was* a degenerate lush."

"Right. And I don't want to become that. So I'm going to get my shit together, starting with making better choices about men. Which is why I only let your veterinarian get to second base last night."

Reese blinked, processing her cousin's words. "Dr. Wally?"

"Yes. I met him at some art thing last night and we hit it off and one thing led to another and—"

"Um, congratulations?"

Larissa smiled. "Thank you. I figured you weren't going to be dating him since you're madly in love with Clay, so we should recycle the vet and I can date a nice guy for a change."

"Very environmentally responsible of you," Clay pointed out.

Larissa nodded and looked at Reese. "So are we good?"

"We're good." Reese bit her lip. "I'm sorry, 'Riss. For the things I said yesterday."

"I'm sorry, too. You're a grump sometimes, but you're still my third-favorite cousin."

With that, Larissa lunged and tackled Reese in a perfume-scented bear hug. It felt warm and messy and absolutely perfect, so Reese let Larissa topple them both onto the couch. She felt Clay let go of her hand, but he sat down beside them on the sofa.

The front door burst open again, and Reese remembered her cousin's words about the others arriving. She heard the thud of footsteps in her foyer and wriggled free from Larissa's hug as June marched in with Jed on her heels. "Honey? Reesey?"

Reese spit Larissa's hair out of her mouth. "Doesn't anyone in this family ever knock?"

June ignored her and hustled to her side. Jed followed as Axl and an unfamiliar man with a necktie and a neatly trimmed beard came through the wide-open front door.

"Come on in," Reese muttered. "Make yourselves at home."

Axl scratched his armpit and grinned at the three of them sprawled on the sofa in various states of undress. "Your grandma always liked a good threesome, too."

"Morning, everyone," Clay said, adjusting his boxers. "Good to see you."

"You guys, can we maybe do this later?" Reese asked, folding her arms over her chest. "Like after I've had time to shower and put on something besides pajamas?"

"No dice," Axl insisted. "We've got serious vineyard business to discuss."

"Should we call Eric?" Clay asked.

"Hell, yes," Reese muttered. "That's just what this situation calls for. My ex-husband."

Her father shook his head a little sadly. "Eric's going to be tied up for a while with Sheila."

"And not in the good way," Axl added.

"There's a lot to deal with," June said. "The police and fire marshal and all. But we've been talking it over, and we agreed as a family we don't want to press charges. How do you feel about that, honey?"

Reese swallowed. "You want to forgive and forget?"

"Not forget," Jed said. "But forgive, yes."

"I don't know that the police will be as forgiving," Reese pointed out. "There's the whole arson thing and all."

"We're willing to be character witnesses," June said. "We know she's a good person at heart. She just made some really bad decisions."

"Haven't we all?" Larissa said.

Clay nodded. "Amen."

"And if she does go to prison, I can help her out," Axl said. "I got friends on the inside who can get her in with the right gang, teach her to make a knife out of a pork chop bone, all that good stuff."

Reese shook her head, trying to digest it all. "How's Eric handling it?"

"Okay, under the circumstances," Jed said. "We gave him the name of this really good marriage counselor we heard of and—"

"Whatever," Axl said, giving Reese a knowing look before waving a dismissive hand. "That's not important right now. The important thing is that I've got your money."

"My money?" Reese said. She felt Clay grab her hand, and the comforting squeeze reminded her this wasn't some bizarre dream.

"Shit, girl—your money for the construction," Axl barked. "I told you I'd come through. You know those 'shrooms I've been growing?"

Reese closed her eyes. "Axl, I really appreciate everything you're trying to do, but illegal drugs are not the way to fund—"

"Shut up. Who said anything about illegal drugs? I said 'shrooms."

"Oregon black truffles, to be more precise." The man with the necktie stepped forward and offered his hand. Seeming to realize he'd barged into something more intimate than a normal business deal, he flushed bright crimson and began to stammer. "I'm, uh—I'm Tony Gavin, owner of—um, eighteen different fine-dining establishments around the Pacific Northwest."

"Reese Clark," she said automatically, reaching for his hand. "Vineyard manager who doesn't generally hold meetings in her pajamas."

"I'm terribly sorry," he said. "Your family assured me now would be a good time to talk."

"It's fine. Go ahead," she said. "My family has a warped sense of what 'good time' means."

"It's one of our finest qualities," Axl said, grinning like he'd just figured out how to hot-wire a BMW.

Tony regarded him awkwardly for a moment, then turned back to

Reese. "Your grandfather discovered what we suspect is the largest crop of Oregon black truffles ever found in this state, and he found them right here on your property."

"The east woods," Axl added. "The ones Dick's been jonesing for all these years. Aren't you glad I didn't sell?"

Tony cleared his throat. "Not only did he discover a highly sustainable, preexisting crop, he and his, um—crew have been working on a cultivation system of adding lime to the soil to raise the pH and alter the soil chemistry while inoculating trees and—"

"This is what you've been doing?" Reese asked Axl. "When you said you were growing 'shrooms, I thought—"

"Magic mushrooms?" Axl grinned. "Don't worry, I've got those, too."

Tony frowned. "Right. As you may know, Oregon black truffles can sell for more than two hundred and fifty dollars a pound. Given the superior quality of truffles found on your property, I'd like to contract with you to be the exclusive truffle provider for my entire restaurant chain."

"Fuck yeah," Axl said.

June placed a hand on her father's arm. "Tell her the other part, Dad."

"Right. You know my old place, right?"

"Right," Reese said, her head still spinning.

"We're converting it into a joint joint."

"A what?"

Reese's dad cleared his throat. "I believe the correct term is 'bud and breakfast.' With Oregon legalizing marijuana last year, pot tourism is becoming a big draw for this whole region."

"Wait, you mean all those permits were legit?" Reese blinked. "Axl was doing everything legally?"

"Maybe not everything—" he began.

"But the things that matter—the paperwork," June said. "That's all legal."

"Believe me," Jed said. "No one's more surprised than we are."

Larissa bounced cheerfully beside her on the sofa. "So we're saving the vineyard with weed and magic mushrooms. Isn't it great?"

Jed and June clasped hands and beamed. "Wouldn't have been my first choice," June said, "but it does seem like a workable plan."

"So whaddya say?" Axl said, nudging Reese's knee. "I believe we have a proposal on the table."

"A very good one," Tony added. "I can show you the figures if you'd like. All the paperwork is back in the office, if you'd like to review it, but I can assure you it's an excellent proposal."

"What do you say, Peanut Butter Cup?"

But Reese wasn't looking at her grandfather or her parents or her cousin or Tony anymore. She was looking at Clay, who was smiling down at her like they were the only two people in the room.

"Yes," Reese said. "I say *yes*."

ACKNOWLEDGMENTS

Growing up in Oregon's Willamette Valley made me intimately familiar with the geographic setting of this story, and I owe a huge debt of gratitude to the amazing individuals in the wine industry who spent countless months familiarizing me with the nitty-gritty of vineyard operations and winemaking. I've taken some creative liberties with the details, and any errors are mine alone.

Spending time at more than fifty Oregon vineyards while researching this story was certainly no hardship, but a handful of people went above and beyond to make the experience even more incredible. Special thanks to the Ford family at Illahe Vineyards and to Leanna Garrison for helping set up my fabulous time there. Thank you to Michael Lundeen, Forrest Schaad, Michael Caputo, and Peter Rosback for opening your cellar doors and opening my eyes to the incredible passion that drives this industry. You inspired facets of the story and characters that might not have existed if I hadn't met you.

I'm grateful to Alex Sokol Blosser at Sokol Blosser Vineyards and to the fine crew at Stoller Vineyards for giving me insight into the challenges of LEED-certified building at Oregon wineries. And thank you to Rebecca Sweet at Van Duzer Vineyards for offering a glimpse into the life of a female vineyard manager.

Thank you to Angela Perry for the Catholic liturgy, to Larissa Hardesty for letting me steal your name, and to Dan Krokos for help developing Clay in the early stages. Thanks also to Adam Fenske, PsyD, (and awesome cousin to boot!) for your insights into addiction and recovery. I'm also grateful to my veterinarian, Dr. Holly O'Brien, for not batting an eyelash when I started asking questions about alpacas and pot.

I owe a million hugs and sloppy smooches to my amazing critique partners, Linda Brundage, Cynthia Reese, and Linda Grimes, as well as my terrific beta readers, Larie Borden, Bridget McGinn, and Minta Powelson. You all know the challenges I was facing in my life while writing this book, and I thank you from the bottom of my heart for pulling me through both personally and professionally.

Thank you to the Bend Book Bitches for your unwavering friendship and love of good books. I'm eternally grateful to the readers of my blog, *Don't Pet Me, I'm Writing*, for being the best cheering section a girl could ever ask for.

I owe so much to my amazing agent, Michelle Wolfson, for the extra hand-holding that went on behind the scenes during the creation of this book. Thank you for being my staunchest advocate and most enthusiastic cheerleader. I'm picturing you with a bullwhip and pom-poms.

Huge thanks to Irene Billings, Anh Schleup, Jennifer Blanksteen, Chris Werner, Michelle Hope Anderson, Nicole Pomeroy, Sharon Turner Mulvihill, and the rest of the fabulous team at Montlake Romance for shepherding this story from "that manuscript gathering dust under my bed" to the book I always knew it could be. I'm especially grateful to Krista Stroever for understanding so precisely where I wanted to go with this story and mapping out the perfect route to get us there. Your belief in this book and its characters reignited my passion for it after all this time.

Thank you to my parents, Dixie and David Fenske, for all the love, support, and humor over the years. None of this would be possible without you guys. I'm also grateful to my baby brother, Aaron "Russ"

Fenske, and his lovely wife, Carlie, for buying so many copies of my books even though I would have given them to you for free.

Thank you to Cedar and Violet for being the world's most kick-ass stepkids (a phrase I figure I'm okay using since you aren't old enough to be permitted to read this book yet).

And thank you to Craig for the endless supply of love, laughter, strength, and joy. You are my daily reminder that *happily ever after* doesn't always turn out the way you think it will. Sometimes, it's better.

ABOUT THE AUTHOR

Photo 2013 © Craig Zagurski

Tawna Fenske is a fourth-generation Oregonian who wrote this book as an excuse to roam Oregon wine country sipping good Pinot Noir and rubbing shoulders with all the cool people in the wine industry.

Tawna writes humorous fiction, risqué romance, and heartwarming love stories with a quirky twist. Her offbeat brand of romance received a starred review from *Publishers Weekly*, noting, "There's something wonderfully relaxing about being immersed in a story filled with over-the-top characters in undeniably relatable situations. Heartache and humor go hand in hand."

Tawna lives in Bend, Oregon, with her husband, stepkids, and a menagerie of ill-behaved pets. She can peel a banana with her toes, and she loses an average of twenty pairs of eyeglasses per year.

To learn more about all of Tawna's books, visit www.tawnafenske.com.